Praise f...
bestsellin...

T0012639

"In short, this is the perfect entertainment for those looking for a suspense novel with emotional intensity."
—*Publishers Weekly* on *Out of the Dark*

"Sala's spellbinding narrative follows the reunited Denver couple as they repair their marriage and try to understand what happened to Frankie. Through vague flashes and unsettling nightmares, Frankie slowly begins to remember the missing years and a powerful man from her childhood who is intent, even now, on possessing her at any cost. Veteran romance writer Sala lives up to her reputation with this well-crafted thriller."
—*Publishers Weekly* on *Remember Me*

"Romantic suspense queen Sala (*Blood Trails*) launches a series with this enticing and exciting contemporary.... Skillfully balancing suspense and romance, Sala gives readers a nonstop breath-holding adventure."
—*Publishers Weekly* on *Going Once*

"No one writes small-town communities better than Ms. Sala. The plot is so well crafted that it gets its teeth into you and doesn't let go until the happily ever after. An absolute winner that I thoroughly enjoyed."
—*The Good, the Bad and the Unread* on *Last Rites*

"Emotionally wrenching, sensually appealing, edgy and suspenseful, and hopeful and endearing."
—*USA TODAY* on *Going Gone*

"Vivid, gripping... This thriller keeps the pages turning."
—*Library Journal* on *Torn Apart*

Dear Reader,

Part of the delight I take in participating in the Harlequin 75th Anniversary program is sharing my story *Save Me* with you, but it is also an honor to have been asked to participate.

My writing journey with Harlequin began over thirty-two years ago, and it has been a long and vital part of my career. All of the wonderful editors I got to work with. All of the stories I was allowed to tell. And the readers, like you, some who have been reading me from the beginning of my career, have been a vital part of that world.

I will be celebrating long-distance with everyone at Harlequin on their very special day. I shall lift a glass to the past seventy-five years with thanks and to the excitement of the next seventy-five story-filled years to come.

With so much appreciation,

Sharon Sala

SAVE ME

NEW YORK TIMES **BESTSELLING AUTHOR**
SHARON SALA

FREE STORY BY
K.D. RICHARDS

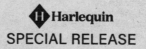

Harlequin
SPECIAL RELEASE

If you purchased this book without a cover you should be aware that this book is stolen property. It was reported as "unsold and destroyed" to the publisher, and neither the author nor the publisher has received any payment for this "stripped book."

Recycling programs
for this product may
not exist in your area.

H Harlequin®
SPECIAL RELEASE

ISBN-13: 978-1-335-01680-5

Save Me
First published in 2024. This edition published in 2024.
Copyright © 2024 by Sharon Sala

Silenced Witness
First published in 2024. This edition published in 2024.
Copyright © 2024 by Kia Dennis

All rights reserved. No part of this book may be used or reproduced in any manner whatsoever without written permission.

Without limiting the author's and publisher's exclusive rights, any unauthorized use of this publication to train generative artificial intelligence (AI) technologies is expressly prohibited.

This is a work of fiction. Names, characters, places and incidents are either the product of the author's imagination or are used fictitiously. Any resemblance to actual persons, living or dead, businesses, companies, events or locales is entirely coincidental.

For questions and comments about the quality of this book, please contact us at CustomerService@Harlequin.com.

TM and ® are trademarks of Harlequin Enterprises ULC.

 Harlequin Enterprises ULC
22 Adelaide St. West, 41st Floor
Toronto, Ontario M5H 4E3, Canada
www.Harlequin.com

Printed in U.S.A.

CONTENTS

New York Times and *USA TODAY* bestselling author **Sharon Sala** has 135+ books in print, published in six different genres—romance, young adult, Western, general fiction, women's fiction and nonfiction. She was first published in 1991, and her industry awards include the Janet Dailey Award, five Career Achievement Awards, five National Readers' Choice Awards, five Colorado Romance Writers' Awards of Excellence, the Heart of Excellence Award, the Booksellers' Best Award, the Nora Roberts Lifetime Achievement Award and the Centennial Award in recognition of her one hundredth published novel. She lives in Oklahoma, the state where she was born. Visit her at sharonsalaauthor.com and Facebook.com/sharonsala.

Also by Sharon Sala

Harlequin Intrigue

Save Me

Visit her Author Profile page at Harlequin.com.

SAVE ME

Sharon Sala

Heroes are everywhere.

Love never dies.

I dedicate this book to the brave ones, who keep putting one step in front of another, even though their lives have been shattered, and their hearts have been broken by the actions of others.

Life isn't fair.

But it's ours to live for as long as we exist.

Chapter One

July 2011
New Orleans, Louisiana

It was the rain.

It rained a lot in Louisiana at this time of year, but to-night it was nothing short of a deluge—so loud on the roof that it muted the sound of Hunter Gray's boots as he paced in his room.

He would look back to this evening as the night angels cried, but there was no warning of what was already in motion. For him, it was a night like any other night in his eighteen years of living.

His dad worked on the docks, and always came home from work drunk.

His mother was drawing unemployment, and was already into her third beer of the evening.

Hunt was in his room, thinking about his girl, Lainie Mayes. He lived for the times they were together. They'd had a plan during the entire senior year of high school. All they were waiting for was for her to turn eighteen.

Hunt had a full-ride scholarship to play football at Tulane University, and Lainie would be following in her mother's footsteps at the same university, pledging her mother's sorority. As a legacy pledge, she was a shoo-in.

But Hunt and Lainie lived in two different worlds.

Her father didn't come home drunk. He was a very well-to-do stockbroker. Her mother wore high heels to the supermarket, and had a housekeeper named Millie, who kept order in their world.

Hunt and Lainie were at opposite ends of the socioeconomic scale, but their real burden was the hate their fathers held for each other.

WHEN CHUCK GRAY and Greg Mayes were thirteen years old, Chuck's mother married Greg's father. The boys' dislike for each other happened at first sight, and being forced to live under the same roof only made it worse. It carried through every aspect of their teenage years, until Chuck's mother died right after he graduated high school.

Chuck wound up on the street, and Greg was on his way to college, with all the trimmings. Chuck was bitter and homeless, which only added to the hate and resentment between them, until years later, when fate dealt them another low blow. Their children fell in love with each other, and the war between them began anew.

THE CRACK OF a dish hitting the wall stopped Hunt in his tracks. He shoved his hands through his hair, and dropped down onto the side of his bed, listening to the beginnings of another fight. Curses were flying. More dishes were breaking.

He waited in silence as sweat ran from his hair, beaded across his upper lip and ran in rivulets down the jut of his jaw. He often wondered how he'd even been born into this family. He didn't look like them, which had been another bone of contention between his parents, to the point of Chuck claiming in one drunken rage that his wife had been unfaithful.

That's when Brenda pulled out an old family photo of her Cajun grandfather, Antoine Beaujean, and shoved it in her husband's face.

"Look! This is Papa 'toine, and it's like looking at Hunter's face. Our son is just a throwback, and you're a jackass," Brenda said, and helped herself to another beer.

After that, the olive cast of Hunt's skin, his black brows and high cheekbones, the same piercing gaze as the man from the photo, and the distinctive Roman nose, were no longer an issue for Chuck. But Chuck and Brenda were a big issue for Hunt, and 50 percent of the conflict in which he and Lainie were caught.

Tonight, the windows were shut because of the rain, but since their air-conditioning hadn't worked for months, his shirt was sticking to his body. Finally, he got up and went out onto the back porch. Rain was blowing in under the overhang, but he didn't care. His clothes were already wet with sweat, and it felt cool on his skin.

He wanted to call Lainie. He just needed to hear her voice, but it was dinnertime at the Mayes house, and nobody was allowed to take their phones to the table. So, he stood in the rain, while the war inside the house waged on without him.

LAINIE MAYES WAS the epitome of southern charm. Well-groomed, well-dressed, always polite, born blessed with a beautiful oval-shaped face, long auburn hair that lay in waves, eyes as green as her daddy's money and what Hunt referred to as kissable lips. The top of her head fit exactly beneath the curve of his chin. He was the last piece of her puzzle. That one missing bit that made her whole.

Tonight, she was sitting at the dinner table, quietly and politely awaiting the first course, and listening to her parents, Greg and Tina's "oh so proper" conversation, but she could tell they didn't love each other anymore.

She often wondered if they ever had. Mama had just been a sorority girl at Tulane University who scored a rich man's son. A classic match straight out of the Old South.

But Lainie's defiant stance regarding Hunter Gray infuriated them. No matter what, she refused to knuckle under to their demands. She and Hunt saw each other and dated each other, and tried to let their fathers' war roll over their heads. The fact that she and Hunt were now going to be attending the same university made Greg angry, and Tina fret.

On a good day, they offered her bribes to quit him.

On a bad day, they threatened to disinherit her.

But Lainie held a hand they didn't know about, and one they couldn't beat. She was three months pregnant with Hunter Gray's baby, and less than a month away from college.

In two days, she would turn eighteen, the legal age for marriage without parental consent in Louisiana, and they would already be at college before she began to show. It would afford them the distance they needed to escape the lifelong hate of their fathers' feud.

He had his scholarship, and she had the trust fund her grandmother Sarah Mayes left her, which would be hers when she turned eighteen. They'd have each other and the rest of their lives.

When she first suspected she was pregnant, she panicked, and put off telling Hunt, because she was afraid of the consequences it would cause in both families. Then a couple of weeks ago she'd begun spotting, and thought she'd lost the baby. But after the spotting stopped, and she missed her third period, she bought another pregnancy test and used it. The baby was still there! She was happy, but time had crept up on her, and Hunt needed to know.

They'd planned to meet tonight, and then the storm came through. So, then her plan was to call him after dinner, but her phone was upstairs in her room. So here she sat, listening to the rain drowning out the drone of her parents' voices, and speaking only when spoken to, until dinner was over. At that point, she laid down her napkin and looked up from her plate.

"Thank you for dinner. I'm going to my room," she said, and stood up without waiting to be excused, and left the table.

The moment she closed the door behind her, she went to get her phone. She always tucked it beneath the chocolate brown teddy bear Hunt had given her on Valentine's Day, but when she thrust her hand beneath the bear, the phone was gone.

Frowning, she began looking around the room, trying to remember if she'd moved it, when the door to her room flew open. Her mother was standing in the doorway with a look on her face Lainie had never seen before, and she was holding Lainie's phone.

"Are you looking for this?" Tina asked.

Lainie frowned. "Yes. What are you doing with my phone?"

"Making sure you don't inform that bastard of a boyfriend that you're pregnant!" Tina said.

Lainie froze. *How did she...?*

Tina's voice began to rise. "I found the box of a pregnancy test kit. Would you like to prove to me you're not pregnant?"

When Lainie stayed silent, Tina started to wail. "Oh, my God! So, it's true! How far along are you?"

"Three months," Lainie said.

Tina groaned. "How dare you do this to me? To us? You've ruined everything, and we don't have much time to fix it!"

"There is no WE, here, Mother. You're not 'fixing' anything, because nothing is broken, and all you've done is lower yourself to digging through my trash."

"Somebody has to protect you from yourself!" Tina shrieked. "I'm having your father contact an abortion clinic. We're driving there tomorrow. You'll be healed before you have to leave for college."

The words were a roar in Lainie's head, and before she knew it, she was screaming.

"You're out of your mind if you think I'll just meekly go along with this! This baby does not belong to you and Dad. It belongs to Hunt and me. We choose. And I'm not going anywhere with you two. You're so full of yourselves and your hate that you've forgotten what love even feels like."

The truth was painful, and without thinking, Tina drew back her hand and slapped her daughter's face. But the moment blood began seeping from Lainie's bottom lip, she took a step back in dismay.

"Oh, honey, I'm sorry. I didn't mean to—"

Lainie was in shock from the unexpected assault, and reacted in kind by snatching her phone from her mother's hands, then shouting.

"Get out of my room. Get out! Get out!"

Tina was already in tears when Greg walked in.

"You will do as your mother said, and no more arguing," Greg said.

The taste of blood was in Lainie's mouth. The imprint of her mother's hand was still burning on her face when she turned on her father, her voice shaking with rage.

"If either of you lay a hand on me again, or hurt this

baby I'm carrying, I'll destroy you. I'll tell the world that you murdered your grandchild. Your reputations won't be worth shit, and I'll be gone."

Greg Mayes grunted like he'd been punched.

Lainie knew he was angry, but when his face twisted into a grotesque mask of pure hate, she turned to run.

He grabbed her by her hair and yanked her around to face him. His breath was hot on her face—his voice little more than a low, angry growl.

"I'd rather you and that abomination in your belly were both dead than have Chuck Gray's bloodline in my family!"

He was raising his fist when Lainie heard her mother cry out—and then everything went blank.

SEEING HER DAUGHTER unconscious on the floor, and now bleeding from her nose and her mouth, sent Tina into hysterics. She began hammering her fists on her husband's back and head.

"What have you done? What's the matter with you?" Tina screamed.

"I don't want…"

She slapped him. "If you ever lay a hand on our daughter again, I will kill you myself. I don't want her to have this baby, but we're going about this all wrong. She needs time away from Hunter, and time to think about her future. I'm taking her to Mother's old place outside of Baton Rouge. We'll tell friends we're going to Europe. We may be looking at having her take a gap year and give the baby up later for adoption."

"Dammit it, Tina, you know what—"

"Just shut up, get her off the floor, then go get some ice. We're leaving now."

"But the storm—"

"You should have thought of that before you cold-cocked your own child," Tina snapped. "Now go do what I said. I need to pack a few things."

LAINIE AWAKENED IN the back seat of her father's Lexus, with her head in her mother's lap, and something cold on the side of her face. For a moment she couldn't figure out what was happening, and then she remembered.

She sat up with a jerk, shoved the cold pack onto the floor and scooted to the other side of the seat. The silence within the car was as horrifying as the situation she was in. She'd been kidnapped by her own parents.

Tina reached for her. "Lainie, honey, I——"

She yanked away from her mother's grasp. "Don't talk to me. Don't touch me. Either of you. I will never forgive you for this."

Tina started crying. Her father cursed.

She turned her face to the window. There was nothing to see beyond the darkness except the rain hammering on the windows, but she was already thinking about how to escape them.

I will find a way to call Hunt. I will find a way to get away.

THE THUNDERSTORM DIDN'T let up, and even after Hunt finally sent Lainie a text, she didn't respond. He didn't know what that meant. She always answered, so he kept trying. He finally gave up messaging in the wee hours of the morning, and when it was daylight, he got in his old truck and drove straight to her house. Even if he had to fight his way in, he needed to know she was okay.

There were cars in the driveway, but her father's Lexus was missing, which was a relief. At least he wouldn't have to face him, Hunt thought, and got out. He rang the doorbell, then waited, and waited, then rang it again. He was about to walk away when the housekeeper opened the door. She was a tiny little sprite of a woman, with a wreath of curls-gone-astray around her face, and she liked Hunter Gray.

"Morning, Miss Millie," Hunt said. "I know it's early, but I would like to speak to Lainie. Is she awake?"

"There's no one here but me," Millie said. "Apparently, they left last night. I got a call this morning that they won't be back. They're taking Lainie to Europe. Some kind of holiday before she goes away to college, they said."

Hunt's gut knotted. "She never mentioned that to me."

"I didn't know anything about it, either," Millie said.

Hunt shoved his hands in his pockets. "Well, thank you, anyway," he said, and started to walk away when something hit him. "Uh, I know this is a lot to ask, but I was wondering how long they would be gone. Would you know by looking in their closets if they'd packed a lot of clothes?"

Millie sighed. She knew about the war between Chuck Gray and Greg Mayes, and knew Hunt and Lainie were caught in the middle. "I might," she said. "If you don't mind waiting, I'll take a look. It'll take a few minutes."

"I don't mind a bit, and thank you. I really appreciate this," he said.

Millie closed the door while Hunt walked over to a concrete bench beside the front flower beds, and sat down to wait. Within minutes, Millie came out of the house and headed toward him, and he could tell by the look on her face that something was wrong. He stood up.

"What?"

Millie clasped her hands together, then took a quick breath. "Their traveling luggage is still here. I'd guess they took a few things, but not anything worth a trip to Europe, and there's blood on the floor in Lainie's bedroom. Somebody tried to clean it up, but it's a mess."

Hunt groaned. "Oh, Jesus. Was her daddy physically abusing her? She never mentioned it to me."

"I can't say," Millie said. "But for the past two years they have fought something terrible. All three of them. Just don't say I told you. I don't want to lose my job. I know they love her. But—"

There were tears in Hunt's eyes. "I know what loving me cost her," he said. "And I know what losing her would cost me. Thank you for the information. And don't worry about your job. I was never here."

He got in his truck and drove away. He didn't know what had happened, but he had a sick feeling in his gut that the dam had finally broken. Neither of their families had been able to keep him and Lainie from seeing each other, but they hadn't counted on being separated, and he had a feeling that's exactly what happened. He finally parked in a supermarket parking lot and sent her one last text.

Lainie, I know in my heart that something is wrong. But I can't save you because I don't know where you are. I don't know what happened to you, but I know it wasn't your choice to disappear. You are my love—my true north, and you always will be. I gave you my heart a long time ago. Feel free to keep it because it's no use to me without you in it.
Hunt

He had no way of knowing that her phone was lying beneath the bed in her old room where it had fallen when her father hit her. Or that she would never see this message in time to stop him from what came next. If he had, he would have moved heaven and earth to find her.

LAINIE WAS LOCKED in the Queen Anne suite on the second floor of her grandmother's old mansion, with no way out. There was no balcony to that room, no trellis to climb down from the only window.

The old estate was a distance outside of Baton Rouge, and had been closed ever since Sarah Mayes's death a few years back. There was still power on the property, but landlines had long since been removed from this house and she was in a panic, frantic as to what Hunt must be thinking.

She'd overheard her parents concocting the story they planned to spread within their social circle, to make Hunt believe she'd dumped him, and now she feared for what was going to happen to her. She walked to the window with her hands on her belly, talking as she went.

"Don't worry, baby, I won't let anyone hurt you, and I will find a way to let your daddy know about you. You be strong for me, and I'll be strong for you."

One week later

CHUCK GRAY WAS the first to see the photo of Lainie and a handsome stranger in the society section of the local paper. They were standing arm in arm on some beach in the tropics, and he took great delight in throwing it on top of Hunt's bowl of cereal as he was eating breakfast.

"Look at that!" Chuck said. "You've been moping around like a baby, and I told you she wasn't worth the trouble. She's already moved on."

Shock rolled through Hunt in waves, but the longer he stared, the more certain it was part of the lie.

"That's not Lainie," Hunt said.

Chuck frowned. "It, by God, is! Look at her face!"

"Oh, that's her face, all right, but that's not her body, and believe me, I know." Then he shoved the paper off the table and finished his cereal. "I've got to go. I'm going to be late for work."

"Sacking groceries," Chuck said, sneering.

Hunt didn't bother arguing. His dad was mean when he was drunk, but even meaner with a hangover, and he wasn't in the mood to deal with it. He'd already shut down every emotion he'd ever had to keep from losing his mind, and was barely going through the motions.

He was heartsick all day, but he could sack groceries on autopilot. When the day finally ended without a message from Lainie, he clocked out, then bought a rotisserie chicken and potato salad from the deli to take home for their dinner.

On the way home, he detoured by the Mayes estate, but the old mansion looked abandoned. He didn't have to check to see if they'd come back, because he couldn't feel her anymore. She was lost, and he didn't know how to find her. All he could do was hope they'd reconnect next month at the university.

When he pulled into the driveway at his house, his dad's car was already there. He frowned, then grabbed the sack with their food and went inside.

They were head-to-head at the table, whispering in hasty, urgent tones, but then the moment he walked into the kitchen, they hushed.

"What's wrong?" he asked, as he set the sack on the counter.

Chuck and Brenda had already agreed not to tell Hunt about the shocking phone call from Greg. It was better he didn't know Lainie was pregnant, and that they'd taken her away to get rid of it.

So, Chuck shrugged. "I got fired. Drinking on the job."

"And you're surprised?" Hunt muttered.

Chuck shrugged. "I don't know what changed. It's never mattered before," he muttered. "Anyway, you're gonna have to pick up the slack until I can find work again."

"Like hell," Hunt said. "Every penny I make is for college. You get your ass down to the unemployment office and sign up, and Mom can stay sober long enough to make it through the day shift at any number of restaurants in town. This is your mess, not mine."

Chuck jumped to his feet and started toward Hunt, his fists doubled up and ready to brawl, when it dawned on him that Hunt was a head taller, muscled-up to hell and back, well past the age of backing down.

Brenda rolled her eyes. "Sit your ass down, Chuck. Son, you got mail from the university," she said, and handed him a long, cream-colored envelope.

"I brought dinner. I'm going to wash up," he said, then took the envelope and went to his room. He sat down on the side of the bed, slid his finger beneath the flap and ripped it open, then pulled out the letter and began reading.

Within seconds, he broke out in a cold sweat, then took a breath and kept reading. He read it through twice, then laid it aside and leaned forward, his elbows on his knees, staring blindly at the floor through a wall of tears. There was a pain in his chest, and a knot in his belly.

The university had just rescinded his scholarship, and he knew with every breath he was taking that Greg Mayes was behind it. It was a death blow to his future.

The weight of the world was on his shoulders, and

when he stood, it felt like he'd aged a thousand years. His steps were dragging as he washed up and went to the table. His mother had cut up the chicken and put a spoon in the bowl of potato salad. She handed him a plate as he walked by. He put some food on his plate and put ice in a glass, then filled it with sweet tea.

His parents were already moving into their usual round of beer and banter, slinging barbs at each other as they ate, but he was numb. Their arguments didn't matter anymore. Nothing mattered. He tried to eat, but he couldn't swallow past the tears. He'd lost Lainie, and he'd lost his chance to get out of this hellhole life.

He went to bed that night as defeated as he'd ever been. He checked his phone as he did every night, praying there would be a text from her. But there was nothing. He put the phone on a charger and closed his eyes, but all he saw was her face, and the way her breath caught when she came apart in his arms.

HIS PARENTS WERE in their room down the hall, and after all that had happened today, they were as close to sober as they'd ever been.

"You still think it's best not to tell Hunt about Greg's call?" Brenda whispered.

Chuck grunted. "Hell yes. Greg is crazy out of his mind. The girl is pregnant and they're 'dealing with it.' Besides, what good would it do? After all this, they'll never be together again."

HUNT DIDN'T THINK he would sleep, but the next time he opened his eyes it was morning, and it felt like someone had died. He felt sad, and empty, and aimless. He left the house while his parents were still asleep and went to pick up his paycheck from the supermarket, told them he was quitting and then drove without purpose, randomly looking for a miracle. But there were no rainbows left in Hunter Gray's world.

When he stopped to get gas, Jody Turner, one of his friends from school, was on the other side of the pumps. He glanced up when he recognized Hunt's old truck.

"Hey, buddy. Saw a picture of Lainie in the paper. Who's the guy she was with?"

"That wasn't Lainie," Hunt muttered.

"Naw, man, it was her," Jody said.

Hunt looked up. "You think I don't know what she looks like in a bikini? That was not her body."

Jody's eyes widened. "No shit?"

"No shit," Hunt said.

"So, what's going on?" Jody asked.

"Her old man is what's going on," Hunt said, and then looked away, unwilling to talk about it anymore.

Jody finished filling up, then replaced the nozzle in the pump.

"Sorry, man. See you around," he said, and drove off.

Hunt filled up, and moments later got in the truck and began driving around the city, going up one street and down another, saying goodbye to the only place he'd ever known.

He didn't know where he was going, but he wasn't coming back. He drove without purpose for almost an hour before he turned onto City Park Avenue, and as he did, the building up ahead caught his eye. It was a knee-jerk decision that made him turn into the parking lot. He got out of the truck, and walked straight into the office, and up to the front desk.

A uniformed officer looked up, gave Hunt the once-over as he approached and liked what he saw.

"Morning, son. How can I help you?"

"My name is Hunter Gray. I want to enlist."

The officer got up and ushered him into another office.

"Sergeant Morley. We have a new recruit," the officer said.

Morley stood up to shake Hunt's hand. "Have a seat and let's see what we can do about that."

HUNT WENT HOME that afternoon, and walked in on a conversation that ended his last regret about joining the Army. His parents didn't know he'd come into the house and were in the kitchen, each of them with a bottle of beer in their hand, but he heard enough to know the fallout of Lainie's disappearance and the end of his scholarship were connected to what his dad was saying.

"It's all Greg's fault," Chuck whined. "He got me fired because Hunt wouldn't leave his daughter alone!"

Brenda shrugged. "Hunt wasn't chasing her. She loves him, too."

"For all the good it will do either of them now. They're gone and I'm glad. Hunt needs to remember his place," Chuck muttered.

Hunt walked into the kitchen, stared at his parents as if they were strangers, and then walked out again.

Brenda looked guilty, and Chuck cursed.

"Well, now you've done it," she said, and winced when she heard a door slam down the hall.

Hunt was sick all the way to his bones. His knee-jerk decision to join the Army was now his saving grace. The war between the two stepbrothers had destroyed every dream he ever had. He didn't know where he would be deployed, but it didn't matter. He didn't know if he'd have to go to war, or if he'd survive it if he did. But it didn't matter. Nothing mattered without Lainie, and she was lost to him.

ONE WEEK LATER, he was gone. He'd taken all of his personal papers to a lawyer for safekeeping. A birth certificate, a high school diploma, his SAT scores, his high school medals, and the awards that he'd won. And if he survived where he was going, then when he was stateside again, the lawyer would send them to him.

He'd left his truck keys and the letter from the university on his bed for his mother to find. He wasn't telling them where he was going, only where he was not.

IT WAS NEARLY noon before Brenda made her way into her son's room to sweep the floors. The closet door was ajar, and as she went to close it, saw that all of his clothes were gone.

"No, no, no," she moaned, and ran to the dresser. All of the drawers were empty.

There was a knot in her stomach as she turned around, then she saw a note on his bed and ran to get it. But it wasn't a note. It was the rejection letter from the university, and his truck keys were beneath it. A cold chill ran through her, and she began to weep.

WHEN CHUCK WANDERED home that evening from a day of job hunting, she met him at the door, shoved the letter in his face and began to scream. "This is what your war with Greg has caused. He's gone."

Chuck's heart sank when he saw the letter, but wouldn't admit any guilt for his son's absence. "He'll be back," he muttered.

"No, he won't. Because he has nothing to come back for, and it's just as much my fault as it is yours. I condoned your stupid brotherly war. I hope it was worth it because our son became collateral damage."

LAINIE HAD BEEN at her grandmother's house for just over two months, and five months into her pregnancy. Her belly was getting round, and she already felt a tiny kick now and then. She had convinced herself it was a boy, and begged her family to take her to a doctor for prenatal care, but they'd refused. She was onto their game. They were hoping she would miscarry.

She called her baby Little Bear, because her stomach was always growling, and every day she fell deeper in love with a child she had yet to see.

When she began to show, the only person who saw her body changing was Millie. Lainie refused to talk to her parents, and after a while, they quit trying. They'd brought Millie down to the country house over a month ago, and the moment Millie realized what was happening, she was shocked, but said little about it.

Once Millie arrived, Lainie regained a hope of escape, and began marking her parents' routine. She imagined Hunt was already at the university, so that's where she would go when she got free.

Her father had set up an office downstairs, and worked from home every day. Her mother had given up trying to make peace with her daughter, and wept copious tears daily at the situation.

Millie didn't hide her dismay at what was happening to Lainie, and feared for her health and the baby's health, being locked in that room like a prisoner. After a month had passed, she'd had enough.

It was October 3. A day like all the others as she took Lainie her lunch, but when she saw the dark circles under Lainie's eyes, and her drawn expression, it broke her heart.

She set the tray of food on a table by the window, and

when Lainie sat down to eat, Millie put a hand on her shoulder. "What can I do to help?"

Lainie's heart skipped. "Are you serious?"

"Yes. This is wrong. This is criminal, and I won't be a part of it any longer," she said.

Lainie was on her feet, so excited she could barely think. "Can you get the keys to my mother's car? She always keeps them in her purse, wherever that is."

Millie lifted her chin. "Yes, I know where it is. I will do that for you."

Lainie threw her arms around Millie's neck. "Thank you! Thank you! I will never forget this."

"Wait here," Millie said. "I have to get their food on the table. If I come back with the keys, then you'll know they are in the dining room. The rest is up to you. I'm not going to lock your door, but stay here until I get back, understand?"

Lainie nodded, and ran to pack up some clothes. She didn't have money or a phone, but she would go straight to the university and find Hunt. After that, she'd be safe.

Once she'd finished packing, she sat down to wait. It felt like forever, but less than fifteen minutes had passed before she heard footsteps coming up the hall.

The door opened. Millie laid the car keys on the little table by the door and blew Lainie a kiss, then walked away. Lainie shouldered her bag, grabbed the keys, and took the back staircase down to the main level, out a side door, and ran for her life. Once inside her mother's car, she wasted no time, and went flying down the driveway like a bird set free.

GREG HAD JUST taken a bite of shrimp scampi when he happened to glance out to the front gardens, and what he saw stopped his heart. He gasped, choked on his food, and then jumped up and ran.

Tina frowned. "Gregory! What on—" And then she glanced out the window and saw her car speeding away. "What the hell?" And then it hit her! That was Lainie! Tina ran out onto the veranda, screaming at Greg, who was running toward his Lexus. "Stop! Stop! You're going to get someone killed!"

And then Millie walked up behind her.

Tina saw the look on her housekeeper's face, and knew what she'd done.

"How dare you?" Tina screamed.

Millie had her purse over her shoulder, and threw her apron in Tina's face. "No, ma'am. How dare *you*? And I quit." Then she went back into the house and straight out the back to where her little Honda was parked and drove away.

Tina was alone in the house without a way to follow. She was screaming at the world as she began calling Greg.

"What?" he shouted.

"What are you doing?" she screamed.

"I'm going to stop her, that's what I'm doing!" he shouted. "I won't have her shaming our name. Do you hear me! I won't have it!"

The line went dead in Tina's ear! He'd hung up on her!

THE PRIVATE ROAD from the estate to the main road was clear of traffic. Lainie's plan was just to get to the highway and get lost in the traffic. She thought she was free and clear until she glanced into the rearview mirror, and saw her dad's black Lexus less than a quarter of a mile behind her, and closing in fast.

She tightened her grip on the steering wheel, and

stomped on the accelerator. After that, everything became a blur.

The hum of the engine turned into a roar. The thick layers of kudzu hanging from the trees and along the fences became a narrow green tunnel, and the road signs were mere blips as she flew past. Twice she skidded into a curve, and then steered out of it, but she couldn't drive fast enough to lose him. And then she glanced into the rearview mirror and the Lexus was behind her! This felt like a nightmare. The mother who used to sleep with her when she was sick had betrayed her. The father who once played dollhouse with her as a child had turned into the maniac in the car behind her. She had one brief glimpse of the enraged expression on his face, and then he rammed the bumper of her car.

After that, everything began happening in slow motion. The car went airborne, like a surfboard riding a wave, and began rolling. At first, the sun was in her eyes, and then she was sideways, and then upside down, and then everything was quiet. She heard the hiss of steam, and someone shouting, and then she was gone.

GREG MAYES RAGE had quickly turned to horror. He was already calling for an ambulance and the police as he braked to a stop. The car was upside down and smoking, and the silence was terrifying. He grabbed a fire extinguisher from the trunk of his car and ran, screaming Lainie's name as he unleashed the contents of the extinguisher. When it was empty, he threw it aside, then knelt and looked inside.

She was hanging upside down, still strapped into the seat, her hair veiling her face. He reached to push it aside, then saw her—and the blood, and in that moment wished to God he'd never looked out the front window.

He reached for her wrist, searching for a pulse. It was weak, but it was there.

"Lainie, sweetheart! It's Daddy. I'm so sorry. I never meant for… This shouldn't have…" And then he stopped. She couldn't hear him, and there would never be enough words to take any of this back.

His phone was ringing. It was Tina again.

"Where are you? Where's Lainie?"

"She wrecked the car. I'm waiting for the ambulance." He didn't share the fact that he'd caused it.

Tina moaned. "Is it bad?"

"Yes, but she's still alive."

"Oh, my God! This is all your fault. You and your hate for Chuck," she screamed.

"You're the one who said abortion. You're the one who wanted her 'cleaned out' before she showed up at your precious sorority. You're the one who didn't want to be embarrassed," he shouted.

Tina was sobbing so hard she could barely breathe. "And you're the one who said you'd rather see both of them dead than have her give birth to Hunter Gray's child. Looks like you're about to get your wish!"

"I hear sirens. Shut up and meet me at the hospital. I'll text you which one."

"Well, I can't. There's nothing left here to drive."

"Have Millie bring you," he said.

"She just threw her apron in my face and quit, so don't count on her to keep quiet about this whole mess. We're ruined in New Orleans. We can never go back."

Greg felt sick. The truth of who they were and what they'd done was becoming a painful reality. "I am watching my daughter die, and you're worried about your reputation. Mother of the Year," Greg muttered, and disconnected.

And then Millie's car appeared in the roadway. She braked and jumped out on the run.

"What have you done?" she screamed. "You're a monster! Both of you! Is she alive?"

"Yes, she's alive, and you don't talk to me like that!" Greg shouted.

"I'll talk to you anyway I choose," Millie cried. "I don't work for you anymore, and I'll tell the authorities what you did."

Greg flinched, and without thinking started toward Millie, but she was too fast. She was back in her car and flying past them. He watched in dismay as she drove away. Everything Tina said was already coming to pass.

Millie would talk, but she didn't witness the wreck. Their reputations would be ruined. His lawyer would keep them from any criminal charges, unless Lainie lived to tell another story. But he'd cross that bridge when they came to it.

LAINIE REGAINED CONSCIOUSNESS two days later, to the repetitive sound of soft voices and beeps. She didn't know where she was, or understand what it meant, and slipped back under.

Hours later, she began coming to again, and this time opened her eyes. The light was blinding, and the pain was so intense it hurt to breathe. Her mouth felt funny, and when she licked her lips, they felt swollen. Then she heard someone saying her name.

"Lainie. Lainie, can you hear me?"

She blinked at the stranger who'd just appeared beside her bed.

"Lainie, I'm Dr. Reasor. You're in a hospital. Do you remember what happened?"

She closed her eyes, trying to think past the pain, when she flashed on running from the house.

"Wreck," she whispered, then tears rolled. She felt empty. The baby was gone. She choked on a sob.

"No baby?"

He touched her shoulder. "No baby. I'm so sorry. It was a bad wreck."

"Chasing me," she mumbled.

Reasor frowned. "Who was chasing you?"

"Daddy."

Reasor only knew she'd been in a wreck. Not that she was being chased. "Your parents are here. They've been waiting for days to talk to you."

All of the machines hooked to her body began beeping and dinging, as her fingers curled around his wrist.

"No...never...don't let them..." The darkness pulled her under.

"She passed out," the nurse said. "What do we tell her parents?"

"That she said no."

SCANDAL WAS ALWAYS good press. And finding out that even the rich aren't immune, even better.

When Lainie was finally moved into a private room, her parents were AWOL. She was of age. She didn't need their approval for her own treatments. But they fully understood that since they broke her in every way possible, they were also liable for the costs of what it took to fix her.

Some days she was so miserable she wished she'd died with her baby, and other days she was so angry, all she could think about was getting even. This morning, she was waiting for Dr. Reasor to make his rounds, because she had questions. And when he and his nurse finally arrived, she was ready.

"Good morning, Lainie. Have you been up and walking this morning?" he asked.

"Yes, and I have a question. I need to know if my baby was a girl or a boy."

Reasor put a hand on her shoulder. "It was a boy. I'm so sorry."

All the breath left her body. It took her a few moments to remember to inhale, and when she did, there were tears on her cheeks. "What happened to his remains?"

"They were cremated at your parents' request. I don't know beyond that," he said.

"I have to know which funeral home they were sent to."

He sat down, pulled up her records on his laptop, scanned the text and then looked up. "Schoen and Son Funeral Home picked them up."

"Thank you," she said, and remained silent as he finished his examination, and then left.

Millie had been visiting her every day, and when she came that afternoon, as soon as they'd greeted each other, Lainie blurted out what she'd learned.

"My parents made the decision to have my baby's remains cremated at Schoen Funeral Home. The doctor told me this morning it was a little boy. I always thought it was," she said, and drew a slow, shaky breath. "I need to know if his ashes are still at the funeral home, or if my parents took them. I'm going to call Schoen's and ask if they're there. If they are, would you please pick them up and keep them for me until I get out of here?"

Now Millie was weeping. "Yes, of course. Just let me know if they are, and I'll get them today."

"Thank you. I don't want my parents touching him.

I'd ask Hunt to come get them, but he doesn't answer his phone."

Millie felt like she was delivering another death notice, but Lainie had to know. "Oh, honey, Hunt's gone. He's disappeared, and no one knows why. All anyone knows is that he never showed up at Tulane."

Lainie was in shock. All this time she'd pictured him already at school. She didn't understand it. He'd been so thrilled to get that full-ride scholarship to play football at Tulane. Another piece of her life had gone missing.

As soon as Millie left, she called the funeral home, identified herself, and asked to speak to the director, and was put on hold. She was staring out the window when he finally answered.

"Good morning, Miss Mayes. On behalf of everyone at Schoen and Son, I extend our deepest condolences. How may I be of service?" he asked.

"I was told you picked up my son's remains for cremation. I need to know where his ashes are."

"Yes, of course. Your mother said to keep them on hold and—"

"What are they in?" she asked.

"A small black box. However, if you want to keep, rather than scatter or inter, we have small, ornamental urns for infant cremains."

"Like what?" Lainie asked.

"Ceramic teddy bears in pink or blue. Little brass heart-shaped boxes in pink or blue, or if you'd rather—"

"A blue brass heart," Lainie said. "I'm still in the hospital, so I'll be sending our housekeeper, Millie Swayze, to pick up my baby's ashes."

"Of course. I'll let my people know. All she'll have to do is sign the release form, stating that she's taking them from our premises with your permission."

"And you have it," Lainie said. "Thank you for your help. Millie will be there later today."

She called Millie the moment the call ended, and once the message had been delivered, she put a pillow over her face and screamed into it until she was numb.

A COUPLE OF days later, there was a knock on the door, then as it opened, Brenda Gray slipped inside.

"Lainie, may we speak?"

Seeing Hunt's mother at the door was a shock, but Lainie was hopeful she'd find out where he'd gone. "Yes, please."

Brenda's voice was shaking as she approached the bed. "I'm so sorry for all you've been through."

"Where's Hunt?" Lainie asked.

Brenda's eyes welled. "We don't know. He went into a deep despair when you disappeared, and then a few days after you went missing, he got a letter from the university rescinding his scholarship. A week later, he was gone. No note. No nothing. He left his truck keys on the bed and left the letter for us to see. We don't know where he went, but it wasn't to college. He hasn't responded to any of our calls. We don't know anything. But even after he saw the picture of you and the other boy, he didn't believe it. He said it wasn't you."

Lainie's heart skipped. "What picture? There was no other boy. I was locked in a room in my grandmother's house."

Brenda pulled out the newspaper clipping that she'd kept, as well as Hunt's letter from the university, and handed them to her.

Lainie was shocked by the photo and the letter. She looked up in dismay, her voice trembling.

"Oh, my God! That's not me. That's not my body."

Brenda sighed. "That's what Hunt said. He never thought for a minute that it was. But after the loss of his scholarship, I think he knew your father was behind it, and was never going to stop tearing at the both of you. He had nowhere to go, and nothing to stay for. God knows we didn't give him the family he deserved. We were too busy being mad at each other to see what it was doing to you and Hunt until it was too late. I'm so sorry. Nobody knows I'm here, but I'm giving you the picture and the letter. You deserve to know he didn't walk out on you. He was driven away. We broke him, and I don't think we'll ever see him again."

Lainie burst into tears. She was still sobbing, with the papers clutched against her chest, long after Brenda was gone. Losing Hunt *and* their baby was the final straw.

She had her grandmother's trust fund to help her relocate, and reassess her future. She had to find something that gave her purpose, because right now she was as broken as a soul could be and still be breathing.

ON THE DAY that Lainie was finally released from the hospital, Millie picked her up and took her back to the family home to get her car, and help pack her things. They already knew her parents had stayed in Baton Rouge, so she wasn't worried about running into them again.

"I'll get the suitcases. You go on up to your room," Millie said.

Lainie's footsteps echoed in the grand hallway as she started up the stairs. It was like the house already knew it had no purpose anymore. It felt strange to be back here, and even more so when she entered her room. The bloodstain was still on her floor. She stared at it a moment, then looked away. That had been the beginning of the end. Today was the beginning of her future. Now she had to decide what to take with her.

The first thing she put aside to take was the brown teddy bear Hunt had given her for Valentine's Day. Then she began pulling out clothes and shoes from her closet, and putting them all on the bed, and emptying the dresser drawers.

The picture of her and Hunt was in the wastebasket. Likely, her mother's doing. She pulled it out to take with her. She loved him. She would always love him. Nothing was going to change that. Then she began emptying the drawer in the bedside table, found the charger cord for her phone and tossed it on the bed. She didn't know where her phone was, but guessed her mother had taken it. It didn't matter. She'd get another one, with a new number they'd never know. Then she began taking clothes off hangers and folding them to pack.

Millie returned with four large suitcases and a travel bag. "If you need more, I'll get them."

Lainie sank down onto the side of the bed. "I'm out of breath. I guess I'm not as healed as I thought."

"You're just weak from being in bed so long," Millie said. "You sit, and I'll pack what you want."

Lainie sighed. "I don't know what I would have done these past weeks without you. You have been the best friend I could ask for."

Millie wiped away a few tears. "I have struggled with the guilt of getting you the keys. I never dreamed your father would chase you like that."

"If it hadn't been for you, I would still be locked up in that room," Lainie said. "What happened afterward was entirely my father's fault. I blame them and no one else."

"They got away with it," Millie said.

Anger was thick in Lainie's voice. "I knew they would. I heard about the story he spun. All in my best interests,

I believe. And only destroyed two lives and killed a baby to do it."

"The law let them off the hook, but the media and their friends did not, and that's something," Millie said. "They were crucified in the local papers. I don't think they'll ever move back."

Lainie shrugged. "I don't care. Let's hurry. I want to get out of here as soon as possible."

They were down to packing her shoes when Millie dropped one. As she bent down to pick it up, she saw the corner of Lainie's cell phone beneath the bed, and pulled it out.

"Look what I found," she said.

Lainie turned around. "My phone! It must have fallen there when Daddy knocked me out! I'll try charging it in my car. Maybe there's a message from Hunt. Thank you, Millie! This is the best thing ever! Maybe I'll be able to find out where he went."

Millie smiled. "I hope so, honey. I hope so."

They finished packing, then rolled the suitcases down the hall, with the stuffed bear on top for the ride.

"You better see if your car will start," Millie said. "It's been sitting for months."

"Right," Lainie said, and hurried out to check. She slid behind the wheel of her SUV, and held her breath as she put the key in the ignition. To her relief, it started on the first try. "Thank you, Lord," she muttered, and backed it up and drove to the front of the house.

They put three suitcases in the back, and the fourth one and the travel bag in the back seat. The heart with her baby's ashes was in its own box, and lying on the back floorboard.

"I have to get some stuff out of the safe," Lainie said. "You can leave now if you want. I'll be okay."

Millie shook her head. "I'm not leaving you alone until I know you're ready to drive away. Go do what you have to do. I'll wait out here."

Lainie ran back inside and down to the safe in her father's office. She knew the combination and quickly unlocked it, then sorted through the files until she found the one with her name on it. It had all of the paperwork for the trust fund her grandmother had left to her, her birth certificate, her high school diploma, and her SAT test scores. Then she closed the safe, locked the front door as she left, and dropped the house key through the mail slot.

Millie was waiting by the vehicle with tears in her eyes.

"I'm going to miss you, but I know you're going to bounce. You're a survivor, Lainie. You don't know any other way to be. You have my number. You know my address. I would love it if you stayed in contact, but if you don't, I'll understand. Sometimes a clean break is the only way to begin anew. Either way, I love you, honey, and remember, the best revenge is to succeed when people want you to fail."

Lainie hugged her close. "I love you, Millie, and I'll never forget what you sacrificed for me. Be well, and don't worry about me. I'll be fine."

Then she slid into the seat of her SUV, and put her phone on the charger before driving away. After a quick trip to the bank to empty her personal checking account, and a quick stop at her family lawyer, she left New Orleans. The sun was above her head, and the echoes of dead dreams were behind her.

LAINIE HAD BEEN driving for the better part of five hours before finally stopping in Natchitoches. It wasn't late, but she was too weak to drive farther. She needed food and rest, and found a motel.

Once inside, she dropped her travel bag on the bed and pulled the recharged cell phone out of her purse to see if it still worked, and it did. She ordered food from a local restaurant to be delivered to her room, then sat down on the bed to check for messages.

They were months old, and all from Hunt, with each one sounding more desperate than the last, and all of them taking her back to the night of the storm, relieving her own horror, and seeing his fear for her in the texts. But it was the last message he'd sent that destroyed her.

Lainie, I know in my heart that something is wrong. But I can't save you because I don't know where you are. I don't know what happened to you, but I know it wasn't your choice to disappear. You are my love—my true north, and you always will be. I gave you my heart a long time ago. Feel free to keep it because it's no use to me without you in it.
Hunt

She read it over and over until she was sobbing too hard to see the words, and when she tried to call him, all she heard was a recorded message. *The number you called is either disconnected, or no longer in service.*

After that, the idea of sending a text was no longer an option. She had to face the hard truth that he was truly lost to her.

Wherever she settled, she would get a new phone and new number. It was a scary thought, because then she'd be lost to him as well. But she wasn't losing this text. So, she took a screen shot of it, then sent it to her email and began trying to pull herself back together.

A few minutes later, there was a knock at her door. Her food had arrived, and tomorrow was another day.

DENVER, COLORADO, became Lainie's final destination. It took her two more days to get there because of her constant need to rest. But she'd spent her downtime online, researching nursing schools in the city and looking at apartments to rent.

She had one phone conversation with the family lawyer while she was on the road, and he reassured her that he was well aware of her situation and that everything he did for her was in confidence. He told her to contact him once she was settled and had chosen a new bank, and he would make sure that the first annuities from her trust fund would be deposited in that account, and then twice a year thereafter. The irony of being saved from the grave by the woman in whose house she had been imprisoned was not lost upon her.

Within a week, Lainie had rented a small, furnished apartment and was investigating a nursing school program, preparing to embark on a long journey alone.

The ensuing months were often scary and lonely, and there were days when she was so depressed that she could barely lift her head, but this was her reality, and she would find a way to rise above it.

GREG AND BRENDA MAYES went through their days in silence, or in screaming fights with each other. They didn't know Lainie had been released from the hospital until they received a final bill, and then they panicked.

"This was dated last week! Where is she?" Tina cried.

Greg shrugged. "She probably went home."

"I need to know!" Tina said. "Take me there now!"

"She won't talk to us," Greg said.

"I don't care, dammit! I just need to know!" Tina begged.

They took Greg's Lexus, and rode in silence all the way to their New Orleans home. As they were pulling up, they noticed that Lainie's car was gone.

"Oh, my God," Tina moaned.

"She's probably just out shopping," Greg said, but Tina jumped out of the car and ran, her hands trembling as she unlocked the door.

The first thing she saw when she opened it was a gold key on the floor. She picked it up and turned it over.

"Lainie's house key. It has that little spot of pink fingernail polish on it," she said, and ran up the stairs and down the hall to Lainie's old room.

The door was wide open. Closet doors were ajar. Dresser drawers were half-open, and everything that had belonged to their daughter was gone.

Tina let out a shriek that sent a chill all the way to Greg's soul. The last time he'd heard that sound was the second before their baby crowned during delivery. It appeared the pain of a mother's delivery was equal to the pain of that same child's death. Lainie might be alive in the world somewhere, but she was dead to them, and Tina knew it. He turned his head and walked away.

HUNT'S ARMY APTITUDE tests had labeled him proficient in all the things it took to be a pilot, and the thought of flying Army helicopters was his first choice. Over the ensuing months, he went from Basic Combat Training to Warrant Officer Training School, then to Basic Helicopter training to learn how to fly. At the end of that course, he received his wings and went on to in-depth survival training.

By April of the next year, he was on his way to Fort Bragg for training on the Apache simulators on base. His hand-eye coordination, which had made him a good quarterback, his attention to detail, and a near photographic memory soon put him at the head of the class.

Nearly three years after leaving New Orleans, Warrant Officer Gray was now fit to fly Apache Longbows, the most formidable attack helicopters the US Army owned. But the new had barely worn off his rank when the US Army received new orders.

Troops were being deployed back to Iraq, this time to join in the fight against ISIS. It was a sobering moment of Hunt's existence, and on the day of their company's deployment, he was quiet and withdrawn.

He'd made friends, but none of them knew his story. All they saw was what the Army had made of him, turning body bulk to hard muscle. He rarely smiled, and a quick glare ended the beginning of any argument.

They called him Gator, because of his slow, Louisiana drawl, but it remained to be seen what would happen over there. Would they live to come home? Would they come home scarred and missing limbs? Or would they come home in a coffin?

And that was Hunt's mindset. He guessed he might die there, or come home crippled, but without Lainie, he didn't really care.

Chapter Two

The troops hit the ground running upon arrival. Base camps and communications had already been set up in a vast desert basin surrounded by mountains. The layout was not unlike a wheel, with the helicopters in their own space in the middle, then tent cities and portable buildings laid out accordingly. Medical and medics in their own area. Troops in their areas next to motor pool, and pilots bunking near the choppers that they flew. The entire base camp was fenced, with a single-entry point and rotating guards.

Nearby villages were still inhabited by locals, but after so many homes and buildings had been destroyed by the wars, the survivors lived in little more than hovels cobbled together from whatever was left.

When the pilots weren't in the air, their time on base was about strategy sessions and daily updates from their commanders. Waiting for intel, plans changing on a dime to take down the next group of insurgents.

Troops on the ground dealt with snipers and IEDs, and when soldiers on the ground needed air support, they called in an air strike. For them, the blade slap of Apache Longbows was better than the jingle of Santa's sleigh bells on Christmas night.

The quick strafe of ammo from the choppers always

sent the enemy scurrying for cover. The precision launch of radar-control Hellfire and Stinger missiles blew up enemy tanks and insurgent strongholds.

Hunt's near-perfect record for hitting targets in the simulator had given him the gunner position, which put him in the front seat of an Apache as both gunner and copilot, while the pilot steered from the back seat.

Hunt's pilot was a man they called Preacher. He got the name by quoting Bible verses instead of curses during times of stress.

As the months passed, the violence of where they were had begun to smooth the rough edges of Hunt's grief. Surrounded daily by death, the hunger and hardship of the people of this nation took him out of his own sadness. Humanity was at war with inhumanity, and he was just a heartbeat in the middle of the roar. He still dreamed of Lainie, and made love to her in his sleep. He could still remember the scent of her and the sound of her voice. But he had no tears left to cry.

As the months passed, his dreams became rehashes of battle and bombs, of snipers and death. Of children laughing in a street one moment, and running from gunfire the next. Of witnessing a woman approaching the gate of their base with a child in her arms. They could hear the woman praying aloud to Allah over and over in a high-pitched shriek, while wearing explosives strapped to her body.

The guards had been given orders to fire when she suddenly stumbled, falling shy of the gate by about a hundred yards. The explosion blew her and her child to kingdom come. It rocked the entire compound. Blew the guards off their feet, and left a hole in the land where she fell.

The sadness and madness of war was never-ending, and whoever was still alive when night came lived to fight another day.

LIKE EVERY SOLDIER, Hunt had long ago accepted that what he did in the air also killed whatever was on the ground. He tried not to think of innocents caught in cross fire, or of the children they sacrificed as human shields.

He dreamed of the hot, humid heat of the Louisiana swamps and woke up to blowing sand and a land so dry the sky looked yellow. It was cold in the winter, with snow and rain in the northern mountains, but cold weather didn't ever stop war.

He missed the drawl of the Deep South, and the Cajun accents from the streets. He missed the taste of Creole gumbo that started from a rich dark roux. It bubbled with tomatoes and okra, had thick, fat shrimps and chunks of andouille sausage, and was seasoned with filé gumbo powder that cooked down to a heavenly stew, then was served over a big bowl of rice. He dreamed of promising Lainie the world on their last Mardi Gras together, and woke up wondering where she was.

There was only one real rule that mattered in war, and that was never for a second forget the constant danger you are in. Forgetting could get you killed. Even during a pickup basketball game on base, on a hot windy day.

HUNT'S T-SHIRT WAS drenched with sweat and stuck to his body. Because of his long arms and ability for high leaps, he'd just blocked a shot from a gunner they called Rat. Rat had retrieved his own rebound and was dribbling back out for a long shot.

Preacher was on Hunt's team. He saw Rat dribbling out, and when he turned to make a long shot, Preacher came running up behind him to steal the ball.

Hunt saw the glee on Preacher's face. Then someone else was shouting at Rat, "Behind you! Behind you!" when all expression on Preacher's face disappeared.

It was the bullet hole in Preacher's forehead that sent Hunt running toward him in a crouch, but he never made it. The second shot fired hit Hunt in the back. The blood from Preacher's head wound was already soaking into the sand as Hunt dropped. He heard T-Bone shouting, "Gator's down," saw Rat running for his weapon, and then somebody turned out the lights.

HE WOKE UP in the ICU of a Level 1 medical unit, with an Army nurse standing over him.

"Welcome back, soldier. Surgery went well. The shot nicked a rib, exited out your side and missed all your vital organs."

Hunt grunted, then closed his eyes.

"You kept saying the name 'Lainie,' over and over. You don't have any next of kin listed. Would you like us to notify her?"

A tear rolled out from under his eyelid. "Don't know where she is. She's lost…like me," Hunt said, and fell back under the drugs.

He learned later they'd taken out the sniper up on the rim of a surrounding mountain, but Preacher was still dead. There would be no more Bible verses as he drew a bad hand at poker. No more preaching in Hunt's ear when they flew. Preacher's war was over, and Hunt's was on hold. He spent two weeks off duty before he was cleared again to fly.

The next time Hunt went up, it was with another pilot, with the call sign, T-Bone. Their missions were successful, but Hunt missed the Bible verses in his ear.

After that, life became a blur. Their company was moved so many times he lost count. They'd get sent stateside only long enough to get their bearings before they'd be deployed to another place of unrest.

Being a chopper pilot meant he owed ten years of his life to the Army, but he often wondered what would happen if he didn't make it to ten. Who would pay that debt for him if he died?

THE FIRST FIVE years of Hunt's service flew past, but the last five felt like forever. On base, it didn't matter so much not getting mail, because they had their own housing. But when they were deployed, mail mattered, and he never received letters or any packages from home, even though the other guys who did always shared.

T-Bone's wife sent gummy bears and Werther's caramels.

Rat's mother sent the best ginger snaps on the planet, and Roadrunner's wife often mailed them huge bags of flavored popcorn.

A pilot they called Memphis got chocolate fudge and divinity on every holiday, and they fought over the last pieces and laughed.

Cowboy, who was Memphis's gunner, got boxes of homemade beef jerky—a highly sought-after commodity they used for money in their poker games.

Hunt was the odd man out with nothing to share.

WHEN WORD BEGAN to spread that "Gator" was being discharged, his buddies were all in shock. Even Hunt's commanding officer was rendered speechless by the request. He'd assumed Gator would retire out of the Army, but there was no dissuading him, and he accepted the soldier's rights without questioning his reasons.

"Warrant Officer Gray, I have to say, I am sorry to see you go. You have been a huge asset. I hope you find what you're looking for," he said. "I'll put your papers through."

"Thank you, sir," Hunt said, saluted, and then left.

WHEN THE DAY of Hunt's discharge finally rolled around, he was at his quarters on base, packing to leave. He'd left the boy he'd been somewhere back in Louisiana, and the Army had turned what was left of him into a lean soldier with a rock-hard, war-weary body.

Never had he looked more like the old sepia photograph of his great-grandfather than he did now. Crow-black hair. Skin burned brown by desert sun. The beginnings of tiny crow's-feet at the corners of ice blue eyes. A sharp edge to his jaw, and not an ounce of body fat left on him.

He was emotionally burned out.

Over.

Done.

He'd been a part of death and destruction in a way no human should ever face. But war did that, and there was no way around it except to wade through it and ask God for the forgiveness he wasn't able to give himself.

The men he'd flown with and fought with knew he was leaving, and had gathered at his quarters to watch him pack. Their normal chatter was absent. They still couldn't reconcile the fact of never seeing him again.

He knew them by their call signs better than he did their given names. T-Bone. Rat. Roadrunner. Memphis. Cowboy. Galahad. Duke. Sundown. Chili Dog. Tulsa. Cherokee. They'd flown together. Lived together. Bled together.

"You're gonna be a hard act to follow," Rat said.

Gator was a legend among his peers, but in all the years they'd been together, they were beginning to realize they only knew the soldier. They knew nothing about the man.

Roadrunner still couldn't believe he was leaving. "So, Gator, where are you headed?"

Hunt kept shoving socks into his duffel bag without looking up. "Flagstaff. Got a job flying choppers for a charter service."

Rat frowned. "That's a long way from Louisiana. I kinda thought you'd be headed home to family."

Hunt paused, and this time he looked up and began carefully scanning their faces, imprinting the moment forever in his memory.

"This place was home. You are my family. Don't go and get yourselves killed," he said, then shouldered his duffel bag and walked out, with them following behind him.

A soldier and a Humvee were waiting for him. He tossed his bags in the back, crawled into the passenger seat and never looked back as they drove away.

Rat had a lump in his throat and a knot in his belly. It felt like losing a brother. "Dammit. Somebody slap me. I have a sudden urge to cry."

Roadrunner cleared his throat and swiped at his eyes. "He never did get over losing Preacher."

Rat shook his head. "I think he lost someone who mattered more, long before he came here."

HUNT SPENT HIS first night as a civilian in a hotel in nearby Fayetteville. He had a flight out to Flagstaff the next morning, and after he got to his room, he checked in with Pete Randolph, the man who would be his new boss.

"Hey, Hunt. Where are you?" Pete asked.

"Still in North Carolina. I have a flight out tomorrow. I'll be in Flagstaff sometime late afternoon."

"Awesome! We're really looking forward to you joining the crew, but take time to find living quarters. Tend to whatever business you need to do, and then give me a call when you've settled, and I'll show you around."

"Thanks, Pete. I appreciate this."

"Hey, I'm the one who got lucky. You're the most highly trained chopper pilot I've ever hired. Even with all my years in the air, you've got me beat. You flew Longbows, man. An Apache pilot is an ace in my book."

"Ex-Apache pilot. I like flying, but I can do without being shot at. I'll be in touch," he said, then disconnected.

HUNT WAS AT the airport early the next morning. He grabbed a sweet roll and a coffee on his way to his gate, and without thinking, began searching the faces of every approaching female in the concourse, while ignoring the looks women were giving him.

The aviator sunglasses he wore had a twofold purpose. Wearing them to hide his eyes was like wearing a mask, as well as using them for blocking out the sun. He didn't have civilian clothes that fit anymore, and was wearing dark charcoal tactical pants and a plain gray T-shirt beneath his flight jacket. The shirt clung to his abs like a lover, giving a hint of the dog tags beneath it.

His boots were old, but polished. He was wearing a baseball cap with an Army star insignia, and his black leather flight jacket with an official Army patch on the back, and an Apache chopper patch on his sleeve.

He knew the odds of seeing Lainie again were infinitesimal, but through all the times he thought he would die in a country not his own, luck had been with him. It stood to reason he could get lucky again.

When he reached the gate, he stood near a window to use the sill for a table, and set his coffee on it while he ate. It was the first time in years that the choices he was making were all his own. The weight of duty had been shed, and he felt lighter. If he wanted, he could search for Lainie now. But there was a part of him afraid to find out where she was. He didn't want to know if she'd married someone else. He couldn't bear the thought of her sleeping in someone else's arms. So, he let the thought fade, and decided to let fate play the hand for him.

When they began boarding, he fell in line, and once on the plane quickly took his seat. It felt strange being in a regular passenger plane, but he wasn't flying over hostile territory anymore, and after the plane was in the air, he stretched his legs and put the cap in his lap.

A flight attendant came by later and quietly whispered, "Thank you for your service," as she handed him a beverage.

He grasped the cup and nodded.

And elderly man in the opposite aisle had already seen the patches on Hunt's jacket, and leaned across the aisle.

"Active duty?" he asked.

Hunt shook his head. "Not anymore."

"Ah…headed home, then," the man said.

"I'm already home," Hunt said. "Just looking for a place to be," then finished his beverage, set the empty cup on the tray table and closed his eyes.

After that, nobody bothered him. He changed planes in Atlanta, and then had a straight flight to Flagstaff from there. By the time he landed, it was late afternoon. He caught a cab to the hotel where he'd made a reservation, and as soon as he had checked in and dumped his stuff in his room, he went down to the dining room and ordered steak with all the trimmings, and sweet tea. It wasn't southern sweet, but it suited him. Afterward, he went straight back to his room to shower and shave, then kicked back in bed with the intent of watching a movie, and fell asleep within minutes.

And he dreamed.

LAINIE WAS LYING beneath him, her arms locked around his neck. There were tears in her eyes, and her lips were slightly parted, as if trying to catch her breath. They'd both been scared when they laid down. She'd never had sex. He'd never made love to a virgin. He was fully erect and protected, and she was willing, but this was a hell of a responsibility he didn't want to flub.

"I love you, Lainie, but don't know how to keep from hurting you," he whispered.

"I know that, but I love you, too, and you're worth it," she said, and held her breath as he moved between her legs, and then slipped inside her, felt the barrier and pushed.

Quick tears came with a gasp, and then he began to move, and the pain was gone. She looked up into the face above her, and then wrapped her arms around his neck and closed her eyes. It felt good. It felt right. And it kept getting better. She didn't know what a climax was until it hit, and then she lost her mind.

The blood rush was still rolling through when Hunt raised up and began searching her face, afraid of what she'd think. How she'd feel.

"Did it hurt you, darlin'?"

"Only for a second," she said. "The rest was magic."

His hands were in her hair as he leaned down and kissed her.

"I have dreamed of what this would be like, to make love to you. It was perfect. You're perfect."

Her gaze was locked upon his face. He had that raptor look in his eyes. Like he'd just caught the prey he'd been after, and claimed it. It was the side of him that turned him into a machine on the football field. That fight or die mindset. She loved it and she loved him.

"Hunter James Gray, you are my first love. My last love. My only love. It will always be you."

"God, Lainie. I don't know what I did to deserve you, but I love you so much I ache from it," he whispered, then moved from her, and stretched out beside her instead.

Silence filled the moments as they nestled in each other's arms, but it was Lainie who broke the silence, and her voice was shaking when she spoke.

"If I ever get lost from you, Hunt, don't quit me. It will never be my choice."

He knew where that was coming from. Their fathers' war.

"If they cause trouble, I'll find a way to save you. I promise," he said.

"I promise... I promise... I promise."

HUNT WOKE UP saying the words. "I promise. I promise."

The moment he heard his voice, the old regret rolled through him, but today he was starting over. He threw back the covers and headed for the shower again. He had a thousand things to do today, and finding a place to live was first on the list.

WITHIN A WEEK, Hunt signed a lease on a 900 square foot, two-bedroom, one-bath house on the outskirts of Flagstaff. He just spent the last ten years of his life within an army, responding to orders shouted, the constant chatter of conversation, and when deployed, a multitude of snoring. He needed peace and privacy. He was lost, and looking for the man he would be without the boots and uniforms.

With a new address to his name, he then contacted the lawyer back in New Orleans to have his personal papers sent. He didn't know if his parents still lived where they had, or if they were even still alive, and didn't care. They were part of what broke him.

The job he'd taken with Randolph Tours and Charters was perfect. Nothing was asked of him but to ferry people from one place to another. Wherever he went, he was always home by evening. The churning waters of his life were beginning to calm. He was almost twenty-nine years old, and most days, he felt fifty, but life went on, taking him with it.

SIX HUNDRED SEVENTY-SEVEN miles north, Lainie Mayes was leaving home in a downpour on her way to work at Denver Health Center. She'd long ago switched her studies from nursing to X-ray and radiology, then on to becoming Certified in Radiologic Technology. She was coming up on her ninth year at the facility, and was as satisfied with her path in life as she knew how to be. There was a hole in her heart, and a tear in her soul, but she was still standing. She glanced back at the house as she was driving away.

It was her refuge. The place where she could unload frustrations and tears in the privacy of her own home, and she bought it the second year after she received her CRT certification.

THE THREE-BEDROOM BRICK, two bath house had been a fixer-upper when she took possession, and the first thing she did was hire a contractor to remodel and update it to her style.

The first thing she changed were the old red bricks. She had them painted a soft, eggshell white, then repainted the shutters sage green. The extra-wide door was stripped down to the wood, and refinished in a cherrywood stain to match the fireplace mantel in the living room.

And when the exterior was finished, the contractor began restructuring the interior, taking down walls, remodeling the entire kitchen, retiling the fireplace and the bathrooms, adding a stand-up shower in the en suite, and a soaker tub instead of the old Jacuzzi. She finished all the walls in white, and used furniture and decor to add color.

The fireplace had been converted to gas logs, which suited her, and she also kept the massive cherrywood mantel and retiled the surround. It was her favorite feature in the house. Not only was it striking, but useful in offsetting the harsh Denver winters.

One day not long after she moved, she picked up a child-size rocking chair at a tag sale. When she got home, she set it beside the hearth, then went into her bedroom to get her old teddy bear and carried it back to the fireplace.

She gave the soft, floppy bear a gentle hug. "My treasures forever," she whispered, then set it down in the rocker and stepped back to get a better view.

After all these years, the bear's floppy head had begun to tilt the slightest bit to the right, like it was waiting to hear another secret. Without Hunt in her life, she'd given them all to his bear.

She turned the smallest bedroom into an office, and lined an entire wall with bookshelves, and through the ensuing years, filled them with books. On her days off when the weather was dreary, she puttered around her kitchen, trying new recipes and baking, and when the weather was good, she hiked the trails in the surrounding mountains.

The day she finally moved in, she said a little prayer, thanking her grandmother's generosity in leaving her that trust, and settled in like a little hen in a nest. She liked her job, and had long since mastered driving in snow. In short, Denver had become her home.

She'd framed Hunt's last text message to her, and hung it over the headboard of her bed as a talisman against bad dreams and lonely nights. But it didn't stop the longing. Time had not eased her broken heart.

She was barely twenty when she first began working at the hospital; she'd had to go through the gamut of being the new, single woman on the job. Doctors, interns, co-workers, even patients hit on her, and her friends kept trying to fix her up with dates, until they realized it was futile. They didn't know her story, but it was apparent having a partner of any kind was not on her radar.

Sometimes she'd hang out with friends, but only as part of a group, and wherever she went, she arrived alone and left the same way. She didn't want another man holding her. Kissing her. Making love to her. She'd had the best. And if she couldn't have Hunt, she chose no one at all.

THE RAIN WAS still pouring as Lainie pulled into the employee parking lot, but she'd come prepared. She had a raincoat over her clothes, and an umbrella over her head as she got out running. Once inside, she headed to her locker, stowed her things, grabbed the lanyard with her ID and pass card and put it around her neck. After a quick check of her pockets to make sure she had everything she needed, she locked her locker and went to check the schedule.

Soon, she was on the job, readying a thirtysomething woman for X-rays. After that, it was a succession of patients, and the morning passed. When there was a break in her schedule, she went down to the cafeteria to grab some lunch, and saw some friends eating at a table, and headed over.

"Got room for one more?" she asked.

A little blonde named Charis Colby waved a French fry in the air. "Sit by me," she said. "I need positive vibes. I just weighed myself this morning and it's not looking good for that wedding dress I'm soon going to need."

Lainie smiled at the comment and the French fry as she sat. "So, you've finally set a date, have you?"

Charis rolled her eyes. "I have six months to pull a wedding together. My mother is in hysterics. You'd think she was the one getting married."

They laughed in sympathy, and then picked up the conversation, most of which was hospital gossip, as they ate. Lainie kept an eye on the time and was just about finished when she noticed a heavyset man in scrubs approaching the table with a food tray. He was a bald, thirtysomething man with broad shoulders, and a mat of thick brown hair on his arms, but it was the look on his face that alerted every ounce of self-preservation within her. To her dismay, he stopped at their table. Before she could leave, Charis was introducing her.

"Hey Lainie, this is Justin Randall…a new nurse on our floor. Justin, this is Lainie Mayes. She's in radiology."

"Lainie, it's a pleasure to meet you," he said.

Lainie nodded politely. "You, too. Welcome to Denver Health. Sorry, but I've gotta run. Later, y'all."

She picked up her tray as she went, sorted the dirty dishes and silverware at the station, and left the cafeteria. She didn't have to look back to know he was still watching her. She could feel it, and it gave her the creeps.

Justin frowned as he watched her go, then put down his tray and sat in the chair she'd just vacated. He took note of the warm leather still holding the shape of her backside, and let dirty thoughts roll through his head as he took his first bite.

Her day got crazy, and toward the end of her shift, she wound up down in ER with a portable X-ray, trying to get film on an unconscious child who'd been pulled from a wreck. By the time she headed home for the evening, she'd forgotten Justin Randall even existed.

But Justin Randall hadn't forgotten her. She was exactly his type. Her auburn hair fit into the category of redheads. She was average height, busty and lean, and by the time his lunch with his coworkers was over, he now knew she was single, too. All he had to do was bide his time. She given off all kinds of "don't touch" vibes, but he didn't care. He liked a good fight.

He picked up a pizza and a six-pack of beer on his way home, and settled in to watch the sports channel, while Lainie was in her oversize soaker tub on the other side of the city, up to her neck in lavender-scented bubbles.

THE ARRIVAL OF Justin Randall began to change Lainie's routine at work. He appeared at random times, in random places where she was working, and at first, she thought little of it. But then it dawned on her that while she moved around within the floors and halls of the hospital according to what her job required, his job did not. He was a nurse on an assigned floor, and yet there he'd be, out of place and in her face.

As the months passed, he began upping his approach, trying to include her in group lunches, asking her to go bowling, to take a ride, to have coffee, and every time, she turned him down. Some days, she made excuses. Other days it was a flat no.

But on this morning when she saw him coming, it

was too late to make an escape, and all of a sudden, he was in her face.

"Lainie! You're looking great today! How about a drink after work? I know this place with great bar food and even better drinks."

"Thanks, but I have other plans. Gotta go. They're waiting for me," she said, and kept walking.

Even though he was talking to her back now, he still persisted. "Maybe another time," he called out, and frowned when she didn't respond.

Before the week was out, he'd blindsided her two more times—appearing out of nowhere. All she could think was that he had to be following her. Why wasn't he on his floor?

Finally, she cornered Charis midweek in the cafeteria. Charis was alone at the table, and Lainie immediately sat down.

"Charis, isn't Justin Randall assigned to your floor?"

Charis nodded. "Yes, why?"

Lainie leaned closer and lowered her voice. "Everywhere I go, no matter what floor I'm on, there he is. It's been going on for months. He just appears out of nowhere, asking me out. I make excuses but he doesn't quit. He's in my face. He's in my personal space. And he creeps me out."

Charis frowned. "How long has this been happening?"

"Since almost from the time you introduced us. He's giving out stalker vibes like you wouldn't believe, and you know me. I don't flirt. I'm not sending out any vibes that could be misconstrued."

Charis's frown deepened. "Oh, honey, I'm so sorry. I'll put a bug in the supervisor's ear, and let her know he's not on the job like he's supposed to be. Other than that, I don't know what else to do."

Lainie's shoulders slumped. "Thanks. I've never experienced anything remotely close to this, and it's getting scary. These are the times when I wish to God I still had Hunter Gray in my life," she said, and then went quiet, shocked that she'd actually spoken out loud.

Charis stilled. This was the first time any of them had ever heard her mention a man.

"So, he's the reason you don't date?" she asked.

Lainie nodded.

"I'm so sorry. What happened?"

"Our fathers happened. They were stepbrothers who hated each other, and Hunt and I committed an unpardonable sin. We fell in love. Life happened. And we lost each other. I don't know where he is. I don't even know if he's still alive in the world…if he even lived to become a man, but he was my everything. He stood between me and our fathers' hate until they broke me, and when that happened, I think it broke him, too."

Charis was horrified. "Here I am all gushing about my happy life and pending marriage, and you're living with this. I'm so sorry. That's the saddest thing I think I've ever heard."

Lainie shrugged. "It is what it is. Look, I would appreciate you keeping this to yourself. Hospital gossip is deadly. I don't want this to be my identity because it's not. That was me at eighteen. I'm neither broken nor helpless. All I want is Justin Randall to leave me the hell alone."

Charis nodded. "I promise. And I'll talk to our supervisor, too."

"As long as he doesn't find out that I'm the one who ratted him out, it should be fine," Lainie said, but those were famous last words.

The next day, Lainie clocked in, locked up her things

and was on her way out of the break room when Justin walked up behind her.

"Hey Lainie!" he said, and gripped her shoulder hard enough it physically stopped her in her tracks.

She jerked, then shoved his hand away. "What the hell, Justin? You scared me half to death! Don't sneak up on people like that, okay?"

She knew the minute she said it that he was angry, because his eyes narrowed, and the smile on his face turned into a thin-lipped grimace.

"Sorry! Didn't know you were so touchy. I know you're off tomorrow, and so am I. I thought it would be fun to—"

Lainie held up her hand. "Justin, just stop. I'm not interested in dating anyone. Period. I don't intend to hurt your feelings, but let's not have this conversation again, okay? Now, I have to hurry, and that's not an excuse. I'm doing MRIs all day today, and we don't keep people waiting."

"Yeah, sure. No problem. I understand," he said, and walked off.

Lainie breathed a quick sigh of relief, thinking he'd finally gotten the message, and hurried up the hall.

Her first patient, a fortysomething woman named Renee Reilly, was already in tears from the fear of the test itself, when Lainie arrived, but she quickly launched into patient mode and began talking her down.

"Hi, Renee, I'm Lainie, your MRI technician. We're doing an open MRI with contrast today, right?"

Renee nodded. "My doctor explained the process. I'm just scared."

"That's fair, and I certainly understand. We can talk while I start your IV so we can begin the drip for the contrast."

"Yes, okay," Renee said, and closed her eyes as the needle went in.

"There we go," Lainie said, as she taped it down, and started the drip. "This will take about twenty minutes or so to finish. Are you cold? I can get you a blanket."

"A blanket would be good," Renee said.

Lainie got a fresh one from the warmer and tucked it around her. "I'm going to be just inside the lab here getting things ready. I'll check back with you in a few minutes."

Renee stifled a sob. "I have cancer. I just know it. The women on my side of the family all die from it. I have three children still at home. They're going to grow up without me," she wailed.

Lainie paused, then pulled up a chair and sat down. "I've been at this job in one capacity or another for almost nine years now, and if there's one thing I've learned about medicine, it is that we never assume anything, okay? The only man I ever loved had a saying that always made me laugh. 'Darlin'.'" She paused and smiled. "He always called me darlin'. Anyway, he would say, 'Darlin', you never want to borrow trouble. The only safe thing to borrow is eggs and butter.'"

Renee smiled through tears. "Sounds like a wonderful guy."

"The best," Lainie said. "Now, let's just get through this test, and then you go home and take your kids out for pizza tonight. I believe in using every day to make memories. Nobody knows what their tomorrow will bring. I don't know what awaits me, any more than your doctor knows what awaits him. One day at a time, honey. One day at a time. How about some music while you wait?" she asked.

Renee squeezed Lainie's hand. "Yes, please, and thank you for that."

"Absolutely," Lainie said. "What kind of music do you like?"

"Music from the '80s."

"You got it," Lainie said, slipped headphones on her, pulled up the proper link and started it playing.

When Renee gave her a thumbs-up and closed her eyes, Lainie slipped into the control area, and began checking the orders to confirm the imaging required for the test.

When it finally came time for Renee to be moved into the open MRI, she was calm enough to follow all the directions. It would be an hour-long process of immobility, flat on her back, with the thump and pulse of the machine around her upper body being drowned out by Bon Jovi singing in her ears.

When the test was finally over, Lainie helped Renee out of the machine and then helped her sit up. "Everything okay? Are you dizzy sitting up now?"

"No, I feel fine," Renee said.

"Good. Now, what are you doing this evening?" Lainie asked.

Renee grinned. "Having pizza with the family at Famous Pizza and Subs."

"Yum! Eat a slice for me!"

"Count on it," Renee said, "and thank you."

Lainie helped her into a wheelchair, and signaled for the waiting orderly to take her out.

Before her day was over, she'd done three more MRIs, and was emotionally exhausted. Dealing with patients' stress was always more complicated than the actual act of her job. She knew the job and did it well. She just never knew what drama, if any, the next patient might bring.

She finally clocked out and was walking across the parking lot when she saw Charis, and waved.

"See you tomorrow!" Charis called.

"My day off! I'm hiking Beaver Brook Trail tomorrow!"

Charis rolled her eyes. "Better you than me. Some of us are going to Adelitas tomorrow evening for drinks and tacos. Seven o'clock. You're invited!"

"Deal!" Lainie said. "See you there!"

"Yay!" Charis said and did a little two-step as she got in her car and drove away.

Lainie envied Charis's ebullience as she was driving away, unaware Justin Randall had overheard everything, including her hiking destination.

Chapter Three

Even though it was her day off, Lainie had set the alarm the night before. She wanted to be on the trail just after sunrise. It was her favorite time of day to begin a hike. The air was still cool, and she'd be on her way back down by the time the day was heating up.

She'd packed her backpack the night before with protein bars, snack packs, first aid, bear spray and a hunting knife. All she had to add were water bottles, and did so before zipping it up.

After checking the weather report for the day, she opted for long pants, sneakers, thick socks, a long-sleeve T-shirt and a flannel shirt to use as a jacket. She had her hiking pole, and a compass, a cell phone, and a charger stick in her pack, just in case.

She put her long hair in a ponytail at the back of her neck, and tied a bandanna around her forehead. Her sunglasses were already in the car, and after a quick breakfast, she headed out the door.

Traffic was already moving at a steady pace as she wound her way west out of Denver and into the foothills toward her chosen hiking path. She liked the Beaver Brook Trail for a number of reasons. The likelihood of running into a lot of other hikers at this time of morning on a weekday was slim, and that suited her.

She was already anticipating the hike as she arrived at the parking area below the trailhead. Pleased that there were no other vehicles around, she got out, dropped the car keys in her pocket, shouldered her backpack, reached for her hiking pole and started up the trail.

JUSTIN RANDALL HAD no idea what time of day Lainie liked to hike, but he was betting it was early. He had the GPS in his phone already set, and was hoping to beat her there, find a secluded place to park and wait for her to arrive. As he drove across town, he quickly learned it was cooler than he'd expected, and was wishing he'd worn long pants instead of hiking shorts. But he would warm up as he hiked, and was making good time through traffic when the truck in front of him blew through a red light.

It hit two cars making opposite turns in the intersection, which threw them into other cars, and by the time the crashing and skidding was over, four cars, a police car, a delivery van and the truck were in a tangled mess at the four-way light.

Traffic came to a halt. There was no way to back up, and no way to move forward. Justin was cursing his luck as police and emergency vehicles began arriving, but there was nothing to do but wait. It took almost an hour before a lane had been cleared for traffic to detour on a nearby street. He had to reset his GPS to get where he was headed from another direction, and by the time he reached the trailhead, the one positive of his morning was that her car was the only one in the parking lot. He laid his hand on the hood, but it was already cool, which meant she'd been gone for some time.

He didn't know if the trail forked, and if it did, which way she would go. He was angry and frustrated, but changing his plan never occurred to him. He was hell-bent on one destination, and that was to get between her legs. So, he shouldered his pack and took off up the trail at a trot.

A CARDINAL WAS flitting from tree to tree along the path Lainie was on, and after a while, she decided it was following her. Delighted, she began talking to it as she went, fantasizing about how and why it was happening.

"I see you…flying from tree to tree along my path. Have we met before? You'll have to excuse me. I'm terrible with names."

A flash of red shot across her line of vision about twenty feet in front of her, and landed on a low-hanging branch. It was the cardinal. She watched as it turned its head one way, and then the other, before dropping to the ground below, where it promptly gobbled up a bug.

"The mighty hunter scores!" she said, as the bird flew back into the tree.

She glanced at the sun, guessing it must be nearing 10:00 a.m. by now, and paused to take a drink.

The cardinal flew off as she began moving again, and for a while, she thought he'd finally flown away. It wasn't until the bird suddenly reappeared that she paused, curious as to what it was doing.

It was that pause that saved her.

In that moment of silence, she heard footsteps on the trail behind her and glanced over her shoulder, expecting another hiker. There was a man behind her, hoofing it up the trail at an unusually hasty pace, but when she saw his face, a wave of panic rolled through her.

Justin Randall!

She shouted at him, angry that he'd made her afraid. "Justin! What the hell are you playing at? There are laws against stalking, and I've made myself perfectly clear."

Justin began smiling and waving his hands. "Lainie! Wait! It's not what you think!" Then began moving faster, to get to her before she bolted.

She'd already dropped her backpack and was fumbling for the bear spray when he started running. Her hands were shaking as she popped the top, and got one good spray toward his face, before he knocked it out of her hand.

He had closed his eyes at the last minute, but the spray still went up his nose, and all of a sudden, the inside of his nose was on fire and his throat was swelling. When his eyes began to burn and his vision blur, he swung a fist at her face. One punch landed on her cheekbone below her eye, and another missed her face and hit the side of her neck.

And just like that, Lainie was back in her bedroom with her father, fighting for her life. She couldn't let Justin Randall knock her out. She had no chance of getting through this alive unless she stayed conscious.

She was still in a panic when he grabbed her by her arms and took her down, straddling her lower body and pinning her arms above her head.

But Lainie was fighting for her life, kicking and thrashing beneath him, and in one brief moment when he let go of her hands to rip at her clothes, she stabbed her fingernails into his face, and raked them all the way down his cheek and neck, plowing furrows into his flesh, then began kicking and scratching at his neck and arms until her hand was slick with his blood.

"You bitch," he roared, and then threw back his head and laughed. "I knew you'd like it rough!"

She dug her fingers into the ground, intent on throwing dirt in his eyes, and felt a softball-size rock beneath her palm instead. She grabbed it without hesitation and swung it at his head. The crack when it hit was the sound of sticks breaking.

He grunted and fell backward, stunned by the blow. She rolled to her knees, grabbed the same rock with both hands and smashed it down onto his mouth and nose. Blood spurted from his lips, as he spit out a tooth to keep from swallowing it. He had both hands on his face, rolling and moaning, as Lainie leaped to her feet and started running.

She went flying down the trail, leaving everything behind her but the car keys in her pocket, knowing she had to outrun him to survive, and run she did, until her side was aching and every breath she took was like swallowing fire.

She didn't know he was behind her until she began hearing curses and shouts. She looked over her shoulder in horror. He was covered in blood, carrying both backpacks and her hiking pole, and running like a man possessed about a hundred yards behind her.

Hope sank. "God help me," she mumbled, and ran faster.

It wasn't until she was started down a steep drop on the path that she realized she was in what hikers called "the blind spot."

She couldn't see him when she looked back, which meant he couldn't see her either. And it was becoming all too clear that he was going to catch her before she ever got to her car. At that moment, she remembered something Hunt used to say.

When faced with a hard decision, do the unexpected.

So, she faked her death.

She yanked off her sneakers, then threw one partway down the slope along with her flannel shirt, and left the other one in the path. Then she dropped and rolled in the trail to make it look like she had a bad fall and rolled off into the canyon below.

Still in her sock feet, she leaped across the path on the other side and ran deep into the trees and brush before pausing to get her bearings. She couldn't keep going down, because that's where he was going, so she hunkered down and began moving in a crouch back up the mountain, and never looked back.

THE LAST THING Justin expected to see was one of Lainie's sneakers on the trail, and then he saw where she fell and looked over the slope, saw her flannel shirt first, and then the other shoe.

Holy shit. The bitch fell off the mountain.

He let out a sigh of relief, and then realized he was still carrying her things. The first thing he did was wipe his prints off her hiking pole before he tossed it down the slope, and then he slung her backpack down with it.

His whole face was on fire. He could feel the furrows she'd left on his face and knew he had to get them treated, but he stopped long enough to use a bottle of his drinking water to wash off what he could of blood and bear spray.

He was confident animals would destroy her body, but his DNA was all over her clothes and backpack, so he began concocting an alibi on his way to his car.

They'd gone hiking together and were surprised by a bear. He was trying to protect her when the bear knocked them both down. He sprayed the bear, got caught in some of the blowback, and was unaware that she'd been knocked over the side of the mountain until after the bear ran away.

Then, he sat in his car and watched TikTok videos until his phone went dead, and his wounds wouldn't be fresh, before driving himself to the nearest emergency room. He staggered in, claiming he'd been knocked unconscious after a bear attack, that his hiking partner was missing, and he'd found a shoe in the path and seen some of her gear on the downslope. His best guess was that she'd fallen off the path into a canyon, but he was too weak to search on his own, and when he got to his car, his phone was dead, so he drove himself to the ER.

Within the hour, both the local police and the Denver Park Rangers were in ER taking his statement, while a doctor and nurse continued to clean up his wounds. They put four staples in his head wound, reset his broken nose and told him to see his dentist, and to drink his meals through straws for the next couple of weeks.

A nurse was swabbing out the scratches as he continued to answer questions, but she wasn't buying the whole story. So, while the police were still questioning Justin, she signaled for the doctor to come out into the hall.

"What's wrong?" he asked.

"Those scratches on his face and neck don't look like bear scratches. They look like fingernail scratches. And he has them on his wrists and neck, and upper arms, too. If his hiking partner is missing, he might be the reason why."

The doctor frowned and went back into the exam room. "Mr. Randall, I want to take another look at the wounds on your face to make sure we've gotten out all of the debris."

Justin didn't say anything, but he was worried. When the cops began whispering between themselves, and then one of them requested the wounds be swabbed for DNA, then took possession of all of the swabs they'd used to clean the scratches the first time, he knew they weren't buying all of his story. But since it was the only one he had, he was sticking to it.

LAINIE'S SIDE WAS ACHING. She was exhausted and stumbling, and out of breath. It felt like she'd been running forever. There was an outcrop of rocks in an open space just ahead, and her focus was just getting to the patch of shade beneath it when she stumbled again, and fell forward before she had time to catch herself. Her head hit the side of the outcrop as she went down, and she was unconscious before she landed.

It was late evening before she woke up with dirt in her mouth and a huge cut on her lip. Her head was one solid ache, and when she moved, everything spun around her. As she rolled over to sit up, something ran down the side of her face. She thought it was sweat and gave it a swipe, only to have her hand come away covered in blood.

"No, no, no," she whispered, and put her head between her knees to keep from passing out.

She couldn't figure out where she was, or what had happened, and began looking around for her backpack, and that's when she remembered. The last time she'd seen it, Justin Randall had it. She groaned, remembering now that she'd tried to throw him off her trail by pretending that she had fallen into the canyon. But what if he was still out there looking for her? What was she supposed to do?

Her hands were trembling as she took the bandanna off her forehead, refolded it and tied it over the bleeding cut, then thought about trying to get up. But when she looked down and saw bear tracks in the dirt all around where she was sitting, she was on her feet before she thought. The motion was too fast, and she nearly went down again.

Her best guess was that she had a concussion, and steadied herself against the outcrop until the world stopped spinning. After that, she took a closer look at the tracks. She couldn't decide if they were old tracks, or if a bear had sniffed around her while she was unconscious, then wandered off. The thought was terrifying, and her biggest fear now became the bear. What if it came back looking for her?

Without thinking, she charged off, staggering and stumbling as she went, until the sun began going down, taking warmth with it. Her head was pounding, and she needed a place out of the wind for the night, and began keeping an eye out as she walked. When she came upon a ledge of rocks with just enough space beneath to crawl under, she stopped. The possibility of a snake crawling up beside her in the night was real, so she began gathering dry brush and small branches, then crawled beneath the ledge and pulled the branches in all around her.

She wanted a drink of water so bad she could almost taste it, and everything hurt, and she was so cold, but exhaustion overwhelmed fear. She curled up, closed her eyes and dreamed.

She was running and then she was driving, and then she was walking, and every time she saw a stranger she'd stop and ask, "Have you seen Hunter? Have you seen my man?" And every time, they would shake their heads and leave her standing.

Then the dream morphed, and she was in a boat on a river, and fog was so thick she couldn't see the shore. The boat had no motor or oars, and she was screaming, "Help me! Help me!" but to no avail.

Then from a distance, she heard a voice. She knew that voice, and stood up in the boat and began to scream. "Help, Hunter! Help. I'm here!" But the boat kept floating farther and farther away, until the world around her was silent once more.

WHEN SEVEN O'CLOCK came and went at Adelitas restaurant and Lainie still wasn't there, Charis called her. The call went to voice mail. Thirty minutes later, she sent a text that wasn't answered, and then another one, and by the time the evening was over, and Charis was headed home, she was still worried enough to drive by Lainie's house. Yet, after she got there, she couldn't tell if the car was in the garage. But her lights were out, so she drove home, telling herself everything was surely okay, convincing herself that when she saw Lainie tomorrow, she would have a logical explanation.

WHEN LAINIE WOKE up again, it was morning, and a raccoon was staring at her through the brush she'd pulled in around her. As soon as she opened her eyes, it waddled away.

The moment she took a breath, she knew something was wrong. It hurt to breathe, and her skin felt hot. When she felt her head wound, her fingers came away bloody. This meant the cut was still seeping blood through the bandanna, and now she had a fever. It was all she could do to crawl out from beneath the ledge, and the only thing on her mind was finding water. There hadn't been any behind her, so up she went.

She was still sad from the dream. And it took everything she had to put one foot in front of the other, but she was lost. Not dead. Surely someone would miss her at work. Charis knew where she'd gone. She had to believe someone would find her. She just needed to be found before she was past help.

WHEN LAINIE DIDN'T show up for work, Charis panicked and went straight to Jennifer Wilson, Lainie's boss.

"Have you talked to Lainie? Has she called in?"

"No, and it's not like her to miss work without calling," Jennifer said.

"She went hiking yesterday and was supposed to meet us for dinner last night, but never showed. I drove by her house on my way home, but all the lights were off, and I couldn't tell if her car was in the garage or not. Please, call the police and ask them to do a welfare check. Something's wrong! I just know it!"

Jennifer made the call, but the moment she mentioned Lainie Mayes's name, she got the shock of her life and quickly put the call on speaker so Charis could hear the officer's reply.

"I'm sorry, ma'am, but that person has already been reported missing by her hiking partner last night. He showed up in an ER with severe wounds. He said he and Miss Mayes were hiking together when they were attacked by a bear. He was injured, but managed to spray it in the face with bear repellant before being knocked unconscious. When he came to, she was missing. He found one of her shoes on the path, and saw some of her other belongings on the slope down into the canyon. He drove himself to ER to report the incident. There is already an ongoing search party, and we're still questioning him."

Charis gasped, and then interrupted the officer.

"No, Officer, no! She would never have gone hiking with that man. He's been stalking and harassing her at work for months. If he showed up in an ER with wounds, it wasn't from any bear. I promise it was Lainie, fighting for her life."

There was a moment of silence, and then the officer spoke. "I'm going to need your name and contact information, and we'll be asking you to come to the station to make a statement."

"Anything! I'll do anything for Lainie," Charis said. "Just don't turn that man loose."

The call ended. Charis and Jennifer stared at each other in disbelief.

THE PARK RANGERS were already in search mode. They had Randall's statement about where the attack happened, and followed the path up to the spot. They found a shoe on the path, as he'd stated, and then another shoe and a shirt on the slope, farther down. They also found a hiking stick, but what they didn't find were bear tracks.

After that, they took the search down into the canyon below, expecting to find her, or her body, but the only other thing the searchers found was her backpack hanging from a tree. It was too far away from the other stuff to have fallen with her, and there was no body, and no sign of drag marks or footprints walking away anywhere beneath it.

They were already suspicious of Justin Randall's story, and were now fairly certain of foul play. She'd obviously been attacked on the trail, but not by a bear, and the bigger question was, was she even still on the mountain?

By midafternoon, the local-hiker-gone-missing story was all over the local news, and by evening, the national news had picked it up.

Justin Randall was in his apartment, so sore he could hardly move, and drinking soup from a cup, when there was a knock at the door. He set the cup down and hobbled to the door.

A detective and four policemen were in the hall.

"Mr. Randall, we need you to come with us," the detective said.

"What the hell? Why?" Justin asked.

"Because your story is full of great big holes, and we need you to come fill those up for us."

Justin was blustering and arguing all the way out the door, and still cursing as they put him in a squad car and drove away.

HUNTER GRAY HAD flown a group of tourists to the South Rim of the Grand Canyon earlier in the day, and he'd just set down to unload them. They were already on their way to the office, and he was doing a final systems check as he shut down. When he finished, he climbed out of the cockpit and started across the tarmac, as the sun was setting behind his back.

He entered the office, signed himself out, and then sat down to wait to talk to Pete before going home. The television on the wall behind him was on, and he wasn't paying much attention to it until he heard a name that stopped his heart. He spun, his gaze immediately fixed on the monitor, and the journalist doing an on-the-spot commentary of what was happening.

"…Lainie Mayes, an employee of Denver Health Center has gone missing. She was last reported to have gone hiking with a friend in the mountains west of the city on Beaver Brook Trail. According to the report, they were attacked by a bear, and in the ensuing drama, she was knocked off the trail and down into a canyon, while the friend was still fighting the bear. He wound up in ER and they are combing the area as we speak. A search has turned up articles of her clothing, and a backpack down in the canyon off the trail, but Miss Mayes's body has yet to be located. Searchers are…"

But it wasn't until they flashed a photo that reality hit. He grunted like he'd been gut punched, and nearly went to his knees, then headed for Pete's office.

Pete was on the phone, a little irked and surprised by Hunt's abrupt entrance, until he saw his face.

"Hunt! What's wrong?"

"Someone I love is lost in the mountains west of Denver. They're searching for her now, and I have to go. I won't be back until I find her."

His eyes widened. "The woman hiker who went missing?"

Hunt nodded. "I'm sorry, but she means everything to me. I have to—"

"Do you need a ride? I can fly you there in the morning," Pete said.

"I can't wait that long. I'm driving up tonight. Thanks, boss," and then he was gone.

As he was driving home, he kept thinking of how close in proximity he'd been to her. He'd been here for months and all the while she was within driving distance. Now, he felt sick that he hadn't searched for her sooner. He couldn't bear the thought of it being too late.

As soon as he got home, he began to focus on what to do first. He needed to pack survival gear, including his SAT phone. He needed to know where she'd been hiking, and where the search site was located, so he did a little online research to see what he could find out. Army life had taught him to never go into a fight unprepared. If she was still alive, he had to accept that he couldn't just go storming into her life as if he still had a right to be there, but he'd made her a promise. If she ever got lost, he would save her. Even if she belonged to someone else now, he still owed her that vow.

BUT HUNT WASN'T the only one in a state of shock about Lainie's fate. Her parents had already heard the same report earlier in the day. They'd had no idea where she was or what she'd been doing since she disappeared, and learning this now was horrifying. Their biggest regret was fearing they were going to be too late to ever speak to her again.

"What do we do?" Greg asked.

Tina was in tears. "We go there. We abandoned her once at her request, but she's not around to ask permission, and I need to know if my daughter is alive or dead."

They caught the last flight out of New Orleans, with a plane change in Dallas. They wouldn't arrive in Denver until after 2:00 a.m., but they didn't care. They just wanted to be on-site.

It was nearing four in the morning by the time they reached the hotel where they'd booked a room. It was too late to sleep, so they showered, changed clothes and went down for an early breakfast before asking the concierge about renting a car.

UNAWARE THAT GREG and Tina Mayes were en route to Denver, Hunt was showering and packing, getting ready to make the drive. It was nearly an eleven-hour trip from Flagstaff to Denver, so he'd be driving all night, but there were things he needed to know. It was just past sundown when he sat down at his laptop and typed her name in the search bar.

Within moments dozens and dozens of links popped up. Surprised by the number of them, he began with the ones in the year she went missing. And to his horror, every paper in New Orleans had the answer to what had happened and where she'd been. He was reading about the parental kidnapping, and how Millie had finally helped her escape, and as the story continued, learned that she'd been chased down by her own father.

And then he saw the words "five months pregnant... lost the baby..." and froze. His ears were ringing, and the pain in his chest was so severe that he thought he was dying.

"Why didn't I know? Why didn't I know?"

Without hesitation, he picked up his phone and made a call. He didn't know if the number was still good, or if they were even alive, but he had a question only they could answer. The call began to ring, and then an answer. For the first time in eleven years, he was hearing his mother's voice.

"Hello?"

"Mom, it's me!"

Brenda started screaming, "Chuck! Chuck! It's Hunter! He's on the phone." And then he heard his father shouting at him, and realized she put the old landline on speaker.

"Hunt! Where are you? Why haven't you—"

"All those years ago, did you know Lainie was pregnant?"

He heard a gasp, then he heard his mother crying, and his father cursing. He hung up and walked outside.

The lights of Flagstaff lined the horizon to his right. A coyote yipped from somewhere nearby. He looked up. Heaven was littered with stars twinkling within the inky blackness of space. He'd spent more of his adult life in the air than he had on the ground, and always felt lighter and weightless there. But tonight, he'd fallen to earth, and the pain was so great he wasn't sure he could get up. He curled fingers into fists as the stars blurred before him, then the pain came out in a roar, and he kept screaming into the night until the pain bled away.

When he could think without wanting to throw up, he stormed back into the house in long, angry strides, coming out minutes later with his arms full of gear. He threw it all into the back of his Jeep, threw a jacket in the front seat, then went back to lock up and turn out the lights before heading north.

BACK IN NEW ORLEANS, his parents were in an uproar, fighting over who was to blame, and why he'd even asked that question now, after all these years. What happened? What had changed?

It wasn't until they turned on the television for the local evening news that they got their answer. There was a photo of Lainie Mayes behind the news anchor as he delivered the story.

"One of New Orleans' own has gone missing on a hike in the mountains outside the city of Denver. Twenty-nine-year-old Lainie Mayes, now a resident of Denver, is the object of a massive search. They've been combing the mountains for…"

"Oh, my God. Chuck! Hunt must have seen this report, too. I don't know where he's been, but it's obviously not with her. He's done some digging. But how would he know about…"

"The papers, Brenda. Remember all those ugly stories after her wreck? That shit's on the internet forever now, isn't it?"

"He'll go there, won't he? If she's lost, he'll want to be part of the search," she said. "We need to go now. It may be our only chance to ever see him again."

"I'm not going to drive all the way Denver just to get spit on by my own son," Chuck muttered.

"Fine. I'll go by myself," Brenda said, and left the room.

Chuck followed her to their bedroom. "What are you doing?"

"Packing," she snapped.

He rolled his eyes. "Okay, fine! I'll take you, but I'm telling you now, it's going to be a huge waste of time. We'll leave first thing in the morning."

"If you're going with me, you're leaving tonight," Brenda said.

JUSTIN RANDALL WAS in lockup, still sticking to his story until they gave him reason not to. He sold the same story to his court-appointed lawyer, and wasn't budging. This wasn't his first rodeo, and he'd gotten away with rape accusations before. Granted, none of the other women had gone missing afterward. Whatever happened to Lainie Mayes after she clocked him with that rock was a mystery to him, too. Last time he'd seen her, she was running full tilt down a hiking path.

Chapter Four

Lainie was lost and didn't know it.

It was nearing the end of her second day on the mountain, and she'd stumbled into enough creeks to get water, but her fever was still rising. She had long since lost sight of hiking trails, and while she thought she was traveling long distances, she was actually walking in circles and passing out. She'd forgotten about Justin Randall.

Her focus was on the bear she was convinced was hunting her, and the higher her fever went, the more vivid her hallucinations became. She kept running and hiding, and falling and praying, and when she'd sleep, Hunt was always in the dream.

The bottoms of her socks were beginning to wear. They kept getting caught in rocks and rough ground, and when she sat down, she saw bloody spots seeping through.

Her feet hurt. Her body ached. And the world kept spinning. She'd pass out and wake up on her back, staring up through a maze of green, leafy spires to the clear, cloudless sky above and cry, and then pray.

"Please, God, after all you've taken from me, don't let this place take my life."

GREG AND TINA MAYES reached the Beaver Brook trailhead early, and went straight to the communications station where the searchers were regathering. They'd taken a hiatus after it got dark last night, and this morning, they were going over the maps to the new search grids.

"Excuse me, who's in charge?" Greg asked.

A man in uniform turned around. "That would be me, Scott Christopher. I'm a ranger with the Denver Park Service."

"I'm Greg Mayes, and this is my wife, Tina. We're Lainie's parents, from Baton Rouge. Do you have any news?"

"Beyond finding some of her gear and shoes yesterday, we do not. If you'll give me your contact information and where you're staying, then I can let you know if we have anything new to report."

Greg quickly wrote it all down on a pad the ranger handed him.

"Thank you both. You can wait beyond the roped-off perimeter," he said, and turned his back.

"That was rude," Tina muttered, as they shuffled back to their rental. "Do they expect us to wait out here in the sun all day?"

Greg gave her a look. "We came uninvited. They're searching for our daughter, not asking you to tea. If this is all you can think about, then why the hell did you want to come?"

Tina flushed beneath the sting of his words. Truth hurt. They went back to the SUV in silence, raised the back hatch and crawled inside, then sat down to wait.

Less than an hour later, a dusty black Jeep with Arizona license plates came flying into lot, wheeled into an empty space beyond the perimeter and parked.

"Someone's in a hurry," Greg mumbled.

Tina watched as a tall, dark-haired man unfolded himself from inside the vehicle. He grabbed a hiking pack from the back of the Jeep, then headed toward the communications van at a run.

"Oh, Lord! That's Hunter Gray," Tina said.

Greg frowned. "The hell it is," he muttered, jumped out of the SUV and took off running, with Tina right behind him. Greg cut Hunt off in the middle of the parking lot and put his hand in the middle of his chest. "What the hell do you think you're…?"

Hunt punched him in the face.

Tina gasped, as Greg hit the blacktop on his butt—in shock at the blood spurting from his nose. Then he looked up, past the long legs and broad shoulders into the face of a very angry man with an icy blue glare.

Hunt gave Tina the same look, then toed the bottom of Greg's shoe.

"You don't talk to me. You don't speak my name. Either of you. You don't ever look at me again. I know what you did to Lainie. I know you're responsible for the death of our child. I'm going up that mountain to find her, and alive or dead, I'm not coming back without her. I know you put your hands on her. I know she bled on her bedroom floor. But I didn't know then, what I know now. If she's dead, I will kill you."

It was pure reflex that made Greg flinch as Hunt walked past him, and then he crawled to his feet with blood dripping down the front of his shirt.

Tina was horrified and scurried away, leaving her husband to get himself back to their car. She got her laptop from a tote bag in the front seat, and crawled into the back again. She wanted to know where Hunter Gray had been, and what had happened to turn him into such a savage.

STILL REELING FROM the full-circle moment, Hunt ignored the fact that the perimeter was roped off, and ducked under it before heading to the communications van.

"Who's in charge?" he asked.

"I am," Ranger Christopher said. "Ranger Scott Christopher. And you are?"

"Former Army Warrant Officer Hunter Gray. I spent ten years in the military flying Apache Longbows. Half of that service was spent in Iraqi war zones. I am highly trained in survival and tracking, and I know the woman who's missing. If she's on that mountain, I will find her. May I see the search map? I'd like to know what areas have already been searched, and where you're going today, and your contact number."

Scott blinked. "Uh…do you have some identifications to—"

Hunt whipped out his wallet and started pulling out all kinds of licenses and info, including a wallet-size photo of Lainie's senior year picture, a photo of Hunt and Lainie together, and a photo of Hunt and Preacher on base in Iraq, standing beside their Longbow.

"Miss Mayes's parents are already on-site and—"

"We've spoken," Hunt said. "Now about that map?"

Scott led Hunt inside the communications van, showed him the map with the grids marked off, then handed him an unmarked map and gave him a contact number.

"Thank you," Hunt said, entered the number in his SAT phone contacts, left the van, shifted his backpack and started up the trailhead.

The sky was clear, and the breeze on the right side of his face was slight and intermittent as Hunt began the climb. Now he'd seen the areas that had already been searched, and the grid they were searching today.

But he was beginning at the spot where her shoes and gear had been found. That was where she disappeared. He needed to stand where she'd stood.

He was two miles up the trail before he reached it. The rangers had marked it with crime scene tape strung along the area and partway down the slope. He stopped and looked around, eyeing the trail above, and then down the slope, trying to imagine her falling. It didn't compute.

There were no divots in the vegetation, no signs of her having been grabbing at things trying to gain foothold, no brush was torn up or broken off. And he already knew that the backpack had been found in the lower branches of a tree, not on the ground. So, someone threw it. The other hiker?

There were tracks all over. Rangers. The searchers. And God knew who else had walked through here. He looked farther up the trail and on impulse started jogging. Nearly another mile up, he saw all kinds of debris in the path before him, and a bloody rock lying off to the side. Then he saw a torn piece of brown plaid flannel with a white button attached, large boot prints and smaller sneaker prints. He knelt for a closer look and found three long strands of hair caught in the bark of a broken limb lying on the ground. Auburn hair, like Lainie's.

"You were fighting him, weren't you, baby?" Hunt muttered. "So, is this his blood or yours on this rock?"

When Hunt called down to the communications van, Scott answered.

"Ranger Christopher speaking."

"Scott, this is Hunt Gray. How high have you searched above the place where Lainie's belongings were found?"

"What do you mean, above?" Scott asked.

"Like farther up the trail from where her shoe was found?"

"Well, we haven't, because our initial search began where Justin Randall said they'd been attacked by the bear. But we just got word that the police have Randall in custody. His story isn't checking out. The scratches he has on his face that he claimed were made by the bear were from fingernails."

"I'm close to a mile higher on the trail from where her gear was found. The ground in and around the trail is all torn up. There's debris in the path. I saw three long strands of hair caught in the bark of a branch on the ground. The strands are reddish brown, like hers. There are boot prints and sneaker prints, and a remnant of torn fabric with a button still attached. Looks like from a shirt. There's also a bloody rock on the ground. I think he attacked her here. They fought. She took him out with a rock, disabling him long enough to get away. I don't know if she really did fall, but the tracks I saw while I was going up look like she was coming down at a fast clip."

"Oh, my God. Okay, look, just leave all that as is. I'll get the crime scene crew up there to gather the evidence."

"Will do. I'll continue my searching. If I find anything else, I'll let you know," Hunt said.

"Say, Hunt…what made you think to do that?"

"I don't know. A hunch. Instinct? But I know Lainie. I don't think she fell into that canyon. I'm operating on the fact that she's still alive somewhere until I know different. I'm out."

He put his SAT phone back in his pack, then stood a moment, trying to put himself in Lainie's place and decided to follow the path back down, seeing it from her viewpoint as she was running toward the car park.

When he got back to the point where the first shoe had been found, he stopped, then looked around, then up the trail again, and when he did, this time he realized there was a big dip in the trail. A virtual blind spot.

And then it hit him! What if she knew she couldn't

outrun him? What if she faked her own death to escape? But where would she go?

Now his thoughts were spinning, and he was thinking to himself, if she threw her things down the slope, then what? He turned around, looked into the brush and trees on the far side of the trail and started walking.

The ground was littered with pine needles and leaves, and he saw nothing that led him to believe she could have gone this way, but he kept moving, eyes down, looking for footprints, for anything that would tell him she'd been this way.

And then he almost stepped on it. One single footprint, but not a shoe, like a moccasin, or a sock! A few yards farther, he found another and then realized the prints were going up the mountain now, instead of down, and he remembered something he used to tell her all the time.

When faced with a hard decision, do the unexpected.

"Way to go, baby," Hunt said, and started moving up, following the footprints she was leaving behind. He followed her trail with some ease, and as he approached a large outcrop he could tell from the length of her stride that she was running. And then he saw where she slipped, and the imprint of her body, and blood on a rock, and then the faint imprint of bear tracks, and groaned.

It took a few minutes for him to find the same little footprints leading away from the site. So, she was alive and moving after the fall. The bear tracks were older than her tracks. He needed to believe it was coincidence that they'd crossed, not that she was being followed.

By now, the sun had passed the apex and was moving down toward the treetops. It would be dark in just a few more hours, and he hastened his pace. As long as he could see tracks, he wasn't stopping.

But when he realized he was passing the same dead

log a second time, his heart sank. She was walking in circles. Was she hurt and confused from a head injury when she fell? Was she ill? Hallucinating? Or was she just lost and in a panic? He couldn't tell.

Just before dusk, he spotted a large pile of dry brush up against some rocks, studied it for a moment, then walked toward it. That wasn't just random deadfall. The brush had been gathered. After a closer look, he saw handprints in the dirt, and drag marks where she'd crawled beneath a ledge and used the brush as a deterrent against snakes. He admired her foresight, and decided to make a dry camp in the same spot. It was going to be cold, but there was no camping up here. No fires allowed.

He got an LED lantern from his backpack and checked out the area for snakes, then used the deadfall she'd gathered and began pulling it into a circle around him for the same purpose. As he was working, something snapped in the woods behind him. He pulled the 9 mm pistol from his shoulder holster and swept the area with the lantern, suddenly spotlighting a deer in the brush. The animal froze. Hunt immediately turned off the light and heard the deer bounding away in the dark.

He couldn't help but think how helpless Lainie was—injured and alone in the dark, without food, shelter, or any kind of weapon. He wanted to keep searching, but in the dark, it would be a waste of time, so he turned his lantern back on, pulled a blanket from his pack, then some water and jerky. He sat down with his back against the rocks, wrapped the blanket around him, left the lantern on long enough to eat and drink, then turned it off.

He sat in silence while his eyes adjusted to the shadows moving within the moonlight filtering down through the trees, then looked up between the leaves and saw a single, shining star. He hadn't prayed to God in years, but tonight he was asking for a miracle.

"Please, God, I feel her. Just keep her alive until I find her. I'll take it from there."

IT WAS HER on the mountain.

Lainie was curled up in a ball beneath a cluster of deadfalls, created by the hand of Mother Nature, and maybe a little from the hand of God. Over time, branches that had frozen and broken off during past winter storms had formed a kind of shelter for the smaller creatures of the forest.

When she'd first found the spot, she'd crawled into the area on her hands and knees to make a space for herself, and then began breaking off leafy branches from the surrounding underbrush to use for cover over her body before crawling back inside with it.

Now she was lying on her side with the leafy branches over her body, her hands tucked beneath her cheek as the only cushion between her and the cold ground. Her fever was still high, but the cold felt good against her face. She was exhausted, but afraid to close her eyes.

Her body still ached from the brutal attack she'd suffered, but it was her feet that had finally slowed her down. Her frantic need to run had ended. The bottoms of her socks were torn and threadbare; her feet were shredded. The cuts that began healing during the night would only break open every morning when she stood on them, but she'd endured it until she couldn't bear it anymore, and so she'd stopped.

She heard a coyote yip, and another answer, and reached for the chunk of a limb she'd been carrying for a weapon. She didn't have much strength left to swing it, but she had no other options.

The faint scent of skunk drifted past, and then faded. The sound of running water was nearby. She'd walked as far as she could go. The water was close enough to crawl to when she was thirsty, but here she would lie until she was found, or this was where she would die.

She cried a little at the thought. She'd never given up believing they would find each other again, and if she died here, Hunt would be her last thought. She would spend her last breath on his name.

She thought of the ashes of their little baby and cried again. There was an order in her will to be buried with them. The thought of that made her approaching demise less tragic. She'd held the baby in her belly, but she'd never held him in her arms. Dying would remedy that. It would no longer be about leaving this world. It would be about joining her Little Bear in his.

She closed her eyes and drifted off, and suddenly Hunt was before her. When he held out his hand, she took it, and let him lead her into the land of dreams.

It was Hunt's second night on the mountain and he hadn't slept more than an hour or two. He'd already packed up his camp and was just waiting for enough light to track by.

He was eating a protein bar when a porcupine ambled by. His presence startled a gray fox heading back to its burrow for the day. The night birds had gone to roost, and the birds who came with sunrise were already flitting from limb to limb, then dropping to the ground for bugs and grubs. Life abounded, and all he could do was hope Lainie was still part of it.

His wait came to an end in the blink of an eye. The forest went from shadows to daylight, like God walked into the room and turned on a light. He shouldered his pack and started walking in the direction of the last tracks he'd seen—his head down, sweeping the area before him with a clear-eyed intensity. He couldn't afford to miss a clue. Her life depended on it.

LAINIE HAD FALLEN asleep in the night and woke in daylight, burning with fever. Her lips were cracked, and her mouth and throat were so dry she didn't have spit to swallow. She knew enough about the human body that she was severely dehydrated, and if she didn't keep drinking water, her organs would begin shutting down.

She could hear the water in the nearby creek, and getting to it today was her only goal. But when she raised up on her elbow to push the branches aside, the pain that shot up the back of her neck and head was so sharp and sudden that, for a moment, she thought she'd been shot.

"That hurt," she muttered, as she pushed past the pain and started crawling.

But the twenty yards from her shelter to the water might as well have been miles. By the time she got there, her arms were trembling. She went belly down at the water's edge and drank until she could hold no more, and then she ducked her face into the flowing stream over and over, trying to cool the fever, until she finally gave up and crawled the rest of the way into the creek.

The water was barely knee deep, but she floated on her belly to a partially submerged rock. Using it for an anchor, she wrapped her arms around the projection above the water and held on, letting the cold mountain water be the ice bath she needed.

She was still hanging on to the rock when a possum waddled out of the underbrush and went down to the water to get a drink. The irony of her fighting to stay alive, side by side with a little possum simply quenching its thirst, was a most perfect analogy of life. After it moved back into the underbrush, Lainie began the painful journey of getting herself out of the creek.

By the time she reached the bank and began to crawl up the slope and back to her shelter, she was exhausted. She pulled the branches back around herself, and as she did, realized she'd lost a sock in the creek, then accepted that it no longer mattered. Exhausted beyond words, she rolled over into a ball and closed her eyes. The last thing she remembered was feeling her clothes beginning to dry, and thinking how hungry she was.

GREG AND TINA MAYES were back at the search site again, only this time they'd come prepared. They had folding chairs and a cooler full of drinks and snacks, and were sitting in the shade of a nearby tree.

After they'd gone back to their hotel last night, neither of them had mentioned the obvious, but they both assumed that their daughter was dead. As they sat at the search site this morning, they were actually discussing where Lainie would be laid to rest when an older model Buick drove up.

The moment Greg saw the car, he cursed.

"What in hell makes Chuck Gray think he has business here?" he said.

Tina glanced up and shrugged. "Probably for the same reason we are. Their son. Somehow, they know Hunt's here. You will be civil. They have as much right to be here as we do. You do not get into a shouting match. Do you understand me?"

Greg gave her a look. He knew better than to challenge her with that tone of voice.

"Whatever," Greg said.

CHUCK AND BRENDA GRAY were holding hands as they started across the parking lot when Brenda saw Lainie's parents.

"Greg and Tina are here," she said.

Chuck stopped, stared at them a few moments and then started walking toward them, but it was the women who spoke first.

Brenda nodded at the couple. "Have you been here long?"

"A few days," Tina said.

Brenda hesitated. Her voice was shaky as she spoke. "Do you know if Hunt is here?"

"We saw him," Tina said, then glanced at Greg. His nose was still red and swollen, and he had a fat lip.

"Did he do that?" Chuck asked.

"His version of 'hello,'" Greg snapped.

Brenda ignored him and refocused on Tina. "Did you talk to him? Did he tell you where he's been?"

"He spoke. We listened. It appears he didn't know anything about the past until recently. He is beyond enraged. He's gone up the mountain to look for Lainie. Said he wouldn't be back without her, and if she was dead, he was going to kill Greg when he got back."

Brenda gasped and reached for Chuck's hand. "I told you we should have told him." Tears rolled, and then she wiped them away. "Is there any news about Lainie today? We've heard nothing since we left home."

Tina shrugged. "Not about Lainie, but they arrested the hiker. They think his story was faked. They think she wasn't hiking with him, and that he faked the bear attack to cover up what he'd done to her. They're still searching, but I don't think they believe she's alive."

Brenda was sobbing. "I'm so sorry. We wouldn't be intruding on your space, but we don't know what happened to Hunt." Then she glared at Greg. "He disappeared without a word after his scholarship was rescinded. It's been what…eleven years? We had heard nothing until three nights ago when he called to ask us if we'd known Lainie was pregnant. I didn't know what to say, and I guess our silence was the answer. He hung up, and after we found out about Lainie, I guessed here is where he would come."

Tina glanced at Greg, but he was staring at the ground, so she kept up the conversation. "Hunt doesn't look like he used to. He was a big kid, but now, very much a grown man. And hard...the look in his eyes was frightening. After he went up the mountain, I went online to see if googling his name brought up any answers, but got nothing. Whatever he was involved in, it changed him."

"Probably has a prison record," Greg mumbled.

Chuck's fingers curled into fists. "Well, that's how stupid you are. That would have been part of public records if you were in a mind to look there. And you're one to talk. He didn't kill his baby. You did that."

Greg started cursing, and Tina dragged him back to where they'd been sitting, while Chuck and Brenda went back to their car. All they could do was sit and wait for Hunt to appear.

PER RANGER CHRISTOPHER'S REQUEST, a crime scene crew from the Denver police had gone up the trail yesterday following Hunt Gray's report. They retrieved hair strands, fabric that matched the flannel shirt they already had in evidence, the bloody rock and took pictures of both sets of footprints. That additional evidence had already been sent to their lab, and if it backed up their suspicions, Justin Randall's story had just blown up in his face.

Ranger Scott had a new search grid for the rescue teams, but hope was fading. It was looking more like they'd be moving from rescue to recovery. He kept hoping he'd hear more from Hunter Gray, but after his initial call, the man had gone quiet.

By noon, Hunt was finding threads from the socks in her footprints, and sometimes blood on the leaves. He was sick, just thinking of how many times her feet must have been pierced. Her steps were closer together now, and sometimes dragging. He'd quit counting the number of times he'd seen where she fell, and how many times she'd turned around and backtracked after getting up. Following her path was like following a drunk afoot who was trying to find the way home.

And then Hunt crossed a deer trail and lost her. The animals had obliterated all signs of her passing. It was like she disappeared in mid-step. The last time he'd felt this kind of panic was that rainy night in New Orleans, waiting for a phone call that never came.

He did a 360-degree turn, looking for something, anything that would tell him where she'd gone, but there was nothing. He took a deep breath and then shouted. "Lainie! Lainie! Can you hear me?"

He paused, listening. The woods had gone silent. Birds quit calling. Even the breeze had laid.

He shouted again, louder. Longer. "Laaiinnieee!"

Nothing. He started walking in an ever-widening circle for over an hour before he found himself above a creek, and moved down the slope to the water's edge. There were plenty of footprints there, too, but none of them were human.

Heartsick and frustrated, he was about to climb back up when he saw something white caught between the rocks in the middle of the rushing stream. He dropped his backpack on the bank and waded into the water in long, hasty strides all the way to the rocks. Even before he picked it up, he knew what he was looking at. A single white hiking sock, with the sole ripped to shreds. His heart sank as he looked upstream.

"Ah, God…where are you, baby?"

He called her name again, then wrung the water out of the sock and headed back to shore to get his pack. Now he had a trail again. It was vague, but it was something, and he began walking upstream.

He was still in search mode when he realized the light was beginning to fade. He started running, as if he was trying to outrun the dark, and was about a quarter of mile up the creek when he came full stop, staring at the handprints and crawl marks right in front of him. There were tracks where she'd crawled into the water, and others coming out.

If she was crawling, she couldn't be far!

Shadows were growing longer as he leaped up the creek bank and began following the trail, but he was no longer looking down, he was searching the tree line. She had to be here somewhere.

"Lainie! Lainie! Can you hear me?" he shouted, but the forest had gone silent. He was moving faster now, following the drag marks all the way to a huge pile of dead brush. Stopped by the barrier, he leaned in and then he saw her, curled up on her side, so still and pale he feared the worst.

"Please, God, no," he cried, and began tearing into the brush and limbs, clearing a path to get to her, then dropped to his knees beside her to search for a pulse.

Chapter Five

The pulse was there! A sign of a heartbeat was all he needed. It was a little rapid, but strong and steady beneath his fingers. It was the answer to his prayer. God had kept her alive for him.

"Thank you, Lord. I've got her."

She had the remnants of one sock on her right foot, and her left foot was bare, revealing the wounds. They were red, inflamed, and in a couple of places, oozing pus. But it was the head wound, the horrific bruising from the attack, and the level of fever in her body that frightened him most.

He slipped a hand beneath her neck. She was his Lainie...but different. A woman now, not the girl she'd been. And she was hurt—so hurt.

"Lainie, darlin', it's me, Hunt. Can you hear me?"

She groaned, then sighed as she rolled over and slowly opened her eyes, and stared straight into a piercing blue gaze.

"The raptor found me," she mumbled. "You're here again, Hunt. Are we dead?"

The skin crawled on the back of his neck. Had she been seeing him in her hallucinations?

"No, baby, we're not dead, and I've been looking for you."

She grabbed his hand. "You're really here? My Hunt? You found me?"

"Yes, darlin', I found you. Easy now… I need to see what all has happened to you," he said, and pulled a bottle of water and the first-aid kit out of his pack.

But Lainie wouldn't let him go. She couldn't believe he was real. This was just another awful dream, and he would disappear. In her mind, she needed to keep him talking so he would stay.

"How did you know I was lost?"

"You're all over the news. I heard your name on TV, and I came to find you." He was holding the bottle of water as he lifted her head. "Just a sip, darlin'."

She took a drink and then another one before he set it aside, and pulled out a digital thermometer. The reading came back 104 degrees plus. His heart skipped. That bordered on seizure level. He dug out a bottle of Bactrim tablets, and over-the-counter fever meds, and set them beside his knee.

She couldn't believe he was real and kept staring at him, touching his leg, reaching for his hand, staring into the face of a boy who'd become a man.

"Hunt…all those years ago… I know why you left, but where did you go?"

"To war, Lainie. I went to war."

"In the military? You were in the military?" She shook her head, trying to make sense of what he was saying, still in fear that he was another fever hallucination as he began applying a balm to her lips.

"Army, darlin'. I mustered out months ago. Been flying helicopters for a charter service in Flagstaff ever since," he said, then he reached for the Bactrim and pain and fever meds.

"If I help you sit up, can you swallow these? They're for fever and infection."

She nodded, then shuddered as he moved her to a sitting position.

"Open your mouth, Lainie," he told her, and she did, like a baby bird waiting to be fed. He dropped in the pills, then held a bottle of water to her lips. "Just sip. Don't want to choke you."

She sipped and swallowed, then reached toward his face, running her fingers along a three-day growth of stubble as black as his hair.

"You know how to fly helicopters?"

"I flew Apache Longbows in Iraq for the better part of four years, then off and on elsewhere for the other six."

Her voice shook. "You could have died, and I would never have known it."

He cupped the side of her face. "If it hadn't been for a news report, you could have died, and I would never have known it."

She sighed. "Touché." Then something snapped in the woods behind them, and she went into an all-out panic. "The bear...is it the bear?"

"The bear is gone, baby, and I have a gun. You're safe now. I promise you are safe."

Tears rolled as she began to tremble. "It hurts, and I'm tired, Hunt. I'm so tired of being afraid." Then she touched him again. "Are you real? Is this happening?"

Her confusion was troubling. It could be from the fever, or the head wound, or a combination of both. "I'm as real as it gets," he said, then he took off his jacket and eased her arms into the sleeves. "Here, put this on. You're shaking."

"I crawled in the creek. I thought maybe the cold water would help take down the fever." The weight and the warmth from the jacket was like his hug, as she wrapped herself in it.

He kept thinking of what she'd done to survive, and then realized this wasn't the first time she'd had to run to get away from a monster. He took the bandanna off her forehead and then the other sock off her foot, eyeing the wounds in dismay as he reached into his pack for disinfectant. The last thing he wanted to do was hurt her more, but he had no choice. It was getting dark, and soon be too hard to see. He turned on the LED lantern.

"I need for you to lie down, honey. I'm going to clean up this head wound a little, and I don't want it getting in your eyes."

He made a pillow of his blanket, then eased her down on it.

Her voice was shaking, her eyes welling again with unshed tears. "If I close my eyes, do you promise you won't disappear?"

He leaned down and brushed a kiss across her cheek, then moved the lantern above her head. "I promised you forever. This is me, Lainie. Put your hand on my knee. You'll feel me beside you. You can talk and I'll answer," he said.

He felt her hand on his thigh as he knelt beside her, then began opening packets of gauze swabs, and dousing them with antiseptic. "Here goes," he said, and began dabbing them along the cut on her forehead. He heard her take a deep breath, then she closed her eyes, but she didn't cry out.

"Did you know the hiker?" he asked, trying to distract her from the pain.

"Stalker from work. Didn't know he'd followed me up the trail. He attacked me, I got away and ran. I tricked him. Made him believe I fell into the canyon, then I did what you always said to do."

He paused and looked up. "What's that?"

"When faced with a difficult situation, do the unexpected. I backtracked on myself and ran up the mountain, instead of trying to get down to the trailhead. When it worked, I thought to myself, Hunter saved me." -

Three simple words... *Hunter saved me*, put a lump in his throat. All those years ago, and she'd remembered.

Lainie was still talking. "Then I really did fall later. Hit my head against some rocks. When I woke my head was bleeding, and there were bear tracks all around me. It scared me. I was dizzy and confused and started running. The next morning, I woke up with a fever. I kept getting sicker, then I got lost...so lost, but you kept finding me in the dreams and bringing me back."

Hunt swallowed past the lump in his throat. "Because we belonged. I gave you my heart a long time ago. It will always be yours."

Her hand was still on his thigh when he began making a bandage for her head. "I'm so sorry, Hunt. Sorry I never answered your texts. I didn't see any of them until months later, after I was released from the hospital. Millie took me home to help me pack and get my car, and found my phone under my bed. I guess it fell there when Dad knocked me out."

Hunt frowned, pulled a leaf from out of her hair and then finished wiping down the cut on her head. "I loved you then. I love you now. Nothing will ever change that." He glanced up. It was full on dark now, and he shifted the lantern enough to get a bandage over the cut in her forehead and tape it down. "I'm going to move down to your feet now," he said, and moved the lantern with him.

As he did, he began seeing the rips and tears in her

pants and could only imagine how bruised and scratched her legs must be, but he was leaving that to the doctors. Right now, he was most concerned about her feet.

"Lainie, darlin'…you have a lot of open wounds here. I need to clean them out, but you're too hurt. The best I can do is kind of drench them with alcohol. It's going to burn like the devil, but I won't have to touch them."

"It's okay, Hunt. I've outrun the devil before."

In that moment, he felt defeated. He knew what she meant. Despite all of his military service, he had not been a part of their greatest war—the war she'd fought with her family to stay with him. The war that cost them their child.

He opened the bottle, then took a breath. God, he hated doing this. It was going to hurt her even more.

"Are you ready, baby?"

"I'm ready," she said, and held her breath, waiting for the inevitable. But when the alcohol hit the cuts, it felt like she'd walked into fire. She screamed, and then fainted.

The shriek stopped his heart. He was on his knees in seconds, checking for a pulse, but it was steady. He dropped his head, then laid a hand beneath her breasts just to feel her heartbeat.

"I am so sorry, baby. Maybe this way is best. At least you're not going to feel it."

He quickly moved back to where he'd been sitting, put on a pair of surgical gloves and began sluicing alcohol over the bottoms of both feet, pouring slowly, and carefully, making sure he'd gotten it into all of the cuts, then put the lid on the bottle and went back to the first-aid kit for tubes of antibiotic ointment. Working quickly, he liberally applied the contents of the tubes to the bottoms of her feet. Then he stripped off the gloves, dug a clean pair of his own socks from his backpack and slipped them on her feet before rocking back on his heels.

It wasn't nearly all she needed, but it was all that he could do. He was in the act of policing the area for the medical debris he'd discarded, packing it all into a bag to dispose of later, when she woke up screaming his name.

Her panic scared him, and within seconds, he had her in his lap. "I'm here, baby, I'm here."

Lainie opened her eyes, saw his face and went limp.

"Thank God! I thought all of this was another dream. I was afraid to open my eyes and still be alone."

He pulled her closer. "I know we're still sitting in a pile of brush, but you did good finding this place. I'm here and I'm real." He took her hand and put it in the center of his chest. "Feel that heartbeat? That's panic. You passed out from pain and woke up screaming. Damn sure got my attention," he said, then kissed the back of her hand and held it close. "Your feet are all cleaned up, and you're wearing a pair of my socks. Do you feel like you could eat something? I have MREs…meals ready to eat. It's military stuff. Spaghetti, stew, or chili, I think."

"Oh. My Lord. Spaghetti. I choose spaghetti," she said.

"I always knew the way to your heart was to feed you," he said.

"I'd deny that, but it's so the truth."

It was the first time in three days that he'd smiled. "Let's get you settled first," he said, and scooted her out of his lap, and then down between his legs, letting her lean against his chest while he sorted through the food packs. When he found the MRE she wanted, he opened it, handed it to her along with a disposable spoon.

"Lean against me, darlin', and here's your drink. You eat. I'm going to call the ranger in charge of the search parties and let him know I found you, okay?"

"Okay," she said, and then took her first bite of food in three days. It was manna in her mouth.

It was full-on dark, but the lantern shed good light. Good enough for Hunt to see the numbers on the SAT phone. He was relieved by the gusto with which she was eating. She was a raggedy, bloody mess, but she wasn't too sick to eat. He was trying to remember if it was "starve a cold and feed a fever," or the opposite, when the ranger suddenly answered.

"Hello? This is Scott."

"Scott, this is Hunt. I found her. She's alive, mostly cognizant except when she's afraid I'm going to disappear, and wolfing down an MRE as we speak. But she's not out of the woods. She's definitely suffering from dehydration, hypothermia and fever. She wore out her socks walking and running. Her feet are shredded, and infection has set in to some of her wounds. She's running a 104 degree fever, but I just gave her some Bactrim tablets for infection, and some meds for fever. I hope that will offset the worst until we get her down. She's also a lot farther up the mountain from where her belongings were found, but my initial impressions were right. Take my GPS location. She's okay to wait it out until morning, and she's safe here with me now."

"Man…this is the best news ever. I've got a fix on your location. We'll have to pack her back to a trail and then bring her down to where one of the Life Flight choppers can pick her up. You stay put. We'll head your way at daybreak."

"Understood," Hunt said, and disconnected. "Okay, the authorities have been notified, and there will be a lot of happy people tonight. They have been searching hard for you for three days."

She had finished the spaghetti and was licking her

spoon when a thought occurred to her. "How did they know I was missing?"

"Not sure why, but the hiker, Randall...took himself to an ER and told some big story about hiking with you and being attacked by a bear."

Lainie tried to laugh, but it came out in a groan. "The bear was me." And that's when she began to describe the attack in detail.

Hunt could only imagine what Randall must have looked like when he walked into the ER, and kept staring at her. The defiant girl he'd loved had grown into a warrior. But there were pending battles she knew nothing about.

"Your parents were at the trailhead with the search crew when I arrived."

She went pale. "I don't want to see them, ever. Don't let him near me. Please, I—"

"I won't, darlin'. I promise," he said, and then began unrolling the sleeping bag he hadn't used the night before. "It's getting colder, and I need to keep you warm. I'm going to slide in, and then you nestle in against me, and I'll zip us in, then cover us with the blanket, okay?"

Her face was in shadows, but she had an odd expression on her face, and she hadn't answered.

"Lainie...darlin', what's wrong?"

"We've made love a hundred times, but we've never slept together. I never imagined it would happen when I look like and feel like this, or that it would be on a mountain under a pile of brush."

He grinned. "What do we do when faced with a difficult decision?"

She sighed. "The unexpected."

"So...we're right on target," he said. He took the lantern to the sleeping bag, spread it out, then carried her there and laid her down on the outside edge. Then he began pulling all the limbs and brush back into place so they were once again enclosed. He situated his backpack and gun within reach before scooting himself into the bag behind her.

After that, it was a simple matter of zipping them in, spreading the blanket and the sleeping bag over their shoulders before turning off the lantern. Now they were lying on their sides, her back to his chest, with her head beneath his chin, enfolded within his arms.

"My poor, darlin', what a nightmare you have had. Are you okay? Do you need to move to a more comfortable position?"

"I'm okay," she said, but he knew she was crying again.

"I love you, Lainie. Time hasn't changed any of that for me." His voice was a rumble in her ear. She was glad it was dark, and he couldn't see her face, because she had yet to talk about the elephant in the room.

"Hunt...there was a baby."

He took a breath, careful to choose the right words without sounding like an accusation. "I know, honey. I found out after I learned you were missing, but why didn't you tell me?"

His arm was across her shoulders, holding her close. As she reached for him, his fingers curled around her hands.

Her tears were rolling in earnest now.

"I didn't realize it myself until I'd missed my second period, which meant I was nearly two months along. I panicked. I knew what hell the news would unleash, and kept trying to find the right time to tell you, and then I started bleeding, and I thought I'd miscarried."

He hugged her closer, waiting. It was her story to tell.

"But then I didn't have my third period, either, and so

I took another pregnancy test, and it was still positive."
The timbre of her voice lifted. "I'm not going to lie. I
know we didn't plan it, but I was happy. I knew it would
be hard, but I figured we'd find a way to make it work
once we were both at college. I told myself I could start a
year later, and you'd already be there on your scholarship
and…well…then it all became moot. Remember when I
disappeared the night of the storm?"

He shuddered. "Like it was yesterday. I'd never been
so scared."

"That was the day I knew for sure I was still pregnant.
I went upstairs to call you, and couldn't find my phone.
Then Mother came storming into my room with my phone,
screaming at me for being pregnant and ruining all her
plans. Dad was worse. They vowed they were going to
take me to an abortion clinic the next day. I was screaming at them, telling them if anything happened to me or
the baby, I would tell the world what they'd done, and that
I would destroy them, and it would ruin their precious social standing." Then she took a deep, shuddering breath.
"That's when…that's when…"

Hunt heard the pain in her voice and knew there was
something more—something ugly that she couldn't get
said.

"What happened, Lainie?"

"Dad flew into a rage. He told me he'd rather the baby
and I were dead than have Chuck's child in his family. And
then he knocked me out. I woke up in the car. They took
me to Baton Rouge to my grandmother's old house and
locked me in an upstairs room. I'd been kidnapped, and I
was there for two months before I got a chance to escape."

Hunt felt the breath leave his body. There was a roar
in his head and a pain in his heart too sharp to bear, and
then the sound of his own voice pulled him back.

"Three days ago, I punched Greg Mayes in the face the moment I saw him. I told him if I found you dead, I would kill him. I thought I hated him before, but there are no words for what I'm feeling now. I know he chased you. Did he also cause the wreck?"

Lainie was sobbing now. "Yes. He ran me down and rammed the back of my car trying to make me stop. I lost control. The car went airborne, then rolled and rolled. Our son died, but I didn't. He's a monster and my mother abetted every decision he ever made."

And once again, Hunt was sideswiped. "Son? It was a boy?"

"Yes. I always thought it was a boy, but I didn't know, because they never took me for prenatal care. I asked the doctor after the wreck. He said it was." She paused. Even though she felt the weight of Hunt's body, it was as if he'd turned to stone. He was tense, silent and motionless, and she didn't know how to help him. She'd had all these years to come to terms with what happened, but for Hunt, it was happening now. The only thing she could think to do was make the baby as real for him as he'd been for her. "You know I was alone in my room all the time, except the last month I was there, when they brought Millie down to cook and clean. My mother was such an ass…all pretense of hiding me and my shame, but she still couldn't bring herself to do menial labor. So, I talked to the baby all the time. I called him Little Bear, because every time I got hungry, my stomach would grumble and growl, and I'd chide him for making such noise."

Hunt buried his face at the back of her neck. All the walls he'd put up were crumbling. Four years in Iraq and watching the life leave Preacher's eyes. The suicide bombers. Scrambling to get choppers in the air with sirens blaring. Flying into a hail of ground fire to provide backup for soldiers barricaded in bombed-out villages. Raining Hellfire and Stinger missiles on insurgents while Preacher quoted the Bible from the pilot seat, and people died on the ground. To now, and the shock of learning he'd been a father, and fearing he'd never find Lainie alive. Knowing there'd been a baby, and then hearing her talking about the real baby, the one living within her. The one he'd never known. They'd made a baby, and their fathers' hate for each other had brought his brief little life to an end. He didn't know how to handle all this hate, and at the same time love her this deeply.

His voice was ragged. He had been shattered by what she'd suffered on her own. "I should have been there. I should have found a way. I should have known."

"No, Hunt. He would have killed you. I'm never going to be sorry our baby was here…even if it was just for a little while. I'm sorry you didn't know it then. I'm sorry our parents broke us. But we didn't do anything but love each other. I loved you then. I love you still. Nothing is ever going to change that for me. I'm here now if you still want me."

Hunt groaned. "Want you? Like I want my next breath. I need you to be whole again. I will never make peace with how you've suffered. But I will find peace with you again, and that is enough. Sleep now, darlin'. Tomorrow we get you off this mountain, and we go from there."

Lainie felt lighter. Eleven years of guilt had been a heavy load to carry, and it was gone. "I love you, Hunt."

His voice was a rumble against her ear. "Not a damn ounce more than I love you."

GREG AND TINA MAYES were watching TV in their hotel room when Greg's cell phone rang. When Denver Park

Rangers popped up on caller ID, he grabbed it. "Tina, it's the park service!"

"Put it on speaker," she said, and then started weeping. "I'm afraid of what they're going to say."

Greg glared because she was crying again, and then answered.

"This is Greg."

"Mr. Mayes, this is Ranger Christopher from the search site. Hunter Gray just called in. He found Lainie. She's alive, suffering from exposure and some injuries, none of which are life-threatening. He is tending to her immediate needs, and we'll be bringing her down in the morning."

"Thank God," Greg said. "And thanks for letting us know."

"You can thank Warrant Officer Gray and his tracking skills."

Greg frowned. "Warrant officer? What's that?"

"Basically, that's the rank given to Army helicopter pilots who didn't go through OTS. That's Officer Training School, you know. He spent ten years with the Army before he was mustered out. I know because I checked up on him a little. He flew Apache Longbows in Iraq and Syria in the fight against ISIS."

Greg was so stunned he forgot to respond.

"Mr. Mayes, are you still there?"

"Yes, yes, just taking in what you'd said. Thank you for calling," Greg said, and disconnected.

Tina glared. "So much for your prison theory. Are you going to call Chuck?"

"So he can gloat about his fucking hero son? Hell, no."

She shrugged. "That's okay. I'll call Brenda."

"You don't call her. Do you hear me?" Greg shouted.

"You don't tell me what to do," Tina said. "Not anymore." Then she picked up her phone and locked herself in the adjoining bathroom to make the call.

BRENDA GRAY WAS a mother in mourning. She feared the day Hunt disappeared that he would never be back, and became certain after all the years that had come and gone without a word. She had already accepted he could be dead, and they would never know.

And then he called.

One question. He'd asked them only one question, and her hesitation was their downfall. She could only imagine the shock he'd received, and the hate he must feel. Only after he hung up in her ear did she realize the immensity of damage they'd done. She knew in her heart that seeing him now wouldn't change anything between them, and there was a part of her wishing they hadn't even come.

And then her cell phone rang, and that tiny spark of hope flared as she looked at caller ID. *Tina? Why would she—oh my God... Lainie!*

Chuck hit Mute on the TV remote and looked up. "Who's calling?"

"Tina. It must be about Lainie," she said.

"Put it on speaker. I want to hear," Chuck said.

Brenda nodded, then answered. "Hello?"

"It's me, Tina. I just wanted you to know the ranger called us. Hunt found Lainie alive."

"Oh, my God, Tina! That's wonderful news. I'm so happy for you."

"Well, Lainie won't believe we give a damn about what happens to her, but I'm happy. I just wanted you to know. She has injuries, but none are life-threatening. They said Hunt had administered first aid and was taking care of her. They're bringing her down in the morning."

"Thank you for telling us. We're hoping to get to speak

to Hunt then, so we'll see you at the trailhead in the morning."

Tina rolled her eyes. Greg was hammering on the bathroom door and cursing her, but she wasn't finished and went on to tell her what the ranger had told them about Hunt's military service. As she was talking, Greg kicked the door.

Tina rolled her eyes again. "I gotta go. Greg's pitching a fit because I locked myself in the bathroom to call you."

The call ended.

Brenda looked at Chuck. He was smiling.

"That's a son to be proud of," he said.

"If you had been prouder of him before, and less focused on the stupid war with your stepbrother, none of this would have happened," she snapped. "I'm going to bed. We need to be at the trailhead early. I don't want to miss our last chance to see him."

Hunt couldn't sleep. He'd given Lainie a couple more pain pills in the night. She turned to face him and slid her arm around his upper body as he tucked them back in.

"If this is another dream, I don't want to wake up," she mumbled, and fell back to sleep again with her cheek against his chest.

"Just rest, love," he whispered, and pulled her close.

Night had never been darker. The stars had never been brighter. And the slice of moon was mostly worthless when it came to shining. But it didn't deter the mountain nightlife.

A coyote yipped, and another answered.

Hunt watched a small herd of mule deer move past their shelter, and there was an owl hooting in a nearby tree. Once, he thought he smelled bear, but he didn't hear or see it, and was thankful Lainie was asleep when the odor dissipated.

He kept thinking of all he'd learned, and if anything could be done about it. It enraged him, and it frustrated him that all of it was old news. His only satisfaction was punching Greg Mayes in the face, even before he'd learned the depth of his betrayal.

Then he felt her breathing change. She was dreaming again. He cupped the back of her head and began whispering in her ear.

"Shush, baby, shush…you're okay. I'm here, I'm here."

She sighed, and then she was still.

THE NIGHT SHIFT was making an exit, and the day shift began arriving. A squirrel was scolding them from a nearby tree, and a little fox passed by them on his way to the creek, and Lainie was awake.

"This is embarrassing, but I need to pee."

He grinned. "Honey, we've seen each other stark naked so many times, I can't believe you'd even utter the word *embarrassing*."

She winced as she tried to move. "Well, it's been a while."

"Better me than the team coming up to get you down the mountain," he said. "Give me a sec."

He tossed their blanket on the pile of deadfall, unzipped the sleeping bag and got up, then began moving aside the limbs to clear their way.

She sat up. "Lord, but I dread walking."

"You're not walking. I'm carrying you into the bushes. As for the rest, I'll close my eyes."

As soon as he had moved enough brush, he grabbed a roll of toilet paper from his pack.

She stared. "What else do you have in there?"

He grinned. "Enough to get by on, and I know what I'm doing, so hush your worries. Today, we blow this Popsicle stand." He handed her the toilet paper, then scooped her up in his arms and headed for the bushes. "Okay, I'm going to ease you down on your feet. I know it's not going to feel good, but those thick socks will help. I'll turn my back, and you let me know when you're done, then I'll go."

He put her down, then held on to her until she'd steadied herself.

"I'm good, and we'll both pee in the bushes. This is my bush. You go find your own."

He was grinning as he walked a couple of yards to comply with her orders, then waited until she called him.

"I'm done."

She was holding the roll of toilet paper when he turned around. It was the first time he'd seen her standing, and he could tell how beautiful her woman body had become. In two strides, she was in his arms again.

"Your Uber has arrived. Where to, lady?"

She smiled. "First pile of brush on your right, please."

He kissed her cheek. "The affection is complimentary. There's no charge for that."

She was still smiling when he put her back down on the sleeping bag, and then reached into the magic backpack again and pulled out a little bottle of liquid hand cleaner. He squirted some in his hands, then handed it to her.

"Wash up, darlin'. Breakfast coming up. We have beef stew with potatoes and vegetables, or chicken and rice with vegetables."

"Chicken and rice, please," she said, as she cleaned her hands.

He glanced at the time, then felt her forehead. It was

still too warm, but better than yesterday. He wouldn't rest easy until he had her in the hands of the medics.

But Lainie saw the worry on his face. "It will be okay, Hunt. You already did the hard part. You found me. Once they start pumping me full of antibiotics, then I will be fine."

"You better be," he said, as he opened her food, handed her a spoon and set her drink within reach before choosing beef stew for himself.

Lainie took her first bite, sighing in quiet delight to have food in her belly again. She chewed, swallowed, then licked her spoon.

"You do know that in other circumstances, camping out with you would be a dream. A tent in lieu of dirt. Real food, and a big teddy bear to sleep with. A girl couldn't ask for more."

He was almost smiling. "So, I'm your teddy bear now?"

And just like that, Lainie's teasing ended. "You're my everything. The next time we sleep together, we will make love."

His eyes narrowed, and when she began drawing him a picture, a muscle jerked at the side of his jaw.

She waved her spoon in the air, like a conductor leading an orchestra, illustrating every comment. "I will look and smell pretty then. I will have had a bath and brushed my teeth. My hair will be clean and shiny, and I will wear something sheer and sexy just so you can take it off me."

Hunt's gaze never left her face. "And I will have showered and shaved off this beard, and you must be prepared for me to peel that sexy whatever off of you with my teeth…if it so pleases you."

She shivered. "It pleases me."

"Then it's on my agenda. However, it will please me

now if you finish your food, instead of giving me an itch I can't scratch."

"I can do that," she said, and shoveled another spoonful of food into her mouth.

Once they finished eating, Hunt gave her more meds, then settled her on top of the sleeping bag to rest while he went about packing up camp. After that, he sat down beside her and cradled her head in his lap. They talked about nothing, and everything, and he watched her fall asleep in the middle of a sentence and thought he couldn't love her more.

About an hour later, he began hearing voices, and then caught a glimpse of men in the distance, moving toward them through the trees.

"Lainie, honey. They're here."

She rolled over and sat up. "Now what?"

"They'll pack you back to the trail and carry you down to wherever the chopper can land."

"Can you come with me?" she asked.

"Not in the chopper. I'll go back down with the rescue crew after you're loaded, then as soon as I get down the mountain, I'll head straight to whichever hospital they're taking you."

"Surely it will be Denver Health, where I work. If you see my parents down at the trailhead, tell them to go home. I don't want to see them."

"I'll find you wherever you are, and I will send them packing, I promise."

She could see the men now, coming toward them at a jog. "Don't disappear on me."

Hunt stood and then picked her up in his arms. "Don't get lost from me, again."

She wrapped her arms around his neck and started to cry.

"It's okay, love. It's okay," he whispered.

"I know…it's just scary letting go when we just found each other again."

"No more hard decisions to make here. We were always attached at the heart, and nothing has changed. I'll come straight to the hospital. I'll find you there a hell of a lot easier than finding you here."

And then the crew arrived, with Ranger Scott Christopher in the lead. They were elated to see their missing hiker, and praised her for her fortitude, but wasted no time. As they were strapping her down on the stretcher, one of the men handed her a park ranger cap.

"To keep the sun out of your eyes while we're carrying you down," he said. "If it hurts the wound on your forehead, we can adjust the size."

"Thank you," Lainie said. "Much appreciated, and it will be fine." Then she looked around for Hunt.

He was standing just beyond the stretcher with the magic backpack on his shoulder, his gaze focused on her, and everything they were doing.

"I'm here," he said. "The path will be narrow, so even if you can't see me, remember I've got your back."

Then they picked her up and started walking.

Hunt gave the giant brush pile one last glance, thankful it had been a shelter and not a grave, then fell into step.

BOTH SETS OF parents were on the scene, but sitting on opposite sides of the parking lot.

Greg and Tina were still fussing.

Chuck and Brenda were silent.

None of them knew Lainie was being airlifted, or that it would be Hunt who reached the trailhead alone. They kept glancing at each other and then looking away. They'd come to this place because of guilt and duty, but everything about this day felt wrong. They'd gate-crashed a reunion to which they no longer belonged.

IT HAD TAKEN the recovery team a little over an hour to hike out of the woods and back onto the trail. They'd been walking it for a while when Hunt began hearing the familiar blade slap of rotors. His pulse quickened, and then he heard Scott talking to Lainie.

"The chopper's inbound. We're almost there, Miss Mayes. Are you okay?"

"I'm okay. Where's Hunt?"

He glanced over his shoulder. "Behind us. He took the flank position, but you will see him before you leave. He'll help load you up."

Her throat tightened with yet another overwhelming urge to cry, but she wouldn't. She didn't want his last sight of her here to be in tears.

A small clearing on the south side of the trail became visible as they came out of the trees. A Classic Air medical copter was already down, rotors still spinning, with the doors open, waiting to hot load. The recovery crew immediately left the trail with Lainie and headed toward it.

Hunt dropped his pack on the trail and ran to catch up. She reached for his hand the moment she saw him, and then he ran the rest of the way with her. One quick kiss, and then he helped lift her up into the chopper. He got one last look at her face before the doors shut between them, and then he was running to get away from the downdraft as it lifted off.

Scott and the recovery crew were already heading down the trail when he grabbed his backpack and caught up.

"Where are they taking her?" he asked.

"Where she works—Denver Health Hospital," Scott said. "They will be waiting for her."

"I'll find it. A big thanks to all of you, but here's where we part company," he said, and started down the trail at a lope.

"Damn, does he think he's going to run the whole way down?" one man asked.

"He's Army, man. He can probably run circles around us and then some," Scott said. "Besides, I think he's got a woman to see about the rest of his life."

Chapter Six

Lainie felt the chopper lift off, and then an EMT began taking vitals, while the nurse on board started an IV. They were talking to each other on their headsets, but the noise inside the chopper made hearing them impossible, so she laid still and closed her eyes. The end of this journey was where her healing began.

The trip was brief. The landing, little more than a bump, and they were down. The doors opened then they were pulling her out on the gurney and pushing her toward the hospital on the run.

The spinning rotors whipped the air into a frenzy, while the heat coming off the roof washed over her in a wave. She closed her eyes against the glare, and only knew they were inside the building by the sudden waft of cool air and people saying her name. Then they were on the move again, pushing her to the dedicated elevator that would take her down to ER.

IT WAS CHARIS's day off, but she'd heard the new update early this morning that Lainie had been found alive, and the rescuers would be bringing her down the mountain today.

Charis had cried buckets when Lainie went missing, and now, knowing she had been found by the man she'd loved and lost, was like something out of a fairy tale. She was guessing they were using a chopper to pick her up somewhere along the trail, but without knowing the schedule or the ETA, she just went straight to the emergency room to wait for her arrival.

A couple of hours passed before they got word the chopper had landed. At that point, the ER erupted in a scurry of doctors and nurses readying for her arrival, along with a detective from the Denver PD, and a crime scene investigator.

Suddenly the paramedics appeared with their patient and rolled her into an exam room then transferred her to the bed as they were debriefing the waiting staff on her stats and condition.

Between the pain and fever, the trip down the mountain and then the chopper noise, Lainie arrived in the ER with a pounding headache and was on the verge of nausea. The room was spinning, and she was afraid she'd pass out when she suddenly spotted Charis at the door.

"Charis. I need to talk to Charis."

Charis hurried into the room. "I'm here, honey… I'm here."

"Hunt will be coming. Can you watch for him, and tell him what's happening and where I am so he doesn't tear up the hospital looking for me?"

"Of course, but how will I know him?" Charis asked.

"Look for tall, dark and handsome, ice-blue eyes, devil-black hair and stubble to match, and if you hear Louisiana coming out of his mouth, that's him."

"Consider it done," Charis said, and left on the run, while one of the other nurses looked at Lainie and groaned. "Dang, girl. Does he have a brother?"

"No, and hands off," she mumbled.

All of the staff in the room knew Lainie, which made

what was happening personal to everyone, including her, but when they began cutting off her clothes, she had no recourse but to let it happen.

Clay Wagner, the ER doctor, quickly moved to the side of her bed. "Welcome back, Lainie, and apologies upfront before we start. This is Della Pryor, a detective with the Denver PD, and she's brought a tech from the crime lab with her. They'll be taking photos of your injuries to back up their case against Justin Randall."

Lainie winced as they kept cutting off her clothes. "Whatever it takes to put him away. And don't lose the car keys in my pocket!"

Wagner continued his examination as every garment was cut away, and when more injuries were revealed, photos were quickly taken. They had her down to socks and panties when Detective Pryor asked them to turn Lainie on her side long enough for them to get photos of her back.

The scrapes and bruises visible there were purple, telltale evidence of the fingerprint bruises on her shoulders and neck where Justin Randall tried to hold her down. Being manhandled exacerbated the pain, but Lainie said nothing, and then they took off her socks.

There was a mutual gasp at the sight and then she heard someone crying. It wasn't as if they hadn't seen worse. It was just because they knew her, and knew everything she'd endured to stay alive. Lainie felt tears welling, and blurted out a joke to change the emotionally charged moment.

"Come on, guys, they feel even worse than they look, so nobody gets to cry but me."

Joking among themselves was how doctors and nurses got through the trauma of what they saw, and the ensuing laughter shifted their emotions.

"Do we need to do a rape kit?" Pryor asked.

Lainie shook her head. "No, ma'am. He only wished. All we had was a nasty wrestling match, and I took him out with a rock before he could unzip his own pants."

"Noted," Pryor said. "We do need to collect DNA from beneath your fingernails. It won't take long." She then signaled her tech, who quickly gloved up and began taking scrapings from under Lainie's nails.

"Apologies for invading the ER and your personal space, but I think we're done here," Pryor said, and she and the tech left the room.

The staff covered Lainie with a sheet, as a tech rolled in a portable X-ray, followed by a lab tech who'd come to draw blood.

Dr. Wagner moved to the foot of the bed to check her feet and the depth of the cuts, but at the first sign of pressure, Lainie screamed.

Wagner jumped. "I'm so sorry. I didn't realize... As I look at the damage here, I think I'll be better able to treat you if we do this in surgery, so we're going to put you under."

Still reeling from the pain, Lainie's voice was shaking, but it was the best thing she'd heard since her arrival. "I second your suggestion, but you might want to run me through the car wash before you start."

They laughed again.

"Having spent four days lost on a mountain, you don't look so bad," Wagner said.

"It was probably the soaking I took from that last creek I crawled into trying to bring down my fever. You know what they say in Texas about women's big hairdos? The higher the hair, the closer to God? I can testify in all honesty that God did not pipe in hot water up there."

They were still laughing when they wheeled her out of the room.

By the time Hunt reached the trailhead, he was exhausted. His clothes were drenched with sweat, and he was in no mood for the reunion he knew was waiting. What he didn't expect were his parents on the scene, as well, but there they were, all running toward him with panicked expressions on their faces. His first thought was, *What the hell?* then he tuned in to what they were saying.

"Where's Lainie? What happened?" Tina screamed.

Hunt dropped his backpack, started to reach into an outside pocket for something to wipe off the sweat, then used his shirtsleeve, instead.

"Nothing happened. A med-flight chopper picked her up halfway down."

"What hospital? Where?" Greg shouted.

The moment Hunt heard that voice, he turned to face him, his voice deepening in anger with every word that he spoke.

"I told you, never look at me again. Never talk to me. Never speak my name." Then he stared Tina down until she took a step back. "Lainie sent you two a message. She doesn't want to see you. She doesn't want to hear your voices, or see your faces. Ever. You don't go to the hospital. You don't interfere in any part of her existence, ever again. You lost the right to her the day she was knocked unconscious in her own bedroom. You kidnapped her like a criminal and locked her up in a velvet jail."

Hunt's rage was frightening, and Greg made a crawdad move backward as Hunt moved toward him, so close now that Hunt could see blood pulsing through a bulging vein in the old man's forehead.

"I don't know who you paid off to get away with what you did, but I know the truth. You ran your daughter down, rammed the back end of her car and caused the wreck."

Greg's face was flushed. His eyes were bulging with a level of fear and anger that he didn't dare turn loose, then when Hunt took another step toward him, it was all he could do not to turn and run.

"You killed my son. And you tried to kill Lainie because of your bullshit feud with my father. The only reason you're still breathing is because she's still alive. Now get in your car and get the hell out of my sight. Both of you!"

The rage in his voice sliced through them. Tina slid her hand under Greg's elbow as Hunt turned to his parents.

"I don't even know what to say to you, but I don't know you anymore. You betrayed me in a way that should haunt you for the rest of your lives. Your silence abetted Lainie's abduction. Your continuing silence led to the death of your own grandchild. You all fed off a war that had nothing to do with the children you both bore. You gave us life, and then you broke us. Lainie and I were pawns. You tossed us about like grenades, daring each other to pull the pins. And when you finally did, we became collateral damage."

Chuck was pale and Brenda was weeping.

"I'm sorry, son," Chuck said.

"No, you're not, and don't call me 'son.'"

Hunt shuddered. He felt empty. Like all the negativity they'd fed him was gone. They were staring at him, pale-faced and silent. His parents. Her parents. All of them. For the first time holding and owning their guilt.

"I don't know how your lives are going to end, but I know Lainie and I will thrive without you. You men are worthless. Whatever tiny bits of good you have put out into this world, you have negated it a thousand times over with your hate. When you die, they should burn you into ashes, bury you both in the same unmarked hole, then forget you ever existed. You have wasted your entire lives fighting over nothing but a common dislike for each other, so you should spend eternity together. And if God wants your sorry souls back, He'll know where to find them."

Greg shuddered, and Chuck was slack-jawed in disbelief. Had Hunt just heaped a curse upon their souls? They wouldn't look at their wives, and they wouldn't look at each other. But they were all watching Hunt as he picked up his backpack and walked away, and they were still watching when tossed his backpack inside his Jeep and began stripping down to his briefs.

Even from a distance, they could see the man and muscle the Army had built, and to their horror, the scars it had left behind. They were still watching when he retrieved clean clothes from the back seat, then put them on and drove away.

The parents parted company without a word. It was going to be a long silent drive back to Louisiana for all of them, with plenty of time to reflect on what they'd wrought.

As they were driving away, Hunt was entering the hospital address into his GPS. He followed them all the way to Denver Health, eyeing the massive edifice as he pulled into the parking lot, then drove to the emergency room entrance and parked. He grabbed his backpack as he was getting out, and hurried inside.

CHARIS HAD BEEN in the ER lobby for hours, eyeballing every man who walked in. She knew it would take time for Hunter Gray to get off the mountain and then back into the city, but it didn't matter. She was here for Lainie.

And then she saw a man coming toward the entrance.

His head was up, and he was moving at a fast pace, with a trail-dusty backpack slung over one shoulder.

The moment he entered the lobby, she knew it was him. Tall, dark and handsome didn't cover it, and even though she was close to the date of her own wedding, just looking at him sent shivers up her spine. She jumped up, running.

"Excuse me! Excuse me! Are you Hunter Gray?"

Hunt skidded to a stop and turned around. "Yes. Who are you?"

Charis sighed. "The scout your girl sent to find you."

His relief was evident. "She's okay?"

"Yes, or will be. They took her to surgery to—"

He panicked. What had he missed? Did delaying her retrieval make it worse?

"Why surgery? What happened?"

"I'm sorry. Nothing dire. They decided anesthesia was the best option before they began treating her feet."

"Oh, right," he said. "She passed out last night when I started pouring disinfectant on them. It scared the hell out of me. Can you tell me where she is?"

"Consider me your escort. I work here, too, although this is my day off. I'm to take you to her room."

"Yes, ma'am. Lead the way."

"Oh, by the way. My name is Charis, and Lainie is one of my best friends."

BETWEEN THE DRUGS, the shampoo, and the bed bath they'd given her, Lainie was feeling no pain—or at least, not much. But being a patient here was the flip side of her daily life. In here, she felt isolated from everything.

She frowned as she fingered her scalp around the head wound. They'd shaved a little bit of hair away to staple it up, so she'd chosen not to look at herself in a mirror. The expressions of horror on her friends' faces when they'd first seen her said it all.

She quit fiddling with the staples, and was staring at the ceiling and thinking about Hunt when someone knocked, and then the door swung inward.

Charis came through, then stepped aside. "Mission accomplished, dear friend. Rest well. We'll talk another time," she said, then blew her a kiss and left the room as the door swung shut behind Hunt.

Seconds later, he was at her bedside. He dropped his backpack to embrace her, then froze. Between the stitches in her head, the bandages on her feet and the cuts still healing on her lips, he was afraid to touch her body at all, and took her hand instead.

"Hey, baby…what did they say? What all did they do? Are you hurting?"

"Pain-wise, I'm better now. I have a concussion, which is healing in spite of me. Bruised ribs but nothing broken. The obvious staples in my head. I'm told that after they cleaned my feet, they glued the deep cuts, and left the rest to heal on their own. A couple of places were infected, as you know, but I have double doses of antibiotics in me, and enough pain meds in me to make the world look pretty in pink."

He smiled. "I'd almost forgotten your sense of humor, and now I'm wondering what kind of description you gave to your friend that made her identify me so fast."

"Oh…basically just look for the best-looking guy with black stubble," she said, and ran her fingers against his chin.

"Ah, yes… I'm going to have to deal with all that."

"They're going to let me go home tomorrow. I'm still here only because they administered anesthetic. When do you have to go back to work?"

His eyes darkened. "Never. I'm not leaving you."

"But your job?"

"Darlin', I can fly choppers anywhere. However, I may be ahead of myself. I guess I need to ask, is there still room for me in your world?"

"Dumbest question ever, and yes," she said. "I have a house. I bought it years ago. I love the house. Everything I did to it was with you in my heart. I guess I should have sent out an SOS years ago, but I think I was afraid to face you."

"Well, that's bullshit, and now you know it," Hunt said. "Then it's settled. I'll call my boss, Pete, and tell him I'm staying. I can catch a quick flight back in a few days to pack up my clothes, and we'll go from there."

Tears quickened. "Go from there… We finally have a future, don't we?"

"Yes, ma'am, we do, but we can't go back. Life happened. We both changed, but without each other to monitor the changes. We're gonna take this slow and this time, do it right. No running. No hiding. We already love each other. We just need to feel the solid ground beneath our feet here as well," he said, and brushed a kiss across her forehead.

She was crying again. "Thank you for coming to find me. Thank you for still loving me even after all the chaos my parents caused. I'm so sorry about your scholarship. I cannot imagine how that felt."

Hunt slid his hand beneath her palm and felt her fingers curl around it. Just like they were before—always needing that feeling of connection. She'd bared her soul to him on the mountain, and he was still living with his hell. It wasn't fair to her, and there were things he needed to purge. They were already talking about their future, and he was still buried in the past.

"I need to tell you stuff, but at the same time, I keep thinking, wait until she's better. Only we both learned the hard way what happens when you wait."

Lainie tightened her grip on his hand. "Lower this bed rail and sit down beside me. Whatever it is will never change how I love you. Give *me* your demons to hold. I know how to handle them."

Hunt lowered the railing, then scooted onto the side of the bed. He glanced at her once, then dropped his head.

Lainie reached for his hand as she waited. She could feel the tension in his body and gave his hand a little tug. "Hunter, it's okay."

He took a deep breath and started talking.

"I've never talked about this before, and you deserve to know. Because there can't be secrets between us again. Ever. I have nightmares that will never go away. Just as I'm sure you do. But you told me yours. And I need to tell you mine."

"I'm listening," Lainie said.

Hunt nodded. "I shut down after I left New Orleans. I packed up the boy I'd been and tried to forget he'd ever existed. There were days in Iraq when I thought I would probably die. Looking back, I think I joined the Army expecting it to happen. By a twist of fate and an aptitude test, I wound up in Aviation training and came out good at what I had learned to do. The whole time I was deployed, I carried out my job in the cockpit of an Apache Longbow, the Army's most impenetrable helicopter. I occupied the front seat as gunner and copilot, with my pilot, Preacher, behind me quoting Bible verses as he flew. Every pilot has a call sign. They called me Gator because I was from Louisiana. There were days when we felt invincible, and days it felt like not even God could save us. Yes, we got shot at every time we went up. And yes, they threw everything at us from ground fire to blasting at us with RPGs, and MANPADS. But we were in Longbows, and what we didn't evade was deflected. We were not on the ground like foot soldiers, being moved from place to place in truck convoys, riding along with your buddies in the middle of nowhere and getting blown up by an IED while you're in the middle of laughing at someone else's dirty joke. But pilots did die. And war sucks. You know?"

Lainie's heart was hammering. She could feel every nuance of the nightmares within him, and yet there were no platitudes that fit. No words to take away the pain, so she did what he needed most, and just listened and watched the shadows come and go on his face.

He was staring out a window now as he talked. She knew he'd gone back there in his mind, and there was no way for her to follow.

He glanced back at her face. She hadn't flinched, and this was good, because it was her permission he sought, to be able to continue.

"We'd been in-country for almost eighteen months and were having a little downtime at the base. It was hot and sunny, and the endless wind was blowing sand in our hair and in our eyes, and if we laughed, we had grit in our mouths, but on that day it didn't matter. We were just hanging out, playing a game of pickup. Rat had the basketball. I was defending under the basket. T-Bone was dancing around in the corner, waving his hand for a pass, and Preacher was coming in behind Rat for a steal when a sniper hiding in the surrounding mountains fired a shot. Preacher had this look of surprise on his face." Hunt stopped, swallowing past the lump in his throat. "And then I saw the hole in his forehead about a second before the next shot hit me in the back."

Lainie flinched. He'd never said he'd been shot!

Hunt looked up and out the window again. "I watched him die in front of me. The last thing I saw before I passed out was Rat running for a weapon. Preacher died and I didn't, and guilt set in. I didn't want to get close to anyone like that again. I'd lost you and then him, so I shut down emotionally and focused on nothing but what I'd signed up to do. Even after we were stateside again, and then deployed in different places during the ensuing years, I began to burn out. Ultimately, I left because I was tired of running away from the past. Then I saw your story on the evening news, and the rest you know."

TEARS WERE RUNNING down her face. "Oh, Hunt… I need to hug the hurt out of you so bad I can't stand it, and they've hooked me up to everything in this hospital except WiFi. Come lie down beside me. You've stayed awake for days because of me. Let *me* hold *you* now while you sleep."

He damn sure wasn't leaving her and didn't have it in him to refuse that offer. And, since she hadn't thrown up her hands in shock at what he'd told her, he guessed she'd decided to keep him.

"You know it's against the rules?"

"You leave the demons and the rules to me," she said, and scooted over until her back was against the bed rail.

Hunt kicked off his boots, lay down beside her and pulled up the bed rail, then turned to face her with the railing at his back. He searched her face for doubt and saw none. All he felt was love. He'd bared his soul, and now his heart was in her hands.

"I love you, Lainie."

She sighed. "I love you, more."

"We're breaking all kinds of hospital protocol," he said.

"I am a dear and beloved employee here, and you're already everybody's hero because you found me, so, in their eyes, you can do no wrong. I love you. Close your eyes."

So, he did.

Chapter Seven

It was time for evening meds.

Lainie's assigned nurse, Maggie Rae, was making her rounds when she entered Lainie's room, then came to a full stop. There was a grown-ass man in bed with her patient, sound asleep and stretched out beside her with his feet hanging off the side. Then she realized it must be Hunter Gray, the man who'd found her.

Gossip was they'd known each other before, and it must have been something special for him to come from so far away to search. Even now, he'd put himself between Lainie and the door, with his arm across her waist in a gesture of protection.

Lainie heard footsteps approaching her bed and opened her eyes, then put a finger to her lips and whispered, "He never slept until he found me."

Maggie lowered her voice as she began checking Lainie's stats. "Bless him. He's quite the hero. How are you feeling?"

Lainie sighed. "Everything hurts."

"This should help," Maggie said as she injected the syringe full of pain meds into Lainie's IV port. "There you go, honey. You'll get easy soon. Do you need anything?"

Lainie looked down at the man beside her. "Not anymore." Then closed her eyes.

JUSTIN RANDALL HAD been taken in handcuffs from his jail cell to an interrogation room. The guards seated him at a table, then one stayed on guard with him. All Justin knew was that his lawyer was coming, so he settled in to wait, but not for long.

Minutes later, the door opened, and Richard Stovall, his court-appointed lawyer, entered the room.

"I'll need some time alone with my client," Richard said.

The guard left the room as Richard sat down and flipped open a file.

"I'll get right to it. You have problems," Richard said. "Lainie Mayes was found alive this morning. She has a large number of injuries, some of which back up the police's theory that you attacked her, and she had plenty to say about that. The lab reports came back regarding DNA found on evidence from the scene of the attack, as well as DNA taken from her backpack they found in the canyon. It's yours."

"Okay, so there wasn't any bear attack, but I didn't try to kill her," Justin said. "She got herself lost."

"Running away in fear for her life after you assaulted her," Richard said. "I'm told the cops were at the emergency room when they brought her in. They took scraping from beneath her fingernails to test for DNA." Then he looked straight at the scratches on his client's face. "We both know how that's going to turn out. And that's not all. About twenty-four hours after your name was mentioned as a suspect of interest in the local and national news, four other women have come forward, claiming you both raped and assaulted them, and threatened to kill them if they talked."

Justin blinked. "They can't prove any of that. It will be my word against theirs."

"So, it's true?" Richard asked.

"Can I fight this?" Justin asked.

"You have no grounds to fight with," Richard said. "Whatever happens, you're going to prison. It's the sentencing that will determine the time you will serve."

Justin shrugged. "Win some. Lose some."

SOMEONE LAUGHED IN the hall outside Lainie's room.

The sound woke Hunt abruptly from a dreamless sleep, and the first thing he saw was her face. She was sound asleep with lashes fluttering, and a tear on her cheek. She was dreaming. *This is real. This is happening.* Bruised and battered, and she'd never been more beautiful to him. *Thank you, God.*

He eased over onto his back to lower the bed rail and stood up, then slid his hands beneath Lainie and slowly eased her back to the middle of the bed. She moaned, then sighed as Hunt pulled the covers up over her shoulders, brushed a kiss across her cheek, then pulled up the bed rail and headed for her bathroom with his backpack.

LAINIE HAD A brief moment of fright when she woke up alone, then she heard water running in the adjoining bathroom and relaxed. Hunt was in the shower. All was right with her world.

She listened, taking comfort in the sound of his presence until the water stopped, then she heard him moving around and thought of all the mornings of their life ahead. Going to bed together. Waking up the same way. And the sound of a shower. She'd never had the pleasure of his company in this way, and was anticipating the simple acts of life that came with love.

And then he emerged, dressed all but for the clean T-shirt he was holding, and she forgot to breathe. The stubble was gone, and the man he'd become was standing before her. Zero body fat. Chiseled abs. A jawline to die for. Blue eyes flashing. The same sensual mouth and thick black hair. And the remnants of war on his body and in his gaze.

She sighed. "So. You have grown into a magnificent man."

The corner of his mouth tilted, just enough to pass for a smile as he approached the bed. "I guess we can chalk it up to Uncle Sam's good cooking," he drawled.

"Nope. I knew you when, remember? This was always you, just waiting to turn into this."

"If you say so," he said, and smoothed the flyaway strands of hair from her face.

"Show me," she said.

He frowned. "Show you what?"

"Where the bullet went in your back."

He turned, then raised his arm a little. "It went in there and came out here." Then he pulled the T-shirt over his head and ended the search as he glanced out the window. The sky was changing. Evening, and they were no longer on the mountain.

The door opened behind him, bringing the scents of food with it. Meal carts were in the hall, and nurses came into her room with two trays. One for Lainie. One for Hunt.

"Maggie Rae ordered two trays for this room," the nurse said.

Hunt glanced back at Lainie. "Who's Maggie Rae?"

"The nurse who caught you sleeping in my bed."

He grinned. "So, I'm not going to be shot at sunrise, after all?"

"I told you I had friends here," Lainie said.

They put Lainie's tray on her tray table and the second one on the window ledge for Hunt.

He lifted the food covers. "Thank you, ladies. This looks and smells way better than the MREs we were eating, doesn't it, darlin'?"

Lainie frowned. "I don't know about that. That first packet of spaghetti with meat sauce tasted like heaven after three days with nothing but water." Then she gave Hunt a look. "Or maybe it was just the chef that made it so good."

"Yeah… I fed you, then poured alcohol on your feet and made you faint. I'll never get over that," he muttered.

The nurses left, and as soon as Lainie raised the head of her bed and moved her tray table toward her, he pulled up the big recliner and sat down beside her with his tray.

"I don't always pack MREs," he said. "When I have to, I'm a fair cook."

"No worries, sweetheart. I love to cook, and I'm better than good." Then she took her first bite. "Um, almost Salisbury steak."

Hunt grinned. "So, a hamburger patty in sauce?"

She nodded and took another bite, and so it went. They were down to scraping the bottom of their pudding cups when Dr. Wagner came in with his nurse, making rounds.

"Good evening, Lainie. Who's your dinner partner?" he asked.

"Hunter Gray. Childhood sweetheart. Man of my dreams. Also, the man who found me. Hunt, this is Dr. Wagner. The man with the staple gun and anesthesia."

Wagner grinned. The hospital staff was well aware of Lainie Mayes's wicked sense of humor.

Hunt immediately stood and shook the doctor's hand. "It's a pleasure, sir."

Wagner arched an eyebrow. "That was very military. Did you serve?"

Hunt nodded. "Ten years. I'm out now. Been flying

charters for Randolph Charter Service in Flagstaff, but I'll be staying here in Denver."

"Good. That means you're not sweeping Lainie away from us. She is a very valuable employee, as well as a good friend. We'd hate to lose her." Then Wagner switched focus and moved closer to Lainie's bed. "The wound in your head looks good. Shirley is going to unwrap your feet for me. I need to make sure everything looks okay before I let you go home tomorrow."

Hunt moved out of the way, but stayed close enough to get a good view after the bandages were removed.

"The antibiotics are already working," Wagner said. "The infected areas are looking much better, and the more superficial cuts are already starting to seal up."

"How long will it be before I can walk?" Lainie asked.

"Don't rush it, but I'd say, as soon as you can comfortably bear weight. You'll need to be cleared before you come back to work, but take the time to heal without worry. Your job isn't going anywhere."

"What happened to the clothes I was wearing when they brought me in?" she asked.

"We cut them off, remember?" Wagner said.

"I had a set of car keys in my pocket. I'm going to need them. And now that I think of it, my car is still parked at the trailhead."

"I believe your keys were bagged and tagged and are at the nurses' desk. Shirley will check for you when we're done here," he said.

"Will I need to change bandages daily?" Lainie asked.

"Maybe for another day or so. After that, I think heavy socks should suffice. Definitely no shoes until you can walk comfortably, and then something like a slipper."

"She's got me," Hunt said. "I waited eleven years to find her. I've got no problem carrying her."

Wagner nodded.

Lainie teared. She made jokes to hide her fears, while Hunt simply blurted out his truths. When the nurse began putting fresh bandages on Lainie's feet, Hunt reached for her hand. She clung to him without words, and soon they had the room to themselves again.

"Don't worry about your car. Once we get you home and I get you settled, I can take an Uber back to the park to get it," Hunt said.

Tears rolled.

Hunt groaned, and then lowered a bed rail and slid onto the bed beside Lainie. He slipped his arms around her. "Honey…what's wrong?"

"Nothing. Just a little PTSD, and not used to having anyone help me do anything."

"Understood," he said. "Tomorrow is the beginning of us again. You and me. For the first time in our lives, we'll be together and on our own."

As PROMISED, Lainie was released the next morning after Wagner made rounds. Hunt had already filled her prescriptions at the hospital pharmacy, and was waiting outside the hospital entrance with the passenger door open. Lainie was wearing borrowed scrubs and another pair of his socks when the orderly brought her down in a wheelchair. It was gray and cloudy, with a forecast of thunderstorms, and Hunt wanted to get her home before they hit.

"Did they give you your keys?" he asked as he picked her up and settled her into the front seat.

"Yes, right here," she said, and held up a plastic bag with her release papers and the keys safely inside.

He buckled her in, then kissed the side of her cheek. "Love you," he whispered, then stepped back and closed the door as the orderly took the wheelchair back inside.

Moments later, he was behind the wheel. He reached across the console and gave her hand a quick squeeze, then reached for his phone.

"I need an address now, darlin', because I don't know where you live."

Lainie blinked. "Oh, right! I guess you do."

He entered it into his GPS and then drove away, following the route, while the clouds continued to gather and the sky began to darken. Twenty minutes later, he pulled into her driveway.

"I'm going to guess the remote control to your garage is in your car," he said.

"Yes, but there's a keyless entry pad on the outside. The four number code is your birthday—1010. Just key it in."

He smiled, gave her a thumbs-up and got out running. The wind was rising, and the first drops of rain were already falling as he keyed in the numbers. When the door began to go up, he ran back to the Jeep and drove into the garage.

"Just in time," Hunt said.

She sighed. "Home. There was a time when I didn't think I would make it back here."

"Will the door into the house be locked from here?"

She shook her head.

"Then sit tight. I've always dreamed of carrying you across the threshold, just not exactly like this."

Lainie was still smiling when he lifted her from the front seat and headed for the door. She hit the Down button on the keypad to lower the garage door as they went by, and then they were going through a utility room and into the kitchen/dining area.

Hunt paused, admiring the open concept of the house. "This is incredible. It feels like you. Where do you want to be, darlin'? Your bedroom, or on the living room sofa for a bit?"

"The sofa."

Outside, the sprinkles were turning into a torrential downpour as Hunt carried her toward a blue upholstered sectional.

She looked toward the window and shivered. "Thank God I am not still lost on that mountain."

"I don't want to think about it," he muttered as he put her down. "I'm going to get my gear. I'll be right back," he said, and bolted back toward the garage.

When he came back carrying it, she waved him down the hall. "My bedroom is the big one at the end of the hall. You'll have to give yourself the grand tour."

He made quick work of the trip, eyed the king-size, four-poster bed, then dumped his stuff just inside the door and returned to where she was sitting.

"Do you need anything, honey? Bathroom? Something to eat or drink?"

She glanced at her little brown teddy with the wobbly head. "Not now, love. Come sit with me for a bit."

Hunt was wondering how he would fit into this place of calm and peace. This was her space. He'd played no part in her life here, but he had no words for how grateful he was to be here.

He was moving toward the sofa when a little wooden rocker at the corner of the hearth caught his eye, and then he recognized the teddy bear sitting in it.

"Lainie…is that the one I gave you? Your Valentine bear?"

Her heart was beginning to race. She'd dreamed of this moment for so many years, and now that it was here, she was scared of how he would react.

"Yes, it is. Would you bring it to me, please, and then sit down with me for a bit?"

"Sure thing," he said as he picked it up and then sat down and put it in her lap. "Here you go, darlin'. Kinda cool to know you still have it."

Lainie's hands were trembling as she picked it up and laid it in his arms. "The ashes of our son are in a tiny brass heart inside this bear. You're holding your son, Hunt. It's not much of him…but it's all I have left to give you."

Hunt's heart stopped with a kick, and then raced to catch up. He could no longer hear the storm, or the rain pounding on the roof. He couldn't see her face for the tears.

The brown pelt was soft beneath his fingers. The bear's shiny black eyes seemed to be looking at him, and right where a heartbeat would be, he felt the tiny metal heart.

"Jesus, Lainie. Oh, my God. Oh, my God." Then cradled it to his chest and broke into sobs.

She wrapped her arms around him, holding him and the little bear until he had no tears left to cry, and the silence was deafening. Without a word, he reached for her, pulling her into his lap, and rocked her and the bear where he sat.

She hurt for the shock that had untethered him, and for grief she knew all too well. Finally, she moved enough to see his face.

"Look at me, love. This isn't your fault. It wasn't our war. And when you disappeared, I wasn't sure I'd ever see you again. But I hoped. You gave me the bear, and then you gave me the baby, and even after I lost you both, I had the solace of knowing that what was left of him was within the last thing you gave me…like he was being held in your arms for safekeeping."

Hunt knew if he opened his mouth that he'd choke on the words, so he just shook his head and hid his face against the curve of her neck.

"This is so painful for you because it's new. But the day your mother came to my hospital room to tell me she didn't know where you were, and how sorry she was, her words became noise in my head. After she left I cried until I made myself sick. We've been through hell, Hunt. We were so lost…and now we're not…because of you. You found me. You saved me. It's okay to grieve. It's the only thing that will heal, and in the meantime, I'm your backup. A little the worse for wear, but I'm here, and I'm not ever losing you again."

Hunt took her words into his soul. She'd always been his compass to sanity, but he'd seen the warrior she'd become. He already knew how fiercely she fought for who she loved. In his world, it was the people who had your back that mattered most, and she was it. He took a breath, cleared the tears from his face in two angry swipes, and then looked her in the eyes.

"Thank you, darlin'…for holding on to who we were. So, this is who we are, and now it's up to us to create who we're going to be."

"Happy. We're going to be happy," she said.

As they sat, sheltered from the ongoing storm and the rain blowing against the windows, Hunt had a flash of déjà vu.

It was the rain!

Just like the day he los her.

He'd been standing in he rain, waiting for a phone call that never came. And now they'd come full circle. She was in his arms again.

When she fell asleep in his lap, he carried her to her bedroom with the little bear and covered them with the blanket draped across the foot of the bed. As he was turning to walk away, he noticed something framed, hanging above the bed. He took a step closer, and then stared in disbelief.

His last text to her! She'd seen it, after all. And kept it.

He looked down at her then, healing wounds and bruises, curled up on her side in such a state of peace, with the Valentine bear tucked beneath her chin. She kept saying that he'd saved her, but it was her who saved him.

He left the room, taking care to leave the door open in case she called, then went into the kitchen to call his boss.

Pete Randolph answered on the second ring.

"Hello."

"Pete, it's me, Hunt."

"Hey! I've been expecting you to call. We've been keeping up with your search through the news. We know the hiker was arrested. His first alibi fell through like a rock, didn't it?"

"Yes, sir," Hunt said.

"Congratulations on finding your girl. I hope she's okay."

"Thanks, and yes, she is. She has some healing to do, but she's getting there. The reason I'm calling is to let you know I'm not coming back. I'm staying in Denver with Lainie."

"I'm sorry to hear this, but I'm not surprised. I could tell she meant a lot to you, and we all wish you the best. Your last check will go into your bank account as always. Take care, son, and have yourself a happy life."

"Thank you for everything," Hunt said, and then stood in the middle of the room, trying to decide what to do next.

Food would be happening, but he didn't know what was here, and she'd been missing so long, some things might have expired, or gone bad. So he began going through the pantry to see what was available, then he dug through the contents of her refrigerator before sitting down to make a list.

It became obvious they would order in for supper, but he'd wait to talk to her about the groceries. He didn't know if she did her own shopping, or ordered online for them to be delivered. There were so many little day-to-day things they were going to learn about each other. It was an exciting thought. All the days ahead of sharing laughs and frustrations—of having someone to come home to. It was Hunt's dream of heaven on earth, and it was coming true.

Fort Liberty North Carolina

A TABLE FULL of soldiers were on base, eating their evening meal and trading digs and laughs with their buddies in between mouthfuls of food. Wall-mounted televisions provided the background for their meals and conversations, while what was airing wasn't always noticed.

An evening news show was airing a follow-up to their previous story about the missing hiker in Colorado, celebrating the fact that she had been found and rescued by none other than a man from her hometown of New Orleans. They went on to explain that the man, an ex-Army helicopter pilot named Hunter Gray had been her childhood sweetheart. The news anchors were listing a quick rundown of his attributes, then followed up by making a joke about "Hollywood will come calling on this story!" when one of the men sitting at that table—a chopper pilot they called Rat—jumped up from his seat, pointing.

"Did you hear that? Did you hear that?" Rat shouted.

T-Bone frowned. "Hear what?"

Rat was running around the table with his fork still in his hand, shouting every word that came out of his mouth. By now, he had the attention of every person in the room.

"The guy who found that missing hiker lady in Colorado! It was Gator! Gator, by God, Gray found her! Using the skills he'd learned in the Army, they said. A former warrant officer with the freaking 82nd Airborne Division, they said! His childhood sweetheart, they said! Hot damn, y'all. That's why he mustered out. He'd left his woman behind, and he, by God, went and found her!"

The room erupted in cheers!

Rat and T-Bone were hugging and slapping each other on the back. Cherokee and Memphis were grinning from ear to ear. Dallas and Roadrunner were high-fiving Cowboy. Tulsa and Chili Dog were staring at the TV in disbelief. Everyone in the room who'd served with him was cheering. Everyone who'd even heard of the ace gunner from the 82nd Airborne was on their feet cheering and whooping. Gator Gray had represented!

NEARLY TWO WEEKS had passed since Lainie's release from the hospital. She was finally back on her feet for short periods of time, and moving slowly. She'd gotten as far as the living room before needing to sit down, and was still there when she saw a delivery van from a local florist shop pull up in her drive.

A man got out, took a huge floral bouquet from the back of the van and headed toward her house. She could walk, but not walk and carry something like that on her own, so she shouted at Hunt.

"Hey honey! Can you come help? There's a delivery guy coming toward the house."

At that moment, the doorbell rang.

Hunt had been unpacking his things from Flagstaff when she called.

"On the way!" he shouted, and came running through the foyer and straight to the door.

"Delivery for Lainie Mayes."

"Thanks," Hunt said, pulled a five-dollar bill from his pocket and tipped the man as he took the vase then toed the door shut behind him. "Wow, darlin'. These are beautiful! Where do you want them?"

"They're gorgeous, and that's the biggest bouquet I've ever seen! How about the dining table? We'll see it every time we walk past, and it's big enough to accommodate it."

"Good call," he said, and headed for the dining room with Lainie right behind him. He put down the vase then pulled the card and handed it to her, then saw her eyes widen in surprise.

"Oh, honey…oh my… I think these are for you as much as for me. Look," she said, and handed him the card.

For Gator's girl,
Rat, T-Bone, Roadrunner, Memphis, Cowboy,
Tulsa, Chili Dog, Cherokee and Dallas, and the
82nd Airborne, sending our love.
Gator Gray…you did good.

Hunt was stunned. "Never thought I'd hear from them again."

Lainie was elated. This was part of who he'd been, and evidence of how much they'd thought of him.

"We've been all over national news for some time. That's probably how they found out. And that last update I saw, news anchors were really playing up your

Army background and the childhood sweetheart connection." She hugged him. "They love you, Hunt. Maybe
not as much as I do, but they love you, and you made
them proud."

"All I wanted was to find you alive. The flowers are
for a special lady, and that's you." He read the card again,
picturing their faces as he saw the names, but then he
kept going back to "Gator's girl," and finally frowned.

"Lainie, I don't want you to just be Gator's girl. That
should read, 'Gator's wife,' but she doesn't exist, and
that's all wrong. Can we talk about getting married?"

Lainie slid her arms around his neck. "You already
proposed to me once, remember?"

He frowned. "Yes, and you said we'd walk that road
after we got to Tulane."

"Because I still wasn't eighteen, and you know my
parents would never have given their consent. I thought
we had time." Her voice broke. "I was wrong."

"So, you're a grown-ass woman and I'm asking you
again. Will you marry me, darlin'?"

"In a heartbeat."

He grinned. "I love how you play hard to get."

She shrugged. "There's no waiting period in Colorado. You can get a marriage license and get married in
the same day, if you want to."

He blinked. "Another plus for this state beside the fact
that you're living in it. What kind of ID do we need?"

"A simple driver's license will suffice," she said.

"Do you want the ceremony with all the trimmings?"
he asked.

"I just want to be your wife. I want the right to call
you husband. But I do want to wait until the bruises are
gone before we do it, because when we get someone to
take our picture, I don't want to look like I'd been in a

dogfight, and have people a hundred years from now wondering why."

Hunt kissed the little scar on her forehead, then ran his thumb along the curve of her chin. "It's a deal. But right now, would you like to take a ride?"

"I'm good with taking a ride. I haven't been out of this house since you brought me home from the hospital, except to have the staples taken out of my head."

"Then let's do it. And wear your fuzzy leopard slippers. They're my favorite," he said.

She laughed. "I'm going to need a few minutes."

"Take all the time you need. We've got the rest of our lives to fix the mess our parents made." But then he thought about her walking back through the house just to get shoes and a jacket, and swung her up into his arms and carried her down the hall and into the bedroom. "Consider it taking a shortcut," he said, brushing a kiss on her lips and leaving the room.

Chapter Eight

When they pulled into the drive-through at Freddy's Frozen Custard and Burgers, Lainie beamed.

"Oh, Hunt! Freddy's! Back home, it was our place to go."

"I know. I saw it the other day when I was picking up groceries. Thought of all the times we spent eating their burgers and fries, and the hot fudge sundaes made with the frozen custard."

"Do you remember what I liked?" she asked.

He frowned. "Darlin'. I remember everything about you."

"Then you order for me," she said.

He pulled up to the speaker. "Two original combos, no onions, extra ketchup for the fries and two large, sweet teas," he said, and then drove around to the pickup window for their order.

He drove them to a nearby parking lot, distributed the food, and then they sat watching traffic as they ate.

"This is so good," Lainie said. "All these years I've lived here, and I've never come to Freddy's."

"We're here now, and we'll be back," Hunt said, and dunked his fry into a puddle of ketchup.

Before long, they began playing the traffic game they used to play when they were teens.

"See that old red truck with the dented fender rattling

by? He's headed to Dallas, Texas, to see his grannie on her birthday," Lainie said.

Hunt remembered the game and jumped in. "Yeah? Well, take a look at that black Porsche darting through traffic. It belongs to the banker's wife, but she's on her way to meet a guy on the side, and she's gonna get caught, because the banker found out."

Lainie frowned. "Poor wifey. She should have settled for the Porsche and forgot about extramarital sex."

Hunt snorted. "Darlin'…if somebody's not getting enough of it, they'll always go huntin' for it."

Lainie grinned. "I suppose you have a point, unless you're one of those ladies who's had the best and isn't willing to settle for second-rate. Like me."

He licked a drip of ketchup off his lip and stared. "You didn't—"

"Not even tempted. I kind of turned it off, I think. Did you date?"

"Not even once," he said. "I'm a one-woman kind of guy."

"So…you turned it off, too?" she asked.

"I didn't know how to turn off wanting you. I just made love to you every night in my dreams, and suffered through the reality that you were gone," he muttered.

The faint brush of despair in his voice made her sad all over again for what they'd lost. Timing couldn't be worse. She still looked like she had one foot in the grave, but they were together again, sharing food and space, and a future of possibilities.

She wiped her hands and turned to face him.

"Hunter?"

His eyes narrowed. She never called him by his full name unless it was serious. "Yes, darlin'?"

"I know I promised you a sexy nightgown and a pretty

body, but if we turn off the lights and you'll settle for as is, you know how to turn me back on."

He took the statement like a fist to the gut, then inhaled to make sure he was still breathing. "Are you finished with that burger?"

Her whole body quickened. "I can be."

He nodded. "I'll gather up the trash."

Today was a day for moving forward, and this moment had been a long time coming.

The drive home happened faster than when they'd left. No sightseeing, or calling attention to points of interest. Just a heart-racing need to be together.

When they pulled into the garage, Hunt ran to her side of the car and picked her up to carry her inside.

"Honey, I can walk," Lainie said.

"If you can say that again in a couple of hours, then you're on your own. But this is me, clearin' the way to paradise."

She said no more and settled for the bird's-eye view she had of his face. Upside down or backward. Front view or silhouette…he was beautiful in her eyes.

He carried her into the house, all the way down the hall to their bedroom before he put her down.

"I'm going to wash up first, or I'm going to taste like ketchup," she said.

"Fine, but don't wash it all off. I like ketchup, too."

Lainie laughed as she walked into the en suite and shut the door. She knew what he was doing…wanting her to forget about how she looked and remember the fireworks when they were together.

When she came out, the shades were down and the covers pulled back on the bed. He was waiting in the shadows, and when she walked into his arms, the removal of their clothing became a dance.

A head bowed to remove a shirt.

A foot lifted to step out of their pants.

The stroke of his hand down the middle of her back.

The rhythm of his heartbeat against her palm.

The fall of her hair across his arm.

The sensual stroke of his tongue in the valley between her breasts.

The catch in her breath when he stretched out beside her.

The glitter in his eyes as he gazed down upon her.

The scars they bore were both outward and inward, but the bond between them was timeless, unbreakable.

He was the same, and yet different.

It wasn't their first kiss…but it was the last remnant of regret for what had been.

"My darlin' Lainie, you never quit me…even after I quit myself. Words do not exist to explain the depths of what you mean to me."

He had that piercing-eye raptor look again, and she was his willing prey. "I love you, Hunt, and that is all."

His heart was pounding as he moved over her, and then he was inside her. Hard as a rock, and throbbing from the blood rush, he began to move.

She closed her eyes, wrapped her legs around his waist and pulled him deeper. *I am whole again.*

It began like it always had between them—with a slow, steady stroke in perfect rhythm. Their bodies fit, like two halves of a perfect whole, turning up the volume as the need grew stronger.

Minute by minute, they chased the heat, always just a little ahead of them, until feel-good turned into need. Need turned into frenzy, and right in the middle of heartbeat, the slam of a climax, wiping out all sense of thought.

In the aftermath, they became each other's anchor until the final quake had stilled.

Still inside her, Hunt rolled onto his back, taking her with him, and within seconds felt the first drops of her tears on his chest.

His voice was but a rumble in Lainie's ear.

"You're crying. Please tell me I didn't hurt you."

"No pain. Tears of joy. Making love to you didn't hurt. It healed."

"Okay then," he said, and slid his hands down the ridge of her spine and cupped her backside.

Lainie felt boneless. She couldn't have moved then if she'd tried, and there they laid, heart to heart, as the minutes passed. She was almost at the point of sleep when she heard him groan, and then move within her.

He was hard again, and still inside her.

She raised up just enough to see his ice-blue eyes catch fire.

"What are you waiting for, Gator?"

"Permission to proceed, ma'am."

"Permission granted."

Three days later

LAINIE DIDN'T HAVE a way to thank each and every person responsible for the flowers from Hunt's squadron, so she turned loose of her ego and had Hunt take a picture of her standing by the bouquet and holding a sign that read,

TO THE GUYS IN GATOR GRAY'S SQUADRON, AND THE 82ND AIRBORNE BATTALION IN FORT LIBERTY
THANK YOU FOR THE FLOWERS.
WITH LOVE—GATOR GRAY'S GIRL.

And then she posted it on her Instagram account.

There was no denying what she'd suffered. But the sweet smile on her battered face said it all. She'd survived.

The post went viral, but all she cared about was making sure Hunt's friends received her thanks.

That evening, she was in the kitchen chopping up vegetables for a casserole when she heard Hunt's Jeep in the driveway. He'd had two separate interviews today with med-flight services, and she was curious to find out what he thought, and what they'd said.

She heard the front door open, wiped her hands and went to meet him.

"I missed you," she said as she gave him a hug.

"I missed you more," he said, and kissed her soundly.

"Get comfy then come talk to me," she said. "I'm chopping veggies for a casserole."

A few minutes later, he was back in his sock feet, minus the boots and flight jacket, but still wearing the jeans and shirt he'd left home in. He walked up behind her, slid his arms around her waist and kissed the back of her ear.

"I have dreamed of this life with you forever. Still have a need to pinch myself that it's real," he said.

She leaned against him, reveling in the embrace. "Fairy tales were always my favorites when I was little because everyone lived happy-ever-after. And I'm also hardheaded. I refused to give up on this dream. I didn't know how it would happen, but I wanted you back in my life."

"And you got me," Hunt said, then reached over her shoulder and grabbed a carrot chunk and popped it in his mouth.

"Give me a couple of minutes to finish this so I can get it in the oven," she said.

"Need help?"

"I might like to look at you now and then while I work, so feel free to lurk about. Grab yourself something to drink, love. I've been standing long enough. I need to sit down soon."

He nodded, took a longneck beer from the fridge, popped off the cap, took a quick sip, and then carried it to the window overlooking her backyard.

"Looks like rain coming in. Earlier, I thought I could smell it in the air," he said.

"I like the rain when I'm snuggled in at home. Not crazy about driving to work and back in it," she said, and dumped the veggies she'd just cut into the brown sauce on the stove, stirred it all together, then poured it over the seared beef tips in the casserole dish, covered it with foil and put it in the oven. She set the timer for an hour, then started to clean up when Hunt turned around and noticed what she was doing.

"I can do that, darlin'," he said, and set her down with his beer.

She didn't argue. And she had a confession to make.

"I posted the thank-you card photo on Instagram this morning. I don't know if any of the guys have seen it yet, but one hundred forty-three thousand other people have."

He turned, staring at her in disbelief. "What? Are you serious?"

She nodded.

He grinned. "Proper southern lady that you are, that is one hell of a thank-you card."

"The spirit of my grandmother Sarah would have haunted me for life had I not sent a thank-you of some kind. One of her well-repeated adages was 'Proper ladies must have proper manners.'"

He gave her a look. "Well, I don't need a damn thing

about you to change. In my eyes, you've always been perfect, and the improper parts are what I love most."

He winked, then finished loading the dishwasher and wiped down the counters.

"Let's go sit where it's comfortable," Lainie said. "I want to put my feet up."

"Uber coming up," Hunt said. "Bring my beer." He scooped her up in his arms.

"You don't have to keep doing this," she said.

"What if I like it?" he said, and then carried her out of the room, eased her down on the sofa so she could stretch out her legs, then sat at the other end and put her feet in his lap. "There now, darlin'. Is that better?"

"Very much so," she said, and handed him his beer. "Now, tell me about your day."

He began lightly rubbing the tops of her feet as he talked. "Both interviews were good. Both companies offer about the same package. I also checked into EMS pilots for hospitals. It's three straight days of twelve-hour shifts, and then six days off. I have the hours, skill and experience to qualify."

"You choose. This is home base. This is where you go when you're not in the air. As long as I'm still Gator's girl, all will be right in my world."

"Gator's wife," he corrected.

She smiled. "Yes…that."

He nodded. "I'm leaning toward the EMS thing. I'll see what's available, and go from there."

"I have something to talk to you about, too," Lainie said. "It's about the baby's ashes."

His hands were still on her feet when he looked up. "What about them?"

"In the beginning, I kept them because of you. I always thought you'd come looking for me one day, and I wanted to give you that moment."

His fingers swept across the tops of her feet and curled around them.

"You did, and I am so grateful."

"But now, every time you see the little bear sitting in the rocker, does it make you feel sad? Is it a hard reminder of the loss, or does it give you comfort to keep it?"

He glanced at the rocker, and then back at her. "What are you asking, darlin'?"

She took a breath. "If you want to lay him to rest."

"What do you want?"

"I don't want to ever hurt you, but in my heart, I feel like keeping the ashes in view, even though we're the only ones who know they're there, isn't fair. Every day we work on putting the past behind us, but it will always be with us, because it was part of our journey. I don't have to hold ashes to remember I carried your child. And our baby was already in the arms of angels before they pulled me out of the wreck."

"You want to scatter them?" he asked.

Lainie's eyes welled. "No. I want to leave the ashes right where they are, and bury the teddy bear. I would like remembering him that way."

Hunt took a deep breath, swallowing past the lump in his throat. "There are days when I think you couldn't get any dearer to me, and then you up and say something like this. You break my heart…in a thousand little pieces. And I would have given anything if you'd never been hurt like this. But you are right. He'll always be with us. We should do this."

Lainie swung her legs off the sofa and then scooted up beside him. "But no funeral service. Just us and a preacher at the gravesite, okay?"

He hesitated. "With one request."

"Name it," she said.

"That I'm his pallbearer."

She nodded. "It is your right."

THAT NIGHT, Lainie was already in bed when Hunt came out of the bathroom. She could smell the scents of his shampoo and body wash as he crossed the room and slid into bed beside her. Her silence was telling, and he knew what it was about.

"I love you, lady, and there is no right or wrong decision here. It's a choice, and if you haven't changed your mind, then we'll start the process tomorrow, okay?"

Her voice was shaking. "And some day, maybe we'll make another baby?"

He kissed the back of her neck. "Well, we certainly know what makes babies, and we do love the practice of it, and I'm damn good at it, so I can't imagine why we'd choose not to."

She chuckled under her breath. "We're going to have to do something about that inferiority complex."

"Hush yourself, girl. You taught me everything I know."

She laughed, then rolled over into his arms. "Well, maybe not everything," she said, and proceeded to prove it.

THE RAIN HUNT predicted came after midnight, and by morning, Denver was sopping wet. Water was still running in the streets when they headed out to Fairmont Funeral Home.

A couple of hours later, after explaining what they wanted, they purchased plots, chose a casket, ordered a headstone, and set a date and time for the service.

Michael Taylor, the funeral director, had recognized

them the moment they walked in, and was quite taken by their request.

"I just want the both of you to know I will do my best to make this service special for you. My deepest sympathies for the tragedy of this loss. I long ago learned there is no expiration date for grief."

"Thank you," Hunt said, and shook his hand. "Until this coming Friday, then?"

"Yes, sir," Taylor said.

THE NEXT FEW days for Lainie were like waiting for the other shoe to drop. She wouldn't even look in the direction of the rocking chair, then one afternoon while Hunt was helping her fold clothes, she caught herself whispering about the service, and was so horrified at herself that she threw her hands up in despair.

"What's wrong with me? Why did I just do that? Like I'm afraid the bear will hear me? Maybe that fall on my head knocked the good sense right out of me!"

He dropped the towel he was folding. "Come here to me, Lainie."

She walked into his arms and laid her head on his chest.

"You're fine," Hunt said. "You know what's happening, right?"

"No, I don't," she mumbled.

He buried his face in the fire of her hair and held her close. "Close your eyes, love, and imagine this scene. Family and friends have just gathered for a meal after burying Grandpa. At first everyone is quiet and reverent. They get their food and start eating, and they begin to feel better. Somebody mentions how good the food is. And then someone else reminds them of how their people made it different, and then someone else reminds them of how much Grandpa loved pie, and they laugh. And then the shock of having laughed at such a moment when they're supposed to be sad is suddenly an embarrassment, and the room is silent again."

She could see the image he was painting.

"Well, darlin', that's where you are right now. Your reality hasn't caught up with your truth. There's no one left to judge you, and it sure as hell won't be me. And we know ashes don't hold a soul captive. You know that little guy went home a long time ago. And a stuffed bear isn't going to judge you. If toys went to heaven, I think that bear would be happy with the job you have given him."

Her face crumpled. "How did you get so smart?"

"I don't know, darlin'. Maybe it's because I know you better than you know yourself?"

She looked up, and when she did, he kissed her, soft and slow, then set her free.

"You're right," Lainie said. "I'm not second-guessing my choice. I'm just not good at letting go."

"Good. Then that means you won't be one of those wives who has a constant urge to get rid of her husband's treasures…like the old jersey from his football days, and the cleats he wore in the homecoming game."

She blinked. "Do you still have that stuff?"

"I might."

She sighed. "God, how I love you."

"Feelin's mutual, darlin'. Now can I ask you a question?"

"Absolutely," she said.

"Can I have that last piece of lemon pie in the fridge?"

She grinned. "Been eatin' at you, has it?"

"Is that a yes?"

She laughed out loud, and then blinked. "Oh, wow. This is me laughing at the family dinner, isn't it?"

He nodded. "I'll give you the first bite."

"I never could tell you no."

IT WAS THE morning of the funeral. The day was clear, but a little cool. Lainie dressed for warmth, choosing a pair of black winter slacks, a blue cashmere sweater to wear under the matching jacket and soft black socks with a pair of black loafers.

A quick glance in the full-length mirror was the assurance she needed. She mostly looked like herself again. Same long auburn hair hanging below her shoulders. Same arched eyebrows and thick lashes. Same oval face and straight nose. Same lips. Hunt called them kissable. But he also considered her entire body kissable, so there was that. Considering Hunt liked her best naked, then she only had to please herself, and turned away.

Hunt was still in the bathroom shaving, so she went to the kitchen for a cup of coffee. It was hard to figure out how to feel. This wasn't a new loss. And for her, it wasn't fresh grief. Maybe it was about turning loose. Of giving up. All she knew was that the hole in her heart would be real.

She took her coffee to the kitchen table, then sat with her view to the backyard. Before long, the first snow would fall. It wouldn't last. It was just a forerunner of the long winter to come.

She could hear Hunt opening drawers and doors down the hall, and knew he was getting dressed. She smiled. The sound of his presence was her blessing. She would never ask God for more. Then she heard him coming up the hall and turned to look, then forgot to breathe.

He was a sight to behold—the soldier he'd been, in full-dress warrant officer uniform, holding his hat. A black dress jacket, adorned in gold braid and stars. Blue trousers with a gold stripe down the outside of each leg. A white, semiformal shirt with a turn-down collar. A black bow tie. The array of service medals was a roadmap of his accomplishments, then she saw the Purple Heart. She knew he had one. But she'd never seen it.

He was searching her face for approval. "To honor our son," he said.

Lainie put a hand on her heart. "You honor us all. I don't think I ever said this aloud, but…thank you for your service."

He nodded. "Are you ready, darlin'?"

"Almost," she said.

He followed her to the living room, then to the rocking chair by the hearth. She picked up the little bear, gave it a hug, then handed it to Hunt.

His eyes briefly closed as he held it to him, and then they were gone.

The ride to the funeral home was silent.

Lainie held the bear in her lap all the way, and when they arrived, the director was waiting.

"Follow me," he said, and led them into a viewing room, and up to the tiny, satin-lined casket and the small nosegay of white roses lying on top of it.

Lainie laid the bear inside, as if she was putting a baby to bed, then Hunt stepped forward, and to their surprise, removed his Purple Heart and pinned it onto the bear's chest, right above the metal heart within it.

"He fought his own war," Hunt said.

They were holding hands as the director closed and locked the casket, and then they followed its passage through the winding halls of the funeral home and out to the waiting hearse in the adjoining garage. They stood in silence, watching as the casket and flowers were loaded, and then were escorted to the family car.

Mr. Taylor seated Hunt and Lainie in the back, and as soon as the doors shut behind them, Hunt put his hat in his lap and turned and kissed her.

"This is the hardest day, and you're the bravest person I know. Stay with me, darlin'. I've got your back."

Her eyes were welling with unshed tears, but she had no regrets. "This is why I waited. I could never have done this without you."

"The same people who broke us, broke him. We're free from them now, and he deserves the same level of release."

Mr. Taylor got behind the wheel as the pastor took the seat beside him. The drive was brief, and as soon as they stopped behind the hearse, they all exited the car.

Once again, Hunt was steadying Lainie's steps as they approached the hearse. Upon their arrival, he handed Lainie over to the director.

"Mr. Taylor, I would appreciate it if you would steady my lady's steps. She's still healing from her ordeal."

"It would be my honor," Taylor said, and offered Lainie his arm.

Hunt put on his hat, then leaned into the back of the hearse and picked up the casket. There was a brief moment of clarity as he measured the weight of it. The pack he'd carried throughout basic training weighed thrice this, maybe more, but the absence of life within it was a weight he would forever bear.

He'd already seen the little tent on the hill where the grave had been dug and started toward it, with the rest of the entourage behind him.

He would remember later, the crunch of dead grass and pebbles beneath his feet. Sunlight glittering on a tombstone in the distance, the chill of the wind against his face, and then they were there. With yet another step of the finality of the moment, he set the little casket on the framework of the casket lowering system and moved back to her.

The pastor they didn't know began reading a psalm.

Lainie was weeping silently.

Blinded by his own tears, Hunt reached for her hand.

The act of burial was the final rite of passage, and Hunt was moving through the service in the same way he'd followed orders—in duty and silence.

Eleven years he'd been a father without knowing it. The unborn child had been given his name, and today, he carried him to the grave.

Hunter James Gray II had never taken a breath, or let out a cry, but today, his mother and father were crying for him.

And then the pastor stopped talking.

The grave attendants moved to the CLS and began lowering the casket until it stopped.

Lainie stepped forward, picked up a handful of dirt from the grave and tossed it onto the casket. Hunt did the same, and then they stood vigil at the site until all of the dirt had been replaced.

In her heart, they'd just put their baby to bed. Leaving it behind was the hard part for her, but he was already with the angels. This parting was for them.

The white roses were on the grave now, and they were driving a temporary grave marker into the ground when Hunt heard Lainie moan beneath her breath, then grab his arm to steady herself. One look, and he knew she was done.

"Darlin', are you hurting?"

She nodded. "I've been standing too long."

Hunt looked around for Taylor, and then called out to him.

"Sir, I need to get Lainie home."

Taylor jumped into action and headed toward the car, as Hunt swung her up in his arms.

"I'm sorry," she whispered. "All of a sudden, I just gave out."

"You don't apologize to me. Doing this for you is my joy."

The director took them back to the funeral home and pulled up beside their Jeep.

"Here you are, but can I get you anything before you leave? Some water, maybe?"

"We have some in the Jeep," Hunt said, "but thank you for everything."

"This is a service I will never forget," the director said.

"You gave us everything we asked for. It was perfect," Lainie said.

"We are always here for you," Taylor said, and drove away.

"I can walk from here," Lainie said.

"Yet, I will carry you," Hunt said, and the moment she was in the seat, he slipped the shoes from her feet, and then brushed a kiss across her lips.

"Buckle up, darlin'. We're going home."

Chapter Nine

The ensuing week was about moving forward.

Hunt carried the little rocking chair to the attic, and Lainie put a potted plant in its place.

After a last trip to Dr. Wagner, he declared her feet healed and cleared her to return to work. She was put back on the roster for the following Monday, but her car had been sitting in the garage for so long that Hunt took it to a garage to be serviced before she started driving it again.

"You're as handy to have around as a pocket on a shirt," Lainie said, when he came back and dropped the car keys in her hand.

"If I'm gonna be a pocket, I want to be the one on the backside of your pants," he said, and kissed her soundly.

She laughed and the Universe took her joy, bound it with a thousand others and sent it out into the world.

He was still reeling from the joy on her face as he stroked the tip of his finger along her cheek. "No bruises left."

"I know. I'm me again," she said.

"Are you ready to take another ride?" he asked.

It was the tone in his voice. "Where to?" she asked.

"The courthouse. To get that marriage license."

Lainie gasped. "Yes, oh yes, but my hair's a mess. I need to change clothes, and..."

He pulled a little black velvet box from the pocket of his flight jacket and opened it, revealing the diamond-encrusted wedding band inside.

Her throat tightened with emotion. "Oh, Hunt. It's beautiful. I'll brush my hair and get my purse," she said, then bolted.

He shouted down the hall, "I expect the same level of excitement when I take you to bed tonight!"

He could hear her laughing, and wondered what her reaction would be when she found out he would be flying choppers for the National Park Service in Denver. After their diligence in searching for Lainie, he liked the thought of being part of that.

TWO HOURS LATER, they were standing in the corner of the court clerk's office, before a justice of the peace. Lainie was holding a bouquet of daisies, still wrapped in the cellophane from the supermarket, while the lines of people in the clerk's office waiting to be served, now stood as witnesses.

They'd already figured out who the bride and groom were. Everyone knew her name. And their story. And now they were seeing them in the flesh, witnessing their marriage.

Phones were recording the vows. Pictures were being taken. And when Hunter Gray slipped the ring on her finger and kissed his wife for the very first time, there wasn't a dry eye in the room.

"We're married! We're finally married," Lainie whispered.

"And I get to call you my wife," Hunt said.

"Gator's wife," she corrected. "We need another picture to send the guys!" She turned to face the crowd. "Wedding pictures! Will somebody take pictures of us?"

The volunteers were endless. Pictures were taken on both of their phones, and Lainie thanked them profusely when they gave them back.

"I'd throw my bouquet, but I'm pretty sure these daisies are on their last legs. All I'd do is make a mess for somebody else to clean up, so I'm going to take them home and let them shed on my table."

"And, without a threshold to carry her over, I'll have to settle for the exit," Hunt said, then swooped her up in his arms and carried her out the door.

VIDEOS AND PHOTOS with accompanying stories were hitting the internet before they even got home, but they wouldn't have cared. Their plans involved making love, and opening that bottle of champagne they'd been saving, and making love, then emptying the bottle.

Their wedding dinner was pizza with everything, compliments of SliceWorks and served by DoorDash. There were no pictures involved. They weren't wearing enough clothing for modesty's sake.

BACK IN NEW ORLEANS, a little gray-haired lady named Millie Swayze was sitting in her recliner with her feet up, a laptop in her lap and a bowl of cheese puffs beside her, eating away as she scrolled through Facebook.

When she came to a post she'd been tagged in, she stopped and read it.

Check it out. Meant to be, her friend said, and attached a video.

Millie clicked it. The images of the people in the video were a little fuzzy, and the sound wasn't great, but when she realized what she was seeing, and who they were, she started laughing and crying.

"Praise the Lord! Good for you, babies…good for you! You beat them, and you beat the odds!" She licked the cheese dust off her fingers, then reached for a tissue to wipe her eyes. "Now I can die happy! But in the meantime, I'll be sipping a little wine cooler to toast your long and happy lives."

LAINIE PICKED OUT the best picture from the wedding and once again posted it on social media with the heading…

> GATOR AND LAINIE GRAY
> WEDDING FINALLY HAPPENED!
> UNTIL DEATH DO US PART.
> HOOYAH!

This time it was T-Bone who saw the post first, and quickly shared it to the team with a caption. This is how you do happy-ever-after.

WHEN LOCAL MEDIA in New Orleans picked up the final chapter to their story, both sets of parents saw it.

Greg and Tina were in the throes of a divorce, so the news only added to the bitterness between them. The acrimony within their lives had destroyed their marriage, destroyed their family, and coming from old money wasn't enough to save their name. And the worst blow of all was that in spite of everything they'd destroyed, they'd never been able to change their daughter's heart.

Lainie loved with a passion far stronger than their hate.

CHUCK AND BRENDA hadn't changed their spots. He was driving a forklift at a warehouse down by the river, and

Brenda was waiting tables four days a week. They came home angry and went to bed drunk, still following the path of least resistance. Knowing Hunt and Lainie were married was what they'd expected to happen. There was no coming back from their part in any of it. They'd lost his love when they broke his trust, but if their son was happy, then it was enough.

IT WAS STILL dark when Hunt kissed Lainie goodbye.

"Happy first day back at work," he whispered, and pulled the covers up over her shoulders.

"What time is it?" she mumbled.

"You still have a couple of hours before your alarm goes off. Love you, darlin'. I'll be late coming home."

"Doesn't matter, as long as you do. Love you forever. Fly safe."

"Always," he said, and then he was gone.

She listened until she heard his Jeep starting up, and then rolled over and closed her eyes.

WHEN SHE WOKE up again, the house was quiet. She rolled over and stretched, then threw back the covers and headed for the shower. The rat race was on.

When she got into the car and backed out of the garage, it felt strange to be back behind the wheel, but that sensation quickly faded. By the time she got to the hospital and parked, she could have almost convinced herself it had all been a horrible nightmare, but for Hunt's presence in her life and the ring on her finger.

From the time she entered the building, all the way to the staff lockers, she was greeted with big smiles and warm hugs. When she got to her office, there were flowers on her desk.

She pulled the card and smiled: *Love you, Hunt*

After that, the morning flew by. When it came time for lunch, she headed to the cafeteria.

Charis saw her coming and waved, indicating she'd saved her a chair.

The moment Lainie sat down with her tray, Charis squealed. "Girl…you're all over social media, and you beat me to the altar. Let me see that ring!"

Lainie lifted her hand, eyeing the circlet of diamonds glittering on her finger.

"It's so you," Charis said. "Gorgeous, elegant and understated. I was kind of hoping Hunt would drop by with you."

"He left for work before I did. He sent flowers. They're on my desk."

"Oh, wow! What's he doing?"

"Flying helicopters for the National Park Service here in Denver."

Charis leaned in and lowered her voice. "Can we talk about Randall for a sec?"

Lainie frowned. "Only if it's bad news for him."

"He got ten years with no possibility of parole, and there are other women who've come forward to file similar charges against him."

Lainie picked up her fork and jammed it into the slice of meat loaf on her plate. "Shame they don't still hang people," she said, and popped the bite into her mouth.

Their lunch was quick, and they both headed off in separate directions—Charis back to the fourth floor, and Lainie to set up for an MRI. After that, time passed quickly.

Lainie clocked out and headed for her car. Winter hours made for short days of daylight, and she still needed to go by a supermarket before she went home.

Even the simple act of shopping for Hunt was a joy. She had a husband she loved to take care of.

He liked Snickers bars and Pepsi, and big salads with everything in them. He didn't like anything to do with peppermint, and loved her soaking tub, and Creole blackened fish, fried a little on the crisp side.

She drove home in the dark, and was grateful when the garage light came on as she was pulling in. Once the door was down, she carried in the groceries, then paused to flip on the wall switch to the gas fireplace as she headed to her room to change. Within seconds, flames were dancing behind the glass.

It was habit that made her look toward the end of the hearth. Little bear had always been there to greet her, but no more. She sighed, then put her hand over her heart.

"It's okay, baby…you're in here now," she whispered, then went down the hall to change clothes.

She wasn't sure when Hunt would get home, but when he did, she'd be waiting. This was their new normal, and it was good. As soon as she changed, she hurried back to the kitchen and started making a roux. It would take a good thirty minutes to get the dark, rich flavors she was looking for. She'd bought shrimp that had already been cleaned, and had all of the other components on the shelf, or in the freezer. This was the perfect night for some Creole gumbo and rice.

A couple of hours later, gumbo thick with shrimp, okra and andouille sausage was simmering on the back burner, rice was in the steamer and a pitcher of sweet tea was in the fridge. She'd already had a shower and changed into warm sweats and fuzzy socks, and was sitting in the recliner with a glass of tea when she saw headlights flash through the curtains.

Her heart skipped. He was home.

HUNT CAME RUSHING into the house, trying to outrun the cold before it snuck in behind him. Even as he was closing the door, she was coming to meet him.

"Louisiana in the house!" he said, then kissed her soundly. "Thank you, Lord, for the woman I come home to," he said. "What is that heavenly smell?"

Lainie grinned. "You mean besides me? It could be the gumbo simmering on the stove."

All the teasing ended. The smile slid off his face, and then he hugged her.

"What's that for?" she asked.

"In Iraq… I dreamed of gumbo and rice, and endless glasses of sweet tea."

She shivered. "Talk about being on the same wavelength. That's our dinner tonight."

He hugged her again. "Is it done…ready to eat?"

"Yep."

"Lord, have mercy…give me a few," he said, and bolted down the hall.

"I'll just be in the kitchen," she said, to no one listening, and went to get the pot of gumbo off the burner.

She had dishes at the ready, glasses filled and rice in the bowls when he came back.

He leaned over to smell the gumbo and closed his eyes. "It smells as good as you look," he said, then kissed the back of her neck. "You worked all day, and then it's obvious you've been working ever since you came home. You sit. I can ladle gumbo over rice without making a mess."

"Deal," she said, and carried their glasses to the table, then watched the play of muscles on his back as he dipped and poured.

He carried the bowls to the table, then sat down beside her. "I gotta taste this before we start talking," he said.

"It's hot. Don't burn your mouth."

He winked. "Yes, ma'am."

Since he'd been warned, the first taste was tentative, but from the look on his face when he chewed and then swallowed, Lainie knew she'd hit a home run.

"Darlin', I'm not just blowing smoke here. This might be the best gumbo I've ever had. Thank you for making this. You brought us home."

"You are most welcome, love. Enjoy. We can talk later."

He nodded, and took another bite, scooping rice and gumbo, and going through two glasses of tea before his bowl was empty.

"I'm gonna want seconds, but I gotta sit a minute to let it settle."

She grinned. "So, what was your day like? Do you think you're going to like it?"

"Yeah, what's not to like? I'm in the air. No one's giving me orders. No one's shooting at me. I flew some people from the Department of the Interior in DC back and forth over a specific area they wanted to see. Something to do with new growth from an old burn zone. What about you? Did you make it okay? Did your feet bother you?"

"I was fine, and some sweet man sent me flowers. They were on my desk when I arrived. Thank you, honey. You are the best. Oh… Charis thinks my ring is beautiful, and she thinks you are, too."

Hunt sat, watching the way her expressions changed with what she was saying, and how green her eyes looked when she wore blue, and how soft her hair was against his skin when they made love. She was all soft and southern sweet until threatened or crossed. Unleashing the wild in a redheaded woman was a dangerous thing, but she was everything he wanted.

He ate that second bowl of gumbo before they cleaned up the kitchen. They made love on a rug in the firelight before taking themselves to bed. Even as she was curling herself against him, he wanted her again, but it was late, and there was always tomorrow.

THERE WAS SNOW on the ground, and Christmas was in the air.

Hunt and Lainie had just put up their first tree together, and had two different Christmas parties on the calendar to attend. Their world was expanding—their lives growing richer—and fuller, in more ways than one.

LAINIE WAS SITTING on the edge of their bathtub, staring down at the test stick she was holding—waiting. The sensation of déjà vu was so strong she couldn't breathe without wanting to cry.

She kept muttering, "Please, God, please. Let it be. Let it be."

She kept glancing at the time, and was so scared at one point that she thought she was going to faint, and put her head between her knees. Afraid to look. Afraid not to. Then the feeling passed, and when she looked up, she had an answer.

"Oh, my God," she mumbled, and started to cry, then headed for the living room.

HUNT WAS KICKED back in the recliner with his feet to the fire, half-listening to the music Lainie had playing in the kitchen. The weekend was always the best, because that's when they had time off together, even though he'd been grounded for two days because of a blizzard, and it was still snowing. He was watching snow fall outside the windows when he heard Lainie coming up the hall. He glanced up as she walked in, saw the tears on her face, and was on his feet and moving toward her.

"Darlin', what's wrong? Are you hurt. Are you sick?"

She held out the test stick. "No, I'm just pregnant. We're going to have a baby, Hunt. Merry Christmas, love. You're going to be a daddy."

Hunt froze, then an explosion joy rolled through him. Seconds later, she was in his arms.

"Oh, my God, Lainie, this is wonderful! Are you happy? Please be happy."

She was laughing through tears. "Yes, I'm happy. I still dream of a little version of you."

He smiled. "Or a little version of you," he said softly.

She put her hand on his chest, feeling the steady hammer of his heartbeat against her palm. "It doesn't matter. All I know is you gave me another baby to love. You're my lifeline to joy. Merry Christmas, Gator."

"Merry Christmas, darlin'," he murmured, then lowered his head and kissed her.

* * * *

A Q&A with Sharon Sala

What or who inspired you to write?
I had always thought of writing the stories in my head, but I never acted on it until the death of my father and sister within two months of each other. Their loss was a heartbreaking shock, as well as the realization that my tomorrow wasn't promised. It was the wake-up call I needed to act upon my dream.

What is your daily writing routine?
The first thing I do every morning is read my local paper and work the crossword puzzle. It's like turning on my brain to the need for words. After that I read and answer email and messages. Within an hour of being up, I'm at my laptop, pulling up the work in progress, rereading and editing the previous chapter from the day before, and by the time I get to the place where I'd ended, I am completely into the story and the characters and what has to happen next. I write for as long as the words come, and when I come to a pause, I take it. Diet Dr Pepper and the excitement of telling what comes next keeps me focused and writing until I choose to stop.

Who are your favorite authors?
When I was young, it was Zane Grey and anything and

everything about Edgar Cayce. As I grew up, I read everything and had no particular favorites. Today, I would say Robert Crais and John Hart.

Where do your story ideas come from?

I dream most of them. They're like movies in my sleep. All I have to do is wake up and write what I saw. Once in a while, something I see triggers the story.

Do you have a favorite travel destination?

I don't particularly like to travel. Going on vacations was never a part of my childhood or my adult life. I was a farmer's daughter, and then a farmer's wife. When everyone else was going on vacation, we were either planting, or harvesting, or tending to the animals we raised.

What is your most treasured possession?

My family. Always.

What is your favorite movie?

Avatar, and a movie called *Stolen Women: Captured Hearts*, based on a true story.

When did you read your first Harlequin romance? Do you remember its title?

I honestly don't remember, nor do I remember the title, but my sister gave me my first one to read.

How did you meet your current love?

I don't have a current love. He passed away in 2005. But we met when I was nine and he was ten. We were childhood sweethearts and then lost each other, only to reconnect in later years when I was single again.

What characteristic do you most value in your friends?
Honesty.

How did you celebrate or treat yourself when you got your first book deal?
I called everyone I knew, and then I cried, and went to the kitchen to cook supper.

Will you share your favorite reader response?
I was at the book signing at a Romantic Times Book-lovers convention in Nashville years ago when a young woman came running toward me, clutching a copy of my first Silhouette romance, a book called *Annie and the Outlaw*. Before I knew what was happening, she was crying and hugging me and telling me that reading that book had taken away her fear of dying, and she wanted to thank me. (I learned as she was telling me the story that she had an inoperable brain tumor.) She wanted a picture of us together, and asked me to sign the book. I was stunned, hardly knowing what to say, and then she hugged me again and was gone. I laid my head down on the table and cried. I learned later she was a bookseller who worked for Waldenbooks. Her name was Steffie Walker, the person for whom the RWA National Bookseller of the Year Award is named.

What are your favorite character names?
Charlie Dodge and Jade Wyrick, the couple from the Jigsaw Files, which was the last series I wrote for MIRA.

Other than author, what job would you like to have?
An artist. I used to paint (in oils) and sell a lot of my work in the '70s and '80s before I began writing.

K.D. Richards is a native of the Washington, DC, area, who now lives outside Toronto with her husband and two sons. You can find her at kdrichardsbooks.com.

Also by K.D. Richards

Harlequin Intrigue

West Investigations

Pursuit of the Truth
Missing at Christmas
Christmas Data Breach
Shielding Her Son
Dark Water Disappearance
Catching the Carling Lake Killer
Under the Cover of Darkness
A Stalker's Prey
Silenced Witness

Visit her Author Profile page at Harlequin.com.

SILENCED WITNESS

K.D. Richards

To Allison Lyons, an amazing editor.
Thank you for believing in me and
making me a better writer.

Chapter One

Alexis Douglas awoke with a start and listened. She'd heard something, or she thought she had, but all was still in her darkened bedroom and there was no sound in the house. She closed her eyes and settled deeper into her soft mattress.

She was on the cusp of falling asleep when she heard the sound again.

Her eyes flew open.

A thin beam of light snaked through the blinds on her bedroom window. Her neighbor's security lights. Maybe Ronnie was out on his back porch. He liked to have a cigarette from time to time and his wife wouldn't allow him to smoke inside their home.

Alexis focused, listening again for the sound that had awakened her. She heard nothing. But she couldn't shake the feeling that something was off.

A minute ticked by. Then another, with each moment increasing the apprehension twisting her stomach into knots.

Creeaak.

She knew that sound. It was a loose floorboard, one of many in the sixty-year-old house she'd bought a year ago with the intention of fixing it up. She'd been too busy with her business as a personal chef to do any renovations other than to the kitchen, which had become her favorite spot in the house.

Alexis bolted out of bed, crouching down in the narrow space between the wall and the bed frame. Her eyes darted over the darkened room for a weapon or a way out. The bedroom was on the second floor, so jumping from the window was a last resort. Unfortunately for her, she liked to keep her space clean and the clutter minimal. No random cutlery sitting around from a midnight snack. Her clothes were hung, by color and season, in her closet or folded neatly in the dresser. The only thing on her nightstand was the hardback she was slowly making her way through. She'd even left her cell phone downstairs to charge rather than plugging it in next to the bed, which was supposed to be the healthier choice according to an article she'd read earlier that week.

Now, she was looking at facing an intruder with nothing but the latest Naomi Hirahara thriller to defend herself with.

But she couldn't just stay cowering next to the bed. She'd be cornered if the intruder came into the bedroom. Same with hiding in the closet.

Another floorboard creaked down the hall.

She grabbed the book from her bedside table, and as quickly and quietly as she could, hurried toward the bedroom door. Flattening her back against the sliver of space between the doorframe and the dresser, she listened for sounds of the intruder entering the room.

Time felt as if it were moving in slow motion. Sweat beaded on her skin, making it sticky even though she'd turned the thermostat down to sixty-six before she'd gone to bed.

The faintest sound of rustling material came from the hall, followed by the soft fall of footsteps.

Trembling, she held the book against her chest as the bedroom door slid open slowly.

Her chest tightened even as it seemed to her as though every breath rumbled into her lungs with the force of a locomotive.

The intruder, a man based on the build, in dark-colored pants and shirt, crept toward the bed. She wasn't a small woman, five-seven with ample curves and she worked out regularly, but she could see that the man had several inches and at least thirty pounds on her. And although it didn't look like he had a weapon on him, there was no way for her to be sure of that. Still, she had to do what she could to protect herself.

She didn't move until the man's back was fully to her. Then, lifting the book high above her head, she raced forward with a battle cry she hoped would catch him off guard.

He turned, his eyes wide in the eyelet cutouts of the ski mask he wore over his face.

She slammed the book into his jaw with all her strength, then let it fall to the floor as she turned and ran. Three-hundred-fifty pages might stun, but it wouldn't incapacitate a man of his size. She had to get out of the house fast.

Her bare feet slapped against the wood floor of the hallway. She made it to the top of the stairs before a hand grabbed her roughly from behind and she was thrown to the floor. She landed on her back and the intruder was on her before she could make any attempt to get to her feet.

His hand clamped down over her mouth, muffling the scream that tore out of her throat. She bucked and thrashed, trying to throw him off or free an arm or leg to lash out with, but she'd been right about his size being no match for her.

Tears leaked from her eyes as he leaned in close. He smelled of whiskey, tobacco and something else. Something foul and more than a little threatening.

Fear ricocheted through her body.

The man smiled maliciously, and she knew that he was getting off on terrorizing her. Was that what he was there for? To terrorize her? Assault her? Worse?

Her heart thudded so hard it felt like it was only seconds away from beating right out of her chest.

The man pressed himself against her, and her entire body shuddered.

His smile grew wider, sending her fear spiking. He brought his face within centimeters of hers. "Stop asking questions about your brother or you'll end up just like him."

He lifted his hand from her mouth, but her scream was cut off by his fist connecting with the side of her temple.

She was only vaguely aware of his weight lifting off her before she was plunged into darkness.

Chapter Two

Sitting at his desk at West Security and Investigations in the late afternoon, Thaddeus Jeremiah Roman—TJ to everyone except his mother—put the finishing touches on his report to the wife of a wealthy Manhattan hedge fund manager who suspected her husband of cheating. Mrs. Hedge Fund Manager had good instincts. She was dead on with her suspicions about her husband cheating, but she'd suspected the wrong woman. Her husband wasn't seeing the twenty-something female associate he worked with but his secretary.

TJ had a feeling Mr. Hedge Fund Manager was about to find out the true meaning of cheaters never prosper. Mrs. Hedge Fund Manager had explained in no uncertain terms when she'd contracted with West Investigations for their services just what she would do to her husband's nether regions if they found evidence he was cheating. And that was before she took him for everything the courts would allow.

And that was reason number 1,582,392 why TJ was never, ever getting married. Not that he'd ever cheat on his nonexistent wife or any other woman he was seeing. He was always up front with the women he dated. He didn't want a serious relationship, and he wasn't looking to have his mind changed at this point. The only woman he'd ever loved had died right as they were on the cusp of building a life together. He hadn't been sure he was going to make it through the loss. And he wasn't interested in feeling pain like that ever again. No, it was better to keep his relationships nice and easy. Surface level. If a woman couldn't deal with that, he wished her well and went on his merry way.

TJ filed his report and sent it off to his boss and co-owner of West Security and Investigations, Shawn West.

West Security and Investigations was one of the best private investigations and personal security firms on the East Coast, and with the recently announced Los Angeles office, the firm was poised to expand its reach nationwide. They'd investigated and gotten to the bottom of cases that included everything from corporate espionage to organized crime. They also provided personal security for some of the wealthiest and most recognizable people in the world, most recently Brianna Baker, one of the hottest actresses in Hollywood at the moment. Most of the investigators who worked for West Security and Investigations preferred to take on the sexier, high-profile assignments, but not TJ. If it was between a case that was likely to see him dodging bullets or a good old-fashioned adultery investigation, he'd take the adultery, please and thank you. A decade in the Army had been more than enough excitement to last him a lifetime.

Now he just wanted to collect a steady paycheck, cheer on the Nets, and make a pretty woman smile from time to time. A simple life.

The sound of the door to the office opening and heels clicking over the tiled floors caught his attention. It was after five. Serena Wells, their receptionist, had already left, and most West employees didn't keep regular hours, coming and going as needed. He was the only West employee currently occupying a desk in the open floor plan office space.

He peeked over the top of the partition surrounding his desk.

A woman with dark micro braids cut into a swingy bob framing her face swept into the office. The first thing he noticed was her curves. She had them for days, and she apparently knew how to make the most of them. Dark blue jeans stretched over a round behind and a bronze V-neck sweater clung to an ample bosom. She marched to the reception desk wearing brown leather boots that matched her sweater, with a black wool coat thrown over her arm. Smooth, dark caramel skin that looked like it had never seen a blemish covered her heart-shaped face.

Even from several feet away, though, he could read the tension in her body. She paused at the empty reception desk, her eyes glazing over the space.

Her gaze landed on him before he could fall back behind the safety of the partition. He didn't like engaging with the clients any more than he had to. Generally, he interacted with them just enough to get the information he needed to do the job and to convey his results. But for some inexplicable reason, he found himself rising and moving toward the woman before he fully comprehended that was what he was doing.

The woman's brown eyes bore into him as he drew closer to her. There was something about her. Something familiar.

"TJ? TJ Roman?" Her gaze shifted over him from head to toe and back in open assessment.

The sound of his name from her lips gave him pause. He knew that voice. Alexis? It couldn't be and yet it was.

Surprise sent his brow into an arch. "Alexis Douglas?"

She smiled crookedly. "I didn't know if you'd remember me."

"Of course." He started toward her, his arms outstretched to give her a hug. It was awkward.

Alexis was the sister of his best friend. Well, he guessed former best friend now. He hadn't spoken to Mark Douglas in over two years, although the loss of the friendship that had begun in grade school still stung. It had been even longer since he'd seen Alexis. More than ten years had passed. She was barely legal back then, a fresh-faced eighteen-year-old heart-stopper. But now... He stepped back, letting his gaze roam over her. She'd grown up to be flat-out gorgeous.

Alexis was four years younger than her brother Mark, which made her five years younger than TJ. The distance in their ages and the fact that she was the sister of his best friend had meant he'd barely noticed her as they'd grown up. But he was noticing her now. The attraction he felt for the woman standing in front of him was instant and strong. Strong enough that he had to remind himself that she was still his friend's sister and still off-limits. That was good for another reason. Based on the anxiety he saw in her dark brown eyes, Alexis hadn't sought him out for old times' sake.

"What are you doing here, Alexis?"

She licked her plump lips nervously. "I need your help."

It took him an extra second to process what she said, given the amount of blood that had moved from his brain to his groin while he'd been looking at her lips.

"Let's go into the conference room and you can tell me about it." He finally managed to get out.

He led her into the conference room, offering her coffee or water, both of which she declined before taking a seat. She sank into the black leather chairs at the long conference table, moving her purse from her shoulder to her lap.

There were plugs in the center of the table for laptops and tablets, and he knew a lot of his colleagues liked taking digital notes, but he preferred pen and paper when he had the choice. He grabbed one of the yellow legal pads stacked on the table and a pen.

"Okay," he said, "start from the beginning."

Alexis took a shaky breath and let it out slowly. "I guess it began with Mark's death."

Chapter Three

Alexis gave TJ a minute to process what she'd just said. She hadn't been sure if he'd heard about Mark passing. She knew that her brother and TJ had had some sort of falling out a couple of years earlier, but Mark would never talk about exactly what happened. Mark had always seen her as his little sister. Someone he had to protect, no matter how old she'd gotten. That protection had extended to bullies, boys, and any information that he thought she didn't need to trouble her pretty little head with. But Mark was gone now and he couldn't protect her from whoever had broken into her house two nights earlier.

"Mark is dead?" TJ cocked his head to one side, saying the words as if he was trying them on for size. Like they didn't fit.

Because they didn't. It had been two months, and she was still trying to process living in a world without her brother in it.

She pushed back the tears threatening to spill from her eyes. "I didn't know if you knew. Or if you wanted to know. I'm sorry to spring it on you like this." This was harder than she'd imagined, but she didn't know who else to turn to.

"How?" TJ's voice came out as little more than a whisper.

"Officially? Suicide." She gripped the strap of her purse so tightly now that her knuckles whitened. But she didn't think Mark had committed suicide, a belief she suspected was at the root of her current troubles.

TJ's eyes went hard. "No way. No. Way."

Buoyed by his categorical rejection of her brother's official cause of death, she slid closer to TJ. "Mark died two months ago. Before he died, he was under suspicion for several crimes."

"What kind of crimes?"

"I'm not sure exactly. All I could get out of him was that there had been a theft of some sort at the company where he worked and he'd been suspended pending an investigation."

TJ frowned. "I don't believe Mark would steal from anyone."

Hearing his conviction that her brother was innocent felt like a thousand pounds had been lifted off her shoulders. She leaned toward TJ, sitting in the chair next to her. "Me either. Mark wouldn't tell me much about it. You know how he was about protecting me from anything and everything even remotely unpleasant."

TJ gave a small smile. "I do remember he was a bit overprotective of you, yes."

"More than a bit," she grumbled. "He hadn't been arrested or anything, but I know he'd hired a lawyer."

"So it was serious." TJ rubbed his chin with the hand not holding the pen.

"Very." She nodded. "And that seems to be the basis for why the authorities believe that Mark committed suicide. He was found in the apartment he rented. It looked like he swallowed a bottle of Valium." She caught a sob before it bubbled out.

For the first two weeks after she was notified of her

brother's death, she hadn't stopped crying. She didn't know if she would be able to stop if she let herself start again. Mark needed her to be strong now. To prove he hadn't committed the crimes he'd been suspected of and that he hadn't killed himself.

TJ gave her a moment to collect herself before asking, "Where did Mark work?"

"TalCon Cyber Security. The company is a major government contractor headquartered in Virginia. Most of the work they do is for the US military."

"I've heard of it," TJ said with a frown.

"Mark did something with computers for them similar to what he did when he was in the Army. I don't really understand what he did, but I know my brother. Mark was an honorable man. He wouldn't have done anything to disgrace himself, and he wouldn't have killed himself. He intended to prove his innocence."

"That sounds like Mark."

Alexis sucked in another deep breath. The conversation with TJ was going well, but if it was going to go off the rails, it would be with what she said next. "TJ, I think Mark was murdered."

He said nothing for a long moment.

"Alexis—"

"Listen, I know what you're going to say. I've already heard it from the cops handling Mark's supposed suicide. And his lawyer. But I know…" her voice caught, "knew my brother. I'm hoping that because you knew him too, you'll help me."

TJ shrank back in his seat away from her.

Damn him, he wasn't going to help her.

"I don't know what I can do to help you," TJ started. "I chase after cheating husbands and people who are trying to defraud their insurance company."

"You work for one of the best private investigations firms in the city," she said incredulously.

"I chase after *very rich* cheating husbands and wives," he repeated with emphasis. "I don't investigate theft and potential murder."

"You could," she said, hating the desperation in her tone. But she needed help, and she was willing to do whatever it took to get it. "I looked into this firm, and this should be a walk in the park for West Investigations. Didn't your boss bring down an organized crime syndicate in the city last year?"

"I am not Ryan West," TJ grumbled.

This had been a waste of her time. He wasn't going to help her.

Alexis threw her shoulders back and stood. "Fine. I want to talk to him then."

TJ remained seated. "Sit down, Alexis."

She sat, the fire suddenly going out of her. She was so tired. Tired of the grief. Tired of the not knowing. She needed to move on, but to do that she had to know the truth, and to get that, she needed help.

"If I'm crazy, if I'm just a grieving sister looking to excuse her brother's bad decisions, why did someone attack me in my home two nights ago?"

She had his full attention now.

TJ leaned forward in his seat. "Attack you? What are you talking about?"

"Two nights ago, someone broke into my house and attacked me." Her voice caught again, thinking about the man's weight pinning her to the floor. "He threatened me, then knocked me out so he could get away."

She'd done what she could to cover the bruise on her face with foundation and had styled her hair to fall over it. She pushed her braids aside now. The makeup helped but couldn't hide the injury completely.

Something akin to a growl rumbled from TJ as he inspected her face.

She let her hair fall back over the mark.

"What kind of a threat?" he barked.

"The man said if I didn't stop asking questions, I'd end up just like Mark."

TJ's expression turned even darker and, although she knew it wasn't aimed at her, deadly.

"Did you call the police?"

She nodded. "I did. They took a report, but I don't think much will come of it. The lock on my front door had scratches, like it had been jimmied, but nothing was taken and I couldn't give the officers a description of the man who attacked me. He wore a mask."

"Give me a description. In fact, walk me through that night. Every detail you can remember."

She did as he asked, pushing aside the fear that ripped through her anew as she recounted the man throwing her to the hallway floor and climbing on top of her.

"Did he…" TJ shook with rage, unable to complete his sentence, but she knew what he was asking.

She shook her head again. "No, thank God."

The man hadn't been there to hurt her, not in any serious way, at least. She knew that now. His objective had been to terrorize her, and he'd succeeded.

She finished telling TJ about that night, watching his jaw flex in anger as she did. She knew she shouldn't, but she found it sexy. TJ had always been a handsome man. She put him at six two or three, taller than Mark had been at six feet, but they'd both developed the lean, hard bodies of soldiers. It looked like TJ kept up his physique. Powerful biceps filled out his pullover. He still kept his hair in the short cut favored by the military, but the hard line of his square jaw was dusted with stubble.

She remembered Mark catching her admiring TJ on the sly one time when they'd both been home on leave. He'd forbid her from dating TJ, which had led to an argument. He didn't have any right to tell her who she could and couldn't date. After all, she had been eighteen at the time, a grown woman and fully capable of deciding who to date.

It hadn't mattered, anyway. TJ hadn't so much as looked twice at her on the several occasions they'd met previously. Mark had made a point of making sure she knew that TJ was a player who never kept a woman around for long.

She'd glimpsed his naked left ring finger now. Unmarried. It didn't seem like much had changed over the years for him. It was just as well. Her last relationship had ended disastrously, and she wasn't sure when, or if, she'd even be ready to jump back into the dating pool.

"Look, I'm not going to give up on clearing Mark's name. If you won't help me, I'll go to Ryan West. And if West Investigations won't help me, I'll keep looking until I find someone who will."

TJ sighed. "Are you sure about this? I mean, someone has already broken into your house. I know Mark wouldn't want you to put yourself in any danger. Maybe the best thing to do is to let the cops handle this."

She leaned forward and looked him in his eyes. "I'm more sure than I've been about anything else in my life. Mark protected me when he was alive. It's my turn to protect him the only way I can now."

TJ looked away from her, staring out of the conference room window for so long she was sure he was coming up with a gentle way to tell her to get lost.

She was nearly ready to tell him to forget the whole thing and go find another private investigator when he turned back to her.

"Okay, I'm in."

Chapter Four

TJ looked up at the sound of a knock and spotted Shawn West on the other side of the glass door.

"I need to step into the hall for a moment," he said to Alexis before getting up, leaving her to review West's standard contract on her own.

"I hear you've bought in a new client," Shawn said, craning his neck to see inside the conference room.

TJ stepped into Shawn's line of sight, blocking his view of Alexis. "Something like that. She's the sister of a friend."

Shawn stepped back and gave him a searching look. "I see. And what does this sister of a friend want us to help her with today?"

"Her brother may or may not have committed suicide after being accused of stealing from his employer. It looks like her questions have drawn some unwanted attention."

Shawn co-owned West Security and Investigations with his brother Ryan. Ultimately, it was up to the two of them which cases West Investigations took and which they passed up, although they gave their investigators a lot of latitude.

TJ gave Shawn a quick rundown of everything that Alexis had told him, including the break-in at her home and the attack on her.

Shawn whistled sharply. "That sounds like a more complex case than the ones you normally take on. Are you sure you're up for it?"

No, he wasn't sure at all. But he was sure that he couldn't just palm Alexis off on another West operative.

"I can handle it," TJ growled.

Shawn gave him a knowing smile. "Why is it that all our cases lately seem to revolve around beautiful women in trouble who tie our male employees up in knots? What's going on around here?"

TJ cocked his head to the side. "Isn't that how you met your wife?"

Shawn chuckled. "Touché. I know you are used to being a lone wolf and all, but let me know if you need any help."

A lone wolf. The idea sparked a moment of sadness in him before he pushed it away. "Will do. I'll probably need to make a trip to Virginia. It's where Mark, my friend and Alexis's brother, lived and worked."

"When are you thinking about leaving?"

"Tomorrow, if that works for Alexis. I don't want to leave her alone, though, so I will take you up on that offer of help and ask that you assign someone to stick with her until I'm sure she's not in any danger."

"No way." Alexis's voice boomed behind him.

He turned, annoyed with himself for being oblivious to the sound of the conference room door opening.

Alexis squared off with him, her hands on her hips. "I'm going to be right by your side for any and all investigating."

TJ sighed. "Alexis—"

"Nope." She held her hand up in a stop motion. "I don't want to hear it. Mark is my brother. I'm the client, so it's my rules or I go to another private investigations firm."

TJ looked to Shawn for help but quickly assessed he'd be getting none from his boss.

Shawn shrugged. "She is the client, and it wouldn't be the first time we let a client tag along."

TJ cast his eyes to the heavens, hoping for some divine help, although none appeared forthcoming.

"Fine," he growled, remembering something Mark had once told him about his sister. She could be incredibly bossy. And she almost always got her way. TJ recalled thinking that was because she had Mark wrapped around her little finger, but now he wondered whether that was it at all. Alexis Douglas was a force.

"I was just saying to Shawn that our first stop should be Virginia."

She nodded. "That's fine with me. The police finally released his apartment and his landlord has given me until the end of the month to move Mark's stuff out so we should have no problem with access."

Since she seemed to be in a somewhat agreeable mood, TJ pressed on. "And, in light of the attack at your place, I am going to suggest you have a bodyguard tonight and any time I'm not with you."

She nodded again. "You won't get any argument from me. That creep getting into my home was terrifying." A small shudder worked its way through her body.

The urge to pull her into his arms and assure her he wouldn't allow anything to hurt her hit him.

"Great," he said and instead of acting on his impulse, he turned to Shawn. "Is Tess or one of the other female operatives available?"

"I'd prefer it if you took the job," Alexis spoke up. "That is, if it's okay with you."

He turned back to her. "It's okay with me. I just assumed you'd be more comfortable with a woman staying with you overnight."

Alexis gave a lopsided smile. "I think we'll manage." Sobering quickly, she added. "Mark trusted you and so do I."

The air between them charged. He wasn't sure if she was right about Mark trusting him, but it made him unexpectedly happy to hear that she did.

"It does make things simpler since you will be headed to Virginia tomorrow," said Shawn, breaking the tension smoldering between TJ and Alexis.

TJ dragged his gaze from Alexis's face with Herculean effort, but he still couldn't seem to get words to form, so he simply nodded his acquiescence to the plan.

"Good. Now that that's all settled," Shawn said, with a clap of his hands and a salute before sidling away toward his office.

"Now that that's all settled…" TJ mimicked his boss. He wasn't sure, but he thought he heard Shawn chuckle before he disappeared around the corner at the end of the hall. "I have a go bag in my car, so I just need to grab my laptop from my desk and I can follow you back to your place."

"Yeah, sure. Great. I'm parked in the garage right next to this building."

"Come on." He stepped to the side of the hall to let her pass in front of him. "Let's go find out what happened to Mark."

ALEXIS PULLED INTO the driveway of her small two story. She waited until TJ pulled in behind her and opened the driver's side door before she got out of her car. Ronnie, her next-door neighbor, sat on his front porch in a puffy orange vest and a pair of shorts, even though it was mid-

October and the temperature hovered just above fifty degrees outside. Ronnie was what her mother used to call "a character" but, with the exception of his penchant to talk far too long about anime, he was harmless.

She threw a wave to Ronnie, then moved to the front door quickly in an effort to avoid being pulled into an endless conversation.

TJ threw his duffel bag over his shoulder and met her on the porch. "Your neighbor seems awfully interested in your comings and goings." He glared at Ronnie. "Or do you so rarely bring a man home that we're causing a neighborhood spectacle?"

Alexis opened the door and stepped inside her home before answering him. "I've never brought a man home before."

A quick flash of surprise swept across TJ's face before he smiled. "I'm honored to be the first."

Alexis pulled her gaze away from his, ignoring the pluck of awareness she felt when he smiled at her. A smile that made his already handsome face even more so.

He stood close. Her foyer wasn't large, and between the two of them, there was a mere sliver of space. She yearned to close it. He was big and strong and she knew he had training she couldn't conceive of. Ever since the break-in, she hadn't felt comfortable in her own home, but now, with TJ here, she finally felt safe.

And maybe a little something else too, but she wasn't sure she wanted to explore those feelings. Not so soon after Lamar. Well, soon might be a stretch. It had been a year since she'd walked in on her then fiancé in their bed with another woman. She and Lamar had been heading for a breakup for months, riding the downward wave of the relationship neither one of them had the courage to officially end. Coming home to their shared apartment and finding him with another woman hadn't hurt nearly as much as it should have, but her self-confidence and her belief in her ability to judge people had taken a significant hit.

She cleared her throat and looked away from TJ's penetrating gaze. "So, let me show you around the place." She did a sidestep and hurried farther into the house. "There isn't much to it. This is my office." She pointed to the room to the right. "It's supposed to be a formal living room, but what do I need with a formal living room?" She could feel herself babbling, but couldn't seem to rein it in. "Back here is the kitchen, dining nook and informal living space. I guess the family room, but of course it's just me. No family."

A shard of grief knifed her when she realized how true that was. Her mother died when she was nineteen, and she and Mark had never known the father who walked out on his family when Alexis was still an infant. Now, with Mark gone, she was well and truly alone. But it wasn't the time to wallow in that thought.

"Um, the two bedrooms are upstairs. We'll have to share a bathroom, but I don't think that should be a problem. It will be like we're back in college." She laughed awkwardly. "Or I guess the military for you."

Shut up!

Her brain seemed to have finally hit the switch that shut off her mouth.

"Your place is nice," TJ said after a moment. He sat his duffel bag on one of the kitchen chairs.

"Thanks. I know it needs some work. I bought the place last year with the intention of doing it all, but you know how life is." She shrugged and let out another nervous chuckle.

TJ's mouth quirked upward in a sexy half smile. "I know how life is."

She moved farther into the kitchen. "The one room, of course, I had to renovate, even before I moved in, was the kitchen." She swept her hand out as if she was a showgirl introducing the headlining act.

For a chef, the kitchen was kind of like a stage. And she'd wanted to make sure her kitchen had everything she could ever dream of. Or at least everything she could afford to dream of at this stage in her career.

TJ did a three-sixty turn, taking in the entire space. "It's stunning. I remember how you liked to cook when we were growing up."

"I've turned it into a career," she said, moving behind the large center island. "I'm a personal chef. I have several private clients in Manhattan and Brooklyn. A couple in Connecticut and Westchester." She hesitated for a moment before blurting, "A friend of mine has even invited me to partner with her to start our own restaurant. I'd be the executive chef."

TJ's smile grew. "Wow. I'm impressed, but not surprised. I'm sure you're a fantastic cook and you'll have people flocking to your restaurant."

A warmness flooded her insides at his praise. "You should probably reserve judgment until you've eaten something I've cooked. Sit. I'll get started on dinner."

He moved his bag to the floor and sat. "You don't have to cook for me. We can order something in."

She pressed a hand to her heart. "You wound me, really you do. Just sit there and keep me company."

His laughter filled the space. "You're the boss. In the kitchen, that is."

Now she laughed as she got to work making penne all'arrabbiata, which was a spicy pasta that was an uncomplicated yet tasty dish she was used to making for several of her regular clients.

While she cooked, TJ worked on his laptop.

After a silence that was far too comfortable, she plated pasta and carried both plates to the table.

"It smells amazing." TJ closed the laptop and set it aside.

She slid into the chair across from him. She'd pointed him to the wine rack in the corner of the kitchen while she'd been cooking and had had him open a bottle of red. She'd had a glass and a half while she'd cooked and TJ topped off her glass now.

"You don't drink?"

"Not when I'm on the job. Just water for me." He tapped the rim of the water glass next to his plate.

"That's too bad," she said, reaching for her glass. "This is a really good year."

TJ smiled. "After this job is over, we can share a bottle."

A smile slid over her lips and she realized she actually liked the idea of going out on a date with him.

The meal was starting to feel too much like a date. She sipped her wine and reminded herself that getting involved with TJ was a horrible idea. He'd been a ladies' man when they were young, and men like that didn't change. Not to mention the very fact that she was attracted to him was enough reason not to pursue anything. Her judgment in men was atrocious, hence her self-imposed hiatus from dating.

She needed TJ's help to prove Mark's innocence, and that was all she needed him for.

"This doesn't just smell good, it tastes out of this world. Wow! You are an amazing chef." TJ said, forking another bite into his mouth.

She felt herself preening under his praise. The dish

showcased her cooking style perfectly. She was all about flavor and taste. Of course, there was something to be said for creating dishes that looked appetizing too, but what people really remembered, and what kept her clients coming back for her services, was tasty comfort food.

"I remember you cooking all the time with your mother. She was an amazing cook, too. Is that why you became a chef?" TJ asked.

She circled the rim of her glass with her index finger. "In part, I guess. I think I associate cooking with taking care of people. I know my mother did. I don't know if I have the maternal gene like she did, but I have a talent in the kitchen and good food makes people feel good. If I can put more good in the world, that makes me happy."

TJ swallowed another bite and reached for his glass of water. "Why do you think you don't have the maternal gene?"

"Oh." She waved a hand in front of her face. She wasn't sure why that comment had slipped out. Too much wine maybe. "I don't know."

"You've never been married?" TJ pressed.

"Never married. I got close, kind of, a year ago." Now she knew she'd had too much to drink. She hadn't meant to open that door, but now that she had, the look on TJ's face made it clear he wasn't going to let her drop it without getting the whole story.

She sighed and took another sip, fortifying herself. "It's pretty much a cliché at this point. I came home early one day and found my fiancé in bed with another woman."

"You're better off without him."

"That's what Mark said." She knocked back the remaining wine in her glass. "But you didn't even know Lamar."

TJ shook his head. "Don't need to. He's a moron and you deserve better."

"Thank you."

A frisson of electricity passed between them.

After a long moment, TJ spoke again. "So currently, no serious boyfriend?"

"No serious boyfriend. No boyfriend at all." Her voice snapped with tension.

"Why not?"

"I don't know," she said, avoiding his gaze now. "I guess I'm just not ready to jump back into the dating pool yet."

She rose and carried her still half full plate to the sink. She hadn't finished her pasta, but she'd lost her appetite. Hopefully, she'd eaten enough to soak up some of the wine that had loosened her lips. "I'm exhausted. I'm going to go to bed. Leave the dishes. I'll clean up in the morning."

TJ rose, bringing his empty plate to the sink. "You cooked. I'll do the dishes. And I'm sorry if I made you uncomfortable."

She tried for a smile, but it felt tight across her face. "Don't worry about it. You don't know uncomfortable until you've been a woman working in a five-star restaurant kitchen." She stepped around him and headed for the stairs.

"Alexis," TJ called out.

She turned.

He looked at her for a long moment, as if he wanted to tell her something. Then the moment passed. "I booked us on a seven o'clock flight to Dulles. I hope that's not too early."

"Not too early at all. I'll be ready."

"Goodnight, Alexis."

"Goodnight, TJ."

Chapter Five

Alexis went to her room after dinner with every intention of finally getting some rest. She hadn't had a good night's sleep since the break-in and attack. That plan was sidelined by a phone call from her best friend, Karen Hall, known to her friends as Kitty.

"So, how did it go?" the ever-vociferous Kitty asked without preamble.

Kitty knew about the break-in at Alexis's house and her plan to enlist TJ's help to investigate Mark's death and the accusations of theft against him.

"TJ's on board," Alexis said, settling in under her duvet. Calls with Kitty tended to run long. "Actually, he's here now. He's staying in my guestroom tonight, and tomorrow we're headed to Virginia."

"Wow, that was fast. I tried looking him up online, but I couldn't find anything on a Thaddeus Roman. Zero social media presence, and there's no staff directory on the West Investigations website."

Alexis chuckled. "Well, there wouldn't be. He's a private investigator. Emphasis on the private. Wouldn't exactly be private if he had a ton of photos of himself floating around on the net."

"I guess," Kitty said sulkily. "Okay, then tell me about him."

It occurred to Alexis that TJ and Kitty might be just each other's types. Kitty shied away from serious romantic relationships, just like TJ, preferring to "cast her net wide," as she liked to say.

"Hello? Alexis, are you still there?"

Kitty's voice pulled her out of her reverie. "Yes, I'm here. Sorry, spaced out for a moment. What do you want to know?"

"What does he look like? Paint a picture."

"I don't know. I guess he's handsome. He's about six foot two, broad shoulders. I think I remember Mark mentioning he played football in high school and he looks like it. He can be kind of surly, but he's got these light brown eyes with flecks of yellow in them and sometimes when he looks at me there's such gentleness in them."

"Flecks of yellow, huh? Sounds like you've been staring into Mr. Roman's eyes quite a bit," Kitty teased.

"It's not like that," Alexis said quickly. "It's just something I noticed."

Kitty laughed. "Okay, if you say so. You know it's okay to have feelings for a man," she added soberly.

Kitty had been there for her through the breakup with Lamar. She'd been gently nudging Alexis to get back into the dating game for a while.

"I know."

"Have you thought any more about my offer?"

Alexis had met Kitty in culinary school, but while Kitty was an adequate chef, she really flourished at restaurant management and finance. Her financial acumen was most likely a result of being the daughter of a prominent investment banker, but whatever the cause, Kitty's knowledge of food, finance and marketing had made the restaurants she currently owned two of the most popular dining spots in Jersey City at the moment. Kitty was currently in the process of opening a third restaurant, this one in Manhattan's Financial District and pressuring Alexis to sign on as partner and executive chef.

"I'm still thinking." When Kitty sighed, Alexis added, "It's a big deal. I'd have to let go of my current clients, give up the business I've already built in order to take on a restaurant."

"I know, I know. I told you to take all the time you need, and I meant it, but it would be so great to run a restaurant together."

She and Kitty spoke for a half hour longer about the restaurant and what they'd do together if Alexis agreed to sign on before hanging up.

Talking to Kitty usually invigorated Alexis, but tonight thinking about what her future could be only made her think about Mark and the future he'd never have. More than just having his future cut short, his name would be forever sullied if she wasn't able to prove that he wasn't a thief who'd committed suicide rather than face the consequences of his actions. She couldn't let that stand.

After receiving the call that Mark had killed himself, she'd made the trip to his home in Virginia. Mark rented one side of a duplex apartment, but she hadn't had the strength to clear out his stuff then. Mark's landlord had offered to do the job, but just the idea that all that was left of her brother could be placed into boxes and shipped to her had kept her from taking him up on his offer.

Maybe she'd be strong enough to go through a few of his things on this trip. Take the things she wanted to keep for herself and bring everything else to the Salvation Army or donate them to local families in need. Mark would have liked that.

She plumped her pillow and willed her mind to shut

down so she could get some sleep, but two hours after she'd gotten into bed, she was still wide awake.

It wasn't just that she'd be going to Virginia tomorrow and, hopefully, getting some answers about her brother's death. Every time it felt like sleep was on the horizon, her mind drifted to TJ in the room across the hall and her brain perked right up again, as well as other parts of her body.

No matter how many times she told herself she should keep things on a friendly level with her brother's former best friend, she couldn't keep her mind from entertaining other ideas. Every time she looked into his perceptive brown eyes, she felt as if he could read her mind. Not a good thing, given the activities that were in her head when she looked at him.

She hadn't been attracted to a man since Lamar. But based on what Mark told her about his friend, TJ might be the perfect man to test the waters again with. After all, his no-strings-attached approach to relationships meant neither of them would end up hurt when it inevitably ended between them.

But finding answers about Mark's death was the most important thing she had to do at the moment. Getting involved with TJ now might jeopardize that. She needed him. It had been no accident, her seeking him out. While his friendship with Mark had seemed to wither, the neighborhood grapevine hadn't. She knew that he'd left the military and gotten his private investigator's license. From there, all it took was an internet search to find him. It was her good luck that he worked at one of the best investigation firms in the city. And because of her very wealthy clientele, she could afford to pay top dollar. At least for a while. She hoped that TJ's status as a military veteran would help open doors and loosen lips she hadn't been able to open or loosen on her own.

She rolled over onto her back and looked at the ceiling. "This isn't going to work." But she desperately needed to sleep if she was going to be any more help than a walking zombie tomorrow.

She got out of bed and slipped on her robe. A mug of warm milk always helped her to relax enough to fall asleep.

She opened the door to her bedroom and came face-to-face with TJ. He stood in the doorway of his room in his jeans and sock feet, but bare chested.

"Are you okay?" he asked.

She struggled to pull her gaze away from the curls of hair on his hard chest. But when she did, she found herself even more enthralled by his face. The shadow of stubble that had lingered on his face during the day was thicker now, propelling him from merely handsome to ruggedly sexy. The urge to jump him and have her way with him right there in her hallway was nearly overwhelming.

After much too long a pause, she finally got her brain to circumvent the lustful thoughts and form words. "Fine. Just couldn't sleep."

She turned away from him and moved toward the stairs. Space. That's what she needed right now. A whole lot of space between her and TJ Roman.

Unfortunately, it didn't look like she'd be getting it. TJ followed her down the stairs and to the kitchen.

She circled the large island, putting it between herself and TJ, and reached inside the refrigerator for the milk. "I'm making myself a cup of warm milk. Would you like some?"

"Sure."

"Why are you still up?" she asked as she got started on the milk.

"I was doing some research on Mark and the theft he was suspected of."

She set the pot of milk on the stove and turned the burner on before turning to face him. "Did you find anything?"

TJ shook his head. "Not much, but that's not surprising. If the charges hadn't yet been placed against him when he died, his name isn't likely to appear on public sources."

Alexis put the milk back in the fridge and closed the door with more force than was necessary. "I can't believe anyone would even think Mark could do what they are accusing him of."

She grabbed two mugs out of the overhead cabinet. A companionable silence fell over the kitchen in the couple of minutes it took for the milk to warm. She wasn't used to having another person in her space and was happy to find that TJ didn't feel the need to fill every moment with chatter.

"Can you take me through everything you know about the case against Mark? Everything Mark told you and everything you found out on your own?" TJ asked.

She poured milk into the two mugs. "I've already told you everything I know, which sadly isn't a lot, but I'll happily tell you again if it helps."

She slid one of the mugs across the counter to him, then turned off the burner and settled onto the stool next to TJ.

"You served with Mark in the military."

TJ nodded.

"I don't know much about it, but he was involved in cyber security. He got out of the Army a few years before you did and joined TalCon doing basically what he'd done for the Army, from what I understand."

TJ nodded again. "TalCon is a major military contractor. They employ hundreds of ex-military personnel, so that makes sense."

"Basically, Mark worked his way up until he was head of TalCon's cybersecurity unit. Several weeks ago, an important program Mark had been working on was stolen. Mark wouldn't tell me all the details, but he was accused of the theft. TalCon suspended him."

"It must have been a pretty important program," TJ mused. "Is that when he got a lawyer?"

Alexis nodded. "Yes, I think so. He hired Sanjay Atwal."

"But Mark wasn't charged with the theft right away?"

"No, but I know the police were putting a lot of pressure on Mark. I could tell he was under a lot of stress. He was worried."

"Sounds like he might have had reason to be."

Alexis frowned. "The Alexandria police department took the lead on the investigation into Mark's death, but I know they've spoken to the executives at TalCon. The detective on the case all but told me that she believes Mark killed himself because of the guilt he felt about stealing the program and because he didn't want to face the consequences of that." She pushed her now lukewarm cup of milk aside. "My brother was no coward, TJ."

He reached for her hand and gave it a squeeze. "I know he wasn't. I know firsthand how courageous your brother was. He saved my hide more than once when we were deployed."

Something shifted in his gaze.

"What happened between you and Mark? You used

to be so close and then it seemed like almost overnight you guys grew apart."

Sadness swam across TJ's face. For a moment, she thought he might tell her, but then he fixed his face back into a neutral expression. "Let's stay on topic. Did the Alexandria police department give you any other information?"

She shook her head, resigned to the fact that she might never know what went down between her brother and his friend. "No. I know that they haven't officially closed the case because the medical examiner hasn't gotten the full toxicology screen back from the forensics lab. I've called Detective Elaine Chellel—she's the detective in charge of Mark's case—every week since getting the news of his death, hoping that the toxicology report will come in and prove Mark didn't take his own life, but so far nothing."

"Even when the tox report comes in, it may not disabuse the detective of her theory." TJ voiced her fear. "She may still close the case as a suicide."

"I know," Alexis said quietly. "And if she does, we may never know what happened to Mark."

Chapter Six

The next morning, they caught a seven o'clock flight out of LaGuardia and into Dulles airport just outside of Washington, DC. West Investigations had accounts with all the major rental car companies. With a few swipes on the app on his phone, TJ was able to rent a midsize sedan. He'd discussed his game plan for the investigation with Alexis on the plane. Their first stop would be to TalCon. TJ didn't hold out much hope that they'd get any straight answers from the company, but they had to at least try. Alexis had met Nelson Bacon, the CEO of TalCon, when she'd come to DC to claim Mark's body and organize his affairs. Bacon had given her his personal cell phone number then, and she'd called that morning to set up a meeting with him and Mark's direct supervisor, Arnold Forrick, at TalCon's offices. He was interested in what Mark's employer had to say about the situation.

TJ pulled up to the gates at TalCon's headquarters at ten minutes to ten that morning and gave his and Alexis's names.

The guard at the gate checked their IDs against his list, then gave them directions to the visitor's parking area before waving them through.

TalCon's headquarters was composed of three, three-story cube-like white buildings with windows too dark to see inside. They formed a U-shape around a large parking lot.

After another round of ID checking at the receptionist's desk in the lobby of the building, he and Alexis were allowed to take the elevator to the third floor. After a brief wait, Nelson Bacon's assistant, a young woman with sun-kissed blonde hair, led them down a long hall to a corner office.

Bacon rose from the chair behind a large black desk as they entered the office. In his sixties, with gray-brown hair and posture so straight, TJ would have pegged Bacon as a former military officer even if TJ hadn't used West Investigations resources to look into the backgrounds of Bacon and Forrick.

Bacon had been a decorated retired Army General who'd left the military for an undoubtedly lucrative position in the private sector with TalCon. He'd been with TalCon for the last twenty years, working his way up to the position of CEO. His second-in-command, Arnold Forrick, had a similar military background with several awards and commendations to his name as well.

"Miss Douglas. It's a pleasure to see you again." Bacon stretched a hand across his desk, which Alexis shook. Bacon turned to TJ. "And you must be Thaddeus Roman."

TJ shook Bacon's hand.

"Thank you for seeing us on such short notice, Mr. Bacon."

Bacon waved at the chairs in front of his desk. TJ and Alexis sat.

"As I said when we met some weeks ago, anything you need, we at TalCon are here for you, Alexis. I hope I can call you Alexis?"

"Yes, please do."

"What can we do for you today, Miss Douglas?" Arnold Forrick had stood stoically beside his boss's desk while they'd engaged in opening chitchat with a scowl that looked to have been etched onto his face.

Bacon's eyebrows arrowed down in a frown. "Please forgive Arnold's abruptness."

Alexis gave a weak smile. "Nothing to forgive. I'm sure you are both very busy, and we'll try not to take up too much of your time."

"So what can we do for you?" Bacon said, reclaiming his seat behind his desk.

"I've hired Mr. Roman to help me look into Mark's death. He's a private investigator," Alexis said.

Since neither had asked what he was doing there with Alexis, TJ had already surmised that they'd checked him out, and the lack of surprise from either man when Alexis pegged him as a private investigator convinced him he was right.

Now, though, Bacon did look surprised. "I'd been told that Mark took his own life."

Alexis gritted her teeth. "I don't believe that. It's a conclusion based largely on the premise that my brother stole from this company, which I know he wouldn't do."

"I don't know who you've been speaking to," Forrick started angrily, "but the details of the projects this company is involved in are confidential. If you share any proprietary information, TalCon will take any and all legal steps to—"

"Mr. Forrick," TJ interrupted, more than a bit irked himself. "Why don't you hear Alexis out before you start threatening legal action?"

Forrick began to speak again, but Bacon raised his hand, stopping him. "Arnold, let Miss Douglas speak, please."

Alexis glared at Forrick. "Mark was not a thief. Mark

was a soldier, as were you, Mr. Bacon. You know how much the Army values honor, integrity and truth. Those values meant something to Mark in, and out of, the military."

"I knew Mark," Bacon said. "I would have never believed he was capable of any of this. I don't know what you have been able to turn up or what the police have shared with you, and I'm not at liberty to share information myself, but I will say the evidence is pretty damning."

"TalCon has been cooperating with law enforcement and will continue to do so," Forrick interjected. "If you know anything about what your brother may have done with the missing program or who he might have sold it to, I strongly suggest you share that information with the authorities."

"I assure you I have been questioned by the police," Alexis growled. "Thoroughly. Mark never told me about the missing program because it was confidential and he didn't take it."

TJ scooted forward in his chair. "You can't tell us about the program that went missing, but can you tell us more about why you are so sure Mark is the one who took it?"

"As I said, we can't reveal—"

Bacon held up his hand a second time. Forrick fell silent, but his scowl deepened.

"TalCon was alerted that there had been an unauthorized download of the program. The warning was supposed to alert in real time, but it was delayed several days because of a system failure. Arnold is right that I can't get into the exact nature of the breach, but we took the report seriously and immediately opened an audit."

"And the audit implicated Mark," TJ said.

Bacon gave a slight nod. "Unfortunately, our security

cameras were down for maintenance on the night in question. But we employ some of the most advanced computer security available here at TalCon. Mark's computer, ID, and randomly generated fob code were used to access the system and download the program."

"Fob code?" Alexis prodded.

Bacon reached for a small gray square about the size of an eraser and held it out for her to see. "A key fob, or fob as we affectionately call it around here. It generates an eight-digit code that, along with an employee's ID, must be entered into the computer in order to gain access to our system. The code changes every three minutes and is unique to every employee."

TJ's heart sank. Bacon was right. The evidence against Mark did appear to be damning, but that wouldn't stop him from turning over every rock looking for an answer that didn't involve Mark being a thief. He didn't have to ask to know Alexis felt the same way.

"Can you give us some general information about your company? What kind of contracting do you do for the military, that sort of thing?"

"We can't—" Forrick started.

"You're a prominent weapons development company and a large government contractor," Alexis said. "We're not asking for any information we couldn't find on our own, but getting it from you now would be a help."

Forrick looked at Bacon, who stayed silent for a long moment before nodding. He launched into a mostly useless recitation of the company's history.

"When did you realize that the software was missing from your inventory?" TJ finally interrupted.

Bacon's expression tightened. "We were alerted by an internal source."

"An internal source? What does that mean?" Alexis pressed.

"I'm afraid we aren't at liberty to share that information," Forrick said. "And I'm afraid Mr. Bacon has to leave now for his next meeting."

Bacon stood, underscoring Forrick's point. Meeting over.

It appeared they'd struck a chord, one TJ intended to keep stroking until he got a sound he liked. Who brought the theft to the company's attention?

TJ and Alexis stood and turned for the door.

"Oh," Alexis said, turning back to Bacon and Forrick. "I'd hoped to speak with Mark's assistant, Lenora Kenda. She had such kind words to say about Mark on the condolence card she sent. I haven't had a chance to thank her."

The tightening in Bacon's jaw was so slight TJ could almost convince himself it hadn't happened. Almost.

"I'm sorry, but Ms. Kenda is out of the office. She decided to take a few weeks off. She and Mark were close coworkers. His death hit her hard."

Bacon's assistant was waiting for TJ and Alexis outside of the office. She stayed at their side until the elevator doors closed.

He and Alexis walked back to the rental car in silence, but once they were safely inside the car and headed back for the gate, Alexis spoke.

"That was a waste of time."

TJ shot a glance across the car. "You think?"

"You don't?" she shot back at him.

TJ chuckled. "Well, I learned that Bacon is hiding something. And that Forrick is his attack dog, so whatever it is Bacon is hiding, Forrick likely has a hand in it."

"You learned all of that from the little bit those two said up there?"

"It wasn't what they said, it was more what they didn't say and how they didn't say it."

Alexis's brow rose. "Okay. I'm going to have to trust your expertise on that."

"More importantly, they gave us a lead to follow." He navigated the car off of TalCon's campus and turned onto the road leading to the highway.

Alexis's eyes widened in surprise. "They did?"

"Lenora Kenda."

Alexis's expression took on a shade of skepticism. "Lenora? I only met her at Mark's memorial, but he talked about her a little over the years. It seemed like Mark trusted her."

It wouldn't be the first time Mark had trusted the wrong woman, but he kept that thought to himself. "I'm not saying she had anything to do with the theft or what happened to Mark. But I do find it curious that she's suddenly decided to take an extended vacation."

The skepticism remained on Alexis's face. "It could be just what Bacon said. She's just taking some time to process everything."

"It could be," TJ said, keeping his focus on the road ahead of him. "But I'd like to hear that from Ms. Kenda."

Chapter Seven

For now, Lenora Kenda would have to wait. Their second appointment of the day was with the attorney Mark had hired after being suspended from TalCon. TJ was hoping the lawyer could fill in some of the blanks Bacon and Forrick couldn't or wouldn't.

TJ allowed the voice on the GPS to direct him through the Alexandria streets. The lawyer's office was in the Old Town Alexandria area, and TJ could immediately see why it was called that. He drove down narrow, cobblestone-lined streets and passed quaint houses that had easily reached the century milestone and were still standing. Alexis sat in the passenger seat—her thoughts, though silent, filling the space in the car. Her frustration was palpable, but this was what investigations were like. Slow and steady, asking questions until someone gave you the answers you were looking for. Not nearly as sexy as they made it out to be in the movies.

TJ pulled the rental car to a stop in front of a two-story red brick house on a quiet, tree-lined street not far from King Street, Alexandria's main thoroughfare. A green sign with gold lettering stood in the front yard announcing, Law Office of Sanjay Atwal. Several of the other houses on the block had similar signs on the front lawns. Alexis had made an appointment for them. According to Alexis, who had spoken with him when she'd come to town to make Mark's final arrangement and several other times on the telephone thereafter, he appeared to be competent and to have had Mark's best interests at heart. She'd said that he'd seemed devastated when they'd spoken initially, which TJ hoped meant he'd be more helpful than Bacon and Forrick.

The receptionist greeted them, offering coffee, which he and Alexis declined, before leaving them to wait in what would have been a living room. Fifteen minutes later, the receptionist returned and led them into the back of the house, knocking briefly on a set of closed French doors, the glass shielded by closed blinds, before pushing the door open and showing them into Atwal's office.

"Alexis. It's so good to see you again." The man behind the desk stood, smiling, and took Alexis's hand in his, holding it longer than necessary. Atwal's gaze held a look that was unmistakable. The lawyer hoped to provide more than just legal services to Alexis. The realization sent an unexpected surge of jealousy through TJ.

Never gonna happen, buddy. The words surged through TJ's mind before he could remind himself that he had no claim over Alexis or who she chose to spend her time with. Still, until they got to the bottom of Mark's death and identified whoever had broken into Alexis's home, she was under his protection. And that meant no lecherous lawyers on his watch.

"Sanjay, thank you for seeing us on such short notice. This is TJ Roman. He and Mark were friends, and he's helping me sort out the events around my brother's death."

Atwal extended his hand toward TJ with a lot less enthusiasm than he'd had in greeting Alexis. "Mr. Roman.

Nice to meet you." Atwal looked him over slowly. When Atwal's gaze returned to TJ's face, he could immediately tell that the lawyer had sized him up as a potential rival for Alexis's affections.

Good.

No, not good. Not good at all, he admonished himself.

He and Alexis took seats in front of Atwal's desk. TJ studied the attorney while the receptionist made a second offer of coffee. He appeared to be in his mid-to late-thirties, dark brown hair just starting to show a bit of gray and light brown eyes that kept straying to Alexis's face. Mark had trusted the man enough to hire him, so despite the lawyer's obvious interest in Alexis, TJ tried to keep an open mind.

"So, Alexis, what can I do for you?" Atwal said once the receptionist closed the door, leaving the three of them in the room alone.

"I have some questions about Mark's…situation before his death. I'm hoping you can help me."

"I'll certainly do what I can."

"I don't think Mark stole anything and I don't think he killed himself," Alexis said.

Atwal sighed. "I had a feeling you were going to say something along those lines. I'd hoped you'd be able to let this go and move on with your life."

"I can't just let it go. I know Mark would never steal from anyone. And the idea that he'd take his own life? No. I know my brother. He wouldn't do what he's been accused of, and I can't let the world think that he did."

"Mark was never charged with a crime. His record was technically clean when he died."

"Technically, maybe, but we both know that TalCon, the police, and several others think he stole some sort of program from the company. And I can't even get anyone to tell me what kind of program went missing."

Atwal sighed again. "I can tell you that the program Mark is accused of having stolen is not just any computer program. It's more like a weapon."

A buzzing began in TJ's ears. "A cyber weapon."

Atwal nodded.

TJ was shocked but not surprised. TalCon held a number of known contracts with the US military, and who knew how many unknown contracts they had. Conventional forms of warfare were giving way to more technologically advanced weapons every day. And not just when it came to guns and rockets. The military recruited men and women who understood computers, programming, coding and all that computer jazz faster than the universities could graduate them.

"What kind of cyber weapon?" Alexis asked.

Atwal shook his head. "I don't know all the details. Some of it, I suspect, is highly confidential, possibly even classified. Mark was rather circumspect despite the pressure the company and the authorities were putting on him. TalCon had dubbed the program Nimbus. Technically, NimbusScriptPro. It's some sort of computer program that the company had hoped to sell to the military when it was operational."

"So the program wasn't actually being developed under a military contract," TJ said.

"No, which was good news for Mark," Atwal answered.

Alexis glanced between them with a confused expression on her face. "Why was that good news for Mark?"

Atwal folded his hands on top of his desk. "Because then the program would have technically been property of the US government and the consequences for Mark would have been far more serious than what he was looking at."

Alexis frowned. "I'd say the consequences were extremely serious as my brother is dead."

Atwal's expression softened. "I'm sorry if I sound callous. It wasn't my intent. Of course, the consequences of the accusations were very serious. I just meant that the matter was being treated as stolen private property rather than stolen government property. While TalCon is anxious to get the program back, they are also mindful of the damage to their reputation and stock price that couldn't be sustained if it becomes widely known that they've lost a significant piece of technology. It could have major effects on their current and future government contracts."

"So TalCon would like to get its property back and to keep this whole episode as quiet as possible?" That fit with the brush-off he and Alexis had received from Bacon and Forrick. With Mark dead, he was the perfect scapegoat if they could just find the stolen program.

"That's about the size of it," Atwal confirmed. "I planned to do my best to defend Mark if it came to that, but I have to tell you there was significant evidence that didn't weigh in his favor."

"We already know about Mark's ID card and fob being used to download the program, but those could have been stolen from him, right?" Alexis asked, sounding hopeful.

Atwal shook his head. "Mark didn't think so." He gave Alexis a sad look. "He was adamant his ID and fob were never out of his possession. But there's more." Atwal flipped open the manila file folder on his desk. "TalCon was tipped off to the fact that the program had been stolen when someone in the company's cybersecurity unit discovered a posting for it on a black market website for these kinds of things."

"An online weapons auction?" TJ said.

"Weapons, drugs, pretty much anything illegal." Atwal's face twisted in disgust, and TJ didn't have to imagine what other things were being sold online.

"I'm sorry. I think you two have gotten ahead of me," Alexis said. "What auction?"

"He's referring to the dark web," TJ explained. "It's like an alternative internet where criminals of all stripes buy and sell contraband and other illegal items, often using cryptocurrency."

Alexis nodded, seemingly having caught up. "And the program that TalCon thinks Mark stole is on this website? Why can't their cyber computer people just track the posting back to whoever put it up there? Then they'd know that Mark isn't the person who stole the program."

"I wish it were that simple." Atwal shook his head again. "The dark web is anonymous. That's why it works so well for moving illegal stuff. TalCon has enlisted the best of the best to try to track the posting, but so far they haven't had any luck in determining who posted it or even where it was posted from."

TalCon may have enlisted the best of the best, but TJ was pretty sure he knew someone better. Tansy Carlson, West Investigations' computer whisperer, had done things with a computer no one had ever dreamed possible. If the person who'd offered that program up for auction could be traced, she'd find them.

TJ made a mental note to ask Shawn for Tansy's help and returned his focus to the conversation at hand.

"What made TalCon focus on Mark?" TJ asked, redirecting the conversation back to what the lawyer did know rather than what he didn't. Even though Atwal had said he couldn't tell them much, it appeared he knew quite a bit about the case, and TJ wanted to keep him sharing information.

"The computer logs from Mark's work laptop. They show someone made an unauthorized download of the complete program from Mark's computer a week before the posting went up on the dark web. That was the only download of the program since Mark completed the most recent upgrades, and it wasn't authorized."

"Forrick and Bacon mentioned that they were alerted to the download by an internal source," TJ said. "You have any idea who or what that source was?"

The attorney shrugged. "I don't, and I don't expect TalCon or the cops will divulge that information without a court order, and we don't have grounds to get one."

"So an anonymous source. That's not hard evidence," Alexis scoffed.

How difficult would it be for someone at TalCon to have accessed the program using Mark's credentials, or how hard would it be to cover up an unauthorized download? TJ suspected those questions were beyond the scope of the attorney's knowledge, but West Investigations had resources the attorney didn't. He'd put the problem to Tansy as soon as he could. Hopefully, she'd make more headway than TalCon's techs had.

Atwal closed the file. "It was enough for TalCon to put Mark on leave. And for the police to question him and get search warrants for his home and personal devices."

"And did they find anything?" Alexis spat.

"No. No, they didn't," Atwal conceded.

TJ got the sense that they'd gotten just about all they could from the lawyer. "Mr. Atwal, I was hoping you could give us the names of a few people we could talk to who might have more insight into this situation. You must have spoken to someone in the course of your investigation."

Atwal frowned. "As I said, Mark hadn't been charged with a crime yet, so I hadn't really started my investigation. I'd really only spoken to him about the case. But Mark did mention his personal assistant as someone I'd want to speak to if the matter moved forward." Atwal opened the file again and flipped through several pages inside. "Ah, yes, Lenora Kenda."

It seemed that Ms. Kenda's name was on the tip of everyone's tongue. "One more question and we'll get out of your hair. Do you happen to have a copy of Mark's autopsy report?"

Alexis shifted uneasily in the chair beside him.

He knew that aspects of this investigation might be difficult for her to hear and deal with, but reviewing Mark's autopsy report was crucial to determining whether or not the medical examiner made the correct call in categorizing Mark's death as a suicide.

Atwal seemed surprised. "Why…no. As far as I know, there wasn't a reason to do so."

Alexis slid forward in her chair and pinned Atwal with a look. "I think there is a reason. Can you get the report?"

"I… Well, I guess so. As Mark's next of kin, you're entitled to it, and I do know the medical examiner. Professionally." Atwal added quickly. "In my capacity as a criminal defense lawyer, I've had to speak with her on several occasions."

"Do you think you could convince her to make a little time to speak with us?" TJ pressed.

Atwal frowned. "I don't know."

"Please, Sanjay." Alexis reached across the desk and grabbed the lawyer's hand. "I couldn't tell you how grateful I'd be. I have to be sure about what happened to Mark."

Atwal's chest puffed out, and he gave Alexis's hand a squeeze. "She's always very busy."

"We'll only take up a few minutes of her time," Alexis pressed.

Atwal sighed. "I'll see what I can do."

Chapter Eight

Alexis was cautiously optimistic as TJ put the car in gear and pulled away from the curb. They'd gotten more information from Sanjay than they had from TalCon, and he was going to try to help them get even more. It was a start.

"It's after one," TJ said, breaking her from her thoughts. "How about we stop for lunch?"

The mention of lunch sent a pang through her stomach, reminding her that she hadn't eaten since before boarding the early morning flight to Virginia. "Sounds good." She took her cell phone from her purse and pulled up nearby restaurants. "There's an Indian restaurant with good reviews not too far from here."

"I do love biryani."

Using the directions on her phone, Alexis directed TJ to the restaurant.

Soft rock played from the overhead speakers and the smell of curry, saffron, and chicken swirled inside the space when they walked in. The lunch crowd, if there had been one, appeared to have already cleared out, and the hostess seated them quickly. A waitress in the standard uniform of black pants and a white shirt slid a plate of naan onto the table and took their drink orders. She returned a minute later with their drinks, having given them just enough time to scan the well-apportioned menu and decide on their meals, biryani for TJ and korma for Alexis.

For several minutes after the waitress left to put in their orders, they sat without speaking. They seemed to have entered into some sort of silent agreement not to talk about Mark or the investigation into his death and the theft, which suited Alexis just fine at the moment.

Alexis reached for a piece of naan and studied TJ.

"What happened between you and Mark?"

TJ coughed, choking a little on the sip of Diet Coke he'd taken just before she'd asked the question.

She supposed it was a little out of left field, but she'd always wondered. She'd asked Mark once, and he'd brushed her off, saying that they'd just grown apart, but she'd never bought that excuse. TJ and Mark were as close as brothers, growing up certainly closer than she and Mark had been, a fact that had led to more than a little jealousy on her part when she was younger. They'd even gone into the military together and, although Mark hadn't re-enlisted like TJ, she knew they'd kept in touch after Mark moved on, so it wasn't the Army that had driven them apart.

TJ had regained his composure, but he still hadn't answered her question.

"Why weren't you two as close as you used to be when we were growing up?" Alexis pressed. "And don't tell me you just grew apart."

"You're awfully bossy." TJ frowned.

She shrugged and waited.

"What did Mark tell you about it?" TJ responded finally.

"Not much. He always avoided answering whenever I asked about you."

He leaned back in his chair and gave a small smile. "I guess we still had some things in common then."

"I'm not going to let you joke your way out of answering the question," she responded pointedly. "Come on. You were like brothers. Brothers don't just stop speaking to each other."

The door to the kitchen opened and their waitress pushed through with a tray full of plates. TJ wore a hopeful expression, probably as much due to the ability to get out of the current conversation as to hunger. But his expression fell away when the waitress headed for a table on the other side of the dining room.

Alexis reached across the table and covered his hand. "Please. I feel like there's so much Mark kept from me. I know he was trying to protect me, but now that he's gone, it feels like I didn't really know him."

TJ's features tightened and the muscle in his jaw worked as he thought. Finally, he let out a haggard sigh. "I don't know if you ever met Mark's girlfriend, Jessica Castaldo."

Alexis's stomach tightened, and not due to hunger. She'd met Jessica. Mark had brought her along on one of his rare trips to New Jersey to visit her. Alexis had found Jessica to be spoiled and entitled. From what she saw during that short weekend, Jessica seemed more interested in the things that Mark was willing to buy for her than she was in Mark.

Alexis had forced herself to keep quiet, though. Her brother was a habitual monogamist. He only dated one woman at a time, but the relationships didn't seem to have much staying power. Most rarely lasted a full year. She'd prayed Jessica wouldn't be any different and had put on a happy face while they'd been in town.

"We met. I can't tell you how happy I was when Mark broke things off with her."

"I had a job that took me to DC two years ago and on my way back to New York, I stopped in Virginia to have a drink and catch up with Mark. He brought Jessica along. We all had a few drinks and...you know Mark."

She did. "He didn't handle his liquor well." It was the one thing she and her brother were in constant conflict about.

"No, he didn't, and Jessica, well, she was coming on pretty strong that night. I didn't encourage it, but I could tell Mark was getting angry." TJ looked away. "I should have ended the night early, walked away and gone back to my hotel, but I was concerned about leaving the two of them given how much they'd drank. Anyway, one thing led to another and Mark and I exchanged words. Honestly, I think Jessica enjoyed it. I suspect she instigated it a bit. Two men fighting over her, at least that's how I'm sure she saw it. I was just trying to get Mark to calm down and see reason."

"But he wouldn't." It wasn't the first time Mark had gotten himself into trouble with his drinking. She'd had to lend him money several years ago to bail himself out of jail after he was arrested on a DUI charge. She'd been livid. He could have killed himself or someone else. Mark swore it would never happen again and, as far as she knew, it never had. Her brother was such a kind, loving, thoughtful person when he was sober, but when he drank, it was like he was a totally different person.

Alexis had tried to talk to him on more than one occasion about his drinking and the possibility of getting some help, but Mark didn't believe he needed help. Instead of risking pushing him further away, she'd dropped the issue each time.

"We got kicked out of the bar, but I was able to get Mark and Jessica into a cab. Mark called me a couple of days later after I was back in New York to apologize. By then I was pretty angry myself. I called him out for thinking I'd ever disrespect him by going after his girl, and I told him his drinking was out of control."

"Let me guess, that didn't go over well."

TJ's brows went up. "You tried to talk to him about it, too?"

"Several times, but what is it they say? You can lead a horse to water…" she said sadly. She let the rest of the sentiment hang in the air.

TJ exhaled heavily. "That was the last time we spoke. I can't tell you how many times I've thought about picking up the phone, but honestly, I was more hurt than angry at Mark for even suggesting I'd hit on his girlfriend."

Alexis reached across the table again, this time squeezing TJ's hand, hoping it provided some comfort. "Hey, when he was drinking, Mark wasn't himself, but he knew you would never do anything to hurt him."

The expression on TJ's face said he wasn't so sure.

She gave his hand another squeeze. "I know you would never do anything to hurt Mark. You loved him as much as I did, which is why I knew I could come to you for help clearing his name and finding out what really happened to him."

"You can come to me no matter what. I hope you know that."

A spark of electricity shot between them. TJ turned her hand over, tracing a line from her ring finger to her wrist. His face had softened and Alexis wondered what his finger would feel like pressed against the pulse thundering under her skin.

"Excuse me."

They pulled apart at the sound of the waitress's voice. She slid their food onto the table and hurried away.

Alexis watched TJ's face morph into a mask of neutrality. She mentally cursed the waitress. Whatever moment she and TJ were having before the woman's appearance was clearly over, and Alexis couldn't help feeling disappointed.

Her phone chimed in her purse.

She fished it out and read the message on the screen.

"Sanjay says the medical examiner can see us at 2:30 today."

TJ glanced at his watch.

"Great. Maybe she'll have more of the answers we need."

Chapter Nine

TJ drove to the modern glass and concrete building that housed the northern district headquarters of the Virginia medical examiner's office. He parked in the parking lot shared with the forensics lab next door and walked with Alexis into the lobby. After giving their names to the security guard at the front desk, they signed in, passed through the metal detectors, and followed the guard's directions to the third floor.

When they stepped off the elevator, they were greeted by a second reception area manned by a male employee with a shiny silver name tag on his shirt announcing his name was Robert.

"Oh, yes, Dr. Bullock said you'd be coming in this afternoon," Robert said when he and Alexis gave their names a second time. "I'll let the doctor know you're here."

Robert rose and headed down a short hallway. After a moment, he reappeared. "Follow me, please."

They followed him into an office cramped with bookshelves and file cabinets, but that boasted two large windows overlooking the front of the building. A wide desk sat in front of the window and a woman with her long dark hair in a braid that hung over her shoulder sat behind it.

"Dr. Bullock, your guests." Robert waved a hand in the general direction of TJ and Alexis as if he was revealing a prize on a game show.

The medical examiner stood. Dr. Jane Bullock was in her late forties or early fifties, petite and fine boned, with pale blue eyes that shone with intelligence.

He and Alexis introduced themselves and shook hands with the medical examiner before settling into the visitor's chairs in front of her desk.

Dr. Bullock let them get settled before speaking. "Miss Douglas, let me start by saying how sorry I am for your loss."

"Thank you," Alexis said quietly.

"I understand from your attorney, Mr. Atwal, that you'd like to see the preliminary autopsy report on your brother. It includes the standard blood tests we run in-house, but in this case Detective Chellel has ordered a more extensive toxicology report from our forensics lab." The doctor shuffled through a stack of files on her desk before pulling one free. "Here it is. I had my assistant make a copy for you to take with you if you'd like. I caution, though, that I am still waiting on the full toxicology results to come in. We're still pretty backed up from Covid, and suspected suicides don't get priority." The doctor passed the entire folder across the desk to Alexis.

TJ leaned over so he could scan the pages along with Alexis. The kind of investigations he typically took on didn't require reading autopsy reports. He had no idea what he was looking at. From her expression, neither did Alexis.

"I'm sorry, Dr. Bullock, would you mind summarizing the report for us?"

"Of course."

TJ handed the report back to the doctor. She ran

through Mark's height and weight, deeming them normal before running through her assessment of his vital organs.

TJ glanced at Alexis. Her face had taken on a gray, almost deathlike pallor. The medical examiner didn't seem to notice.

"Doctor," TJ interrupted. "We just need to know if you found anything unusual in the autopsy."

Dr. Bullock frowned. "Mr. Douglas's liver was beginning to show signs of liver disease. And of course, I found several undigested Valium pills in his stomach. That was consistent with the empty prescription bottle the police found in Mr. Douglas's apartment."

"But there were no signs of chronic drug use, right?" TJ pressed.

The doctor sighed. "I know where you're going with this line of questioning, and I won't have a definitive answer for you until the toxicology results are back. But I will say everything I've seen so far points to a diazepam overdose. I will be able to make a more definitive determination about cause and manner of death once I have all the test results back."

Not many people knew the distinction between the cause of death and the manner of death, but it was important. The medical examiner could rely on her examination of the body and the battery of tests that were standard in an autopsy to tell her what the cause of death was, such as a heart attack, gunshot, or as the cops suspected in Mark's case, an overdose.

The manner of death, though, required her to examine the totality of the circumstances to make a determination. A gunshot wound, for instance, could be self-inflicted or inflicted by a third party. The former would lead to the manner of death being listed as a suicide, while the latter would be a homicide. The same held for an overdose.

While it was the cops' job to track down the source of pills that had been the cause of Mark's death, the medical examiner was likely to be more forthcoming with information than the cops, which was why he wasn't upset that he and Alexis were able to speak to Dr. Bullock before seeing Detective Chellel.

"That I can't tell you. I do know that the only fingerprints that were found on the bottle of pills were those of Mark Douglas," she said pointedly.

Alexis frowned. "If someone had the wherewithal to try to make it look like Mark killed himself, I'm sure they'd have the foresight to wear gloves or wipe their fingerprints from the murder weapon."

Dr. Bullock looked as if she was ready to argue the premise. They needed the doctor on their side and willing to continue to answer their questions, so challenging her findings directly wasn't the best idea.

"Dr. Bullock," TJ interrupted whatever the doctor might have been prepared to respond to Alexis. "Did the toxicity screen turn up any other unusual substances in Mark's system?"

Mark's wasn't the first autopsy he'd read, but he was no expert. There were people he could tap at West Investigations to help him make sense of all the technical mumbo jumbo in the report and he would, but Dr. Bullock was here now.

"I ran the usual blood screening test and, except for the Valium, nothing unusual turned up."

"But the standard blood screening is limited, right?" TJ pressed gently. "It doesn't look for the more exotic potential substances that could debilitate a person."

Irritation flashed across Dr. Bullock's face. "Of

course, blood screening is much more limited than the full toxicology, and we can't test for every possible substance anyway. If there was any hint that something like that had been administered to Mr. Douglas prior to his death, the protocol is for the police to notify me and I can order the requisite tests to confirm the existence of such a substance or rule its use out. The police, in this instance, made no such notification."

"Of course," TJ said, backing off. "We're not suggesting that anything is amiss."

A soft snort slipped from Alexis, but the medical examiner either didn't hear it or chose to ignore it.

TJ couldn't help but wonder what Sanjay Atwal had told the doctor about his and Alexis's interest in Mark's death. "We just want to make sure we understand the scope of your report."

Dr. Bullock's steely expression softened marginally. "That is prudent of you. But I assure you that everything was done according to policy." The doctor turned her gaze on Alexis. "I am very sorry for your loss. My findings are supported by the evidence. Your brother took his own life."

Chapter Ten

It was after three, which meant they were able to check into the hotel TJ had booked for them. Alexis considered Dr. Bullock's findings as TJ drove, her mood dark. She'd pulled up the medical examiner's bio on the state website, so she knew the doctor was experienced and well trained. Still, she must have missed something because, deep in her heart, Alexis knew her brother. No matter what, he wouldn't have given up on life or on her. There had to be an explanation that fit with the medical examiner's findings and also proved that Mark hadn't killed himself. The question was, how did she find it?

She glanced over at TJ. He hadn't said much since they'd left Dr. Bullock's office, and Alexis was beginning to wonder if he regretted agreeing to help her. So far, they'd run into nothing but flashing signs declaring Mark's guilt.

TJ had made a reservation at a boutique hotel on the outskirts of Alexandria. It was a two-story structure, on the older side, but recently renovated. The rooms each had a window next to the door that looked out onto a shared courtyard and an outdoor pool. TJ had reserved a corner room on the second floor, a roomy one-bedroom, one-bath suite.

"This is a sofa bed," TJ said, tossing his duffel bag

onto the wide sofa in the living area of the suite. "I'll sleep here and you can take the bedroom."

That didn't seem fair at all. She wasn't a delicate flower who couldn't handle a night on a sofa bed. "That doesn't sound comfortable. I'm happy to alternate. One night on the sofa, the next in the bed for each of us, for as long as we're in town."

TJ shook his head. "The last thing I want is to get too comfortable. That's how mistakes are made. Plus, I'd rather be out here where I can keep an eye on things."

She shuddered as the memory from the night of the break-in rolled through her mind. She'd pushed the terror from that night into the recesses of her mind, trying to focus on clearing Mark's name, but it came thundering back at the worst times, reminding her that this wasn't just about Mark. She was in danger as well.

She and TJ settled into the suite and spent the rest of the afternoon working on the case. TJ called into West headquarters and, together with Tansy Carlson, West Investigations' computer whiz, was able to find a phone number and address for Lenora Kenda, along with a bunch of background information on the woman. Lenora didn't answer the phone when they called, so they had to leave a message. Alexis reached out to Detective Chellel with no success. She was sure the detective was avoiding her calls on purpose. The detective had made no secret of the fact that she believed Alexis was a grieving sister unwilling to accept that her brother had committed a crime and taken his own life to avoid the consequences of that act as the law closed in.

TJ sent the copy of Mark's autopsy report that Dr. Bullock gave them to Shawn West, who had more experience with such reports, hoping he'd see something the doctor missed. She and TJ sat on the pullout sofa on a video call going over the autopsy report with Shawn. Unfortunately, he only confirmed what Dr. Bullock had told them. They'd have to wait for the toxicology report to come in before any definitive conclusions could be made.

"We've left a message for the detective in charge of the case asking to meet with her but haven't heard back yet." TJ said. "I know Mark was a heavy drinker, but his using Valium was new information to me and Alexis."

"With everything he had going on in his life, it's not too surprising," Shawn responded. "Valium is an anti-anxiety and stress medication."

"Are you saying you think the police and the medical examiner could be right? That Mark could have taken his own life?" Alexis said, anger vibrating in her tone.

Shawn frowned. "I'm just thinking through the information you've gotten so far. It's too soon to draw any conclusions."

There was that line again. It was too soon to draw conclusions. But Mark was dead, so it seemed to her like they were far, far too late.

She rose and walked to the window. She knew she didn't have a right to be angry at Shawn West. He was only restating the facts. But her attempt to prove Mark's innocence seemed to be doing just the opposite.

Frown lines appeared above Shawn's brow. "I can't say what the cops will find suspicious, but it's definitely a question worth asking when you do get a hold of the detective in charge of the case."

"Thanks, Shawn. I appreciate your help with this," TJ said, signaling an end to their conversation.

"Why don't you go take a nap?" TJ inclined his head toward the suite's bedroom door. "It's already been a long day."

She glanced at her watch. It was just after four, but to

her body, it felt like it could have easily been well after midnight. "If I sleep now, I won't be able to sleep later tonight."

"And if you run yourself ragged, you won't be any help to me, Mark, or yourself. Take a quick nap. I'll wake you in an hour."

A second uncontrollable yawn wiped away all of her remaining hesitation. "Okay. Wake me up in one hour."

TJ held up three fingers. "Scout's honor."

She fell asleep quickly, but her rest was fitful. She awoke ten minutes before the hour was up. The suite's bathroom was a Jack-and-Jill style that had a door opening into the bedroom and a second entrance from the living area.

She could hear TJ moving behind the closed bathroom door.

Her stomach grumbled, and she padded barefoot from the bedroom to the small kitchenette area that housed a coffee maker and, she hoped, something she could snack on while she waited for TJ to emerge from the bathroom so they could discuss dinner plans. She grabbed the bag of peanuts, cringing at the $4.50 price tag before ripping the bag open. She made her way to the sofa, popped a handful of peanuts in her mouth, and froze.

TJ had left the door cracked slightly open. His back was to her and from where she stood, she knew he couldn't see her. But she could see him. Nearly all of him. He was shaving, wearing nothing but a white bath towel around his waist. The dark brown skin of his back was corded in muscles that flexed as he drew his razor along his jaw.

She tried to make herself walk away, head back into the bedroom before he found her staring at him like a museum exhibit, but she couldn't make her feet move.

TJ turned on the faucet and bent forward, washing the remaining shaving cream from his face, and her mouth went dry while her pulse raced.

Whatever thought of moving along she'd had fled, and she stared openly now.

TJ reached for the hand towel on the counter, his eyes catching hers in the mirror, finally breaking her out of the lust-filled stupor she seemed to have fallen into.

Heat flushed her face, while embarrassment at being caught ogling him climbed in her chest.

"Sorry, I woke up. Hungry. Peanuts." She held the bag up as embarrassment continued to heat her cheeks.

The corners of TJ's mouth turned up, only heightening her embarrassment.

"I'm just going to…" She turned and rushed to the bedroom, shutting the door, then leaning against it.

It had been a long time since she'd felt such a strong burst of desire for a man. Well, technically she couldn't recall ever having felt that strong a desire, not even when she'd been in the two relationships she would have defined as serious over the years. But TJ Roman was not a man she should be desiring. He wasn't a man who stuck, even with a faulty relationship meter. She knew that.

"Pull yourself together," she whispered to herself. She couldn't stay in the bedroom all night. Her stomach was already grumbling that the peanuts weren't nearly enough.

"He's just a man." An incredibly handsome, smart, sexy man.

She took a deep breath and let it out slowly before opening the door again.

TJ was fully dressed now and sitting at the small table adjacent to the kitchenette. The small smile was still on his lips, and the glint in his eyes sent another wave of heat to her cheeks.

"Sorry about that." She walked toward the sofa in the living room.

"No problem. I didn't realize the door had opened. The lock appears to be a little hinky, so watch out for that."

"Yeah, I will. I'm starving. Do you have something in mind for dinner?"

TJ cocked his head to one side. "I saw a Mexican place on the drive here. It's only a couple of blocks away. We can walk."

It was a short walk, but she was nearly ravenous by the time they got to the restaurant. Mexican music played softly while they waited for the hostess to ready their table. Alexis noted that the interior design of the space was somewhat more romantic than the outside would lead patrons to believe. Short candles and a single red rose formed centerpieces on each of the tables, and most were set for two.

The hostess sat them at a table in the center of the restaurant and the waitress wasted no time coming to take their orders.

Alexis munched on the tortilla chips the waitress left while she and TJ waited for their food to be brought out. "Mexican is my favorite."

"I remember," TJ said.

Mark and TJ had done everything they could to discourage her from tagging along with them when they were younger, so she was surprised that TJ would remember something as mundane as her favorite type of food.

"I remember that Christmas that Mark saved up and bought you that churro maker and your mother was afraid you'd burn down the apartment building."

Alexis laughed. "I'd forgotten about that."

"Mark started saving in June to have enough money to get you something you'd love for Christmas."

Her heart clenched, grief mingling with the memory of the happiness she'd felt when she'd opened that long-ago gift. She'd never share another Christmas with her brother.

"Hey." TJ reached across the table and took her hand in his. "I'm sorry. I didn't mean to make you sad. I shouldn't have brought it up."

"It's not your fault. Sometimes it hits me out of nowhere that I'm all alone now. I have no one."

He squeezed her hand. "You have me. You can always count on me for anything."

The spark of desire she'd felt earlier as she'd watched him shave returned, even stronger than it had been. She had the urge to lean forward and press her lips against his mouth, to see what he tasted like.

Before she could do anything foolish that she'd certainly regret, the waitress returned with their meals.

They settled in to eat, making small talk and catching up on what had happened in their lives since they'd last seen each other. By the time the waitress cleared their plates, Alexis found that she'd relaxed completely and was enjoying TJ's company.

"You up for sharing a couple of churros? I still have a weakness for them." Alexis reached for the dessert menu the waitress had left at the corner of their table.

"No, I think we should head back to the hotel. Now," TJ answered, his expression serious. His attention trained over her shoulder.

Alexis turned and followed the line of TJ's gaze.

Two men sat at a table on the opposite side of the restaurant. One was slender and balding, the other huskier with a dark mustache. Nothing in particular stood out about them to Alexis, but it was clear that something had for TJ.

The husky man glanced at their table, looking away quickly when his eyes met Alexis's.

"Let's go," TJ said, dropping enough money on the table to more than cover the check.

Alexis stood, letting TJ grasp her elbow gently and lead her to the restaurant doors.

As they hurried along the sidewalk back to the hotel, TJ looking over his shoulder every few steps, apprehension grew in Alexis's gut.

"Do you really think those guys were watching us?"

"I don't know." TJ turned to look behind them again while continuing to move along the sidewalk. It wasn't late, but there weren't very many people out and about.

Alexis glanced over her shoulder but didn't see either of the men.

"Maybe you're overreacting," she said with a note of hopefulness.

"Maybe."

But she could tell by his tone that he didn't think so.

They made it back to the hotel and to their suite.

TJ led her inside, then turned back for the door. "I'm going to circle the perimeter, make sure they didn't follow us or aren't waiting for us to fall asleep. You stay here. Do not open the door to anyone. I'll be back in less than ten minutes. If anything goes wrong, call Shawn, understand?"

She nodded, not trusting the words to work around the fear lodged in her throat.

TJ disappeared out the door and she remained rooted in place. But not for long.

Moments after TJ stepped out of the room, footsteps

pounded on the exterior stairs. She heard TJ's deep voice order, "Stop right there."

She crossed the suite to the window overlooking the courtyard and pulled back the heavy curtain.

Two men with masks pulled low over their faces stood at the top of the step, facing TJ. They had the same build as the men from the restaurant, but there was no way to know for sure if it was them.

Alexis's heart raced as the husky guy lunged for TJ.

She raced for the door, pulling it open despite TJ's admonition not to open it until he returned.

TJ grabbed the man's arm, wrenching it behind his back as he brought his knee up to meet the man's chin. The husky man flew backward into the door of one of the other hotel rooms with a grunt. He slid down the door, one hand pressed to his chest, his breath coming in ragged gasps.

The taller, slender man came at TJ, his punch landing on TJ's jaw and sending him stumbling. The slender man didn't waste any time raining more punches down.

Alexis glanced around for something to use to help, but before she found a weapon, a door opened farther along the corridor.

A woman with large blonde curls stepped out, and seeing the melee, screamed for help.

The slender man froze, his gaze pulled toward the screaming woman.

TJ lurched to his feet, headbutting the slender man and sending him crashing into the railing that stopped him from falling onto the pavers below. TJ threw a punch to the man's jaw, followed by a kick to his gut that took the man down to his knees.

More doors opened along the corridor.

An elderly man peeked his head out of his room, then yelled that he was calling the police.

The huskier man finally made it to his feet. "Let's go," he huffed.

The slender man was still on his knees. He looked up at TJ, hostility shooting from his eyes like laser beams.

"Come on!" The husky man had already started down the staircase.

The slender man held TJ's gaze for a moment longer before getting to his feet and following his friend.

Alexis ran to TJ's side. "You're just going to let them leave?"

TJ's gaze didn't waver from the men. They jumped into a dark sedan and peeled away from the hotel parking lot.

"Yes," he said. "I can't leave you to chase after them. They might just be a distraction."

Icy fear snaked through her. The distraction. That meant that there could be someone else out there coming for them.

TJ threw his arm around her and hustled her back to the room.

"Hey, wait a minute. You need to report those guys to the cops," one of the other hotel guests called out to their backs.

TJ ignored the man, hustling her into their suite and securing the door.

"We need to get out of here. You should go pack up."

Alexis grabbed a napkin from beside the coffee maker and pressed it to TJ's bleeding lip. "We aren't going to report this to the police?"

"I think we will probably have to since I had an audience, but I'm going to tell them that I think those guys were just trying to mug me."

"But you don't think that, really?" Alexis pulled the napkin from TJ's lip, eliciting a grimace of pain. "Sorry."

"It's fine." He waved off her attempt to press the napkin against his split lip again. "No, I don't. I'm pretty sure those were the same guys watching us at the restaurant, and since I know they didn't follow us as we walked back to the hotel, that means they know where we're staying."

"How is that possible?"

"I don't know, but I'm going to find out."

Chapter Eleven

The police were at the hotel for more than an hour, taking his and Alexis's statement, as well as the statements of the neighboring hotel guests who'd witnessed the fight. He'd avoided lying when he recounted the details of the attack, but he hadn't told the officers about the break-in at Alexis's or why they were in Virginia. The officers pretty clearly believed they'd been victims of a crime of convenience, an attempted robbery gone wrong, and his instincts told him it was best to let them believe that for now. It appeared as if the statements of the other hotel guests supported that belief. The officer who'd taken his statement handed TJ his card and informed him that he could request a copy of the incident report in seventy-two hours. He held out little hope that anything would come of the police investigation. No one had been seriously injured and the would-be muggers had gotten away with nothing.

He closed the suite door behind the last officer and turned to Alexis. She looked exhausted. He'd have loved to give her a few hours to get some rest. Hell, he'd have loved to get a few hours of sleep himself, but it was too risky. Those guys could come back with reinforcements. They needed to move now.

"You were amazing fighting off those guys," Alexis

said with a small smile, despite the fatigue that shone in her eyes.

"Thanks. And I'm sorry to do this to you, but we have to get moving. We can't stay here."

"I know. Those guys might have just been a distraction," she said, repeating what he said earlier. She shivered.

"Hey." He reached out and pulled her to him before he realized he was doing it. "Don't worry. I'm not going to let anyone get to you."

"Do you think the cops bought your story about those guys being muggers?" she asked, her face pressed against his chest.

He knew she could hear his heart beating and wondered if she realized that its pace had more than doubled since she'd stepped into his arms.

"They bought it. They want to buy it. They've got bigger issues to deal with than an attempted mugging. Especially one where the muggers got away with nothing of value."

"But don't you think it might be better for us if we explained about Mark's death and our investigation?" She pulled away just enough that she could look up at him. "Maybe with the mugging and the attack in my home, the detective in charge of the case will see that there is something very wrong going on here and take my claim that Mark couldn't have committed suicide more seriously."

TJ considered the idea. "Maybe, but I'd like to meet the detective first. Feel her out a bit before we start sharing information."

"I guess that makes sense." Alexis stepped out of his arms and he fought the intense desire to pull her back against him again.

Where she belongs. The thought popped into his head,

but he was more surprised by the fact that he didn't want to swat it back.

"Are you all packed?" he asked, focusing on what needed to be done and ignoring his libido for now.

"Yes, I packed while you finished up with the police officer. I'm ready to go." Alexis turned and disappeared into the bedroom.

"Good. Me too." In fact, he'd never unpacked. It wouldn't be the first time, and probably not the last, that he'd lived out of a bag.

He took Alexis's bag from her and slung it onto one shoulder, then hiked his own bag on the other.

"We'll call Shawn from the car and let him know what happened. I was able to get a partial plate from the car those guys drove off in, but I don't know how much help it will be. Chances are the car is a rental or more likely stolen, but if anyone can track it down, it's Shawn."

TJ opened the door, scanning the area before waving for Alexis to step out of the room. They walked quickly to the car while he remained on alert. He doubted the guys would return to the hotel so soon, but there'd now been two attempts to get to Alexis, which meant she made a motivated enemy.

"What I don't understand is how those guys knew we were staying at this hotel," Alexis said as they hurried to the rental car. "I mean, you were looking the whole time we made our way back to the hotel from the restaurant and there are more than a half dozen other hotels in this area."

"That's a good question." TJ contemplated the answer as he beeped the SUV's trunk open and placed their bags inside. "Get in. I want to check something."

He waited until Alexis had gotten in on the passenger side and closed and locked the door before walking around the SUV. He ran his hand over the inside of each of the wheel wells. Behind the front driver's side tire, he found what he was looking for.

Alexis lowered the passenger window as he approached. "What is that?"

"A GPS tracker. That's why they didn't have to follow us from the restaurant. They knew where to find us."

He took several photos of the tracker before tossing it to the pavement and stomping on it. In a perfect world, he'd have a West technician examine it to see if they couldn't get some information off it that might tell them who'd bought it or planted it on the car, but he couldn't take the chance of taking it with them while it was still emitting a signal notifying their pursuers of where they were going next. The photos were going to have to do.

He rounded the car and hopped into the driver's side. He peeled out of the parking lot before instructing the in-phone assistant to call Shawn West.

It took several minutes to update Shawn.

"You two are okay, though, right?" Shawn asked once TJ had finished explaining the night's events.

"We're fine. I've got a split lip and will probably have one hell of a shiner tomorrow, but I've had worse," TJ answered. He didn't know where they were going, but driving aimlessly wasn't a bad idea at the moment. It made it easier to spot if they had a tail. So far, they were in the clear.

"What do you need from me?" Shawn asked.

"A secure place to sleep would be great." TJ glanced across the car. Alexis had looked exhausted before, but she was all but wilting now. Her head rested against the back of the seat and her eyes were closed, although he knew she wasn't asleep.

"No problem. I actually have a buddy who lives in

Virginia. It's not too far from where you are. He's over-seas right now, but he's let me use his place as a safe house before."

"That's some good friend."

Shawn chuckled. "Yeah, well, he's in the business, too." The business being the business of elite private se-curity, TJ knew. "Give me a minute to reach out."

Ryan West had once told him that more than being a skilled fighter or being able to hack into computer sys-tems or even anticipating potential dangers, private se-curity and investigations were about contacts. Knowing the right people and being able to call on them when you needed to. That seemed to be proving true now.

"Okay, my buddy says the place is empty, and it's fine for you and Alexis to stay there as long as you need to," Shawn told TJ.

Shawn came back on the line after several minutes. He relayed the address and the details of how to gain entry into the house. TJ was to call a phone number when they arrived and Shawn's friend would unlock the door remotely for them. The joys of technology.

It took about an hour for them to get to the house, but as Shawn had promised, they had no trouble getting in touch with his friend and getting inside. TJ took a quick tour around the home, which he noted was quite nice, before walking Alexis to the room he'd deemed safest for her to claim.

He placed her bag on the bed and was headed for the door when she placed a hand on his biceps, stopping him.

"Just in case I haven't said it before, thank you. For being here with me. For believing me. For protecting me."

He reached out a hand and palmed her cheek. "I will always be here for you, and I will always protect you."

She took a step forward, closing the short distance between them. Her flowery perfume tickled his nose and lit the flame of desire in him.

Her eyes closed, and she tilted her head up. Her plump lips were the most enticing thing he'd ever seen, and it took every punch of willpower he had to force himself to step away from her.

"I'll be across the hall if you need me."

Alexis's eyes opened, reflecting the same confusion mixed with the desire he felt inside.

Falling into bed with her now would be a mistake. An admittedly enjoyable mistake, but still, a mistake. And he couldn't afford any mistakes now. Not when Alexis's life could be on the line.

Chapter Twelve

TJ awoke the next morning to a quiet house. He peeked in on Alexis and found her still asleep. The safe house had three full bathrooms and a half bath, so there was no need for him and Alexis to share here.

He set the water to freezing and climbed into the shower.

He'd managed to keep the desire he felt for Alexis every time he looked at her at bay during the day, but he couldn't stop the erotic scenes that had plagued his dreams during the night. He'd awoken hard as a rock and even grumpier than usual. Hence the cold shower. Unfortunately, it wasn't working as well as he'd hoped. He couldn't stop thinking about the hunger he'd seen in her eyes last night when he'd almost kissed her. He'd been with enough women to know that look when he saw it. She'd wanted him as much as he'd wanted her.

Yet he'd still pulled away.

It was the right thing to do.

So then why didn't it feel right?

He turned the shower nozzle from cold to scalding, hoping the hot water would finish the work of quelling his growing feelings for Alexis.

He'd been right to stop what was clearly going to be a mistake for both of them. Alexis wasn't a woman he could jump into bed with just for fun, even if she agreed to it. He cared about her, more than he liked to admit, certainly more than any woman he'd ever dated. She deserved the white picket fence, two kids, and a husband whose job didn't involve living out of a car for days on end so he could catch other married people cheating on their spouses. It was more than he could, or was willing, to give. So he needed to put his libido in park and focus on the task at hand.

He turned off the water and stepped out of the shower.

He and Alexis still had a lot of work to do if they had any chance of proving that Mark didn't steal TalCon's software program and even more work ahead of them when it came to proving Mark didn't commit suicide. All of which was made more difficult by the fact that he had almost no idea what he was doing.

He got dressed in jeans and a gray pullover while considering, for probably the hundredth time since he'd agreed to take on Alexis's case, whether he'd serve her better by letting Shawn or nearly anyone else at West take the lead. He chased cheaters, deadbeat dads, and disability fraudsters. He didn't know the first thing about software programs and military contracts. And proving that Mark was really murdered?

He stopped himself before his thoughts really began to spiral and took a deep breath, letting it out slowly.

Alexis had come to him and he wasn't going to let her down or pawn her off on someone else. This may not have been his usual type of case, but any good investigator knew that information was key.

Which was why he'd emailed Shawn to ask him to pull background reports on Nelson Bacon and Arnold Forrick after Alexis went to bed last night. And after some internal debate, he'd also asked Shawn to pull a background report on Mark, although doing so had left him feeling as if he was betraying his friend. Still, it had been nearly two years since he'd spoken to Mark. And if their last encounter was any indication, Mark's drinking was worse than TJ had realized. Maybe he didn't know his friend as well as he thought he did. It was possible Mark had gotten himself into something, wittingly or unwittingly, that he didn't know how to get out of. Even though checking into Mark made him feel guilty, as if he was betraying his friend, he couldn't ignore the possibility that the situation was just what the cops and TalCon said it was. Not that he would say that to Alexis unless and until he had concrete proof that her brother was a thief who had ended his own life rather than face the consequences of his actions.

In the kitchen, he popped two of the frozen muffins he'd found in the freezer into the toaster oven and started a pot of coffee before opening his laptop.

He clicked on the email from Shawn that was waiting at the top of his inbox just as his cell phone rang.

"Good timing," TJ answered the phone. "I was just opening up the email with the background reports. Thanks for doing that, by the way."

"Not a problem," Shawn responded. "I told you I've got your back on this. Whatever you need."

TJ skimmed the report. "Has Tansy made any headway on tracing the person who made the posting for Nimbus on the dark web?"

Shawn sighed. "Not so far."

TJ beat back a surge of frustration and focused on the email Shawn had sent him. "I'm just getting a look at these reports. Is there anything in here about Bacon or Forrick I should focus on?"

"Both these guys are good at what they do. Both ex-military. Both highly decorated. Bacon was a Ranger. Forrick a Marine. Doesn't appear they knew each other in the service, but they both landed at TalCon about the same time and rose in the ranks pretty much in lockstep. Bacon is the better diplomat, which propelled him to the top seat as CEO, but he brought Forrick along as his right-hand man. Forrick is the heavy. He does whatever Bacon needs him to do, leaving Bacon's hands relatively clean."

"Not a bad setup."

"No, and there's nothing I could find that suggests either of them is anything other than your typical, sometimes ruthless, corporate executive."

The toaster dinged. TJ put the phone on speaker and carried it with him while he fixed himself a cup of coffee and buttered his muffin. "I've been thinking about the theft of the software. Atwal, the lawyer Mark hired to represent him, said that TalCon's cybersecurity professionals found an offer to sell the program on the dark web. I don't think this is the first rodeo for whoever stole this program."

"You think the thief has done this before?"

"This or something like it. Whoever this is knows way too much about TalCon and this program and how to offload it for this to be the first time they've done this."

"Yeah, but you'd think that if someone were running around stealing computer programs that could be used to wage cyber war, it would make the news."

"Not necessarily. Atwal said that one of the reasons that Mark hadn't been charged was that TalCon is still hoping to recover the program without a lot of fanfare. Maybe this kind of theft has happened previously and TalCon, or whatever company fell victim, worked to keep things just as quiet."

"That makes some sense." Shawn still sounded skeptical. "I'll dig around. See what I can find."

"Thanks. Hopefully, it will generate some much needed leads that don't point back to Mark."

TJ let his cursor hang over the third and final report Shawn had attached to the email. Mark's background report.

"How is Alexis?" Shawn asked.

"Hanging in there. She's strong. She'll get through this."

"How about you? I was surprised to see you asked for a background on your friend. Are you starting to have doubts?"

Was he? He didn't doubt the Mark he'd known would never have done what he was being accused of. But the Mark who thought he'd ever make a play for his woman. The Mark that was drinking heavily the last time TJ had seen him. He wasn't sure he knew that Mark at all.

"Just being thorough." It seemed a safe enough answer, but Shawn was too good of an investigator not to have heard the hesitation.

"I sent the photos of the tracker to our technology team. I'll let you know what, if anything, they are able to find out."

"Thanks. Sorry I couldn't get the actual device to you, but I didn't want to take any chances."

"I get it. I don't want to step on your toes, but have you checked for other devices? That might not have been the only one."

"I did a thorough check of the car last night. Didn't find anything else, but you know this kind of investigation isn't really what I'm used to doing."

"You're doing fine. And like I said, I got your back. And to prove it, after I pulled the backgrounds on Forrick and Bacon, I dug around some more." The laptop chimed with an incoming email. "TalCon's a juggernaut in the military contracting world, but they have a couple of up-start competitors nipping at their heels. I figured it might be worth looking at who would benefit if TalCon does a very public and embarrassing face-plant with Nimbus."

The new email contained research on TalCon's two closest competitors. TJ kicked himself for not having thought of the competition angle himself. "Thanks, man."

"No problem. I'm also sending you a name."

TJ's email chimed again. The name Noel Muscarelli followed by an address. The text also included Noel's phone number.

"Noel Muscarelli is a former executive at TalCon who abruptly left the company six months ago, even though he'd been touted as one of Bacon's possible successors."

TJ was surprised by Shawn's last statement. "Is Bacon on his way out?"

"Umm… That's an open question. Bacon has been in the CEO chair for twelve years. At some point, probably in the not-too-distant future, the board is going to have to start thinking about who follows him."

"What about Forrick?"

"Uh-uh." TJ imagined Shawn shaking his head on the other end of the line. "Forrick has burned too many bridges getting and keeping Bacon on top. When Bacon goes, Forrick goes too."

Footsteps sounded down the hall where the bedrooms were. Alexis was awake.

"Thanks, Shawn. This is great. It gives me a few bushes to beat in hopes that something falls out."

TJ ended the call as Alexis entered the kitchen. She wore a pink T-shirt and pink pajama shorts that showed enough of her tantalizingly creamy caramel skin to have him considering taking yet another cold shower.

"Good morning."

"Good morning."

"I made coffee and thawed out a muffin for you."

"Thanks." She turned away from him quickly and he saw her cheeks pink. "I thought I heard you talking to someone."

"Shawn. I asked him to do some background research for me." TJ filled her in on the conversation. "Shawn found a former TalCon employee who worked in the same section as Mark who might be worth tracking down."

"That sounds great. Speaking of TalCon employees, has Lenora Kenda gotten back to you?"

TJ frowned. "No." Ms. Kenda was proving elusive, and he didn't like it. There was no reason for Mark's assistant to dodge his call unless she was hiding something. She was definitely on his list of people to talk to sooner rather than later. "I think it's time we try being more forward with Miss Kenda. I want to take a drive by her house today. See if we can't get her to chat with us. But I think it might be best to reach out to Noel Muscarelli, the former TalCon employee, first. He's more likely to talk to us since he's no longer with TalCon, and we still need to chat with Detective Chellel. We also need to track down Mark's ex, Jessica."

Alexis carried her coffee mug to the table and sat. "Mark told me they'd broken up a few weeks before he died. I'm not sure she'd know anything that could help us."

"We won't know until we ask."

Alexis frowned.

"I know you didn't like your brother's taste in women. But this is part of investigating. Following all the potential leads, even the ones that don't look as if they will pan out to anything."

Alexis held up her hands in surrender. "You're right. You're the expert. If you say we need to talk to Jessica, we talk to Jessica."

TJ didn't feel like an expert, but Jessica was clearly someone they needed to speak to. "Tansy got Jessica's most recent address. I thought we would pay her a visit this morning before stopping by the police station to talk to Detective Chellel. I'm going to call Noel Muscarelli and see if we can arrange to meet up sometime today."

"Wow, I'm impressed. You got all that done before I even got out of bed."

Pride swelled in TJ's chest at her compliment. "It wasn't that much, but you better hurry and get dressed if we want to get a jump on this day."

Alexis downed the remainder of her coffee, then hurried back up the stairs.

He called Noel Muscarelli while Alexis showered and changed. Noel agreed to meet with them at noon at a small coffee shop not far from his home.

After ending the call, TJ's gaze fell on the email from Shawn that contained the background on Mark. He hadn't opened it. Yet. Once again, his finger hovered over the keyboard, but the sound of Alexis heading back toward the kitchen stopped him.

He closed the laptop and turned, forcing a smile. "Ready to go?"

Alexis returned his smile with a tepid one of her own. "Ready as I'll ever be."

They set out for Jessica Castaldo's apartment complex. The two-story brown boxy building was utilitarian, but it looked well kept.

TJ knocked on the door of apartment 2B and got no

answer. He knocked a second time just as the door to apartment 2A was flung open.

"Ain't nobody there." A rail-thin woman with gray hair in two braids that stopped just above her buttocks stood in the open door of the opposite apartment.

Alexis and TJ turned to face the woman, who gave Alexis a quick once-over, but her gaze lingered on TJ. A smile, likely meant to be seductive, quirked her mouth up.

TJ noted, with more than a little satisfaction, that Alexis's lips had taken a decidedly downward turn. She scowled at Jessica's neighbor.

Thinking it was best that he take the lead, he smiled at the woman and said, "Hi there. We're looking for your neighbor, Jessica Castaldo."

The woman smiled back at TJ. "I never knew what her name was, but she doesn't live there anymore. Moved out a couple weeks ago."

"Did she say where she was going?" Alexis asked, a polite smile replacing her former scowl.

The woman shot Alexis a disinterested look before turning her attention back to TJ. "No idea. She didn't exactly leave a forwarding address with me. Like I said, I never even knew her name. A real standoffish little thing, she was."

"Well, could you tell us how long she lived here?"

The woman waved her hand dismissively. "Oh, about six months. Not long. I know she didn't give thirty days' notice like we're all supposed to do if we're going to move out. Super was fit to be tied. Asked me a bunch of questions about where she went, just like you're doing. And I told him the same thing. I didn't really know Little Miss Thing."

TJ pulled out his cell phone and put up a picture of

Mark. "Did you ever see her with this man?" He turned the phone to face the woman.

The woman squinted at the screen for a moment. "Yeah, yeah. I've seen him around here a few times. Not for a few weeks before Little Miss Thing moved out. I think they were dating, but he must've gotten wise and broken up with her."

"What did he get wise to?" Alexis pressed.

The woman jutted her chin in the direction of Jessica's apartment door. "She was a gold digger. Had a job as a waitress or something. I've seen her in her uniform. But no waitressing job is gonna pay for Jimmy Choo shoes and Fendi bags and all those expensive clothes I'd see her traipsing off to the club in on Saturday nights."

For someone who didn't even know her neighbor's name, the woman sure had seen a lot of the goings-on at Jessica's place.

"Is there anything else you can tell us about your neighbor? Anything that might help us figure out where she moved to?"

To her credit, the woman did seem to think about it for a moment before shaking her head. "Naw, I just told you everything I know about her."

TJ put his phone back in his pocket and shot the woman another smile. "Thanks for your help."

The woman smiled back at him. "You're welcome. Anytime, handsome. If you want to come in, maybe have a drink or two?"

TJ heard the soft growl emanating from Alexis's throat. If the other woman heard it, she gave no indication.

"Sorry," TJ said, placing a hand on Alexis's back and guiding her toward the staircase. "I'm on the clock."

"Too bad."

He heard the sound of the woman's door closing.

"I can wait in the car if you want to get to know your new friend a little better," Alexis groused.

TJ's lips twisted into a smile he was sure wasn't going to make his situation any better. He was right. Alexis's scowl deepened when she saw it.

He opened the door to the car and slid in behind the wheel. Alexis slid in next to him.

"Hey, I can't help it if women find me attractive," he joked, hoping to lighten the mood in the car.

Alexis's lips quirked up slightly. "I'll bet. But your attractiveness didn't do much to help us. We have no idea where Jessica lives."

TJ started the car. "No, but I'm not about to let that stop us. I'll give Shawn a call and see if he can dig up Jessica's new address. But right now, we have a meeting with the detective."

Chapter Thirteen

Alexis didn't read happiness on the face of Detective Elaine Chellel when she walked into the police precinct and found Alexis and TJ in the waiting room. Detective Chellel was a tall, wide-framed woman with blonde hair that was shot through with gray. She wore a dark brown pantsuit, no makeup and a scowl. Alexis had done a bit of checking into Detective Chellel following her interview with the woman after Mark's death. She knew the detective was married with two kids and had spent time on the San Francisco police force before moving to Alexandria, Virginia, several years earlier. In their prior conversations, Chellel had displayed a no-nonsense direct approach, which Alexis might have appreciated more if the detective hadn't been telling her that Mark was suspected of theft and having committed suicide. She'd found several articles lauding her for having closed difficult cases, including homicides. She had hoped that meant the detective would have an open mind, but based on their past interactions, that didn't appear to be the case.

Their first conversation had been rather informal, the detective extending her condolences and asking general questions about Mark. But their second interaction had been much more pointed. More of an interrogation, really. The detective had wanted to know everything Alexis knew about Mark's work at TalCon. Since she and Mark hadn't spoken to each other in several weeks, and work was rarely a topic of conversation when they did, Alexis hadn't been able to help the detective much.

The detective had not been happy.

Detective Chellel had seemed all in on the theory that Mark had stolen from TalCon and taken his own life as the walls closed in around him. Alexis's calls requesting updates on Mark's case had, at first, been met with the perfunctory statement that the "investigation was ongoing." Detective Chellel hadn't bothered returning her last several messages at all.

Alexis introduced TJ as a family friend and private investigator. Detective Chellel excused herself from the room, leaving Alexis and TJ to take seats around the circular conference room table.

She was back a moment later with a thick file folder under her arm. "Miss Douglas, I'm surprised to see you here. What can I do for you?" Detective Chellel said, as she took a seat.

"You haven't responded to my last messages, so I thought I'd pay a visit. I'd like to know if there's been any progress in my brother's case."

Frown lines formed on Detective Chellel's forehead. "As I explained to you the last time we spoke, every indication we have is that your brother took his own life. I know that's hard to hear—"

"It's not hard to hear, Detective. It's utterly impossible to believe. Mark had hired a lawyer. He denied the accusations of theft against him and he was prepared to fight to prove his innocence."

"Be that as it may—"

"Detective, I think there is something else you should

know," TJ interrupted. "Alexis was attacked in her home a few nights ago."

Concern flashed across the detective's face. "I'm sorry to hear that. Did you report the assault?"

"I did," Alexis responded. "Although I'm not sure that the Newark cops took my claims any more seriously than you have."

Detective Chellel frowned. "I'm sure they will do a thorough job of investigating."

"The assailant threatened Alexis," TJ said. "Specifically, warning her to back off looking into Mark's death."

Detective Chellel slipped a notepad from beneath the file and took a pen from her jacket pocket. "Take me through everything that happened."

Alexis did as asked. Detective Chellel listened attentively, asking a handful of questions but mostly letting Alexis go through the break-in. When she got to the part about the assailant's threats, Detective Chellel pressed her. Did she recognize the voice? Was there anything at all distinctive about it? Was she sure about what the man had said?

The detective tapped her pen against the table for several long moments after she'd exhausted all her questions. "I'm not sure how the break-in at your home fits into my investigation. I have entertained the possibility that your brother had an accomplice, especially since we haven't yet recovered the stolen property."

Ire rose in Alexis's gut. "An accomplice? The man who assaulted me is most likely the real thief, not an accomplice. He's framing my brother. That's why he doesn't want me looking into things. That's why he killed…" She choked on the rest of the words.

"Miss Douglas," Detective Chellel said, sliding a little closer in her rolling chair. "I'm afraid there are quite a few things we've turned up that your brother didn't tell you about his life. I'm not at liberty to share everything, as this is still an ongoing investigation, but you may not like what I am able to tell you."

Apprehension tingled down Alexis's spine. "I want to hear it. Whatever it is."

The detective sighed. "It seems your brother had racked up quite a bit of debt."

"That can't be right. I know Mark made a good salary at TalCon. He told me that he'd almost finished paying off his student loans and that he was saving to buy a house. He was very responsible with his money."

Chellel took a sheet of paper from the folder and slid it across the table to Alexis. Mark's bank statement. Line after line showed withdrawals. One to two hundred dollars at first, then the withdrawals got bigger. Five hundred. One thousand. Sixteen hundred. Mark was bleeding money.

"What is this? Where is all this money going?" Alexis looked up from the statement at Detective Chellel.

"I've talked to several of Mark's friends and coworkers. Your brother had developed a gambling problem."

Alexis gripped the arm of her chair. "No. I…he never said anything to me about gambling." She vaguely remembered Mark saying something about going to a local casino for a bachelor party weekend with some friends several months earlier. But one weekend with the boys couldn't turn a person into a gambling addict.

Detective Chellel gave her a sympathetic look. "It's not uncommon for something like this to be kept from family members and loved ones. Either the person doesn't think they have a problem or they are too embarrassed to seek help for it. His bank statements show numerous withdrawals from an ATM in the MGM National Harbor."

There were dozens of highlighted lines showing withdrawals in the pages that Detective Chellel handed Alexis. Struggling to make sense of what the detective was saying to her, she handed the bank statement to TJ.

Alexis struggled for a moment to grab onto a nugget of information that was pushing its way into the forefront of her mind. "The MGM? Isn't that where Jessica Castaldo works?" She recalled now that Jessica had mentioned working there when she and Mark had visited.

Detective Chellel nodded. "Yes. When I spoke to her, she said that was how she and Mark met." Detective Chellel pulled a photo out of the file she'd brought into the room. "We also discovered that your brother had been prescribed diazepam for stress and anxiety by his doctor."

She slid the photo across the table to Alexis. It showed a close-up of an empty prescription bottle with Mark's name on the label.

"The empty bottle we found in his apartment was his own prescription," the detective continued. "We've also developed information that suggests your brother had a drinking problem. A problem you never mentioned when we spoke about your brother in our earlier interviews, Miss Douglas." Chellel's tone was pointed.

Alexis caught the glance TJ shot her way. "It didn't seem relevant. Mark drank too much, yes. But he'd never hurt himself or others."

Mark's DUI and TJ's description of how out of control Mark had been on the night their friendship had fractured played through her mind, but she wouldn't let the detective define Mark by his worst moments.

"This account shows a negative balance." TJ's voice brought her back to the present. "How was Mark paying his bills with this much money going out, presumably to feed his gambling?"

Chellel shook her head. "He wasn't. His landlord says he was always late with the rent and often short on money. The financing company for his car had already started the repossession process."

Alexis massaged the growing headache behind her temples. "This is madness."

"I'm sure it's hard to make sense of now," Detective Chellel said.

"So you think Mark's gambling losses were the catalyst for the theft?" TJ asked the detective.

Chellel nodded. "That looks to be the case. We know Mark downloaded the completely updated program a few days before an online posting went up on the dark web offering its sale."

"Mark was working on the program. His downloading it isn't suspicious," Alexis said.

"His coworkers at TalCon say the work he was doing on the program would not have required him to download it. And the system shows that it was downloaded to an external drive. That is expressly prohibited by company policy according to the people we spoke with."

Frustration bubbled in Alexis's chest. She gripped the arms of her chair tighter.

TJ covered her hand with one of his. A warning to keep her cool.

"Have you been able to trace that posting back to Mark?" he asked the detective.

Detective Chellel frowned. "No. It's incredibly difficult to trace anything on the dark web."

"So you still have no proof Mark made the posting," TJ pressed.

Chellel focused her frown on TJ. "No. But we are sure he is the only person who downloaded the complete program."

Alexis worked to keep the scowl off her face. The detective's eagerness to ignore all the inconsistencies in her theory irked her. "And you don't think it's at all suspicious that TalCon's security cameras were offline on the night the program was stolen?"

"No, I don't," the detective responded forcefully. "The system was down for scheduled maintenance. If anything, that hurts your brother's case. He was one of only a handful of employees privy to the company's routine maintenance schedule."

Alexis had no response for that piece of news, so she simply stewed quietly.

"I know this is not what you want to hear," Detective Chellel said after a moment. "But your brother had the means, motive and opportunity to steal the program."

"Even if you're right and Mark did steal the program—and to be clear I don't accept that, but let's assume we're in some bizarro world—that doesn't mean Mark killed himself."

"The charges he would have faced, corporate espionage, theft, cybersecurity violations, are serious felonies. Some of them are federal. He'd have faced decades in prison. It's not a small thing, and when people feel they have no way out…"

Chellel let the rest of the statement hang unspoken.

"But Mark hadn't even been charged yet. He had a lawyer. He was ready to fight to clear his name. It doesn't make sense that he'd just give up."

Detective Chellel looked as if she was fighting to hold on to her patience.

Alexis didn't care. The detective had been far too willing to jump to conclusions when it came to this case. There didn't seem to be anyone pushing her to examine any lines of inquiry that didn't lead to Mark.

"Look, Miss Douglas, I can see how hard this is for you. I'm sure I would feel the same way if the roles were reversed. But I can't ignore the evidence, and right now, all the evidence leads to the conclusion that Mark Douglas stole property from TalCon and took his own life once his theft became known and his arrest was imminent."

"Was his arrest imminent?" TJ interrupted. "Because that's not how Mark's lawyer understood the situation. He was under the impression that TalCon wanted to get the Nimbus program back but to keep the theft quiet at the same time."

Chellel's narrow-eyed gaze shifted to TJ. "I can't speak to what Mr. Atwal understood, but it's not the policy of this police department to spend valuable resources and working hours investigating with the intention of just letting the crimes we turn up go. I'm confident we would have sought and obtained a warrant for Mark Douglas's arrest."

Detective Chellel's statement hit Alexis like a punch in the chest. Her brother had been on the verge of being arrested. How desperate might that knowledge have made him?

No. She knew Mark. No matter what was happening in his life, he wouldn't have gone as far as suicide.

Alexis surged to her feet. "Well then, you would have been arresting the wrong man. And I'm going to prove it."

Chapter Fourteen

TJ guided Alexis from the police station, his arm lightly at her waist. Her determination with the detective had impressed him and, if he was being completely honest, turned him on a little. There was nothing sexier than a strong woman standing up for what she thought was right. Walking close enough to her now that the flowery scent of her perfume engulfed him wasn't doing anything to cool his desire for her, but Alexis didn't seem to be suffering from the same affliction.

She tapped away on her phone, engrossed in whatever she was doing on it, as they exited the police station. He let her be and focused on getting them back to the car.

"We need to go to the MGM and talk to Jessica," Alexis said as he slid into the driver's seat of the rental and turned over the engine.

"We're supposed to meet with Noel Muscarelli, the former TalCon employee Shawn hooked us up with, remember?"

"I know, I know, but you said that meeting was set for noon. That gives us more than an hour and a half. The MGM is fifteen minutes from here. I don't want to wait any longer to find out what Jessica knows."

TJ pulled out of the parking space and headed for the garage's exit. "We don't even know if Jessica is at work now. You really didn't know anything about Mark's gambling habit?"

"No, nothing at all. Jessica mentioned that she worked at the MGM when she and Mark came to visit me last year, but I had no idea. I mean, it didn't even cross my mind that Mark…"

"Of course not. Why would it? Okay," TJ said, shifting into the right-hand lane when he saw the sign announcing the entrance ramp for the highway was less than a half mile away. "We'll head to the MGM and see if Jessica is working. At the very least, we might be able to find out when she is working and we can return then."

He drove the fifteen minutes to the casino and paid the exorbitant parking fee for a nearby garage.

The MGM was located at the National Harbor, an area that had undergone an extensive revitalization, some might say gentrification, over the last decade. The décor was elegant and upscale. In addition to the casino and hotel, the space boasted a luxuriously appointed spa, several bars and lounges, retail stores, and a bevy of high-end restaurants.

"This place is gorgeous," Alexis said, craning her neck to take in the splendor of the main entrance.

"Gorgeous and huge," TJ responded. He closed a hand over Alexis's elbow and led her toward the casino floor. "These places usually have a lounge off the casino floor. Our best bet is probably to sit there and get the lay of the land first."

He was right. There was a lounge that overlooked the casino's main floor. A waitress approached only seconds after they'd taken a table that allowed them a clear view of the floor. She took their orders, a club soda for him and sparkling water for Alexis.

Alexis scanned the casino floor. "I don't see Jessica."

"There's no guarantee she's here," TJ said. "For now, we need to look like we're just a couple enjoying our drinks and thinking about losing a little money."

Alexis looked at him. "Couple? I thought you didn't do the couple thing?"

His lips quirked up. "Just this once."

"Lucky me," Alexis replied, her voice husky.

The waitress returned, putting an end to the charged moment. It was just as well. He needed to focus. He'd seen a photo of Jessica Castaldo in the background, information on her that he'd gathered, but that didn't mean it would be easy to spot her. If she was even there, which was still an open question.

A question that must have been lingering on Alexis's mind too. "Maybe we should ask our waitress if Jessica is working today?" She nodded at the waitress's retreating back.

"Alexis Douglas?"

Alexis's gaze shifted over his shoulder.

TJ turned to find a tall Latino man with dark hair that grazed his shoulder headed for them.

The man swept Alexis from her seat and kissed her on each of her cheeks before stepping back and holding her at arm's length. "Muñeca, what are you doing here?"

"Antonio. It's so good to see you. I'm just down for a visit." Alexis said, obviously flustered, but the smile on her face made it clear she was happy to see Antonio, whoever he was.

"Well, this is an amazing surprise, then." Antonio pulled Alexis in for another hug.

TJ stood, jealousy knotting his stomach.

Alexis pulled out of the other man's arms and stepped back. "Antonio, I want you to meet my friend, TJ. TJ, this is Antonio. He and I went to culinary school together."

TJ moved to Alexis's side and shook the hand Antonio extended.

"Are you two staying in the hotel here?" Antonio asked.

"Oh, no. We got a place somewhere else," Alexis said, uncertainty in her eyes.

"Good." Antonio leaned in and lowered his voice. "This place is way overpriced. Trust me, I'm the pastry chef at a restaurant here and you don't want me to tell you the difference between what it costs to make our signature dessert versus what we charge the guests." Antonio laughed good naturedly.

TJ found himself warming to the man even though he was standing much too close to Alexis and looked as if he should be on the cover of a magazine instead of in a kitchen. "You two must stay for lunch. I'm not on duty until later this evening, but I'll make sure the kitchen takes care of you."

Alexis's gaze slid to TJ's face. It was almost as if he could read the thoughts going through her mind. Antonio could be just the person they were looking for to help locate Jessica.

TJ nodded, letting her know he was on board with her asking Antonio about Jessica.

"Antonio, we're not just here to visit." Alexis pulled her phone from her pocket and pulled up the photo of Mark, her, and Jessica. "We're looking for this woman. Jessica Castaldo. She's a cocktail waitress at the casino here and she was dating my brother. It's very important that we speak to her."

Antonio peered at the photo. "I'm sorry, I don't know her. A lot of people work for the hotel and casino. If she's dating your brother, wouldn't he know how to get in touch with her?"

Sadness clouded Alexis's eyes.

"Mark died two months ago," TJ said.

"Oh, muñeca." Antonio clasped his hands together, prayer-like. "I'm so sorry to hear that."

"There are questions." TJ picked up the conversation again when it seemed that Alexis would not. "We'd really like to talk to Jessica, but we don't have a working phone number for her and she's moved out of her apartment. We were hoping to catch her at work."

Antonio made a face. "That might be tricky, but let me see what I can do."

Antonio strode away into an area behind the lounge's bar where their waitress seemed to have also disappeared. TJ and Alexis reclaimed their seats.

Curiosity and jealousy getting the best of him, TJ queried, "Muñeca?"

Alexis's brow arched. "Antonio calls all his female friends muñeca. It means doll in Spanish."

"His friends?"

Alexis's lips turned up into a smile, and he knew she knew he was jealous. "Yes, his friends. Antonio is something of a flirt, but he's been married for I don't know how long. Since before I met him. And he and his wife are sickeningly in love."

"Oh, well, that's nice."

Alexis's grin grew. "It is."

She was still smiling when her gaze shifted over his shoulder again.

He turned to find Antonio heading their way again, this time with a woman in tow. She wore the same basic uniform as their waitress wore, a short black skirt, white top and heels.

"Guys, this is Stacey. Stacey, this is Alexis and her

friend TJ." Antonio made the introductions. "Stacey knows Jessica."

"Yeah," Stacey said, looking from Antonio to TJ before her gaze finally landed on Alexis. "She used to work here, but she quit about three weeks ago. Maybe a month. I'm not sure. We don't always work the same shifts."

TJ shared a glance with Alexis. "She quit," he pressed. "You're sure?"

Stacey nodded. "Yeah, absolutely. Our manager was pretty upset. She didn't give notice at all. Just called in right before she was scheduled to start her shift and said she wasn't ever coming back. The rest of us had to cover her shifts for the rest of the week. Made a little extra, but it was annoying just the same."

"Do you have a phone number or address for Jessica?" Alexis asked.

Suspicion clouded Stacey's eyes. "I don't know if I should be giving that kind of information out."

Alexis pulled her phone out of her pocket again and turned it toward Stacey.

"This guy, Mark, he's my brother. He was also dating Jessica. He passed away recently, and he left something for Jessica. I want to make sure she gets it."

TJ managed to stifle his surprise at the lie that fell so easily from Alexis's mouth, but Antonio frowned. Thankfully, he kept quiet.

The suspicion in Stacey's eyes evaporated. "Oh, I recognize him. Good guy. I'm sorry for your loss."

"You knew my brother?"

Stacey's forehead crinkled. "Knew is too strong. He played here a lot, though, so I served him a bunch of times. Good tipper. Terrible gambler."

"Why do you say that?" TJ pressed.

Stacey threw a glance over her shoulder. But they were

the only people in the lounge. Even their waitress had disappeared. "Well, I mean, the deck is stacked against you anyway, right? The house always wins and all that. But some people never really get that through their heads. Winning becomes a challenge they just can't let go of. I mean, that's how it becomes an addiction, right?"

"You're saying my brother was addicted to gambling?"

Stacey shot another quick glance over her shoulder. "You're his sister, so you deserve to know. Some of the gamblers with serious problems, they go to this guy, Chamberly, when the casino stops giving them credit."

"A loan shark?" TJ asked to clarify.

A small gasp escaped Alexis's lips.

Stacey nodded. "I saw your brother talking to him once at a bar down the street. Chamberly is persona non grata in the hotel and casino, so he does his business out of the Blue Bull Bar. I think he owns part of it or part of the owner," she scoffed. "That's all I know."

Stacey didn't have a current phone number or address for Jessica or a full name for Chamberly. She wished them luck before sauntering away.

Antonio reissued his offer for lunch, but they took a raincheck. They had a half hour to make it back to Alexandria for their meeting with Noel.

TJ paid their bill and he and Alexis began the drive back to Alexandria. He used the speakerphone to call Shawn on the way, briefly updating him on what they'd learned at the casino.

"So could you see if you or Tansy can dig up a current address and phone number for Jessica Castaldo and whatever we can find on this Chamberly? A full name would be great, for starters."

"Chamberly. I've heard of him, although I thought he operated in Atlantic City. I guess the new casino on the harbor was too good of an opportunity for him to pass up. He's a predator," Shawn said with more than a little disgust in his voice.

TJ shot a look across the car at Alexis. "Is he dangerous?"

Shawn grunted. "No more so than any loan shark. Generally, these guys might work a guy over, but murder is bad business. Brings police attention, and dead men don't pay."

Alexis let out a deep breath. "So you don't think he could have killed Mark?"

"I didn't say that, but it's not likely."

"Can you get us a meeting with him?" TJ asked Shawn. The silence on the other side of the line went on and on. "Shawn, are you still there?"

"I'm here. I can reach out to a few people and see what I can do, but are you sure about this?"

"I think we have to talk to him." He glanced at Alexis again, hesitating to say exactly what he was thinking while she was in earshot.

Shawn didn't have any such misgiving. "We have to consider that Mark might have stolen Nimbus as a means of paying off a debt to Chamberly."

"No!" Alexis exclaimed.

"It's a possibility we have to explore," TJ said at the same time.

Alexis shot a look his way. "Mark would never do something like that."

"Sweetheart, there's only one thing we've learned so far, and that is that Mark had a lot of secrets. If you really want to get to the bottom of his death, we have to look into everything."

The interior of the car was quiet for a full minute. Even Shawn remained silent on the open line.

"Fine," Alexis spat finally. "We'll talk to this Chamberly person. We'll turn over every rock and when we do, I know we'll prove Mark's innocence."

TJ hoped for Alexis's sake that would be the case.

Chapter Fifteen

Shawn ended the call with a promise to get back to them as soon as he'd arranged a meeting with Chamberly. Alexis and TJ made the rest of the drive to meet Noel Muscarelli in silence. The weight of being the only one who believed, no, who knew, that Mark was innocent, pressed down on her until she thought she'd break.

TJ found a parking spot in the small, paved lot next to the café. He held the door open and Alexis stepped into the coffee shop where Noel Muscarelli had agreed to meet them. At a little after noon, there were only a handful of tables occupied. The space was small, but she could tell right away that they prepared their own baked goods. The air smelled of sugar and cinnamon. An instrumental pop song she vaguely recognized played too loudly from the overhead speakers.

Noel Muscarelli wasn't hard to spot. He sat alone, a steaming cup in front of him, his eyes trained on the door of the shop.

Alexis moved toward him, with TJ following closely behind. "Noel?" The man nodded. "Hi. I'm Alexis Douglas. Mark's sister. Thank you for agreeing to speak with us."

"No problem." Noel shook her hand, then turned to TJ. "You must be Mr. Roman."

"TJ, please." TJ shook Noel's hand.

"Can I get either of you something to drink?" Noel asked once Alexis and TJ were seated across the table from him.

"We should be extending that offer to you, but no, I'm fine, thank you," Alexis replied.

"I'm okay."

"Oh, okay." Noel tapped his nails against the side of his cup. "Sorry if I'm a little nervous. When you called to say you wanted to talk to me about TalCon… Well, I don't have good memories of that place."

"I'm sure you heard about Mark. His being accused of stealing from TalCon and…" She let the rest of the sentence fall away. She still couldn't bring herself to say that Mark had committed suicide.

"Yes. It was such a shock. I'm truly sorry for your loss." Noel looked at her with sadness in his eyes.

"Thank you. TJ was also close to Mark, and neither one of us believes that Mark would have done what TalCon is saying he did. We're hoping you can help us."

Noel fidgeted in his chair. "I'm not sure how. I haven't worked at TalCon for more than six months now."

"If it's not too forward, you could start by telling us why you left TalCon. I understand that you worked in the same division as Mark," TJ said.

Noel leaned back in his chair, seemingly considering how to reply. Or maybe whether to reply at all. He was silent for so long, Alexis started to think he wasn't going to answer.

"I guess, if you think it would help prove Mark isn't a thief, which, for the record, I don't buy."

Alexis felt her shoulders relax and realized she'd been worried about speaking to Noel. So far, it seemed as if everyone who knew Mark had bought TalCon's story that he'd stolen from them. She didn't realize just how much stress having her brother's name dragged through the mud had put on her.

"I appreciate that." She smiled across the table at Noel.

"I worked at TalCon in the cybersecurity and engineering division with Mark. We were both senior engineers, and we were both assigned to work on a special program that the company was pouring tons of money into."

"Nimbus," Alexis said.

Noel startled in surprise. "Yes. I don't know how you know that…"

"We spoke with Nelson Bacon and Arnold Forrick yesterday, but they were pretty tight-lipped when it came to Nimbus," TJ said. "Can you give us a bit more detail about what exactly it is we're talking about?"

"I don't know," Noel said nervously. "TalCon let me go, but my nondisclosure agreement is still in effect. They were very clear about that as they frog-marched me from the building."

"Noel," Alexis said, leaning forward and pinning Noel in her gaze. "I promise we won't tell anyone where we got the information. We have somewhat of an idea about what the program is anyway from Mark's lawyer."

Noel hesitated for a moment more before speaking. "It's software that would allow the user to take over another computer system. Countries aren't winning wars anymore based on who has the better guns or the bigger bombs. Everything now is run by computers." Noel leaned forward excitedly. "Think about it. Your electrical grid. The water supply. Every financial institution. All government entities. Everything is online or in the cloud. Everything is on some sort of computer system."

"So you're saying this program would allow the owner to take over the electrical grid?" TJ's voice was laced with the skepticism that Alexis felt. The whole thing felt more like a bad B movie than anything that could happen in real life.

Noel let out a frustrated sigh. "That's exactly what I'm saying. An electrical grid, really any system that's run by a computer, which these days is every system. Look, I know it might sound ridiculous to people not steeped in cyber warfare, but this is what I do for a living. Trust me when I say that not only is the US putting billions of dollars into developing programs like this, so are our enemies. Whoever manages to crack it first will be at a very distinct advantage."

"So how would it work?" Alexis pressed. "I mean, I know that we're always told not to click on links in emails from people we don't know. I assume the US government and whoever is in charge of our electrical and water supply has access to better protection for its computers than I have for my laptop."

"Yes and no," Noel answered. "The biggest weakness in any system is and always will be humans. No matter how much you warn them not to do something, somebody isn't going to listen. But the beauty of this program is that it doesn't matter."

Alexis felt her mouth turn down in a frown. She was getting a headache trying to keep up with Noel.

He must have noticed. "Okay, so here's an example. You remember how the federal and state governments went on hyper-alert a while back and started banning certain social media platforms on government computers that were owned by foreign companies because they worried that the foreign governments might use them to spy on Americans?"

She wasn't a regular user of social media, although she'd been telling herself for ages now that she needed to integrate it into her business model, but she vaguely remembered reading an article online on the subject. "Yeah, I think so."

She glanced at TJ, who nodded. He seemed to be having a far easier time following Noel. Maybe because of his military background, more of what Noel was saying made sense to him.

"Well, social media platforms were downloaded on millions, maybe even billions, of machines all over the world. Now imagine if simply by downloading a popular social media platform or a word processing program or any computer software, it could be infected and give a bad actor, a terrorist state, for instance, complete and total control over your computer or device. No need to wait for some clueless sap to click on a link. Nimbus attaches itself to otherwise useful code that a company pushes out to all its networked computers and bam!"

Noel clapped his hands once loudly, making Alexis jump.

"It goes to work," Noel continued excitedly. "They could see your banking information, emails, what programs you'd opened recently and all the passwords for those programs and you wouldn't even realize it. With enough computers under their control, they could harness the information and gain access to restricted servers."

"Like servers that house national security secrets, run the electrical grid..." TJ said.

Noel made a finger gun. "Exactly. Obviously, the US government would be very interested in getting its hands on a program such as this, as would many other governments."

Alexis finally felt as if she had a handle on what Noel was explaining. "And TalCon would make billions."

Noel made another finger gun and directed it at her this time.

"So that explains why someone might steal it. They could also make a lot of money selling it on the black market."

"Yes, but there is one thing," Noel said, chewing his bottom lip. "Nimbus? It doesn't work."

"It doesn't…" Alexis stuttered.

"It doesn't work. That's why I got fired. I told Bacon that we needed more time. Hell, I wasn't even one hundred percent sure we could ever make it work."

She glanced at TJ next to her, but he appeared to be just as stunned as she was.

"What did Bacon do?" TJ asked.

Noel sighed. "He went off the rails. He and Forrick had been talking up the program to the board. And I heard they'd been buzzing about it to big wigs at the Pentagon and some of the senators and representatives on various congressional committees that would have had to approve the purchase. Bacon wanted the program operational, like, yesterday, but Mark and I just couldn't make it work."

"So Mark knew the program was faulty?" TJ pressed.

Noel nodded. "He knew. He was more optimistic than I was that we could get it up and running. Eventually."

TJ frowned. "So why did you get fired but Mark didn't?"

"I confronted Bacon about hyping Nimbus to the board when he knew it wasn't going to be ready on schedule. I told him that he had an obligation to accurately report to the board, we both did, and that by not doing so we could find ourselves in a lot of hot water, not just with the board but with the SEC and other governing bodies if they felt like we were hiding the program's failures to keep the company stock from taking a hit."

"And Bacon responded by firing you," TJ summarized.

"Pretty much. There were lots of threats to go along with the firing. And blackballing. I can't get a job. People I've known and worked with in the industry for the past ten years won't return my calls. I'm starting to think I should have just kept my mouth shut like Mar—" Noel's cheeks reddened.

"Mark wouldn't have let TalCon lie to the government or the public. I'm sure he thought he had a shot at fixing the program in time."

Noel held up his hands in a surrender pose. "I'm not judging him at all. We all do what we have to do to keep food on the table. But there was no way that program was going to be ready by the end of the year like Bacon wanted."

She started to defend Mark, but TJ spoke before she could get a word out.

"So TalCon knows the program doesn't work but can't say that when they find the posting on the dark web offering it for sale so they accuse Mark of the theft, making him the fall guy?" TJ's tone said he didn't quite buy it.

"That's one possibility." Noel shot a weary glance at Alexis.

"What is it?" TJ asked while sliding his hand over hers and giving it a squeeze. She took it as a sign he knew she wasn't going to like whatever Noel was holding back.

"Look, I liked Mark. Like I said, no judgment at all. But the last couple of months we worked together, he'd been struggling."

"Struggling how?" TJ pressed.

"Drinking a lot. He never came into work out-and-out drunk," Noel added quickly. "But there were times I could smell the booze from the night before still on his breath, you know? And he'd started gambling. Ever since the MGM opened up on the National Harbor. A few of us used to go on weekends. Have a few drinks. Lose a little money. No big deal. But I think Mark got a real taste for it. He started going a lot more often than the rest of us."

Alexis's hands began to tremble.

TJ squeezed the hand he was holding just a little tighter.

"I'm sorry. I have to go." Noel pushed away from the table. "I was lucky enough to get a little freelance work and I can't afford to miss my deadlines." He stood.

TJ let go of her hand and stood as well. "Thanks for meeting with us."

Noel walked away from the table, and seconds later she heard the bell over the door ring, signaling he'd left the coffee shop.

TJ sat. "You okay?" He put an arm around her shoulder.

Alexis shook her head, looking down at the scarred table. "I'm not sure. The man Noel described was not the Mark I knew." She swallowed hard and forced herself to meet TJ's gaze. "I'm not sure I knew my brother at all."

TJ reached out and swiped at a tear that was threatening to fall. A clash of emotions rumbled through her, but desire, a hunger to feel his arms around her, pushed to the forefront.

She could see in his eyes that he was warring with the same emotions and, more than anything, she wanted him to let go. To feel what she was feeling and to act on it.

TJ leaned forward as if he might kiss her, and she moved to meet him.

His phone rang.

He swore quietly and reached for it.

"Roman." His expression hardened a heartbeat later. He rose from the table and gestured for her to do the same, reaching out a hand.

She took it and they hurried from the café and toward the car.

Once inside, TJ switched the phone to speaker.

"It's not ideal," he said. "I'd rather meet him in person."

"He won't go for it," Shawn said on the other end of the phone. "If you want to talk to Chamberly, it's a phone call, now or never."

TJ glanced at her, and she nodded. A phone call was better than nothing. And to be honest, she was a little relieved they wouldn't have to face down the loan shark in person. Proving Mark's innocence was taking her places she'd never have imagined going. She was willing to do it for her brother, but that didn't make it any less scary.

"Okay," TJ acquiesced. "But I don't want him to know Alexis is on the line." He looked at her. "It's for your protection."

"I'm fine with that as long as I can hear the conversation," she said.

After a moment of silence, Shawn spoke again. "Chamberly, I've got TJ Roman on the line."

"Good. Fine. What is it that you want from me?" a voice with an Eastern European accent said over the line.

"Actually, I'd like to meet with you in person. I'd only take a few moments of your time."

"I'm a busy man. I don't meet with people I don't know," Chamberly said, brooking no argument. "I'm only talking to you now as a favor to a friend."

For a moment Alexis wondered just what kind of

friends Shawn shared with the loan shark that made this call possible, but figured it was probably best that she didn't know the answer to that question.

"What is it you want?" Chamberly asked a second time.

Alexis got the feeling he wouldn't ask a third time.

TJ must have too. "I've been hired to look into a suspicious death of one of your clients. Mark Douglas."

"Ah, yes, Mark. I heard about his untimely passing. So sad. But he wasn't my client."

Alexis watched TJ's brow furrow. "He was seen speaking to you at the Blue Bull. That's where you do business, correct?"

There was silence on the other side of the line for a long moment. "I am part owner of the establishment."

"Listen, I don't care about your loan-sharking business," TJ said. "I'm sure that Shawn has already explained that we aren't looking to jam you up unless you had something to do with Mark Douglas's death."

"I'm not a killer. Bad for business. Mr. Douglas used to frequent my business, but our relationship ended three months ago. Amicably."

Alexis had no idea what that meant. She shot a quizzical look at TJ.

"I'm assuming that meant Mark didn't have an outstanding debt with you?"

"That's what amicable means in my business. He paid his bill with interest in March. I haven't seen him since."

Truth? Alexis mouthed at TJ.

He shrugged.

"How much did he owe you?"

Chamberly didn't answer.

"Chamberly, if you're not involved with Douglas's

death, you've got nothing to worry about. You've got my word," Shawn said.

"Thirty-two thousand with interest," Chamberly finally answered.

Alexis covered her mouth just in time to stifle the gasp that escaped. Thirty-two thousand dollars? Where did Mark get that kind of money?

"Did he say where he got the money from to pay you?" TJ asked, his line of thought mirroring her own.

"No. I don't ask those kinds of questions. As long as the client has my money, I don't care where they get it from, you understand?"

"Understood. How about Nimbus? Did Mark ever mention it to you?"

"Nimbus? What is that? I've never heard of it."

"It's potentially very lucrative software. Mark never offered it to you as payment for his debts? Or maybe as security?"

Chamberly guffawed. "I'm not running a pawn shop here. This is a cash for cash operation. Douglas paid me in cold hard cash."

"Right. Thanks."

Chamberly's end of the line dropped without another word.

"You believe him?" Shawn asked.

TJ let out a heavy sigh. "Yeah. I do."

As much as Alexis wanted answers now, she had to admit she believed the loan shark, too. It didn't make sense for Chamberly to have killed Mark, and he'd seemed genuinely baffled when TJ mentioned Nimbus. Of course, it could have all been an act, but her gut was telling her that whatever happened to Mark, Chamberly didn't have anything to do with it.

"Now what?" Alexis asked. "Where do we go from here?":

Based on Shawn's silence and the look on TJ's face, neither of them were any closer to answering that question than she was.

Chapter Sixteen

TJ and Alexis returned to the safe house after meeting with Noel. Alexis went to her room, firmly closing the door behind her, a not-so-subtle hint that she wanted to be alone.

TJ settled down on the sofa with his laptop and dug deeper into Noel, TalCon, and cyber weapons generally. Noel's comments about Mark's drinking escalating and Chamberly's information about Mark's gambling problems only supported what Detective Chellel had told them. There seemed to be quite a bit about his life that Mark had been keeping a secret from his sister.

TJ felt for her. He knew it could be difficult for a family member to find out that their loved one wasn't who they thought they were. He saw it more than he liked. Wives or husbands who came to him to investigate whether their spouse was cheating or hiding money or keeping any number of secrets. Finding out that an upstanding member of the community was actually gambling away the family fortune wasn't uncommon. Neither was discovering drinking or substance abuse problems. The pressure that people found themselves under these days was often crushing, and many people turned to vices to deal with it.

Was that what had happened to Mark? Had the stress

of his job, of being pressured to make Nimbus work on TalCon's timeline, gotten to him? Had he simply snapped, figuring that if he couldn't make the program work, maybe he could still make some money off of it and when his theft was discovered he hadn't been able to deal with the fallout?

Even with everything he'd learned about his friend since starting this investigation, TJ had a hard time picturing it.

He glanced at the ceiling above, wondering how Alexis was faring with the onslaught of new information about her brother.

Even though he knew Alexis had a lot to process, it stung to have her shut him out.

But it shouldn't. She's not your girlfriend.

Definitely not. He didn't do the girlfriend thing. At least not long term. But if he did, Alexis would be exactly the kind of woman he'd want by his side.

He shook the idea from his head. He had to stop with the fantasies. He made a promise to Mark and, despite everything, he kept his promises.

The sound of footsteps overhead then on the stairs signaled Alexis's imminent arrival. But she didn't appear immediately. Instead, he heard her in the kitchen and minutes later she stepped into the living room with a steaming mug in her hand.

She sat on the sofa beside him and handed him the mug. The aroma of green tea leaves wafted under his nose.

"An apology for being so rude earlier," Alexis said, handing over the mug. "And I want to take you to lunch. Whatever you want, your choice."

"No apology necessary, but I will take you up on lunch." Without thinking, TJ set his mug aside and reached for her hand and curled his fingers through hers. "This has got to be an overwhelming situation for you. I think you're handling it as well as could be expected. Better even."

"It doesn't feel that way. I guess I needed time to process everything we just learned about Mark." Alexis dropped her head, her gaze cast down at their combined hands. "It feels like there were two Marks. The one I knew, my brother, and this other person who…" TJ saw unabated fear in her eyes and the urge to do whatever it took to banish it forever hit him like a punch in the chest. "Maybe that Mark could have done what Detective Chellel thinks he did?"

TJ used an index finger to tip her head up until her eyes met his. "Hey, we will get to the bottom of this, and whatever we find, you will get through it. I promise. And I'll be right here to help you as long as you want me."

He realized his last words could be taken more than one way.

Alexis must have heard it too. He watched an unmistakable desire flare in her eyes.

Slowly, Alexis placed a soft hand over his chest. Their gazes locked on each other.

She glided her hands up to his shoulders, leaning in.

TJ's heated gaze searched hers before his eyes fell to her mouth and she swiped her tongue over her bottom lip.

A low moan escaped from his throat, and he reached for her, closing the distance between them. He pressed his mouth to hers, his fingers kneading her back.

He tilted his head, sucking her bottom lip before deepening the kiss. She eagerly accepted him, need and desire mingling with the green tea she tasted on his lips.

Emboldened, he slipped his hands down to her backside and in one swift motion, lifted her onto his lap so she was straddling him.

She moaned as he pulled her firmly against him.

Her breasts swelled against his chest, and he imagined what it would feel like to strip her of her top and take each round bud into his mouth. His erection swelled.

Alexis broke off the kiss and met his gaze, lust swimming in her eyes. "Take me to bed."

Her words hit him like a cold shower.

He grasped her wrists gently and eased her back. "I'm sorry. I can't do this."

Confusion mixed with the lust in her eyes. "Why not?" she said, nearly breathless from his kiss.

Why not? It was a good question, one he suspected she wouldn't like his answer for.

"I'm supposed to be protecting you. Not taking advantage of you."

"You're not taking advantage. I want this, and I think you do, too."

She leaned forward, but he held her firmly. He was pretty sure he wouldn't be able to stop himself from making love to her if he let her kiss him again. "Alexis, I can't. I can't do that to Mark."

She eased off his lap. "What does Mark have to do with you and me being together?"

"You're his sister and, even though we were on the outs when he died, I still considered him my friend. My best friend. I can't do that to him. And I'm not the kind of guy you should be with anyway."

Alexis shook her head, a humorless laugh falling from her lips. "And you know the kind of guy I should be with?"

"Yes," he said, exasperated. "Someone who can give

you everything you deserve. A home. Marriage. Children. I can't do any of that."

"Why not?"

"Because I don't want to." The words burst out of him now. "Because I fell in love my first year in the military. Her name was Lyssa, and I thought I'd spend my life with her. I wanted to give all of those things, but then she died and I just can't take the chance of losing someone I love again." His breaths came out in heavy puffs.

"I'm sorry you lost someone you loved, but I'm sure she wouldn't want you to cut yourself off from the possibility of ever finding someone to spend your life with. Not if she loved you as much as I can see you loved her."

On some level, he knew what Alexis said made sense, but the pain and the grief were just too deep. "I'm sorry, Alexis. I just can't."

The sorrow in her eyes mingled with pity. "I'm going to my room," she said, avoiding looking at him. "I don't think lunch is such a good idea. I've lost my appetite."

As MUCH AS he'd wanted to be with Alexis, TJ knew he'd made the right decision in stopping where they'd been headed. She deserved more than a quick roll in the hay, and he wasn't the kind of man who did relationships. The best thing he could do for her was to keep his focus on helping her find out what really happened to Mark. They'd made some progress, but there was more to do. Going to Mark's apartment to see if they could find anything there that could be of help was next on his to-do list.

He wasn't surprised when he told Alexis of his plan to search Mark's apartment that she wanted to go with him. As angry as she might have been with him, she was determined to find the answers to the questions surrounding her brother's death. She didn't say a single word to him on the drive to the apartment, however. She wouldn't even look at him. It felt like his insides were being scooped out with a spoon, but he knew it was for the best. He had to nip the feelings building between them in the bud now before they got out of hand. As much as he wanted to kiss her and more, he couldn't change who he was.

A man who was afraid of getting his heart broken again.

Mark had rented one side of a duplex in suburban Alexandria. The duplex's owner, Mark's landlord, occupied the other side. The small yard in front of the home was well taken care of, neatly cut grass edged with a flower bed blooming with brightly colored tulips. The driveway looked as if someone had recently touched up the asphalt, and the detached garage TJ glimpsed from the front of the house looked to have been recently painted.

There was no car in the shared driveway when TJ parked at the curb and no one answered the landlord's door when he and Alexis knocked to let the man know they'd be clearing out some of Mark's things today.

Alexis's hand shook as she stuck the key into the lock on the door.

"You okay?" TJ gazed down at her. He was more than a little emotional himself. He couldn't imagine what Alexis was feeling at the moment.

But she nodded. "Yeah. It's time I do this. Mark's landlord has contacted me about getting his things. Knowing what I know now about Mark being late on the rent so much, he's actually been rather kind in not pushing me to clear out the place sooner."

They'd stopped and picked up several boxes and some packing tape on the way to Mark's house. Alexis had been all in on focusing on packing up Mark's things rather than the information Detective Chellel and Noel

Muscarelli had told them about Mark, but packing up her dead brother's things seemed to be hitting her hard now.

The small one-bedroom space was clean and functional. A long black leather sofa with colorful throw pillows faced a large wall-mounted flat-screen television and a glass-top coffee table. Two end tables, each with a porcelain lamp, flanked the sofa. A flowery tablecloth covered the dining table that separated the living room from the kitchen. Frilly curtains hung at the single large window in the living room.

"This place is freezing," Alexis said, turning up the thermostat on the wall.

She wasn't wrong about that, but still a musty odor hung in the air. TJ recognized it as the smell of a space that had sat uninhabited for too long.

"We'll warm up as we work," he said, although he elected to keep his coat on for the time being.

Alexis appeared to have the same idea, pulling the zipper on the padded vest she wore over her thick sweater higher as she ambled to the opposite side of the living room. Keeping her distance. He fought the internal push-pull of wanting her close but needing to hold her at arm's length.

"Is there somewhere you want to start?" he asked, focusing back on the task at hand.

They weren't just there to pack up Mark's things. The Mark that he and Alexis knew and the Mark that Detective Chellel and Noel Muscarelli described were so different, TJ hoped that he'd find something in his old friend's apartment that would help traverse the gulf between the two Marks. Something that would help stem the turmoil he felt. He didn't want to believe that Mark could have done what he was accused of, but Detective Chellel wasn't wrong about financial stress and substance abuse making people do things that they wouldn't otherwise do. If Mark was really in as much financial trouble as Detective Chellel said he was, maybe he'd seen stealing Nimbus as his only way out.

He knew that Alexis would never believe her brother was a thief, though. Not without irrefutable proof.

"Why don't you start by packing up Mark's clothes? I'm sure Mark wouldn't like his sister rooting around in his underwear drawer," Alexis said without looking at him. "I'll pack up the kitchen."

"Okay," TJ answered, hesitant to leave her in the room alone, although he figured that was exactly why she'd made the suggestion. "Remember to be on the lookout for anything that might help the investigation. Papers. Notes. Journals. A flash drive."

Alexis frowned, but nodded.

TJ headed into Mark's room. A mattress and box spring sat on a metal frame, no headboard, with a blue comforter and another bunch of throw pillows covering it. The same frilly curtains from the living room hung on the window in the bedroom.

The closet door stood open. Although Mark may have lived simply in most respects, TJ wasn't surprised to see the closet packed full of clothes. Clothes had always been one area where Mark liked to indulge. His favorite saying was "the clothes make the man."

"Alexis, you should see this," he called, moving over to the nightstand beside the bed.

He picked up a framed photo and turned as Alexis entered the room.

"What is it?"

TJ nodded at the photo in his hand. "Didn't you say Mark and Jessica broke up? Why would he keep her photo by the bed?"

Her hand brushed against his as he handed the photo to her. A charge of desire sparked in him. He met her gaze and found desire that matched his own there. Despite everything he'd said earlier, the attraction between them was undeniable. If she was anyone other than Mark's sister...

Alexis stepped back, taking the photo with her, and looked down at it. When she looked at him again, the moment had passed.

"I don't know," she said. "If she and Mark were still together, where is she? She wasn't at his funeral, and I haven't heard from her."

"That's a good question and one we'll definitely want—"

TJ was interrupted by the sound of glass shattering in the living room, followed by a thundering whoosh.

He ran out into the hall.

Fire raced up the curtains and along the cheap carpeting covering the floor. The gaping hole in the window was evidence of the fire's origin. Someone had thrown a Molotov cocktail through the window.

The sound of more glass shattering and a crash sent him racing back into Mark's bedroom.

A second firebomb had come through the bedroom window, landing on the bed and engulfing it in flames.

Alexis crouched on the floor near the closet, her hands covering her head.

"Alexis! Are you okay?"

She looked up at him from her crouched position. "I ducked," she said, her voice shaky. "It...it just missed me."

"We have to get out of here."

He helped her to her feet.

Thick smoke filled the apartment.

"Cover your mouth," TJ ordered, shielding his own mouth as best he could, using the sleeve of his shirt.

Alexis did the same, and together they made their way into the hallway.

The living room was nearly completely engulfed in flames now. There was no way they could reach the front door without going through the fire.

"Does this place have a rear entrance?" TJ asked, casting about for another means of getting out.

Alexis coughed. "No."

TJ glanced back at the bedroom. The window in the room was big enough for them to get out of, but the fire had totally engulfed the bed and it was far closer to the window than he would have liked when making an escape.

There was only one other possibility.

"In here."

TJ pulled Alexis into the bathroom and shut the door behind them. He grabbed one of the two towels from the towel rack on the wall and stuffed it under the door. He wet the second towel and handed it to Alexis. "Use that to cover your face."

"What about you?" Alexis asked, doing as he told her.

TJ studied the window above the bathroom sink. "I'm going to work on getting us out of here."

He hopped up on the countertop and flicked the latch on the window. It opened, but when he tried pulling the windowpane open, it wouldn't budge. It had been painted over at some point.

He had to get that window open. Hopefully, a neighbor or a passerby had already seen the smoke and flames and called the fire department, but he couldn't wait around. The fire was consuming the duplex, and he and Alexis might not have much more time before the smoke overwhelmed them. The window was their only path to safety.

He jumped off the counter and scanned the bathroom. There wasn't much that looked like it could be of any use, but maybe if he could get the towel rod off the wall.

He grabbed the towel rod and yanked. Catching onto his plan, Alexis joined him, pulling on the other end.

It took longer than he'd have liked under the circumstances, but the rod finally came away from the wall.

"Stand back," he ordered Alexis, hopping back up on the counter with the rod in his hand.

He slammed the rod into the window, shattering the glass. A few more strikes and all the glass gave way.

"Okay," he said, hopping down off the counter again. "Up you go and through the window."

Alexis gave the small opening the once-over. "I'm not sure I'll fit."

TJ placed a hand on either of her shoulders and looked her in the eye. "It's our only way out, so you'll have to."

He steadied her as she climbed on the counter. She stuck her head out of the opening, wiggling until her entire torso was out.

"I don't think I'm going to make it." Her voice floated back through the window.

TJ hopped onto the counter again and placed his hands on her bottom. "On the count of three, I'm going to push. One. Two. Three."

He shoved, and Alexis tumbled the rest of the way out of the window. He had nearly as much trouble getting out of the small window, but he finally managed to squeeze his body through.

TJ crawled away from the house toward where Alexis lay on the grass in the backyard.

"Are you okay?" he asked, scanning her body. There were visible cuts and bruises on her hands.

"I think...my arm." She clutched her right forearm.

Her vest was covered in soot, not unlike his own clothing. But it was the lower portion of her right sleeve that he noticed now. It was burned away and her usually smooth brown skin was red and raw. The second Molotov cocktail hadn't missed her after all. It must have caught the sleeve of her shirt. It was a miracle that it hadn't done more damage.

TJ swore, which led to a coughing fit. He patted his back pocket where his cell phone should be and found that it was missing. He'd probably dropped it in the chaos of trying to get out of the fire.

Luckily, he could hear sirens approaching.

Alexis groaned next to him.

He gathered her in his arms. "It's okay, baby. It's alright. Help will be here any second now."

Help was on the way, and as soon as he was sure that Alexis would be okay, he was going to find the bastard who had just tried to kill them and make him pay.

Chapter Seventeen

TJ paced the hospital waiting room.

The EMTs had allowed him to ride in the ambulance with Alexis but the nurses wouldn't let him go any further than the emergency room waiting area. That had been more than an hour earlier, and no one was giving him any information about Alexis's condition. He was getting desperate.

Alexis's burns had looked serious.

He should have moved faster. Been paying more attention to whether or not they were being followed. All his bravado from the hours before was gone, leaving nothing but guilt and regret for having taken on a case he was utterly unqualified to handle.

He'd spent the last hour beating himself up for not having anticipated the second firebomb. It galled him to admit it, but the truth was that he was in way over his head. The most important thing to him was that Alexis be kept safe, and he knew now that he wasn't the man who could make that happen. As soon as he was sure Alexis was okay, he was going to turn her case over to Shawn or another West operative with more experience in dangerous, complex cases.

The doors to the ER opened and Detective Chellel strode into the waiting room.

"Roman! What the hell have you and Miss Douglas gotten yourselves into?"

"We haven't gotten ourselves into anything," TJ responded, facing the detective down. "Someone tried to kill us."

"You had no business being at Mark Douglas's place. The arson inspector tells me the entire space is a loss."

"Alexis had every right to be there. It's her brother's place, and we were there packing up his things."

"Right," Chellel scoffed. "Packing. And snooping, no doubt. You don't think we scoured every inch of that place before we released it?"

TJ fisted his hands on his hips. "Well, then you don't have to worry. We'll find anything you missed."

Detective Chellel let out a long, slow breath. "I'm not here to fight with you. How is Miss Douglas?"

TJ ran a shaky hand over his head. "I don't know. No one has told me anything since they took her in the back. Her arm was burned pretty badly."

"She's tough. I know that for a fact. She'll be okay."

Alexis was tough, but that did nothing to keep him from worrying about her.

"The officer who took your statements at the scene gave me a brief rundown on what happened, but I'd like to hear the details from you if I could."

The detective led him to a bank of chairs, and they sat.

"We went to Mark's place to pack up some of his things, but also to look around, see if we could find anything that might point toward someone other than Mark as the thief."

"And did you find anything?"

"We weren't in the apartment long enough to find anything before the first firebomb came through the window."

Detective Chellel pulled a small notebook from her purse. "And that was the one that was thrown into the living room, correct?"

"Yes, a Molotov cocktail came through the living room window and about thirty seconds later, a second bomb was thrown through the bedroom window."

Detective Chellel took notes. "And you and Miss Douglas didn't see anyone before the fire broke out. No movement outside the windows? The sounds of someone prowling around outside?"

"No. Nothing, but I was…distracted," he conceded.

"Distracted?" Chellel gave him a knowing look.

There was no way he was going to confirm what she appeared to be thinking, so he told a half truth. "I'd just found a photo of Mark's ex-girlfriend next to his bed. Alexis believed that Mark and Jessica had broken up, so we were surprised to see the photo."

Detective Chellel flipped back several pages in her notebook. "Jessica Castaldo. I spoke to her. She said that she and Mark had an on-again, off-again relationship that was off when he died."

TJ arched his brow. "Are you sure Mark knew that? It would be strange for him to have kept a photo of a woman who wasn't his girlfriend next to his bed."

Chellel looked thoughtful. "I'll have another chat with her, but I'm not sure it relates to the attack on you and Miss Douglas today."

Detective Chellel was stubborn. But so was he. "This is your case too?"

"Someone burns down the house of my suspect in a major theft. Yeah, it's my case."

"At least you acknowledge it's related," TJ mumbled.

"Look, Mr. Roman, I know you and Miss Douglas don't think much of my investigative skills, but I know my job and I'm good at it. I told you earlier that I've always had my suspicions that Mark Douglas had an accomplice. The attacks on you and Miss Douglas support that theory."

TJ shook his head. "But you still think Mark was involved?"

"The evidence is the evidence."

The doors to the waiting room slid open again. A woman in blue scrubs with a surgical mask dangling from one ear stepped into the room, her eyes scanning the seats. "Mr. Roman?"

"Here." TJ raised his hand as if he was in school, his heart rate picking up speed.

"Miss Douglas is asking for you. If you'll follow me."

TJ looked at the detective.

"Go ahead." She waved him away. "I know where to find you if I have any more questions."

He followed the nurse down a long, bright hallway until they reached a curtained-off section. The nurse pulled the curtain back.

His breath caught in his chest when he saw her. Alexis reclined on the bed, her eyes closed. She wore a hospital gown and the lower part of her right arm was heavily bandaged.

She opened her eyes as he made his way to her bedside. "Hi."

"Hi, you. How are you feeling?"

"A little groggy. They gave me the good stuff to take the edge off."

He took the hand on her unbandaged arm and pressed a kiss to her knuckles. "I'm so sorry."

She reached up and ran her hand over his jaw. "You have nothing to be sorry for. You didn't set Mark's place on fire."

"I should have been paying more attention. I should have anticipated the second Molotov cocktail."

"You can't blame yourself."

Maybe she didn't blame him, but he could definitely blame himself.

"I'm going to turn the case over to Shawn. I don't know what I'm doing and I'd never forgive myself if something happened to you because of that. Mark would never forgive me."

"No." Alexis struggled to get into a more upright position.

"Hey, hey, take it easy." He helped her sit up.

"Listen to me. I need you. Not Shawn West or anyone else. I need you to do this. You knew Mark and loved him as much as I did, but you also saw the flaws that I couldn't. I trust you to tell me if my love for him is getting in the way of my objectivity. No one else can do that."

The nurse who'd brought him to Alexis appeared around the curtain. "I'm sorry. Miss Douglas needs to rest. The doctor is going to keep her overnight. You can come back tomorrow."

Alexis gripped his arm. "Please, TJ. Think about what I said. I need you."

He bent and pressed a featherlight kiss to her lips.

He'd think about what she'd asked of him. But he'd do what he thought was best.

TJ WAS TORN. Alexis had been discharged from the hospital the next morning. He'd gotten her settled at the safe house then made a quick run to the grocery store, loading up on food for them with the intention on staying in for the next day or two so she could rest and heal.

He hadn't stopped thinking about what she'd said about needing him to stay on the case. After a lot of back and forth with himself, he'd decided to stick it out on the condition that she spend the morning resting, which she had. But as morning changed to early afternoon, Alexis began to push for them to get back to investigating.

He thought the best thing for her would be to stay in bed and rest. But he also didn't want to waste any more time before speaking to Lenora Kenda. Still, he didn't feel comfortable leaving Alexis alone. Not that it seemed to matter. Alexis made it clear that the decision wasn't his to make. She'd insisted that she was fine and that she couldn't take any more rest. They'd spent some time compiling as much information as possible on Lenora Kenda and planning how they'd go about interviewing her since she was clearly avoiding them. They settled on an unannounced visit to her home and figured since she was a mom, the best time to catch her would be around dinnertime.

Lenora Kenda lived in a modest craftsman-style home in a middle-class neighborhood. The background search he'd done on Mark's assistant revealed that she was a single mother of two. That made the extended vacation Nelson Bacon had said she'd taken more than a little suspect to TJ's mind. Single mothers tended to save their vacation days for things like sick kids, snow days off of school, and other unexpected kid-related events. Based on the lights blazing in the windows of the house, Lenora was taking a staycation.

TJ climbed out of the car and rounded the hood to the passenger side. He scanned the street, looking for signs of anyone who didn't belong. He'd been equally vigilant on the drive to the Kenda home, twisting through less-traveled residential streets to make sure they weren't being followed. He hadn't seen anyone, but given the lengths Alexis's pursuers had already gone through to get to her, he wasn't under any illusions that they'd stop until she dropped her investigation. Since Alexis had made it clear that she had no intention of doing that, he had to step up his game and do everything he could to protect her.

He helped Alexis out of the car and they climbed the stairs onto the wide porch that wrapped around the front of the Kenda home. TJ rang the doorbell, and he and Alexis waited more than a minute before the curtain on the side window was pulled back. A blonde woman with a bob haircut and the same green eyes TJ had seen in the photo that had been in the background report on Lenora Kenda peered out at them.

"Can I help you?" Lenora asked, suspicion ringing in her voice. She was wearing a blue cardigan over a white shirt, black pants and well-worn slippers.

"Ms. Kenda? My name is Alexis Douglas. Mark was my brother. I was hoping I could ask you a few questions."

"Who is he?" Lenora said. Her skittish gaze shifted from Alexis to TJ and back again.

"This is TJ Roman." Alexis gestured toward him. "He's a friend, and he also knew my brother. He's helping me sort out the events leading up to Mark's death. I'm hoping you can help us."

Lenora disappeared from the window. Seconds later, the door opened a crack. "I already talked to the police."

"I know," Alexis said, "but I'm not sure the police are on the right track."

Lenora glanced back inside the house nervously. "It's a school night and the kids have homework." She started to close the door.

Alexis put out a hand, stopping the door from closing. "Please. Mark always spoke highly of you. This will only take a few minutes."

Lenora hesitated for several moments longer. "Okay, but just for a few minutes." She moved aside so they could step inside. The house had a warm, cozy, lived-in feel. Shoes lined the wall by the door and a table next to the stairs was littered with unopened mail, keys and a black leather purse. A formal dining room was to the right of the front door, and TJ could see the kitchen down a hall at the rear of the house. Classical music floated from the back of the house.

A preteen girl with blonde hair the same shade as Lenora's but that hung down past her shoulders stepped out of the kitchen. "Mom?"

"It's okay, sweetheart. These people just want to ask me some questions about my boss."

The preteen let out a put-upon sigh. "The police again? What was this guy, some kind of uber-criminal?"

"Annie, please. Go finish up dinner with your sister and then help her get started on her homework."

Annie sighed again but flounced back into the kitchen.

"Sorry about that." Lenora led them into the living room. "Whoever said the terrible twos are the worst should wait until those toddlers become preteens."

The room was dominated by a large blue sectional that faced an entertainment system. The walls held framed family photos starting with Lenora, with a man TJ assumed was her husband and a baby who must have been Annie. The photos progressed to show a family of four. Lenora's background report showed that she'd divorced her husband five years earlier. The most recent photos showed Lenora flanked by her two girls alone.

Lenora gestured toward the comfortable sectional.

TJ took a seat next to Alexis on one end and Lenora sat on the other end.

"You're a difficult woman to get a hold of," TJ began.

Lenora shifted nervously on the sofa. "Yes, well, I am sorry about not returning your calls. With work and the girls, I get very busy at times."

"We spoke with Nelson Bacon and Arnold Forrick and they said you were taking some vacation time."

"I... I needed time. Mark's death is a lot to process. I'm sure you two of all people understand being his sister and friend."

"It has been a difficult time. That's why I'm here. Trying to make sense of it. Ms. Kenda—"

"Please, you can call me Lenora."

"Lenora." Alexis smiled. "I don't think Mark stole anything and there's no way he committed suicide."

Lenora shook her head. "I only know what the police told me."

"Did you notice anything strange or out of the ordinary in the days or weeks before the theft?" TJ asked. They needed details, specifics that could lead them to the person who had Nimbus now and who had most likely attacked them.

"No. Nothing." Lenora's gaze skipped away to the wall of photos.

"You're lying," TJ barked, sending Lenora jumping in her seat.

He might have gone easier on Mark's assistant if she hadn't been avoiding speaking to them. It was obvious the woman knew more than what she was saying, and he was losing his patience.

"I'm not. I don't know anything."

Alexis scooted forward on the sofa. "You worked with my brother every day for more than five years. You spent more time with him than I did. Do you think he stole the Nimbus program from TalCon with the intention of selling it on the black market?"

Lenora clenched her hands together. "The police say—"

"I know what the police are saying. I want to know what you think."

Torment flashed across Lenora's face. "I have children."

"Is someone threatening you?" TJ asked.

Lenora nodded.

TJ softened his tone. "Lenora, we will keep you safe. I promise you, but we need to know what you know."

A tear slid down Lenora's face, and her hands shook. "I didn't know what I was seeing."

Alexis covered the woman's hands with her own. "What did you see?"

"One night several months ago, I left my cell phone at the office. It was a Friday night, and the girls were going to have a sleepover at a friend's house. After I dropped them off, I went back to the office to get my phone."

TJ wanted to hurry her along but knew it would be counterproductive, so he dipped into his storeroom of patience.

"I saw a man in Mark's office at his computer," she answered softly.

"Did you recognize him?"

"No. I didn't know him, but when I asked what he was doing, he said he was from the IT department and that he was just installing some updates to the computer," she said, her eyes darting around the room evasively.

"But you were suspicious," Alexis said.

"He looked the part, button-down shirt, khakis, wire-rimmed glasses. Even had a pocket protector in his shirt pocket. But it just felt like something wasn't right, you know? I'm not very computer savvy, so I've interacted with most of the people in IT at some point or another. So there was no reason for me to think much of it…"

"Until…" TJ pressed. Lenora's body language screamed that there was something she was holding back.

"The next day I took myself out for brunch before I had to pick up the girls. The man from Mark's office sat down at my table. The IT nerd was long gone. He was in all black and he looked…scary. He asked if I'd told anyone I'd seen him that night in Mark's office, and when I said no, he said if I told anyone, my daughters would have a very bad accident. He threatened my daughters. And then after Mark was accused of stealing the program, the man came back."

"You saw him a third time?"

"He came to my house. With Annie." Lenora's shoulders shook from crying now. "She'd biked to her friend's house and the chain had broken on the way back. He offered her a ride and thank God she knew better than to get in the car with a strange man, but she didn't see any harm when he offered to walk with her to make sure she got home safe. It was only a few blocks but…"

TJ knew the distance wasn't the point. Terror was. A mother's children were always her soft spot. "He wanted to make sure you knew he could get to you and the girls."

Lenora glanced over her shoulder toward the back of the house. They could hear the girls talking in the kitchen. "He reminded me not to do anything foolish. That I had better keep my mouth shut."

"And you did," Alexis said. "You didn't tell Detective Chellel any of this?"

"No. I… I couldn't risk it." Lenora collapsed her hands together in a death grip.

"Not even when Mark was under suspicion? When he died and the police called it a suicide?"

Lenora met Alexis's angry gaze with a direct one of her own. "You don't have any children, do you? I'm sorry about Mark, but I don't know if the accusations against him are true or not. Even if I did, you can't expect me to risk my children."

Alexis scowled. "Is that why you've been on an extended vacation?"

"Yes. I don't know who the man is or how he got into TalCon, but I don't feel safe there anymore. I'm pretty sure I'm going to look for a new job, but the company is being very generous, allowing me to take as much time off as I need in light of Mark's death."

"Mom?" Annie poked her head around the corner of the wall. "Are you okay?"

Lenora wiped her eyes. "I'm fine, honey. Just a little sad about my boss. Remember, I told you he passed away. This is his sister."

"Yeah, ah, I'm sorry about your brother." Annie shifted from one foot to the other.

"We'll be through here in just a minute. If you've finished your homework, you can have a little TV time."

Annie hesitated for a long moment, unsure if she should leave her mother before disappearing back into the kitchen.

"We just need a few more minutes of your time. Can you describe the man who threatened you?" TJ asked.

"Um…he was tall, over six feet. White guy with dark hair."

"Any distinguishing marks? Maybe a tattoo?"

Lenora nodded. "He had a tattoo on his neck. A coiled snake ready to strike." A small shiver stole through her body.

"Lenora, this is really important. I need you to think back. What day, exactly, was it that you saw this man in Mark's office?"

Lenora squeezed her hands together tighter still and

looked at them woefully. TJ knew what she was going to say before she said it. "It was exactly one week before Mark was accused of stealing the program."

Chapter Eighteen

Alexis insisted on heading to the police station to share the information that Lenora Kenda had given them with Detective Chellel. It felt like they had finally gotten a break that might help them prove Mark's innocence, but TJ seemed almost reticent about the turn in their investigation.

"Hey, this is great news. Why aren't you happier about it?"

"I am happy. Lenora's statement gives Detective Chellel someone to look at for the theft other than Mark and that is great."

"So why the frowny face? What are you thinking?"

"There was something she wasn't telling us. It was something in her body language. She wouldn't look either of us in the eye when she answered certain questions, and she was so nervous."

"Maybe," Alexis said, recalling Lenora's actions as she answered their questions. "But with the threats that guy made against her and her kids, she had reason to be scared. That could be all it was."

"It's possible."

But Alexis could tell TJ didn't think fear was all it was. If Lenora knew more, they could get it out of her later. For now, they had a place to start with the information she had given them.

The detective had dismissed Alexis's assertions that Mark couldn't be the thief before, but now Detective Chellel would have to take her seriously. Lenora's statement proved that someone other than Mark had been at this computer station at the time the Nimbus program was downloaded.

Once again, they gave their names to the clerk at the reception desk. TJ's phone beeped with an incoming text while they were waiting for an escort to take them back to meet with Detective Chellel.

"What is it?" Alexis asked.

"Shawn," he answered his eyes still on the phone. "He got an address for Jessica."

The heavy doors leading beyond the station's reception area opened and a uniformed cop barked at them to follow him to the conference room. Detective Chellel was already waiting for them when they arrived.

"Miss Douglas." Detective Chellel rose from her seat at the table when TJ and Alexis entered. "I was just about to contact you."

"Detective, we have new information for you. TJ and I have just come from speaking to Lenora Kenda."

Detective Chellel looked surprised. "Mark Douglas's assistant."

"The very one," TJ said.

"Sit." Detective Chellel waved them toward chairs.

Alexis ignored her. She was too excited to sit. "Lenora Kenda saw someone, not Mark, at Mark's desk, on his computer on the night the Nimbus program had been illegally downloaded. She described the man to us."

TJ broke in then, relaying to Detective Chellel the concise description that they'd gotten from Lenora.

Detective Chellel frowned. "Hang on a minute. What were you two doing talking to Lenora Kenda?"

Alexis fisted her hands on her hips. "We were doing what you couldn't or wouldn't. Looking for the truth about what happened to my brother."

Detective Chellel let out a breath that was half sigh, half growl. "Ms. Douglas—"

"May I suggest," TJ spoke up, "that you listen to what we have to say first? Then you can dress us down however you'd like."

Detective Chellel's eyes narrowed in on TJ, her frown deepening into a scowl. "Fine. Tell me what you know," she said finally.

"On the night Mark supposedly stole Nimbus, Lenora Kenda saw a man she didn't recognize working at his computer. She'd gone back to the office because she'd forgotten her cell phone. She said the man said he was upgrading the computer system, but she found the situation suspicious."

"If she found this man suspicious, why didn't she say something when I questioned her after the theft or after your brother's death?"

"She was scared," TJ said. "She said that the day after she saw the man, he showed up at the restaurant where she was having brunch and threatened her children if she told anyone what she saw."

Detective Chellel swore. "I need to speak to her again."

"You need to look for this man she saw. He's the one who stole Nimbus, and he probably killed my brother."

Detective Chellel sighed heavily. "I will follow up with Ms. Kenda." She gestured again toward a chair. "Ms. Douglas, please sit down. There is something I need to speak with you about."

Alexis had expected more of a fight to get Detective Chellel to listen. The detective giving in so easily sent a shot of nerves through her. She caught a look from TJ. He also seemed to sense something was up.

She swayed on her feet. TJ's arm wrapped around her waist and he guided her into a seat before sitting in the chair next to her.

Detective Chellel opened a manila folder Alexis hadn't noticed lying on the table. The detective scanned the top sheet of what appeared to be several sheets stapled together before looking up at them again. "We got the complete toxicology report back. There was diazepam in your brother's system, but not enough to kill him. It appears the undigested pills he took were the only pills ingested."

Alexis's mind churned in confusion. "What does that mean?"

"It means someone wanted us to think Mark overdosed on Valium. They might have forced him to take a few pills, or maybe they just waited until he'd taken them himself. But that wasn't what killed him. The toxicology report showed that Mark had over fifteen hundred micrograms of fentanyl in his system."

Alexis's stomach dropped to her toes. She felt TJ's hand wrap around hers and hold on tight.

"No! Mark was a drinker, sometimes a heavy one, yes, but he'd never use drugs."

"We know," Detective Chellel said. "We don't think your brother introduced the fentanyl into his system voluntarily. Since the medical examiner is sure there were no injection marks on Mark's body, we believe the drug was introduced orally or nasally when your brother was unconscious." Detective Chellel closed her file. "I'm very sorry."

Hot tears rolled down Alexis's cheeks. She glared at Detective Chellel. "I told you Mark wouldn't have committed suicide."

"I had to follow the evidence." Chellel had the grace to look away from Alexis as she spoke. "Just like I will do now. I will follow up with Ms. Kenda and on the information we've obtained from this report to see if I can trace where these drugs came from. We know the diazepam was prescribed by Mark's primary care physician. Do you have any idea who would know he was taking the drug?"

"No." Alexis wiped at her eyes. "I mean, he didn't even tell me he was on medication. Maybe his on-again, off-again girlfriend Jessica?"

Detective Chellel shook her head. "She said she didn't know about the diazepam. Of course, I'll be talking to her again."

"Maybe Lenora Kenda," TJ offered. "In my experience, secretaries and assistants typically know more about the people they work for than those people think."

Detective Chellel's brow rose to her hairline. "You have a point there. I'll ask her about it."

"What's next?" Alexis asked Detective Chellel.

"Next, I will continue to do my job and investigate this case." The detective's answer was pointed. "You and Mr. Roman have been a big help." The detective struggled to get that last sentence out. "But as you are quite aware, this case is proving dangerous. We have someone out there who isn't afraid of killing people in order to sell this Nimbus program. You two need to back off. Leave this to law enforcement to handle."

Alexis almost responded that if she and TJ hadn't started their own investigation, Detective Chellel and her department would be even further behind in their investigation of Mark's death than they currently were. The detective had wasted weeks investigating the case as a suicide as a result of the theft. Who knew what evidence had been lost in those weeks?

TJ squeezed her hand and Alexis took it as a sign she shouldn't say what she'd been thinking. She stayed silent.

"Thank you for keeping us updated on the case," TJ said, standing as if ready to leave. "I hope we can count on you to continue to keep us in the loop as the case progresses."

Alexis rose along with Detective Chellel.

"I'll do what I can." The detective's tone was non-committal.

Alexis and TJ said their goodbyes to the detective and made their way back to the parking garage.

Inside the car, Alexis broke down.

TJ held her close, whispering in her ear that everything would be okay until the storm of emotion passed.

After several minutes, she slid out of his arms. "Sorry. It's just, I knew my brother would never kill himself and when Detective Chellel finally said she believed that too…"

"You have nothing to feel sorry for. With everything you've been through in the last several weeks… I'm amazed at your strength."

TJ started the SUV and pointed them toward the safe house.

"Are you going to do what the detective said and leave the investigating to the cops now?" he asked after several minutes of driving in silence.

"No way," Alexis scoffed. "I'm hopeful that the detective will have a more open mind now that she knows for a fact that Mark was murdered, but she's bungled this investigation from the beginning. I'm not ready to put my faith in her now."

"Me either. So you're thinking what I'm thinking then. We keep moving forward in our own investigation."

Alexis gazed up at her brother's best friend and the

man she'd fallen hard for. "I'm not stopping until Mark's name is completely cleared and we prove he was murdered."

"So, WHAT'S OUR next step?" Alexis asked.

"Our conversation with Detective Chellel reminded me that we still need to talk to Jessica Castaldo. I say we drop in on her and see what she can tell us."

"Sounds good."

"Her address is on my phone." TJ jerked his head toward his phone in the cup holder in the center console. "Could you get it for me?" He gave Alexis his password, and she checked it out on the screen. A moment later, they had the address plugged into the phone's GPS system and were on their way.

"It feels like we're finally making some progress at least," Alexis said soberly. "I know Detective Chellel doesn't believe Mark wasn't involved in the theft yet, but now that we know he didn't kill himself..." The rest of what she was about to say was swallowed by a sob.

TJ reached across the console and took her hand in his, squeezing it. "Hey, take a breath. You've been dealing with a lot. Should I pull over?"

With her free hand, she swiped at the tears falling from her eyes. "No, no. We need to talk to Jessica and I don't want to waste any more time. It just finally hit me that if Mark didn't commit suicide, that means he was murdered."

TJ had wondered when that revelation would finally sink in, and now that it had, he felt she was strong enough to deal with it. He would help her any way he could.

He glanced in the rearview mirror and spotted a large black SUV speeding toward them. He changed lanes, but the SUV changed lanes with him.

TJ pressed down on the accelerator and the car moved forward faster.

"What's wrong?" Alexis asked, fear edging her words.

"We're being followed. The black SUV behind us has been following for the last several miles."

Alexis twisted in her seat so she could get a look at the car through the rearview window. She reported that the driver was male with dark hair, but the glare from the sun kept her from seeing much more detail.

The SUV behind them sped up and rammed into their car. TJ fought to keep their rental on the road and avoid hitting the car in the lane next to them. He stomped down on the accelerator and the car lurched forward.

"He's crazy. He's gonna get us killed."

"I think that's his plan," TJ said, keeping his eyes on the road in front of him.

The SUV hit their car again, sending the rental skidding across the road. Thankfully, there was not another car next to them, but that didn't stop the horns from the surrounding cars from blaring. Hopefully, one of the other drivers was calling the police and getting help. But until help arrived, they were going to have to try to outrun the SUV.

The SUV slammed into the back of the sedan a third time. This time the car spun, clipping the rear bumper of a pickup truck before TJ got control of the car again. Unfortunately, they were facing the wrong way on the highway.

Car horns blared as the other drivers swerved to avoid hitting them. TJ punched the car forward and turned the wheel so that they did a 180-degree turn and faced the right way again. The engine roared as he raced down the pavement and attempted to get away from the SUV.

"Can you reach your phone?" TJ asked. "Call for help."

Alexis reached toward the passenger floor for her purse between her feet, but before she could grab it, the SUV hit them again and she lurched forward, barely managing to keep her chest from slamming against the dashboard.

A loud pop ricocheted around the interior of the car.

"What was that?" Alexis exclaimed in a voice laden with panic.

TJ's gaze went to the rearview mirror, and he swore. "He's shooting at us."

Another round of gunshots sounded, joining the cacophony of car horns from the other drivers on the road.

Another loud pop and the back of the car fishtailed.

"He shot out our tire," TJ yelled, fighting to regain control of the car, to no avail.

They clipped the side of a BMW, and then they were tumbling. Over and over until the car came to a stop on its roof, the passenger side door smashed against the side of an old oak tree.

TJ groaned and turned his head slowly to look at her. "Alexis, are you OK? Baby, are you hurt?"

She seemed to take stock of her body. "I'm OK. How about you?"

There was an angry red scratch just above TJ's eyebrow. "I'm fine. But my seat belt is jammed."

Alexis pressed the release button on her seat belt, but it would not give. "My belt is stuck too." She looked up from the belt and gasped. "TJ, he's coming." She pointed at the driver's side window.

The driver from the SUV, clad in all black, marched toward them with a silver pistol in his right hand. "We have to get out of here!"

She pressed frantically at the seat belt release, but the buckle held fast.

TJ tried reaching for his ankle. "I can't reach my gun."

Suddenly, the man stopped and glanced over his shoulder. It took a moment before TJ realized why, but then the sound of sirens reached his ears. The SUV driver looked back at them, pure venom in his eyes, before spinning around and running back toward the highway.

Alexis let out a breath.

"He's gone," TJ said.

The sound of the sirens grew closer until they were almost deafening. They could see red and blue swirls at the top of the incline that led back to the highway.

"He's gone, but I recognized him, TJ."

"You recognized him?"

"Yes. That was the man who killed my brother."

Chapter Nineteen

Two police cruisers and an ambulance crowded the breakdown lane that ran along the side of the highway. The sun had already fallen below the horizon, leaving the sky a dusky blue color. A tow truck had arrived only moments earlier to pull their rental car out of the ditch, limiting the drivers on the road to a single lane. The traffic passed by slowly, the drivers shooting curious glances at the commotion on the side of the road.

TJ and Alexis sat between the open back doors of the ambulance. TJ had a gash along his right shoulder from where his seat belt had dug into his skin. The EMTs wanted him to go to the hospital to get it stitched up, but he declined. He'd had far worse injuries and, at the moment, he had bigger issues to attend to than a gash on his shoulder.

He wasn't surprised when a black, unmarked police car screeched to a stop behind the ambulance and Detective Chellel sprung from the car.

"What the hell have you two gotten yourselves into now?" Detective Chellel demanded.

Alexis frowned. "We're both fine, Detective. Thanks for your concern."

"Why should I be concerned for your safety when

clearly neither of you are," the detective growled. "Now, what's going on here?"

"We were forced off the road," TJ said.

"And shot at," Alexis added.

"Did you get a good look at your assailant?" the detective asked.

"I can tell you he drove a black SUV with no license plates." TJ waved away the EMT, who was still fussing with the scratch on his shoulder and shrugged back into his coat.

Alexis stood. "It was the same guy Lenora Kenda saw in Mark's office. The same guy who threatened her."

"How can you be sure of that?" Detective Chellel's tone was infused with skepticism. "I thought you didn't recognize the description of the man she'd given you?"

"I didn't. But the man who forced us off the road and shot at us had a tattoo of a snake crawling up the right side of his neck. I saw it when he ran back to the SUV when he heard the police sirens."

Detective Chellel's expression was still skeptical. "So you're thinking it was the same guy?"

Alexis threw up her hands. "How many guys with snake tattoos on their neck do you think are after us?"

"I'm learning not to underestimate you two," Detective Chellel said with more than a hint of derision.

TJ stepped between the two women. "OK, ladies, we're on the same team here." He looked at the detective. "I checked the car for trackers. There were none. I think Mr. Snake followed us from Lenora Kenda's house. He must have gotten spooked when he saw us go into the police station. He's getting desperate. Running us off the road and shooting at us in broad daylight with multiple witnesses was reckless."

Detective Chellel signaled to one of the uniformed officers.

The officer headed their way.

"I'll send a car to Ms. Kenda's house to make sure everything is OK there." Detective Chellel gave the officer his orders before turning back to Alexis and TJ. "You two should go to the hospital to get checked out."

TJ shot a look at Alexis, who shook her head. "We'll be OK. I think the best thing for us right now would be to go home and let me do my job."

"The best thing you can do for me right now, Detective Chellel, is to find the man who attacked us and killed my brother. The best thing you can do for me…" Alexis pressed her hands to her chest and gave the detective an angry glare, "is to do your job."

Detective Chellel sighed. "I know you've just been through a traumatic accident, you're upset and frustrated, but you should know I'm doing everything I can to find out who killed your brother and who is after you now."

"What are you doing standing here, then?" Alexis gestured toward the highway and the traffic that was crawling by. "We gave you a description of the guy and his car. Why aren't you out there looking for him before he tries something like this again? Or worse."

Detective Chellel's expression darkened. "Ms. Douglas, go home. Rest. Stay out of my way." The detective turned on her heel and marched away.

Alexis turned to TJ, her eyes still simmering with anger and frustration. "She wouldn't be anywhere without the information that we got for her. Now she wants us to go home and rest?" Alexis's voice shook with indignation. "With the way she's bungled the investigation so far, we'll never get answers leaving it to her and the police department."

TJ wrapped an arm around Alexis's shoulder. He didn't disagree with Alexis's assessment of the situation, but Detective Chellel wasn't wrong, either. At least not about them both needing to rest. Being driven off the road? Wouldn't leave any lasting damage, but they would soon have new bruises to add to their growing collection of injuries, and he was sure they both would be sore come morning. He also wanted to talk the latest turn of events over with Shawn and make a plan for the next steps. On a scale of dangerousness, they just jumped up several rungs, and TJ was no longer sure it was safe for Alexis to continue to help him with this investigation. But that was a discussion he wanted to have with her when her emotions weren't running so high.

"Detective Chellel is right about us getting some rest. It's getting late, and we both need to recharge and create a plan for the next steps."

For a moment, it looked as if Alexis was going to argue with him, but then her shoulders slumped forward, a sign of resignation.

When she looked up at him again, her eyes were filled with weariness. "You're not giving up on me, are you?"

He met her gaze directly, hoping she would see the resolve in his eyes. "Never. Let's go talk to Jessica Castaldo."

Chapter Twenty

Detective Chellel assigned a patrolman to take them back to the safe house. Alexis knew there was no way TJ was going to allow anyone, not even a police officer, knowledge of the safe house's location, so she wasn't surprised when he asked the cop to drop them off at the nearest rental car location. This car rental company wasn't the same one they'd used at the airport, which was probably for the best since the car they'd rented at the airport was currently being pulled out of a ditch.

Once they were back on the road, TJ called Shawn and gave him a status update. Shawn agreed to take care of the paperwork hassle that was sure to arise out of their being forced off the road and reminded TJ to call if he needed backup.

The address they had for Jessica led them to a newish high-rise apartment building not far from the Potomac River waterfront.

TJ found a parking garage a half block away, and they walked back to the building, stopping for a moment when they reached the entrance and looking up.

"This is definitely a step up from Mark's duplex and her apartment. Jessica is a waitress. How could she afford a place like this?" Alexis asked, looking from the building to TJ.

"Didn't she move in with Mark only a couple of weeks after they started dating?"

Alexis nodded.

"Well, maybe this isn't her place either, but that's definitely one question I want the answer to." TJ reached for the door and held it open to let Alexis enter first.

There was a reception desk, but the doorman must have been occupied elsewhere. They took the opportunity that had been handed to them and walked past the desk quickly. Their luck continued when the elevator doors opened immediately.

They stepped out of the elevator on the tenth floor and headed to Jessica's apartment.

It took several moments before the apartment door was opened, but when it was, Mark's former flame stood before them in colorful leggings and an oversize T-shirt with the collar cut off. The shirt hung off one shoulder, revealing the smooth, tan skin of one of Jessica's shoulders. Surprise darkened her green eyes.

"Alexis, what a nice surprise." The tone of Jessica's voice didn't match the words. She wasn't at all happy to see them on her doorstep.

Alexis flashed a tight smile at her brother's former girlfriend. "Hi, Jessica. Sorry to drop in on you like this, but I wondered if you have a moment to talk?"

Jessica tipped her head to the side, her expression curious. "Sure, I guess." Her eyes swept over TJ appraisingly, lighting a spark of jealousy in Alexis.

"I'm sure you remember TJ," Alexis said. "He's helping me sort out a few details."

Jessica flashed a sultry smile. "I don't mind at all. I remember TJ well." Jessica's smile was openly seductive and only made Alexis dislike her more.

Jessica held the door open for them to enter.

The apartment was open space, almost loft like, and roomy. She had no idea what the place rented for, but it was clear from the condition of the building and the finishes in the apartment that this was not a place a waitress could afford on her own.

Jessica waved them toward a large black leather sectional sofa, taking a seat herself on one end, while he and Alexis sat on the other side.

"So you said you're sorting out some details?" Jessica asked. "I assume about Mark."

"Yes," Alexis answered. "I know Detective Chellel has already spoken to you about Mark. The police believe that he stole from his employer."

Jessica nodded, but her eyes skated away from Alexis's. "I talked to the detective, but I want you to know that I told her that there was no way Mark stole anything."

She may not have liked Jessica, but at least they were on the same page regarding Mark's innocence. "I told Detective Chellel the same thing but, at least until recently, she seems convinced Mark stole the Nimbus program and then killed himself before he could be arrested."

Jessica glanced away. "I don't know anything about that."

Alexis slid a little closer to Jessica. "I think the police are on the wrong track, so I hired TJ. He's not only a friend of Mark's, but he's a private detective. We've been working to clear Mark's name and, well…" Alexis glanced at TJ.

"A little while ago, the detective in charge of the case informed us that Mark's death was going to be ruled a homicide," TJ said. Alexis still couldn't quite bring herself to say it out loud.

A small gasp escaped Jessica's lips, and she pressed a hand to her chest.

It felt overdone to Alexis, as if Jessica was reacting how she thought they expected her to, but not with genuine shock. "Jessica, I need you to tell me the truth. Do you know anything about the theft or what happened to Mark that you didn't tell the cops when they questioned you?"

"What? No, of course not. Why would I? Mark and I had broken up by then." Jessica squared her shoulders, but Alexis read the fear in her eyes before they darted away.

"You're lying," Alexis growled, her patience running thin.

Jessica shifted nervously on the sofa. "You can't just come into my apartment and call me a liar."

"I just did. And speaking of your apartment, how do you pay for this place? It seems way outside the budget for a waitress."

Jessica glared. "It's a sublet. Look, I'm sorry about Mark, but..."

"You're going to be a lot sorrier if you don't tell the truth," Alexis spat.

TJ interrupted. "Jessica, now that the investigation includes a homicide, you can expect the police will be paying you another visit, and I'm sure Detective Chellel is going to ask the same questions in a far less polite manner. It might be best for you if you get out ahead of this. Alexis and I will do what we can to help you."

If Jessica had a hand in Mark's death, the only help Alexis would give her would be getting her to prison, but she knew better than to say that when they needed the woman to tell them whatever she might know.

"You said that you and Mark broke up, but he still had your photo next to his bed."

Jessica shrugged, petulantly. "Okay, so we hooked up a little sometimes. It didn't mean we were headed for marriage."

"Were you hooking up with Mark around the time he was killed?" Alexis asked.

Jessica crossed her arms over her chest and nodded. "Yeah, I guess so."

She still wouldn't meet Alexis's eyes. It was clear there was something she wasn't telling them. Before Alexis could press the point, TJ spoke.

"Jessica." He reached across the sofa and laid his hand lightly on Jessica's leg. "Whatever it is you aren't saying, it will be a lot better to get it out now than to have Detective Chellel drag it out of you."

"I didn't know!" The words burst forth, opening a well of tears. TJ wrapped an arm around Jessica while she cried.

It took a few minutes before she was able to pull herself together and speak again.

"I swear I didn't know anything about a theft or that they were going to hurt Mark."

"I'm sure you didn't," TJ said soothingly.

All Alexis could think was that she was glad he was there, and that he was sitting between her and Jessica. She was more than ready to shake the truth out of the woman if that's what it took, but she marshaled her patience and let TJ take the lead on this part of the questioning, since he seemed to be getting somewhere.

"Tell us what happened so we can help you," TJ coaxed.

"A man came to the diner and asked if I could get Mark's work identification and key fob for him. I… I knew I shouldn't do it. But he offered me ten thousand dollars. Mark told me he'd help me pay rent on my new place when he broke up with me and I moved out, but he never gave me a dime. I was struggling and so mad at Mark."

Alexis opened her mouth to tell Jessica just how much

it had hurt. Her actions had likely been the catalyst for Mark's murder.

TJ spoke before her, though. "Did the man say why he wanted the ID and fob?"

Jessica shook her head. "Not really. He just said he was a friend of Mark's and he was going to play a joke on him."

Alexis couldn't stay quiet any longer. "You can't possibly have believed that."

Jessica turned a tear-filled glare onto Alexis. "I made a mistake. I needed the money." She waved a hand in the air, indicating the apartment.

Ten thousand dollars wasn't a lot when it came to renting a place like this long term, but it would buy a few months of luxury, which was apparently enough for Jessica.

"I convinced Mark we should talk about getting back together. He agreed and invited me to his place. We had a few drinks and then…" Jessica's cheeks reddened. "After he fell asleep I took the ID and fob and texted the guy to come get them. I don't know what he did with them while he had them, but he only had them for like an hour. Two at the most. He slipped them through the mail slot in Mark's door and I put them back before Mark even knew they were missing. I'm sorry, but I didn't have any choice." She sniffled.

"There's always a choice," Alexis spat.

TJ squeezed her thigh. "Can you describe the man who asked you to get Mark's ID for him?" he asked Jessica.

Jessica wiped at her eyes again. "Um…white. Average height, I guess. Dark hair and eyes. There was nothing really special about him. I mean, he wasn't a looker or anything, you know. The only thing that stood out was the tattoo on his neck." She grimaced as if she'd just bit-

ten into something sour. "I usually go for guys with tattoos, but this one, it was so creepy."

"Let me guess," Alexis said, looking from Jessica to
TJ. "A coiled snake."

"Yeah." Jessica's eyes opened wide in surprise. "How
did you know?"

Chapter Twenty-One

When she and TJ returned to the safe house, Alexis went to her room to shower and change before catching a quick power nap. Despite the renewed sense of hope she felt about clearing Mark's name, she was emotionally and physically exhausted. She only intended to lie down for a few minutes, but she awakened hours later to a darkened room.

She may have needed the sleep, but she wasn't sure how restful it had been. She'd found herself caught in a tantalizingly erotic dream starring TJ that she'd been more than a little disappointed to have awoken from. A dream that had left her libido revved and ready for the real thing.

TJ wasn't the kind of guy who stuck it out for the long term, she knew that. That didn't mean they couldn't enjoy each other's company while they were together. She'd seen the desire in his eyes more than once. She knew he wanted her. And from the way her body was humming at just the thought of taking him into her bed, she couldn't deny she wanted him just as much. She'd never thought of herself as the kind of woman who'd have a fling, but life was about trying new things. And she trusted TJ. More importantly, she wanted him. She was willing to worry about the consequences of that later.

So she was going to try one more time to make him forget his misguided loyalty or that she was Mark's sister. And if he rejected her a second time? She couldn't think about that now. Not before attempting to seduce TJ Roman.

She crossed the room to the adjoining bathroom and ran a brush through her hair. She'd napped in the oversize T-shirt that hit her mid-thigh and that she normally wore as a pajama top with panties, and nothing else. It wasn't the sexiest outfit, but it would do for an impromptu seduction.

The house was quiet when she patted down the stairs. For a moment, fear sprinted its way through her body until a familiar grunt sounded from beyond the kitchen. She found the garage door open and the lights on. TJ's feet stuck out from under the SUV. He lay on some sort of dolly, and based on the swears coming from underneath the chassis, whatever he was doing wasn't going well.

"Everything okay?" Alexis asked, stopping beside the car next to TJ.

TJ rolled himself out from under the car. His gaze blazed a trail up from her legs to her torso, and finally landed on her face.

The lust she saw in his eyes sent a surge of feminine power through her.

TJ pushed to his feet and cleared his throat. "Everything is fine. I'm just checking the car for trackers or bugs."

Alexis stepped forward, leaving only a sliver of space between them. "In case I haven't said it yet, thank you for helping me." She went onto the tips of her toes and pressed a kiss to his cheek.

She pulled back and watched as TJ swallowed hard, his Adam's apple bobbing.

"Alexis, what are you doing?"

She threaded her arms around his neck. "I think you know," she whispered in his ear, pressing her breasts against his chest.

A low moan erupted from TJ's throat and his arms came around her waist. "We shouldn't."

She pulled back again, looking into his eyes. "Why not? And don't say Mark. If you don't want me, that's one thing…"

TJ pulled her closer. She felt the hard ridge of his manhood against her thigh.

"You know I do," he growled.

"So take what you want." She feathered kisses along his neck. "What we both want."

TJ didn't move.

For a millisecond, she thought he was going to reject her.

But then he tipped his head, bringing his mouth to hers in a crushing kiss. His mouth was hot and hungry, surpassing everything she'd dreamed and imagined it would be.

She opened to him and he took the kiss deeper, pulling a moan from deep within her. She leaned forward and felt TJ's erection throb between her legs.

Her heart thundered against his chest, its beat becoming wilder and wilder the more he plundered her mouth.

Far too soon, TJ pulled away, his chest rising and falling with rapid breaths. "Are you sure? Really sure?"

She ran her bare foot up his calf. "Absolutely."

TJ took her mouth again, at the same time hoisting her up.

She wrapped her legs around his waist, and she rocked her hips against him.

He let out a low growl that ripped from his throat. "If you keep doing that, I won't be able to go slow."

She rocked again. "Who says I want you to go slow?"

TJ swung them around and walked them into the house.

He lowered her onto the sofa and made quick work of stripping her of her T-shirt and panties. Then she had the pleasure of watching him as he freed himself from his clothes.

He joined her on the sofa, his mouth covering hers again. His hands moved over her body and then he followed with his mouth.

Alexis closed her eyes and let him roam, content, ecstatic even, simply to allow herself to feel. To enjoy the feeling of TJ's mouth on her left breast, and then her right. He kissed his way down her torso to her core and brought her to an explosive climax with his mouth.

Giving her no time to catch her breath, he settled between her legs and plunged deep.

She cried out.

TJ stilled. "Am I hurting you?"

"No. Don't stop," she panted, rolling her hips and pulling him in deeper still.

He shuddered and began moving again with an urgency that had her crying out a second time as he drove her to the edge.

She opened her eyes and watched his jaw tighten as he thrust into her. It was the most erotic sight she'd ever seen, and she rose to meet each thrust, each of them driving the other higher and higher until she broke. Her back arched, and she came harder than she ever had before.

He drove into her one last time with a shudder and moaned her name.

TJ collapsed on top of her, his weight pressing her back into the sofa cushions.

She ran her hand up and down his spine.

"How do you feel?" TJ asked, his head buried in the crook of her neck.

"Pretty damn fine, thank you." She giggled.

TJ lifted his head and looked her in the eye with a wry grin on his lips. "Glad I could be of service."

Chapter Twenty-Two

TJ woke up with Alexis curled into his side. He and Alexis had reached for each other once more during the night for another passionate round of love making. His feelings in tumult, he got out of bed and showered and dressed for the day. Alexis was still asleep when he tiptoed back through the bedroom and into the kitchen, where he got a pot of coffee started and turned once again to the information they'd collected so far on Mark's case. He tried to stop the memories of making love with Alexis from consuming all his thoughts.

"TJ?"

He started at the sound of Alexis's voice.

She wrapped her arms around him from behind and dropped a kiss on his neck that sent a shiver through him. "I called your name twice. What are you reading so intently?"

"Just thinking about our next steps." He raised his head and did a quarter turn in the chair, pulling her into his lap. He captured her lips in a searing good morning kiss that left them both panting for breath by the time they pulled away from each other. They held each other for several moments.

"Good morning," he finally said.

"Good morning." Alexis beamed.

The coffee maker beeped it was ready. Alexis dropped another quick kiss on his lips before pushing to her feet. "I could use a cup. Should I pour you one too?"

"Sure. Thanks."

"I'm planning to whip up omelets for breakfast if that's alright with you?" She grabbed two coffee mugs from an overhead cabinet.

She carried two mugs of coffee to the table and sat across from him. "Umm…should we talk about what happened last night?"

"Last night was amazing," he said, looking directly into her eyes. "But I don't want to give you the wrong idea. I'm still the man who can't give you what you want."

"I don't believe that and I don't believe you do either."

He tore his gaze away from her and looked into his coffee. "Let's just focus on finding answers for Mark now, okay?"

His phone rang, cutting off her answer.

"Roman."

"Mr. Roman, this is Detective Chellel. I have to ask you and Ms. Douglas to come down to the station for some questioning immediately."

The detective's tone wasn't out-and-out hostile, but it wasn't polite either.

"Questioning about what?" TJ pressed.

"It would be better if I explained once you were here."

TJ shot a glance at Alexis, who'd paused her quest for coffee and was watching him intently now.

"Then we're at an impasse. I assume since you're making this call, you can't compel our appearance at the station and neither Alexis nor I are willing to walk into questioning without knowing what this is about and whether we should bring our lawyers with us."

He could almost feel the frustration and annoyance

emanating from the detective on the other end of the phone.

"Jessica Castaldo was found deceased in her apartment early this morning. I believe you and Miss Douglas were the last two people to see her alive. Now, will you come in voluntarily, or do I send a patrol car?"

TJ DROVE HIMSELF and Alexis to the police station. They were led to separate interrogation rooms the moment they arrived. He was brought to a bland interview room that smelled vaguely of stale beer and vomit. The uniformed officer who led him to the room offered coffee. TJ declined.

He'd also declined to bring a lawyer with him, although he'd called Shawn on the way to the station. Shawn had cautioned them both not to speak to Detective Chellel without representation and had offered to arrange for an attorney to meet them, but Alexis countered that they had nothing to hide. While he agreed that they didn't have anything to hide, Jessica had been alive and well when they left her apartment. He knew that innocence didn't always carry the day. Still, he figured it couldn't hurt to speak to the detective and get a sense of what had happened after they'd left Jessica's apartment the night before.

But he was getting annoyed at the detective's tactics. He'd been waiting in the interrogation room for more than forty minutes.

Finally, the door opened and Detective Chellel walked in. She slapped a file folder on the table between them and sat, giving TJ a long look. "What were you doing at Jessica Castaldo's apartment yesterday?"

"Alexis and I wanted to find out what she knew about Mark's death."

Chellel scowled. "I told you I'd handle things from here on out. I told you to stay out of my investigation."

TJ leaned back in his chair and folded his hands on his lap. "You have your job, Detective, and I have mine."

"Does your job include murder?"

He couldn't see any benefit in antagonizing the detective. At least, not at the moment.

"It does not and whatever happened to Jessica, neither Alexis nor I had any hand in it."

"You snuck into her building."

"We did no such thing."

Chellel snatched a sheet of paper from the file and slapped it down on the table in front of him. "The building sign-in sheet doesn't have you or Ms. Douglas signing in, and the security tapes show you rushing toward the elevators while the doorman was away from his post."

"I wouldn't call that sneaking in. You said it yourself, the doorman wasn't at his post."

Chellel eyed him with open derision. "Why don't you start from the beginning? What time did you arrive at Ms. Castaldo's apartment?"

He took the detective through the details of his and Alexis's talk with Jessica the night before. The detective let him tell the story the first time through without interruption before asking him to repeat it from the beginning. The second time through, it felt like she stopped him every ten seconds or so to ask a question or drill down on some minute detail. It didn't matter, though. The story wasn't going to change, no matter how many ways she asked the same question.

"So you're saying Jessica admitted to stealing Mark Douglas's employee ID and passing it along to someone who you think then used it to download the Nimbus program?"

"Exactly."

Chellel shook her head. "And I've only got your word about this confession."

"You have Alexis's too. I'm sure she's told you, or she will, the same things I have. We confronted Jessica, and she told us about her role in the theft. And there's your motive for why someone might want her dead."

Chellel's brow arched. "Someone like Alexis Douglas, for instance."

Now TJ shook his head. "No. Alexis doesn't have a motive. She needed Jessica alive and willing to testify to her part in the theft."

"Or," Chellel dragged out the word. "She saw Jessica's actions as having contributed to her brother's death and she sought retribution."

"Or, since we're positing theories here, the man Jessica gave Mark's ID to got spooked and decided to eliminate a potential witness."

"I wonder what could have spooked this hypothetical killer. Maybe you and Ms. Douglas mucking around in my case, perhaps?"

It was a possibility. One he couldn't help feeling a little bit of guilt over. It was entirely possible his and Alexis's visit to Jessica's apartment had led to her death, but the only thing they could do about it now was to help find her killer.

Chellel sifted through the papers in the file. "You're licensed to carry a gun, correct?"

"Correct."

"We'd like to run ballistics on your gun."

"So Jessica was shot?"

Chellel didn't answer.

"You're welcome to run whatever test you'd like. Obviously, I didn't bring a gun into the police station."

"I can have a uniformed officer follow you to wherever you're staying. Which is where?"

TJ smiled. He wasn't about to reveal the location of the safe house. "No need. My sidearm is locked in the glove box."

Chellel frowned. "Then I'll have an officer retrieve it."

TJ didn't love that idea either. No doubt the officer assigned would also be told to snoop around in the car, but he didn't see a way around it. He handed the keys to the rental to the detective.

She rose and left the room for several minutes before returning. "Thank you for being so cooperative. It will take a couple of days for the ballistics guys to do their work. I'll get your weapon back to you as soon as possible."

It annoyed him to be without his favorite gun, but he'd brought several others along for the trip in his go bag. "Not a problem. Can I ask one question, though?"

"You can ask whatever you want. I won't promise to answer."

"Fair enough. What time was Jessica killed?"

Chellel shook her head. "I can't share that information with you."

"Fine." TJ held up his hands. "But if the lobby security recordings show Alexis and I going up to Jessica's apartment, they must show us leaving as well. You know Alexis and I didn't have anything to do with her death."

"I don't know any such thing," the detective said. "There are security cameras in the lobby, but not at the back door to the building or in the stairwells. You or Ms. Douglas could have been scoping out the building and then come back later in the evening."

"Come on, detective," TJ said incredulously. "We were smart enough to scope out the building but dumb enough to let ourselves get caught on tape the day Jessica was killed? That makes no sense."

Detective Chellel's eyes narrowed into slits. "Murder never makes sense, Mr. Roman. I'll be in touch."

Chapter Twenty-Three

A uniformed officer escorted him as far as the reception area of the police department. Alexis rose from her seat and hurried toward him as soon as he entered.

"Are you alright?" she asked, wrapping her arms around him.

Relief and something else, a feeling as if his world had been righted the moment she stepped into his arms, washed over him.

He pulled her close. "I'm fine. How about you?"

Alexis pulled back enough to look at his face. "Fine. Detective Chellel was a pit bull, but I just told her the truth. We spoke to Jessica. She told us about stealing Mark's ID and fob. We left."

"Same here. Come on, let's get out of here."

They walked to the car, arms still wrapped around each other.

"Where are we going?" Alexis asked once they were inside.

"First, back to the safe house. I need to pick up another weapon. Or two. Detective Chellel took the gun I had in the car for testing."

Alexis shook her head in disgust. "She can't really believe you or I killed Jessica. That's insane."

"I don't think she does," TJ said, steering them in the direction of the safe house. "But she has to do her job."

Alexis frowned but let it go. "You said first to the safe house. Where to second?"

"I thought we'd talk to Lenora Kenda again. I'm convinced there was something she wasn't telling us. If I'm right, she and her daughters could be in real danger."

Alexis looked at him with wide eyes. "You think the guy with the snake tattoo killed Jessica and now he might go after Lenora?"

That's exactly what he thought. "It's as good a theory as any. Killing Jessica strikes me as a cleaning house move. If Lenora is somehow a part of this too, she could be next on this guy's list."

After a quick stop at the safe house where he grabbed his backup weapon, they headed for Lenora Kenda's home.

As TJ turned the car onto Lenora's street, he saw the woman hustling a girl who looked like a younger version of the teenager they'd seen at Lenora's house a day earlier from the front door to the minivan parked in the driveway in front of the house. TJ stopped the car at the corner, a safe distance away, but close enough for him and Alexis to have a good view of Lenora's house.

"What is she doing?" Alexis asked.

"Running," TJ answered.

The younger girl had a pink backpack slung over her shoulder and dragged her purple suitcase on wheels behind her.

"Running from what?"

"That is a very good question. And exactly what we need to know."

If there'd been any doubt in his mind before, Lenora's current actions would have erased them all. She was hiding something, and TJ could feel that they were running out of time to convince her to tell them what it was.

He and Alexis watched as Lenora threw her daughter's purple suitcase in the trunk and slammed it closed. She shooed her daughter into the backseat and slammed the back door closed before heading for the driver's side door.

Lenora paused, her hand gripping the door handle, and scanned the street. For one brief moment, TJ thought she'd seen them.

Alexis must've thought the same. She slid down a bit in her seat and cast a glance over at him. "Did she see us?"

"I don't think so." He was sure they weren't close enough for Lenora to see them. At least not to see who was inside the car. He may not have extensive experience investigating the big complex cases that West Investigations usually took on, but he knew how to track and follow. It was the bread and butter of his work. Lenora might wonder about the unusual car parked on a street, but she couldn't know they were inside.

After a moment, Lenora opened the door and hopped into the driver's side of the minivan. She backed out of the driveway and headed down the street, away from where they were parked.

TJ shifted the car back into Drive and followed.

Alexis looked at him with a mixture of excitement and curiosity swimming across her face. "We're following her?"

"Unless you have a better idea. We might get more information seeing where she's headed, than we would trying to force her to answer our questions."

Alexis grinned. "You're the expert."

He finally felt like he knew what he was doing, at least when it came to this type of investigation. He knew exactly how far back to stay so that Lenora wouldn't see them, but so that he wouldn't lose her either. He could finally put all the hours he'd spent following cheating husbands and wives to use helping Alexis.

Lenora made a series of turns probably trying to spot if someone was tailing her. He kept following, giving her a long enough tether that he was sure she didn't realize they were behind her.

TJ's cell phone rang.

Alexis peered at the screen. "It's Shawn." She pressed the button to answer the call.

"Shawn, I've got you on speaker. Alexis and I are in the car tailing Lenora Kenda."

"Tailing her? Why?"

"Actually, we just wanted to talk to her, but when we got to her street, we saw her racing from her house to the car with her youngest daughter in tow."

"So what's your plan?"

TJ shot a glance across the car at Alexis. She shrugged her shoulders.

"We don't really have one. It looked kind of suspicious, so we decided to see where Lenora was headed. There's a fifty-fifty chance we're wasting our time. But Lenora is our best lead so far."

"You got good instincts," Shawn said. "I trust them. Think you'll need backup?"

TJ frowned. "You trust my instincts?"

"I do," Shawn said quickly. "But I told you I've got your back, and I meant it. I can hop on a plane and be there in a few hours. You just give the order."

TJ wasn't sure how he felt about Shawn offering to race to his rescue. A bit irritated. A bit relieved to have the offer of backup if he needed it. It had only been a few hours since he noted that the danger factor in this investigation had notched up considerably. And now here he was, going God knows where, and taking Alexis with him. Backup didn't seem like such a terrible idea. But he knew Alexis wouldn't want to wait hours. And neither did he.

"Thanks for the offer but, we don't know where Lenora is going and if we have any chance of getting her to talk to us, it would probably be better if just Alexis and I confronted her. She already knows us."

"Whatever you say," Shawn said. "Just know I'm here for you if you need me. And make sure the GPS on your phone is enabled."

"Copy that." TJ ended the call.

Lenora made a left turn up ahead, and TJ followed several seconds later. Lenora parked the minivan in a driveway belonging to a large redbrick colonial with black shutters and overgrown hedges lining the front of the house. The back door of the minivan opened and Lenora's daughter flew out of the car as the front door of the colonial opened and a man stepped onto the front porch.

The man swept the little girl into his arms and swung her around while Lenora hauled the purple suitcase and the pink backpack from the minivan.

"It looks like she's just dropping her youngest daughter off with her father." Alexis's voice sounded a note of defeat.

"Maybe." TJ wasn't so sure. Everything about Lenora's countenance said she was scared. And if this was just a visitation drop-off, where was her oldest daughter Annie? Something about the situation just felt off.

Lenora made her way up the paved walkway, stopping in front of the man who put the little girl down to take the suitcase and backpack from her.

Lenora and the man spoke briefly before Lenora turned and hurried back to the minivan. The man gave an awkward wave, a curious look on his face, as Lenora peeled out of the driveway and back down the street.

"Where is she going now?" Alexis asked.

"Let's keep following and see." TJ put the car in gear and fell in behind Lenora again.

Chapter Twenty-Four

TJ continued to follow Lenora Kenda at a distance as she drove away from the more populated areas of town and into a decidedly more rural landscape. Alexis was amazed at how far back he could hang without losing her trail.

"Where is she going?" Alexis asked, peering out the windshield at the back of Lenora's minivan.

"I have no idea," TJ responded. "But wherever it is, we can safely say it's off the beaten path."

The wrinkles in TJ's forehead deepened the longer they followed Lenora. Alexis was more than a little worried herself. But she believed they were on the right track following her. Something was definitely up with the woman, and they needed to find out what it was.

The street signs along the side of the road they were on announced they were headed southwest toward the airport. Was Lenora headed out of state? Detective Chellel said that she'd be giving Lenora a heads-up that the man who had threatened Lenora had also run her and TJ off the road the night before. Had the detective's call scared Lenora into running?

Alexis didn't think so. She could definitely see Lenora running, but not without taking her daughters with her.

That meant this trip was about something else. Could

they have been wrong about Lenora not being involved with the theft of the Nimbus program and in Mark's death? Lenora seemed truly broken up by Mark's death, but what did that really mean? She wouldn't be the first murderer to feel remorse for her actions.

Lenora turned off the main highway onto an ill-kept, bumpy asphalt road.

TJ slowed, allowing more distance between their rental car and Lenora's minivan before he too turned onto the road.

"Where is she going?" Alexis muttered just above her breath.

"I don't know." TJ swerved to miss a gigantic pothole in the middle of the desolate street. "But it's going to be hard to tail her without being seen as long as she stays on this road."

Alexis shot a look at him across the car. "We can't lose her." Not after they'd come this far. Not without knowing why she came out here herself.

TJ didn't respond, but the frown lines on his forehead deepened.

The street they were on twisted and turned, heading into an area dense with trees. Alexis's ears popped, indicating that they were also increasing in elevation.

They followed Lenora, seemingly undetected, for another twenty minutes before she made another turn. Moments later they reached the driveway Lenora had turned into, but there was no way they could turn in after her without being noticed.

TJ drove past the driveway's entrance and pulled the car to a stop about a quarter-mile down the road.

Alexis turned in her seat to face him. "Now what?"

TJ reached across her body and opened the glove compartment and pulled out a shiny silver gun she hadn't seen him put inside. "Now you stay in the car and I will see what Lenora is doing here."

Alexis grabbed his arm before he could exit the car. "No way. I told you I wanted to be involved, and I meant every part of this investigation. Where you go I go."

TJ growled in exasperation. "Things have changed. This investigation has gotten increasingly dangerous. I don't want to see you hurt any worse than you already have been, and we don't know what we might be walking into here."

"I understand the potential danger. I'm going to see this through." Alexis gave his arm a reassuring squeeze. "So let's go talk to Lenora."

They got out of the car and Alexis tucked the gun into the waistband of her jeans at her back. Together, she and TJ picked through the overgrowth lining the street back toward the driveway that Lenora had turned into.

"Try to avoid stepping on branches," TJ whispered. "Or making too much noise."

She did the best she could, but it seemed to her that her every footfall thundered through the woods.

Every few steps TJ stopped them and listened to the sound of the birds chirping in the trees above and little critters that Alexis didn't want to think too hard about, scurrying away from the giant humans thundering through their home. Alexis did know what he was looking for, but she could just barely see through the trees to a lake behind the property they were headed for.

Finally, they reached the tree line surrounding what looked to be a ramshackle house in the middle of a clearing. The house had probably, at one point, been a looker. It had certainly been worth something, and probably still was, sitting so close to the lake. Not that the lake seemed to have fared any better than the house. The water was brown and muddy, and Alexis shuddered at the mere thought of swimming in it. Just beyond the waterline was a boathouse, little more than a shack really, and a half-capsized dock. There was no boat in sight.

"What now?" Alexis repeated the same question she posed in the car.

She turned to look at TJ, but he was frozen, perked, as if he was listening for something coming their way. A palpable fear raced through the woods and surrounded her.

TJ whirled, but he was a fraction of a second too late.

Alexis saw the baseball bat, heard the terrifying crunch as it met the side of TJ's head, and watched the man she cared about more than she was ready to admit, even to herself, crumple to the grass.

She processed it all a split second before the man turned toward her, swinging the bat again.

She had just enough time to register the man's sinister glower and the oiled snake on his neck before the bat connected with the side of her skull with a dull thud that reverberated through her body a millisecond before everything went black.

Chapter Twenty-Five

The pain was excruciating. For the first several moments while he regained consciousness, it was all he could think about. His head felt like it had been cracked into a dozen pieces with the sharp edges stabbing into his brain. But pain meant that he was still alive, although that felt like a slim silver lining at the moment.

"TJ? TJ, can you hear me? TJ, you need to wake up."

Alexis's soft voice cut through the pain reverberating through his head.

"TJ, we're going to need your help if we're going to get out of here. Come on, wake up. Wake up, please."

It was a struggle, but TJ finally forced his eyes to open. Thankfully, wherever they were was shrouded in almost complete darkness. The only light emanated from a single bulb hanging from a chain in the ceiling. He was lying on the hard wooden planks of a floor on his side, his hands bound behind his back.

A sudden awareness jolted through him that they were in deep trouble, followed by a terror he hadn't felt since his time deployed in the military. "Alexis?" His voice came out a croak.

"I'm okay." Her voice came from somewhere behind his head. "But Lenora Kenda is here with us. And so is her daughter Annie."

TJ struggled to sit up. A wave of pain surged through his brain, forcing him to bite back a cry. He finally got himself into a sitting position, his back resting against what felt like a wooden post, and took stock of his current situation.

He remembered hearing a sound behind him and Alexis as they crept up on the house they'd seen Lenora Kenda enter. He remembered a searing pain and then nothing.

It was obvious that someone had gotten the jump on them. He turned his head slowly in the direction Alexis's voice had come from.

Alexis sat with her legs stretched out in front of her against the wall parallel to the post he was leaning against. Lenora Kenda and her daughter Annie sat next to Alexis. All three had their hands tied in front of them instead of behind them, as his were. Alexis was the only one of the three women who wore an angry red gash just below her hairline and above her ear.

Rage swam through him. Forgetting for a moment that his hands were tied behind his back, he tried moving closer. A fresh surge of pain ricocheting through his head knocked him back.

"Sit still," Alexis ordered. "He hit you pretty hard, and you've been out for a while."

TJ's head still throbbed with pain, but Alexis was right. They had to get out of here, and it would be easier to do that if his hands weren't tied behind his back. He scanned the room for a weapon or anything else that could be useful. There wasn't much. It appeared they'd been brought to the ramshackle boathouse he'd seen as he and Alexis were making their way through the woods toward the house. From where he was sitting it looked like a good stiff wind could blow the boathouse over, and it was clear that it hadn't been used in any number of years. A threadbare blanket with holes that made it look like an animal had mistaken it for a possible snack lay alone in a corner. A single oar hung forlornly on the wall. Neither would be any help to him.

He flexed his wrists, testing the ropes that bound his hands. They were tight, but not overly so. He started working on getting his hands free, flexing and unflexing his wrists while simultaneously rubbing the rope against the wooden post at his back. Hopefully, the combination of tension would break the twine, or at least loosen it enough for him to slip his hands free.

TJ groaned. "Who? Who hit me?"

"Brock Chavez," Lenora said.

TJ shifted his gaze to Lenora. "All this time you knew who was behind all this, didn't you?"

Annie leaned against her mother, her hands in her mother's lap. Lenora grasped her daughter's tied hands and looked down, but not before TJ saw the guilt swimming in her eyes.

Lenora nodded. "The man I told you about in Mark's office that night... I recognized him. I'd seen him around the office before. Not often, but always in the executive suite."

"So he works for TalCon," Alexis said, disgust in her voice.

Lenora shook her head. "No. Not for TalCon. For Nelson Bacon."

"And you said nothing," Alexis spat, the disgust in her voice now tinged with rage.

"I had to protect my daughters," Lenora shot back. "The threats I told you about were real. I was afraid. And with good reason. He kidnapped my Annie."

TJ's head was clearing quickly, but something about what Lenora was telling them didn't make sense. "You hadn't given up Chavez or Bacon, so why kidnap your daughter?"

"They knew I talked to you." Lenora's angry glare darted from TJ to Alexis and back. "I got a phone call after you left my house yesterday."

Lenora's words confirmed it. Brock Chavez must have been the man who had followed him and Alexis from Lenora's house to the police station before forcing them off the road.

"I planned to pack up the girls and take them to my sister's house in Florida after they got home from school today. But then I got another call." Tears slid from Lenora's eyes. She huddled closer to her daughter. "He had Annie."

"Why didn't you call the police?" Alexis asked, her tone marginally softer than it'd been moments earlier.

"He told me not to. He said he would kill Annie if he even suspected I called the police. I couldn't take a chance. He told me to drive out to this address." Lenora glanced between them again, desperation in her gaze. "I knew it was a trap, but what choice did I have? I dropped my youngest daughter off with her father, and I did what he told me to do. How did you find me?"

"We were coming to talk to you again. We saw you speeding away from your house." TJ continued to work the rope binding his hands. It was loosening, but not fast enough. "It looked suspicious, so we decided to follow."

Lenora glared. "Now your nosiness is going to get us all killed."

Alexis guffawed. "You can't be serious? Chavez and Bacon were going to kill you no matter what."

The sound of footsteps outside forestalled any response Lenora might have made.

TJ looked at Alexis. "The gun?"

Alexis shook her head. "It was gone when I came to, along with my cell phone."

TJ felt the absence of the familiar weight he usually wore around his ankle. Chavez had taken his gun and cell phone as well.

He worked the ropes against the jagged edges of the pole faster and said a silent prayer.

The rope snapped just as the door to the boathouse opened and the man who had driven them off the road stepped through, holding a gun in his hand.

"I see you all have finally awoken. That's great. It'll be easier to dispose of you."

Chapter Twenty-Six

Alexis wasn't sure she'd ever hated a person as much as she hated the man who hovered over them now, holding a gun. The thought had barely run its course through her head before Nelson Bacon stepped into the boathouse and stopped next to Chavez.

"You killed Mark," Alexis spat. It was all she could do to fight back the urge to lunge at Nelson and wrap her hands around his throat.

A sad expression fell over Bacon's face. "Actually, that was my associate here." Bacon placed a hand on Chavez's shoulder, but quickly removed it when Chavez shot a glare at him. "I am truly sorry about Mark, but I was left with no other choice."

"And what exactly are you up to?" TJ asked.

"Well, I plan to sell Nimbus to the highest bidder, of course," Bacon responded, as if his plans should've been obvious to all.

"But it doesn't even work," Alexis spat.

Bacon waved a hand, unconcerned. "My bidders don't know that and by the time they figure it out, I'll be long gone with their money."

"Mark found out and he was going to stop you, wasn't he?" Alexis said.

Bacon sighed. "He overheard a conversation he shouldn't

have. I tried to reason with him. I even offered him a cut. But he couldn't be reasoned with."

"You mean you tried to blackmail him and he wouldn't be blackmailed?" TJ said, feeling a swell of pride for his late friend.

"Why would you do this?" Alexis growled. "You're the CEO of a major military contracting company. You make millions of dollars a year. What more could you want?"

"There's always more to want," Bacon growled. "Especially when the company you've devoted your life to is about to put you out to pasture."

Anger and disgust swelled in Alexis's chest. "So that's it? All this... Mark and Jessica's murders, the attempts on TJ and me, kidnapping, and now what, four more murders? All because you're mad you're being forced to retire with a several million dollar parachute, I'm sure?"

"It sounds terrible when you say it like that." Bacon gave a little shrug. "But it's a matter of loyalty. I've been loyal to TalCon for over twenty years, and now just when the company is about to embark on a new phase in the design of weapons that will send their profits into the stratosphere, they want to cut me out," Bacon barked. "I won't stand for it!"

"Enough chitchat," Chavez said. He handed the weapon in his hand to Bacon and stepped toward TJ. "Keep the gun on them."

As Chavez reached down to haul TJ to his feet, TJ lashed out with a punch that caught Chavez in the nose. Blood gushed.

TJ lashed out with another vicious punch.

Bacon stood frozen, seemingly unsure of what to do about the rapid turn of events.

Alexis didn't waste a moment. She scrambled to her

feet and launched herself at Bacon. She threw her shoulder into his gut and heard the air whoosh from his lungs.

Her hands were still tied together, but she was able to use them to gain purchase by balancing herself against Bacon's shoulders before driving her knee into his torso.

The gun fell from Bacon's hand and clattered to the floor.

Alexis followed where it landed, but Bacon was too fast for her. He grabbed her around the ankle and took her to the floor, pulling her back toward him before she could reach the gun. She flipped over onto her back and with the leg Bacon wasn't holding onto, kicked out, catching him in his jaw.

Bacon swore loudly. "I'm going to make you pay for that."

Bacon lunged for her just as a primal scream reverberated around the small boathouse. "Nobody moves!" Lenora stood, her feet shoulder width apart, the gun held out in front of her, her still-tied hands shaking.

Everyone in the room did as Lenora ordered and froze.

"Annie," Lenora said, her voice shaking almost as much as her hands, "get out of here. Go on. Run, find help."

Tears streamed down the teenager's face. She'd crawled into a corner of the boathouse and curled herself into a ball, tucking her head into her knees. She looked up now at her mother. "I don't want to leave you, Mom."

Lenora sent a soft smile in her daughter's direction. "It's okay. I'll be okay. But I need to know that you're safe. Go now."

Annie hesitated for a moment longer before getting to her feet and heading for the boathouse door. There she paused again, looking at her mother.

Lenora nodded her encouragement. "Hurry."

Annie took off and Lenora turned back toward the adults who were still in the boathouse.

Bacon rose slowly, his hands in the air. "This doesn't have to get ugly, Ms. Kenda. I can make it worth your while if you just let me leave here."

Lenora shot Bacon a venomous look. "You terrorized me. You kidnapped my daughter. You had this thug…" The gun swung in Chavez's direction.

Chavez stuck his hands in the air, the first real signs of fear dancing across his face.

TJ took a step back, away from Chavez. "Lenora, you don't want to do this. Bacon and Chavez will pay. Just hand me the gun."

The sound of sirens pierced the air.

Lenora turned toward the sound.

Seeing his chance, Bacon sprung to his feet and ran for the door of the boathouse.

Chavez also seized the moment. He lunged toward Lenora.

TJ grabbed him before he could reach Lenora and landed a punch to his jaw. Chavez fell to the boathouse floor, out cold.

Alexis eased to Lenora's side. "Come on, Lenora. Let me have the gun." She reached for the gun with a slow, deliberate motion.

Lenora appeared to be in a state of shock. She didn't put up any resistance as Alexis eased the gun from her hand.

The sirens were almost on top of them now.

TJ hobbled to Alexis's side and took the gun. He flung it out of the boathouse door and toward the surrounding trees. "We should go out with our hands up so they know we're not a threat."

Lenora started for the boathouse door with her hands held high above her head.

"What about Bacon?" Alexis said.

TJ pulled her to him and pressed a kiss to her hairline. "He couldn't have gotten far. We'll let the authorities know to be on the lookout for him."

Alexis met his gaze. "I did it. The men who killed my brother are going to have to answer for it."

TJ smiled at her. "You did it, baby. You did it."

Chapter Twenty-Seven

TJ sat next to Alexis's hospital bed and watched her sleep, committing every inch of her face to memory. The doctors had given them both a thorough checkup, and despite nasty bumps on the head, neither had a concussion. Alexis's hands had been bound by zip ties, which had cut into the skin around her wrists and that had required some tending to. She'd gotten lucky and hadn't aggravated any of her prior injuries. The nurse tasked with gathering Alexis's discharge papers had gotten pulled into an emergency. Alexis had fallen asleep waiting for her to return.

TJ was dreading the nurse's return. It meant he would have no more excuses for not doing what he knew he had to do. Walk away for good.

The case was over. Annie and Lenora Kenda had been checked out at the hospital. Annie was rattled but unhurt. He and Alexis had given their statements to Detective Chellel at the scene before being transported to the hospital. It certainly wouldn't be the last time they talked to the cops, but it was all a formality now. Nelson Bacon had been caught speeding down the highway in an attempt to get away from the scene. He wasn't talking, but Chavez was singing like a canary.

An experienced criminal with a rap sheet as long as a book, Chavez knew how it worked. The first to talk got the best deal. Chavez didn't have the smarts or know-how to pull off the theft of the Nimbus program on his own. Bacon was the mastermind behind the plan to steal Nimbus, according to Chavez, which had initially amounted to stealing the program, selling it to the highest bidder and setting up Mark as the fall guy. Bacon didn't have the stomach for the violence, but Brock Chavez had already done time for manslaughter and he had no problem with it. Surprisingly, it appeared that Arnold Forrick hadn't known anything about what Bacon and Chavez were up to.

Chavez copped to kidnapping Annie Kenda, killing Jessica, firebombing Mark's apartment and breaking into Alexis's house in a bid to stop her from investigating Mark's death. He'd also admitted to driving TJ and Alexis off the road and to getting a couple of friends to attack them at the hotel in Alexandria. He'd also administered the overdose of fentanyl to Mark. Detective Chellel cautioned that there was a lot of work still to be done, but it was clear that Mark was nothing more than an innocent victim.

Alexis's eyes fluttered open. She smiled when she caught sight of TJ sitting next to her bed. "Hey, you."

"Hey, how are you feeling?"

"Better now that I've had a little sleep," she said, sliding into a sitting position on the bed. She reached out a hand, but he avoided taking it.

Alexis frowned. "What's wrong?"

A sharp pain pierced TJ's chest at the thought of what he was about to do. He pushed to his feet. "I should go see what's keeping the nurse with the discharge papers."

Alexis sat up straighter and frowned. "No, you should tell me what's wrong. TJ?"

"Bacon and his lackey are in jail. We've proved that

Mark didn't kill himself and wasn't a thief. You're safe now. The case is over. And I think it's best if we both went back to our real lives."

"You think it's best, huh?" Alexis pressed the back of her hand to her forehead and TJ's heart gave a jolt at the sight of the white bandages coiled around her wrists.

"I'm not the type of man who can go the distance," he said, his voice barely above a whisper. Guilt and shame engulfed him, but he knew what he was saying was true. He wasn't the man Alexis needed. The kind she deserved.

Alexis glared at him with a mixture of hurt, anger and disappointment. "So that's it? I don't even get a say?"

"I don't think there's anything to say. We both know this can't be anything more than what it was."

"No, we both don't," she responded fiercely. "I'm sorry that you lost Lyssa, but you're just scared now. I'm asking you to take a risk. With me. Together."

TJ felt as if his chest were being pried open. "I can't. I'm sorry. I'm just not the right man for you."

Alexis stared at him for a moment longer before turning away. "If that's what you believe, then go."

TJ hesitated for a moment, his feet feeling as if they were rooted to the spot. He knew this was one of those moments. A defining moment. One that would change the trajectory of his life.

The door to the room suddenly opened, and Alexis's missing nurse hustled into the room.

"So sorry for the delay," the nurse said breathlessly. She thrust a tablet at Alexis and proceeded to explain how the doctor wanted her to take care of her injuries and where Alexis needed to sign before she could leave.

TJ turned and headed for the door.

"TJ."

The sound of Alexis's voice stopped him before he stepped through the door. He turned back to face her.

Alexis sat up straight, her eyes trained just beyond his shoulders. "Thank you for everything."

His eyes stung. "If you ever need anything, anything at all, call. I'll be there."

Her gaze finally met his. "Goodbye, TJ."

"Goodbye, Alexis."

Chapter Twenty-Eight

Alexis pulled open the heavy entrance door to the upscale soul food restaurant. Her restaurant soon if Kitty's offer was still good. She'd decided to take the leap and invest with her friend. The space was coming along. Tables and chairs set out in no particular order yet littered the dining space. The walls had been painted a creamy beige color and the rich wood trim lining the tops and bottoms of the walls had been stained and glossed to a high shine. The dark mahogany bar was in place at the back of the restaurant space, and two workmen were currently installing the shelves that would hold an assortment of liquors for the patrons.

Her and Kitty's dream restaurant come to life.

If she had learned anything over the last couple of weeks, it was not to take anything in life for granted. Some risks were worth taking even if they didn't work out in the end.

Her thoughts turned to TJ. Falling in love with him had been a risk, and she'd known that from the beginning. It'd been over a month since he walked out of her hospital room and she hadn't heard from him since she'd flown home. Alone.

She didn't expect to hear from him either. But she didn't regret falling in love with him. She couldn't. He'd been a risk worth taking, even though her heart was now shattered into a million little pieces.

Kitty pushed her way out of the kitchen carrying a tray of glasses. A smile bloomed on her face when she saw Alexis standing in the middle of the space.

"Yay! You're finally here." Kitty set the glasses on a nearby table and wrapped Alexis in a hug. "I've been dying for you to see the space. It's come a long way, and we're almost ready to hold a soft open."

"It looks fabulous," Alexis said, stepping out of Kitty's embrace and doing a slow spin to take in as much of the space as she could. Kitty had done a great job. The space was almost exactly as Alexis had imagined it from all of their brainstorming sessions in school and after.

She turned back to face her best friend. "You've done an amazing job, Kitty. I'm sorry I wasn't more help."

Kitty threw her arm around Alexis's shoulder and gave it a squeeze. "What are you talking about? You've been there through all of this. Supporting me. Giving me advice. Listening to me moan and groan. The perfect best friend."

Alexis cleared her throat, her heart pounding. "I'm glad to hear you say that. And I'm hoping that your offer to take me on as a partner is still good."

Kitty squealed. "Good? Of course it's still good! The dream wouldn't be complete without you, and I never doubted you'd come to your senses." Kitty engulfed her in another hug.

Alexis laughed. "Well, I'm glad one of us never doubted it."

Kitty shuffled Alexis over to a table and both of them took a seat. They spent the next hour hashing through the terms of the partnership. Alexis would take over executive chef duties at the new restaurant while Kitty continued to run the food truck and operations in the older space. Kitty had applied for a line of credit on her house in order to cover the remaining expenses of the new restaurant. But now, with Alexis's investment, she would not need to take that extraordinary step.

"I'll have my attorney draw up paperwork outlining everything we've just said ASAP," Kitty said.

"That's great." Alexis grinned.

"Now," Kitty said, her tone sobering, "let's talk about TJ."

Alexis felt the smile fall from her face. "There's nothing to talk about."

Kitty cocked her head to the side. "So you haven't spoken to him since the hospital?"

"No. And I don't plan to. He made it very clear he didn't want to be with me. I'm not going to beg."

Kitty reached across the table and took Alexis's hands in hers. "I'm not suggesting that you do, but I can't help but notice that you've been moping around for the last month. If he's half as miserable as you've been, maybe there's a chance you two can work this out."

"He hasn't called." Alexis felt tears welling behind her eyes. "If he felt anything like I feel, he would've called, right?"

Kitty gave Alexis's hands a squeeze and looked at her with sympathy in her eyes. "Oh honey, men aren't that smart."

Alexis chuckled, knowing her friend was trying to lighten the mood even though her heart still felt as if it had been lined in lead.

"I just hate to see you so unhappy," Kitty said.

One of the workmen called Kitty over. Kitty gave Alexis's hands one more squeeze before she stood and headed for the workmen.

Kitty was right. Alexis had been moping around for a month. Hoping that TJ would call, apologize, and they'd somehow find a way back to each other. But it was time for that to end. She was embarking on a new adventure now, and TJ Roman wasn't a part of it.

TJ WATCHED THE clock on his dashboard tick over from 8:59 to 9:00. He followed the cheating husband West Investigations had been hired to follow as part of the multimillion-dollar divorce between the CEO of one of the biggest conglomerates in the country and his wife. He'd gotten a dozen photographs of the CEO entering the motel, across from which he now sat, with a young, buxom blonde. That had been more than an hour ago and neither of them had come out of the motel room yet.

He'd taken a couple weeks off of work after wrapping up Alexis's case. When he returned, Shawn had offered to put him on one of the more complex cases. Shawn hadn't pulled any punches, stating outright that TJ was wasting his skills, talents and experience photographing cheats and liars. He knew Shawn was right, but ever since he walked out of Alexis's hospital room, he'd had trouble mustering the will to care about much of anything.

He almost called her more than a dozen times, but each time he stopped himself before the call connected. He wanted to be with Alexis more than he wanted air to breathe, but he made a promise.

Someone knocked on the passenger side window, startling TJ from his thoughts.

"Open up," Shawn said.

TJ unlocked the doors, and Shawn slid inside the car.

"You scared the dickens out of me," TJ said grumpily.

"Because you were daydreaming. Or should I say brooding?" Shawn shot him a knowing look.

"I wasn't brooding."

"You've been brooding for the last month and a half. And to be honest it is getting old. Why don't you just call Alexis, tell her what a fool you've been, and beg her to take you back?"

TJ shot a glance at his friend. "There is no back. We were never together."

Shawn guffawed. "You really are a fool if you believe that. You're in love with her. And she's in love with you. I don't understand what the problem is?"

"The problem is, I don't do relationships, and she does. The problem is, she deserves someone better than me. The problem is, I made a promise to a friend and I don't plan to break that promise."

"Look, man, I understand. In general, it's a sound rule to keep your hands off your best friend's sister. But Mark is gone and I doubt he would want to see you in the state you're in over Alexis. I bet if he knew how much you cared for his sister, he'd be ecstatic because I'm sure more than anything what he would have wanted is for his sister and his best friend to be happy."

TJ's heart clenched and unclenched. He and Shawn sat in silence for several long moments before he spoke again. "It's not just the promise. I'm not sure I can go through it all again. Losing Lyssa felt like someone had ripped my heart out."

Shawn sighed. "Losing someone we love, man, is hard for everyone. I can't imagine what it felt like to lose Lyssa. But I think you have to ask yourself, is living right now, without Alexis, the woman you're in love with today, any better?"

The question lingered in the car, but TJ knew the answer. It was worse.

Yes, he made a promise to Mark. But when Mark had

extracted that promise, he'd done so out of love for Alexis and out of a desire to protect her. Mark couldn't do that anymore, but TJ could, and dammit, he wanted to. When Lyssa was taken from him, there was nothing he could do about that. It was fate. But losing Alexis, that was all on him.

TJ groaned.

Shawn smiled. "Glad to see you're on the road to figuring it out. Now, what do you plan to do about fixing the mess you've made?"

"I have no idea. I can't just call Alexis now. I don't even know if she would take my call. I couldn't blame her if she didn't."

Shawn grinned. "I've got an idea, but there's no guarantee it'll work, and I will need help."

The sparkle in Shawn's eyes sent a shot of hope surging through TJ. "Let's hear it. I'm ready to do whatever it takes to win Alexis back."

ALEXIS LET OUT a deep breath and marveled at the crowd of people that filled the restaurant. It was their "soft opening" where they invited all of their investors, close friends, and industry influencers in order to wine and dine them into generating a buzz. So far, the night had progressed well. Everyone seemed to be enjoying themselves, the booze and, most importantly, the food. She'd gotten dozens of compliments about the menu that left her feeling triumphant.

It was a much-needed confidence boost since she wasn't used to having so many people eat her food. Kitty had even insisted she lose her usual armor, otherwise known as her chef's coat, and don a cocktail dress for the event. Alexis had to admit, the dress Kitty had picked out for her made her body look amazing. Sleeveless black lace with a plunging neckline and a pair of Kitty's strapless silver heels had her feeling like a supermodel. And it was clear the men in attendance had noticed. She'd received more than one appreciative glance and had had more men flirt with her in the last couple of hours than had flirted with her in the last year. Still, for some reason, all the male attention had made her melancholy.

There was only one man's attentions she wanted, and he wasn't even there.

Her breath hitched in her chest as she pushed back an impending sob.

Almost as if she'd been summoned, Kitty appeared at Alexis's shoulder. "Smile," she hissed. "It's a party. Happy, happy."

"I am happy." Alexis stretched her mouth into a smile and tried to get into the party spirit. "See."

"Girl, you look like one of those creepy heritage dolls my grandmother used to collect," Kitty said, grimacing. "Why don't you take a moment? Pull yourself together and remember this here is your dream come true. We could use a couple more bottles of champagne. Can you grab a few? There's an open case in the party room."

Alexis accepted the offer of a reprieve, heading down the short hall that led toward the room she and Kitty had dubbed "the party room." They planned to use the room to host larger private parties once they got the restaurant up off the ground, but for now it was being used as a storeroom.

At least that's what it had been used for the last time Alexis had been in it. This time when she stepped into the room, she found that someone had cleared everything out of it except a small table that had been set with a white tablecloth, place settings, roses and candles. The lights were turned down low and twinkling fairy lights hung from the ceiling.

Alexis stepped into the room, confused but curious.

"Kitty said you wouldn't mind being pulled away from the festivities."

She turned toward the door leading from the kitchen into the private room.

TJ stood there in a black tailored suit and an electric blue tie. In his hands was a single red rose.

Alexis just stared for a moment. It was almost as if he were an apparition. It didn't make any sense for him to be there, and yet there he was, looking so much more handsome than she remembered.

Her chest tightened, and her heart pounded furiously. "What are you doing here?"

"I…" The word came out as a croak, and TJ cleared his throat before starting again. "I wanted to see you."

Her heart raced. "Why?"

"To apologize. I'm an idiot."

Alexis felt a small smile tip the ends of her mouth upward. "Great start so far."

TJ took several steps toward her, closing the space between them. "I'm so sorry I walked out on you that day in the hospital. I let my fear of losing you, like I lost Lyssa, overshadow the fact that I love you more than anything else in this world."

Alexis thought her heart might just fly right out of her chest.

"You do?"

TJ moved closer. There were only a few inches between them now. "I do. If you give me the chance, I'll make sure you know it every single day for the rest of your life."

Tears sprang into Alexis's eyes. "Are you sure? I mean,

you made a promise to Mark and your feelings about relationships…"

TJ reached out and took her hands into his. "It took me a while, but I finally realized those are just excuses. I was scared. Of losing you. So scared that I pushed you away and risked losing you anyway."

Alexis chuckled. "Yeah, that didn't make much sense, did it?"

TJ gave her a smile. "No, it didn't. I needed a little help to see that, but I see it now. I just hope it's not too late." He looked at her with a question in his eyes.

Alexis bit her bottom lip, but it did nothing to stop the tears rolling down her cheeks. "It's not too late." She stepped into TJ's embrace, wrapping her arms around his waist. "It would've never been too late. My heart belongs to you, and it always will."

TJ let out a shuddering breath that shook them both. "I love you, Alexis, and I promise I will never leave your side again."

When he captured her mouth with his a second later, she knew she could count on that promise forever.

* * * * *

Look for more books in K.D. Richards's
West Investigations series,
when Lakeside Secrets
comes out next month!

A Q&A with K.D. Richards

What or who inspired you to write?
I'd have to say both of my parents inspired me to write, not because they are writers, but they are both big readers. My mother taught English for thirty years and my dad had an extensive personal library so I think my love of reading and writing came from them.

What is your daily writing routine?
Generally, I start writing around 8:00 a.m. and write until I get hungry. I take a break for lunch. After lunch I'll pick up writing if I need to or I may work on some social media posts or plan for the next day's writing. I usually stop writing at three and if I'm on deadline I'll try to squeeze in more writing after dinner.

Who are your favorite authors?
There are so many. Karin Slaughter. Lisa Unger. Riley Sager. S. A. Cosby. I could name a hundred more.

Where do your story ideas come from?
Pretty much everywhere and anywhere. The other day I saw a very cool-looking, but very steep, narrow staircase and my thoughts instantly went to how I could incorporate it into a story.

Do you have a favorite travel destination?
Spain. I love Barcelona, Spain.

What is your most treasured possession?
I have three. A piano my great-aunt gifted me when I started playing, a little porcelain brown bear my great-grandmother gave me and a teddy bear my mother gave me for Valentine's Day when I was eight.

How did you meet your current love?
I met my husband at a party a mutual friend threw. Didn't like him at first—LOL—but he grew on me. :)

How did you celebrate or treat yourself when you got your first book deal?
I bought myself a violin I'd been coveting for a while. Now I just have to find the time to practice more!

What are your favorite character names?
My favorite character names would have to be the names of the characters in the first West Investigations book, *Pursuit of the Truth*. Nadia and Ryan. I've always loved the name Nadia and I really don't remember why I chose the name Ryan but I love the character.

Other than author, what job would you like to have?
I'd love to be a professional classical violinist. Of course, I'd need to play A LOT better than I currently do.